A Novel Murder

A Novel Murder

E. C. Nevin

Black&White

Black&White

First published in the UK in 2025 by Black & White Publishing
An imprint of Black & White Publishing Group
A Bonnier Books UK company
4th Floor, Victoria House, Bloomsbury Square, London, WC1B 4DA
Owned by Bonnier Books, Sveavägen 56, Stockholm, Sweden

Hardback ISBN: 978-1-78530-606-8
eBook ISBN: 978-1-78530-604-4

A CIP catalogue record for this book is available from the British Library.

Cover design by Bonnier Books Art Dept

Typeset by IDSUK (Data Connection) Ltd
Printed and bound in Great Britain by Clays Ltd, Elcograf S.p.A

1 3 5 7 9 10 8 6 4 2

Every reasonable effort has been made to trace copyright-holders of material
reproduced in this book. If any have been inadvertently overlooked,
the publisher would be glad to hear from them.

Black & White Publishing is an imprint of Bonnier Books UK
www.bonnierbooks.co.uk

To come

Here If Applicable

Prologue

Novels aren't good for you, thinks Jane Hepburn as she stares down at the body of her literary agent.

The Victorians had it right. What good can filling your head with invented horrors do? People like to blame video games for inspiring violence, but Jane is standing in a tent surrounded by books *crammed* with the stuff. Serial killers, assassins, women who murder their husbands, and friends who knock each other off on holiday. Men who trick women with amnesia. Women who fake their own deaths for revenge. Clowns who emerge from sewers to torment children.

And now, there is a real-life corpse on the floor.

It is the second day of the Killer Lines Crime Fiction Festival in Hoslewit, a Cumbrian village on which the entire publishing industry descends once a year. Jane has crept into the bookselling tent at 5 a.m. while everyone else is still sleeping off the excesses of the night before. Her plan was to take this opportunity to . . . rearrange things. Just a little. After all, it's not really fair that her books – all six of the excellent PI Sandra Baker series – are confined to the furthest corner of the highest shelf when they could be on the attractive table in the centre of the tent. People buy what they can see in front of them – and Jane was determined that someone would at least *see* her books.

True, she has been sneakily rearranging bookshop shelves for months now, and it hasn't had any noticeable impact on sales. She isn't one to give up easily though, and today might just have been the day that changed things.

But finding the bookselling tent . . . occupied has thrown a bit of a spanner in the works.

No, reading crime novels can't be good for you *at all*. As she lies on her back, the milky whites of Carrie Marks's eyes stare up at the canvas ceiling of the temporary bookshop, her skin damp with morning dew and smudged coral lips slightly parted, a smear of blood under her nose. Carrie Marks, a literary agent who was revered and feared in equal measure, is still wearing her trademark tailoring – an anomaly in an industry full of floral print maxi dresses – but the silk of her blouse is stained and her mud-spattered skirt has ridden up to show a knobbly knee. Despite this rare glimpse of vulnerability, even in death she looks as if she could eat you alive.

It doesn't take an expert – and after writing six (admittedly poorly selling) novels on the subject of murder, Jane does consider herself one – to realise that Carrie Marks is dead. For the avoidance of any doubt, someone has stuck a large dagger through her heart, and she is covered in blood.

After boldly prodding Carrie's leg with one toe, Jane confirms this isn't some sort of feeble publicity stunt for a new novel. On the contrary, it looks as though this year's Killer Lines Crime Fiction Festival is about to get a lot more interesting.

Chapter One

'You're an author? Are you sure? I don't have you on my list.'

Jane's face burns, but she forces herself to keep her head up, even as she feels her kitten heels start to sink into the grass. The line of authors, publishing professionals, and avid crime-fiction fans waiting to enter day one of the Killer Lines Crime Fiction Festival is lengthening behind her. Two women nearby stop their conversation to listen in.

'Yes. I'm sure.'

'Hmm. Jane Hopper, yeah?' The woman handing out lanyards looks barely older than a teenager. Blonde, beautiful, fresh-faced, well-spoken – the kind of person who has the world at their feet without even realising it. She glances up from her clipboard with one perfect caterpillar of an eyebrow raised in a question mark.

'No, it's Jane Hepburn? With Eagle Wing Books?' Jane hates how she phrases everything as a question when she is nervous, which is most of the time. She takes a deep breath. 'I'm with Eagle Wing Books.'

The blonde looks back down at her clipboard, furrowing her caterpillars and performatively running a pink nail down the row of names. 'Nope. Sorry. I'm afraid you're not on here.' She cocks her head and pouts her lips in pity, as if telling a child it *can't* stay up past bedtime today. Jane smoulders with humiliation, feeling her body tip slowly back as she sinks further into the mud.

'My editor may have forgotten to add me?' It comes out as a whisper; the little confidence there once was draining away.

3

'She is *very* busy. Can I come in as a guest for now? I'm sure I can sort it when I find her?'

'Sure! Then it'll be £175 for the weekend pass.' The keeper of the lanyards stabs the jaw-dropping number into her card reader with a smile, and holds it up for Jane to tap. Fishing around in her bag for her ancient iPhone, Jane furiously hopes that the payment will go through. 'Insufficient Funds' would be a mortification too far.

Thankfully, it dings a happy tone, APPROVED flashing up on the screen. She'll try and claim this back from Eagle Wing as soon as she can get hold of her elusive editor, Frankie Reid. Besides, Jane has plans for this weekend that should mean she will see a return on the investment. These next few days will be the making of her, she has a *feeling*.

As a child, Jane Hepburn had rather fancied becoming a spy, or else a private detective. There would be clingy red dresses, dry martinis and late nights. She'd have trysts with handsome yet morally bankrupt men, from whom she'd coax information before disappearing into the darkness. Long days would be spent tailing people through parks and down busy streets, dodging commuters while wrapped in an elegant camel-coloured trench coat, low heels clicking on the pavement.

However, on reaching adulthood, Jane realised she had grown to fit her name: plain. Too plain for a successful honey trap, and – at six foot tall and as broad as a builder – without the figure for the clinging red dress. Consequently, she'd shut the door on that particular dream, and never mentioned it to a living soul.

Briefly, she'd considered becoming a police officer instead, but that plan was knocked on the head after meeting a harried and furious constable at a school careers day.

'Don't do it,' Jane had been told by PC Imogen Ross.

'Aren't you supposed to be persuading us to join?'

'I'm supposed to be giving advice on careers to young people. And my advice is, don't join the police force. Long hours, shite pay, and mostly you'll either be telling drunk blokes to put their trousers back on, or filling out tedious forms. Don't even get me *started* on traffic duty, which is dull as the proverbial ditchwater.'

PC Ross had wild, wide eyes, and had waved the official police force brochure around violently, hitting a passing student on the ear. 'Be an investment banker. Be rich. Or a teacher, if you want to do good. Just not *this*!'

Looking back, it seemed the woman had been having some sort of mental breakdown, and perhaps Jane should have consulted other police sources. But it's too late now.

She even studied Criminology at university for a term, until she dropped out and returned to the security of living at home with her mother. It seemed the life of a student hadn't quite suited her either.

Jane has cycled through multiple versions of her dream to catch criminals and live a life of high glamour. And, at the age of 42, she has been disappointed many times over.

For the past nine years, Jane has been, as well as a full-time admin assistant in a company that insures white goods, a writer of detective novels. No, you probably wouldn't have heard of her; no, she doesn't know J. K. Rowling; no, none of her books are being made into a film; and no to almost every other question she is asked repeatedly in taxis and at parties or any other time she tells someone what she does. At least she is a writer though. She is proud of that fact.

But now, she thinks to herself as she pulls the yellow lanyard reading GUEST over her head, rather than the green one reading AUTHOR, apparently she isn't even that.

The Killer Lines Crime Fiction Festival has been running for 32 years now. Through rain or shine, fans and professionals have arrived in Hoslewit, booking hotel rooms and B&Bs – even, occasionally, bringing tents – ready to drink, talk and read.

If they are blessed with sunshine, the party mostly takes place outside. But when the festival falls on a rainy weekend – this is England after all – the crowd forces its way into the bar of the Dog and Bone Inn, the pub-cum-hotel at the heart of the festival, where the famous Killer Lines dagger glints above the outer door. The air smells of damp wool, and the noise rises to an almost unbearable pitch as people edge around each other, spilling pints of pale ale and Sauvignon Blanc on their way back to their tables. Devoted smokers huddle under the large willow tree outside, pulling up their hoods against the spring rain, and sharing gossip.

The Dog is an unassuming name for what was once a rather impressive building. In its day, it would have looked more like a King's Head, or a Swan, or even a Grand. But almost as if it predicted its own future, it's always been the Dog, a name that now perfectly suits its scruffy, down-at-heel appearance. In the eighties an extension was added on to the original bar and back rooms, to turn the once enchanting pub into a bigger building with far more space and far less charm.

Despite the peeling wallpaper and outdated carpets, it still looks out over an impressively picturesque vista: a large, bright green lawn – currently scattered with publishers setting up stalls of books – surrounded by carefully tended hedges. Beyond the lawn, fields roll into the distance like an ocean. It reminds Jane, powerfully, of *Teletubbies*.

Ever since she's been writing crime novels, she has considered attending Killer Lines. Each year, as the month arrives, she has excused herself from it – too busy, can't take the time off, there's no point anyway. Despite Hoslewit only being a short train journey from her home, there is always some reason. But really, she has never come before because she is scared.

This year, however, she has finally made it, and is pleased to see the sky is bright, the grass lush, and Hoslewit coming alive with the love of books. The reason for Jane's newfound courage is twofold. First, there was the death of her mother, to whom she was exceptionally close. Without her presence, Jane's life became even smaller and quieter than it had previously been. Realising she'd spent two weeks solid without communicating with anyone, other than emailing people about dishwasher insurance, and subsequently finding herself talking animatedly to a pot plant in her living room, pushed her over the edge.

Second, neither her agent nor her editor has replied to her for two months, and this seemed like the perfect place to pin them down while also making brand-spanking-new contacts. Officially, you see, the whole point of the Killer Lines Crime Fiction Festival is to watch authors answer questions on panels, raise awareness of upcoming titles, and celebrate books. But unofficially, it is a networking event. And, green lanyard or not, Jane is going to network her socks off.

She is currently weighed down with tote bags. She's brought one full of her own novels, in case someone important wants a copy, and her laptop, thinking that if and when she fails to make friends, she can hide in a corner and get some writing done. Who knows? Maybe she'll give the impression of being an author suddenly struck with inspiration rather than an awkward social pariah.

Through the entrance now, Jane pauses to untangle her belongings and put away her phone, trying to calm herself down about the money spent by hyping herself up for what is to come. As she is starting to fantasise about who she will thank first when she finally wins the Booker Prize – her late mother? Is that touchingly down to earth or a little pathetic? – someone smacks into her from behind, sending her notepad and festival programme flying.

'Keep it moving, love! Honestly . . .' grumbles the man, stalking past in a blue-and-white striped shirt so tightly tucked into his belted chinos that it frames the perfectly round baby bump of his beer belly.

Jane pulls her heels out of the mud again and tiptoes to the concrete path at the edge of the grass, bending to scrabble for her pen and notebook in the hedge. Why had she worn heels anyway? Anything that accentuates her height is a bad idea, but she'd wanted to look professional, and she'd forgotten about the grass.

'Janet,' squeaks a tiny voice from somewhere. 'Is that right?'

'It's *Jane*.' With a sigh, she turns to find a woman, or girl really, peering at her, half concealed by the bushy hedge. As the stranger steps out onto the path, Jane notes that she is immaculately dressed in the publishing uniform of flowing, floral dress and bright white platform trainers, but her mousy hair is frizzing in the mild heat, and her lipstick, a cheap bright pink, has smudged onto her chin. Jane immediately feels a kinship with her.

'Jane! Yes, of course, sorry. I'm a bit all over the place. Here.' She hands Jane the festival programme that had become lodged in the hedge. 'I don't think we've met, but I'm the assistant at the Marks Literary Agency. I think I recognise you from Carrie's client list? Oh, and it's Abi by the way!' She laughs awkwardly and gulps at what looks like a plastic cup of Pimm's. 'Gosh, you're tall, aren't you?'

'I'm surprised my photo is still *on* Carrie's list, to be honest with you,' Jane mutters, ignoring the comment on her height and accepting the programme.

'You've got a new agent?'

Jane hadn't meant to say that out loud. She really *has* been alone too long. 'No, I just haven't heard from her in a while. I wasn't sure . . . never mind. Anyway. Nice to meet you, Abi.'

'Books not selling well?'

Jane takes a half step back in surprise, almost sending her whole body into the hedge this time. One thing she has learnt over the years is that no one in this industry actually says what they mean, especially if it is unpleasant. Her editor, for example, is always telling Jane how excited she is to read her work, but then won't respond for months. Jane finds herself matching Abi's refreshing honesty in a whisper. 'You could say that.'

'Righto. She does that. Fawns over the big sellers and new authors with potential, ignores the dead horses.'

Jane starts to suspect that this isn't Abi's first drink of the day, despite it being – she checks her golden watch – 11.15 in the morning.

'Dead horses?'

'Oh, God, I shouldn't have said – I mean, she's super busy. Carrie. And some of the less . . . profitable clients sometimes get . . . well, she tries her best. Anyway, she's dropping some and started foisting others on to me – I mean, I'm actually getting the opportunity to agent some people now. So, like, maybe we'll be working together.' She raises her eyebrows behind her cup as she takes a gulp in what Jane swears is *mock* enthusiasm. Oh, good.

'That . . . would be nice?'

The women both look around them, registering the steady stream of excitable people coming past the gorgeous gatekeeper. Jane looks at her watch again for something to do.

'What's with the yellow lanyard, Janet?'

'It's Jane. And there was a mix up, I'm getting it sorted.' Jane is starting to strongly dislike Abi. When she was this age – she judges Abi to be around 20 – she had been unfailingly polite and borderline terrified during the majority of adult interactions. She crosses her arms defensively over her green polka dot dress, which she'd picked to give a quirky, retro impression. Now she looks around, it seems out of place. She is a giant, spotty toadstool in a sea of lovely young flowers.

'And why so much stuff? Have you brought a *computer* with you?'

'In case I need to write,' Jane says, aiming at lofty but missing the mark and coming across as confused.

'Well, let's get you a drink at least. I need another.' Abi tosses her plastic cup into a nearby bin – what happened to Gen Z being environmentally conscious? – and strides off across the lawn. With few other options available, Jane follows.

Previously, she had decided there was around a 12 per cent chance of her being professionally dumped this weekend, given that neither her agent of the past nine years nor her editor had been returning her calls. Standing in line inside the beer tent, she finds herself recalculating after her interaction with Abi.

Overall, she thinks her chances of being dumped by Carrie Marks have risen, but her chances of being dumped by the agency have shrunk. Wins being few and far between as an author, she decides to take this as one. When Abi pushes a plastic cup of Pimm's into her hand, Jane manages to reply with a genuine smile.

'It's weak. You need, like, four glasses to even feel a buzz.'

If Abi is to be her agent, Jane will bond with her. She might be young and blunt and inappropriately drunk before midday at a work event, but perhaps she is excellent in other ways. Perhaps she is just who Jane needs in her corner. 'Well, bottoms up!'

She isn't relinquishing her dreams today.

Chapter Two

Thursday, 12.10 a.m.

'Oh, God, don't let *him* see me,' Abi says, easily hiding her tiny frame behind Jane's. For the past hour or so, they've been standing under the willow tree watching the crowd swell in front of them, taking it in turns to collect new drinks from the beer tent. Abi's hair has grown increasingly bushy and her lipstick has mostly vanished.

'What's wrong with him seeing you?'

'He's an assistant editor over at Polar Bear Publishing. Just my luck that he's here. We got together at a launch event a while ago. Then he tried to make me show Carrie his terrible romance novel. It's awkward.'

'You'd think it would be quite good, considering he works with books.'

'Oh, *please*. Every one of these people,' Abi wags a finger around accusingly, 'is writing something, from the editors to the publicists to the booksellers. They all dream of swapping their puny salaries for a splashy book advance, and having their colleagues wait on *them* for a change.' She snorts with derision. 'None of them will tell you about their secret novels, and they will *all* be crap. Carrie gets them on submission now and again, always with pleas to keep it secret. They're all at it, mark my words.'

'Oh.'

'Apart from me, obviously.'

'Obviously.'

'Anyway, it's your round.' Abi waves her empty cup.

'Let's wait until the queue dies down? I haven't finished mine.'

Jane is trying her best to keep up with Abi's rather impressive drinking speed by sipping half a cup of Pimm's and tipping the rest of it discreetly onto the grass. With the price of the ticket hanging over her, she is going to have to watch how much she spends, but at least she is getting a surprisingly informative insight into an industry she has considered herself part of for the past nine years. Abi, it seems, knows everything about everyone.

'Fine. Oh, look, here come the Scots.' Abi gestures towards a laughing group of mostly men, a few women sprinkled among them, emerging from the hotel. 'Watch out for the Scottish crime writers. Drunks, the lot of them.' She fishes the chunks of alcohol-soaked apple from the bottom of her cup. 'And they won't be interested in you anyway. Don't like the English.'

'Really? I'm sure I met that one on the end at a book signing once and he was very ni—'

'Oh, and *that*,' Abi says with a jut of her chin, sending the now-giant hair bobbing ferociously, 'is Kimberley Brown. Top American editor. You can tell by the teeth. I wonder if Carrie knows she's here? There's some sort of beef between them so we're told never to contact her.'

'The one in the blue jumpsui—?'

'And them!' Abi interrupts with a shout that makes people nearby move away. 'You see those women?' Jane guesses she is referring to a group of middle-aged ladies sitting together in deckchairs, laughing over glasses of rosé wine. Abi's volume drops to a disconcerting whisper. '*The psychological thriller ladies*. Smug.'

Jane's heart gives a little twinge. They don't look smug to her. In fact, they look lovely. One of them, with wild, auburn curls and thick black eyeliner, looks as if she is telling a story. Her hands are flying everywhere in a theatrical fashion, her eyes are wide. After a dramatic pause, she stands up, extends her arms, and shouts, 'And then I pushed him in!'

The group bursts into hysterical laughter, wiping tears from their eyes and clutching each other's arms. Satisfied, the storyteller tops up their wine glasses and collapses back into her deckchair.

'Don't tell them I said they were smug.'

For one insane moment, Jane pictures walking straight over to the group of smiling, happy women, introducing herself and pulling up a chair. They'd swap stories, vow to read each other's books, and compliment each other's outfits. Jane would tell the storyteller she liked her hair, and she would obligingly pick something about Jane she liked too, solidifying their friendship.

'Not that they'd be up for talking to a *yellow lanyard* anyway,' Abi says with a snigger. Jane turns away from them.

For a moment, she tries to be grateful to Abi, who is still standing next to her despite clearly knowing many people here and having other options. Although, just because you *know* everyone, Jane reminds herself, doesn't mean any of them *like* you.

'Hey, do you see that guy?' Abi asks, spilling Jane's Pimm's with a sharp nudge to her waist. 'The tall one, glasses?' She is pointing to a spindly man with greying blond hair, who is lingering by a hedge. He has the air of a daddy long legs who got lost at a party, and is smiling and nodding at almost everyone who passes.

Jane is approaching her limit. 'What's wrong with him then? Embezzler? Pushes over old ladies?'

'Huh? Oh, no, that's Edward Carter. The reviewer for the *Daily News*? Good person to speak to. Knows everyone, and can make or break a book with a review. He's been around forever. Not a bad bone in his body.'

Well, thinks Jane, that's a turn-up for the books. Behind Edward, she thinks she catches a glimpse of her editor, though she's gone in a flash. She'll have to start a proper hunt for her at some point.

'Hey, Jane? What's it like being so tall?' Abi is staring up at her, squinting her eyes in the bright sunlight and wobbling slightly. She clutches onto a trailing willow frond

After *do your books sell well?* and *so didn't you* want *children?*, questions about her height are Jane's least favourite kind.

'It's . . . fine. A bit of a pain. But fine.' She is blushing, and she looks around, hoping to find another victim for Abi to comment on instead.

'I'd love to be tall.'

'No, you wouldn't.' In her surprise, it comes out with unintended sharpness. 'Not this tall anyway.'

'What are you talking about? It's cool. I bet you get people's attention, that they take you seriously. I'm five foot nothing. Everyone talks to me like I'm a child, but I'm 25 with a first-class degree in Classics. Half the time, people don't even know I'm in the room.'

'Oh.' Jane can't think of much else to say to that.

'You just need some confidence,' Abi says, now chewing on a slice of orange from her glass, sucking the juice and alcohol from the rind. 'Stop hunching your shoulders. I'd love to be your height.'

Momentarily, Jane is a little stunned – both by the tiny jolt of pride she feels and at Abi's sudden kindness.

'Obviously I'd rather be thinner though,' Abi adds.

A young man pushes aside some trailing willow shoots and joins Jane and Abi under the tree. Looking at her companions, Jane feels as though she is centuries old and ageing by the second. These two probably don't even know about Beanie Babies or house phones or choosing top friends on MySpace.

'Abi! There you are!'

'Did you finish unloading?'

'Yep, I've put those boxes of books in Room Three and made sure Carrie has everything she needs.' He is panting, and pushes long dark hair back from his sweaty forehead to reveal startling blue eyes.

'For God's *sake*, Daniel. It's Room *Six*. Upstairs.' Abi turns to Jane with an eye roll. '*Interns*,' she says, as if Daniel isn't standing a foot away from her, or is something inanimate like a tall, sweaty lamp. Daniel apologises, grinning despite Abi's tone. Behind her back, he catches Jane's eye and mimes hanging himself with an imaginary rope, tongue lolling, before speeding off the way he came.

This tiny woman contains so much bitterness in such a small package, Jane thinks to herself. Like a gooseberry. Jane considers following the grinning boy with the blue eyes. Abi is wearing her down, and her feet are hurting from standing for so long.

But there is no use moaning. That was something she'd learnt from her mother. *Buck your ideas up, Jane*, she'd say. *There's no use crying over spilt milk, turn that frown upside down, the early bird catches the worm, a stitch in time saves nine.* Thinking about it, she may have just liked idioms and spouted them whether they fitted the occasion or not. But they've stuck with Jane nonetheless. She is at a writing festival, with a well-connected person at her side. Catch the worm. Sew the stitch.

'So, Abi, it must be exciting to work with Carrie Marks?' she says loudly, bravely speaking over Abi's list of positive attributes to look for in an intern. Her round face has worked its way into a rage, and she is startled to be jolted back to the present.

'Huh? Oh, yes, I suppose so.' Abi points towards two striped deckchairs that have just been vacated, and they collapse gratefully into them.

15

'Suppose?' Though Jane fears the palaver of getting out of this chair, it's nice not to be shouting a foot down to her shorter companion.

'It's hard. Working for Carrie. I know I'm lucky – she's always telling me how thousands of people want my job. How I'm *replaceable in a heartbeat*. But I'm just the assistant. I do what I'm told, whatever that may be, and half the time get none of the credit. I want to be an *actual* agent, but Carrie is kind of blocking me from taking on my own clients. Sorry, I'm talking way too much. I think I might be slightly drunk,' she slurs. And then she belches.

Abi visibly deflates, a morose expression settling over her face, and Jane starts to warm to her again. We're bonding! she thinks. As a team, we will be unstoppable. We'll make each other successful, make each other happy, and rich, and respected. She is considering hugging her maybe-agent when Abi clutches at her arm first.

'There she is! Natasha Martez!'

'Who?'

'Carrie's latest client. Debut author. *Big* six-figure book deal. *And* she's only twenty-six.' Jane follows Abi's eyeline towards a nervous-looking woman, short with pale brown skin and dark hair roughly scraped back into a ponytail. She is standing by a privet hedge clutching the festival programme. Whereas most women are wearing some sort of patterned dress, she's dressed down in a white t-shirt and jeans. At her side is her polar opposite – a perfectly polished, expensively dressed woman with white-blonde hair and vicious pink fingernails that flash in the sun as she speaks.

'I read her book first,' Abi continues in a fast whisper. '*Knew* how good it was, but obviously she gets to be *Carrie's* client. Oh, I'd *kill* to have Carrie's client list. I've been dying to meet Natasha. How do I look?' She thrusts her plastic cup, empty but for chewed bits of orange peel, into Jane's hand and smooths down her frizzy hair with sticky fingers.

'You look good?'

'Great.'

Without another word, Abi leaps up and is confidently marching across the lawn towards Natasha Martez, literary prodigy.

Jane, once again, is alone.

Chapter Three

Frankie Reid is late. She was supposed to be in Room Eight ten minutes ago to assure one of her authors they would be brilliant on their panel discussion, but instead she is lost somewhere in the maze of the old hotel.

She was late for her morning train, because she woke up late, because she had been up late editing someone's novel, which had been delivered to her late. This means she has been late for absolutely everything since. Frankie hates being on the back foot, but these days she finds she perpetually is.

Pushing open the door to the hotel staircase, she finds some urinals. That doesn't seem right. Maybe the next door?

Killer Lines used to be fun. When she first came to this festival, she was a wide-eyed assistant, fascinated by the famous authors walking around like normal people, and the hordes of strangers who came simply because they loved books. This was her world now, she'd thought back then, and she couldn't quite believe they'd let her enter it.

Ten years on, she's feeling jaded. Ten years, during which she's given blood, sweat and tears to a job that pays her poorly and treats her worse. Frankie knows she has the habit of catastrophising, so tries to dial back the self-pity. She is an Aries after all, she reminds herself, and it's in her blood to keep going.

Her job has some perks, and she'd rather be herself than one of the unfortunate authors she is avoiding. She'd neatly dodged poor old Jane Hepburn earlier – such a classic Capricorn – to whom she owes an email and a phone call and an explanation for her silence. For the past month Frankie had been pretending to be sick, but that can't last forever. Unless she fakes her own death?

The stairs have to be through *one* of these doors.

If only Frankie had got that latest Commissioning Editor job she'd applied for. At least now she knows the *reason* she didn't – Carrie Marks. Literary agent extraordinaire, and don't you forget it. Frankie saw her earlier, right after she found out about the sabotage, strutting around on the lawn like she owned it in that inappropriate mint green skirt suit like she was on her way to court. Wasn't she *hot* in that thing? It had made Frankie blind with fury.

Rounding the corner at a light jog, weighed down by bags and boxes, she entertains herself by thinking how the silk shirt Carrie has on must have huge sweat patches spreading across it, effectively trapping her in the clammy suit jacket for the rest of the day.

It must be so easy to be an agent. It's mostly parties and lunches and taking a hefty chunk of a client's earnings. Maybe Frankie should do that instead? She would positively kill to start her career all over again.

'Yes!' she shouts, finally pushing open the door to the dingy staircase with her back. Now, what floor is she on, and which does she need to get to? She is pretty sure it's down. She went past the escape room, which was on six, and she should be in Room Eight, which is on floor three. Or four. She goes down.

By now, Frankie should have an assistant. An office even. Well, maybe not an office, but at least someone to do the running around with boxes of books and make sure she is in the right place at the right time. But her career, so promising in those early days, has stalled. She had never been sure if this was down to her skin colour, a lack of talent, or sheer bad luck. Not sure which option she would hate more, she had tried not to think about it too much. If only she had known sooner that the real reason was mint green and sweaty.

As she skids to a halt at the door to the fourth floor, a faint metallic tinkling announces something important has fallen from her person. Frankie dumps the box of books on the stairs and unloads the tote bags from both shoulders, quickly taking inventory of her belongings. As her hand reaches her right ear, she discovers what is missing.

'Oh, bugger. Not the earring. Not the bloody earring,' she mutters into the echoey stairwell. Frankie has mixed feelings about the Kate Spade earrings she is – had been – wearing. A gift from her terrifying dragon of a boss, who had tired of them, they remind Frankie of her poverty and low place in the grand scheme of things. The receiver of cast-offs. The owner of old things. However, they are still the nicest, and most expensive, piece of jewellery she owns.

Leaving her books, she starts to scrabble on the floor, her silver skirt growing grimy with long-forgotten dust.

This image, thinks Frankie, would be on the cover of her autobiography.

She sees a gleam of neon pink, and then spots the square-cut runaway sitting on a perfect circle of old chewing gum. When she is feeling down, everything takes on added significance to Frankie. The sight of that earring, gleaming in the dirt, makes her eyes well with tears. Unsticking it, and scrubbing at it with the inside of her skirt and her own saliva, she threads it back through her ear.

After this festival is over, she is going to take some days off. Hang the edits her authors are waiting for, hang the agents demanding publishing timelines and marketing plans, hang the vision document her boss is hounding her about. Frankie needs a rest. She can call in sick, or say she has a family emergency – though last time she'd tried that she'd had to tell an increasingly complex web of lies to get herself out of trouble. Her boss still believes she has a stepmother recovering from triple amputation in Wales.

Frankie is going to get to this panel. She is going to manage to not appear wildly stressed and unprofessional. And then she is going to have a little think about how else to untangle all the things that have gone wrong in her life so far.

With a sigh of relief, she sees the door to Room Eight at the end of the corridor, the chatter of the author panel discussion whispering through the wood. Before pushing it open, she takes a deep breath to compose herself. There will be plenty more time to brood over what Carrie Marks did to her career, and plenty of time to get it back on track. And, of course, to contemplate revenge.

Chapter Four

Thursday, 5.30 p.m.

It's not like being alone is a new thing for Jane.

Outside, day is slowly fading to evening, and so she has found an empty booth in the quiet of the bar inside the Dog and Bone. Elsewhere in the hotel, a few early events have been taking place, and every 30 minutes or thereabouts, streams of people walk through the bar area, laden with tote bags full of books and chattering excitedly. Occasionally she turns to stare out of the smudgy glass of the window, where people still mingle on the lawns and the fields roll out beyond them like a patchwork quilt, yellow and green in the early-evening light.

The programme in front of her on the sticky table is as yet unopened, the back page taken up with a large photo of the festival headliner and winner of the Crime Legend award, Brad Levinsky, plus an advert for the few remaining Murder Mystery Lunch tickets. Both Brad's main event and the lunch will take place on the final day at one o'clock, so there is 'something for everyone' according to the advert. Though at £50 a pop, Jane has a ticket for neither.

She has gleaned enough from overheard snatches of conversation to know what else is happening without reading the programme. As well as the authors, readers, bloggers, publicists and publishers filling the beer tent and lawn, a police cell-themed escape room – these make Jane panic so she won't be signing up for that, thank you very much – is located on the sixth floor; people are getting their 'mug shots' taken in the tea room; and in other rooms, various authors are discussing their inspiration, characters and writing process.

Jane isn't on any author panels, nor is she particularly interested in watching her more successful peers answering questions thrown at them by adoring fans. She should go and watch, should try to engage people in conversation that she then brings around to her own writing. That's what self-promotion is all about. But it's not something that comes naturally to Jane, and the excitable fans eagerly running to meet their favourite authors feel like a mockery of her unfulfilled ambitions, glueing her to the spot. Instead, she draws an outline of a badger in some old spilt lager, drinks cold tea and stares out of the window, moping.

She knows she is moping, and believes, given the circumstances, it is perfectly acceptable. Her situation plagues her. Her absent editor, Abi's ominous mention of Carrie letting authors go, the recent loss of her beloved mother, her loneliness.

The first day is rumoured to be the quietest, but it is already far too busy for Jane's liking. The bar smells strongly of the years of ale soaked into the cushions, carpet and table tops, masked unconvincingly by lemon Pledge. But she feels less exposed in here than outside, where happy people laugh, compare notes, and share confidences in the shade of the trees. If one must be alone, it's best to be *completely* alone.

Luckily, Jane is well versed in entertaining herself. Looking out onto the lawn, she chooses a person and decides which animal they most remind her of. A woman with a large nose becomes a toucan; a short, chubby man a mouse. Abi, she thinks, would be a snappy little chihuahua.

Jane doesn't have a pet. She doesn't feel able to get a dog when she lives alone, and cats have never liked her. Maybe Abi is more of a cat.

Earlier, Jane had been watching Abi and Natasha talking on the lawn, but she'd lost sight of them two cups of tea ago. Jane knows who Natasha is, of course she does. She had seen an announcement on the Marks Agency website, linking to an article in the trade press. Natasha Martez, just 26, had secured a lucrative publishing deal with a major publisher and was hailed as being the 'next big name in crime fiction'. How could they *possibly* tell that? She'd only written one book! What if the rest were dreadful?

Jane had read the news after a long night in her living room, laptop on her knees, bringing Sandra Baker to the end of her seventh mystery as the clock chimed 1 in the morning. She'd tried, really tried, to be happy for this person, but she couldn't quite do it. Usually, Jane was good at being happy for others – even if they lost weight without trying or won the lottery after only buying a ticket once. But this was a step too far.

Sitting up straight, she downs the rest of her disgusting tea (not just cold but too weak, with the taste of tap water and the colour of sanded pine) and gives herself a mental and physical shake. Moping is a precise art – too little and you become consumed by unindulged bitterness, too much and you can never shake it off. Her moping time is up.

Don't make a mountain out of a molehill. That's what Jane's mother would have told her. *Good things come to those who wait.*

Fate, which in theory Jane doesn't believe in but in practice thinks about constantly, delivers. Just as she has wiped her eyes, who should burst into the bar but her editor Frankie Reid.

She comes through the door back first, a large box in her arms and bags hanging from both shoulders. Jane doesn't want to *ambush* her per se, but she also doesn't particularly want Frankie to see her. Not yet. Not if there's even the slightest chance she can pretend to be rushing off somewhere.

In an industry full of middle-class white women in floral prints, Frankie stands out. Tall and slim with dark skin and natural, tightly curled hair framing her small, fine-boned face, she shines in the dingy bar in a silver skirt, white t-shirt and trainers.

Jane can't help but notice that her skirt is grubby though – is that chewing gum stuck to the back? – and she looks exhausted. God knows why, all she does is read books and ignore emails.

Jane peels the festival programme off the table and holds it up to hide her face, watching around the side like a cartoon spy. Frankie flops down into an empty booth and puts her head in her hands as if she is about to cry. Perfect!

'Frankie?' Jane sees a slight crease form between Frankie's eyes as she takes a second to register the identity of her assailant. She really does look dreadful, or as dreadful as a striking young woman can feasibly look. Maybe she'd been out on the town last night? She did say she'd been ill lately. Taking pity, Jane deposits a fresh glass of wine – she's come prepared – in front of her editor, and drops into the chair across from her. 'I thought that was you. I've been keeping an eye out.'

Did that sound threatening? Jane makes a mental note to try hard not to sound psychotic. Cool Jane. Casual Jane. *Not* the Jane who has been checking her email inbox every half an hour for the past two months while she waits for Frankie's reply.

The Pimm's she'd drunk earlier is making Jane braver than she otherwise would be. It is creating a war of emotions – her usual embarrassment in the face of boldly imposing herself like this is being pushed down by a metal jacket of boozy self-assurance. Remembering Abi's gigantic hair, she frantically smooths her own chocolate-brown ponytail to make sure it is still vaguely the same shape.

'Jane,' Frankie says with what seems like a sad but genuine smile. 'Oh, wow, I needed this.' She takes a gulp from her glass, grimaces, then takes another. 'Thanks. You won't believe the day I'm having. I'm supposed to be in an author panel right now, but they wouldn't let me in because I was so late.' She takes another large mouthful of wine. 'My boss keeps calling me about some work I haven't had time to do.' Gulp. 'And my flatmate just texted to say the boiler's broken.' She finishes what is left in the glass in one.

'That . . . doesn't sound like a good collection of things to happen.' Jane starts to feel guilty, but reminds herself that Frankie's boiler isn't really her problem, whereas her books *are*. 'I was actually wondering what you thought of my latest? I sent Baker Book Seven to you a while ago, but I haven't heard back? I was thinking of calling it' – she splays both hands in front of her face to show the name in lights – '*Death of Last Hope*. What do you think?'

'Oh, God, I'm so sorry, Jane. I know you sent it weeks ago; I just haven't had time to read it yet.' Jane's hands fall limply onto the sticky wood. *Months*, she thinks, not weeks. 'There have been a lot of things going on. And I'll be honest . . . Listen, let me get you a drink, and we'll chat?'

Jane perks up at this. Frankie is busy, she can accept that – despite not really understanding what she could possibly be doing with her time; she has *all day* to read books, *every* day, and she can't find time for Jane's? Maybe she is just a very slow reader.

Frankie returns from the bar already sipping at a glass of concerningly yellow wine, handing Jane another as she sits back down.

'Look, about the Baker books . . .'

The crash of a shattered glass breaks the moment and Frankie's head whips up to check where it has come from. A *wheeyyyy* sounds from somewhere, despite the room being almost empty. Jane supposes that, in Britain, there is always someone, somewhere, who hears a glass smash and finds the time to cheer.

The sound has clearly come from the only other people Jane can see in the room, standing by a high, round table in one corner. It is the very tall reviewer – Edward, she thinks he's called – leaning on the table next to the particularly shiny woman with white-blonde hair and violently pink fingernails who had been with Natasha Martez earlier. She looks, Jane decides, expensive.

Frankie falls silent, and they both sit in unspoken agreement to listen in.

'. . . I don't *care* about that, Ed. Screw *you*,' the woman hisses. Jane is a little alarmed to see that she is holding the sharp stem of a wine glass, the bowl of which is in shards at her feet. With her other hand, she dabs at her eyes, forestalling any mascara-stained tears that may threaten to run.

'Sarah,' he whispers, stroking the air down with his hands as if it will settle the atmosphere. The man is so tall that he is having to stoop to speak to her, even though she is wearing stacked, white-heeled ankle boots. 'Come on, don't be like that. Maybe it's for the best?'

'It. Is. Not.' She spits out the words, accompanying each with a threatening jab of glass in his direction. 'You need to help me. You owe me after that night. Oh, I could bloody *kill* her.'

'Sarah, stop it,' he says with a little more force. 'Calm down.'

'Don't you tell me to *calm down*.' The blonde raises the glass stem higher and points it at Edward. Jane, on instinct, rises a few inches from her seat. She can't stand by while this woman potentially murders a man with a cheap wine glass. Especially now she *finally* has Frankie's attention. Her chair screeches on the wood as she moves, causing both heads to turn her way. The blonde drops the remains of her glass onto the floor, where it shatters into further pieces, and makes to storm from the room, but Edward grabs her arm. He says something in a low voice that Jane can't hear.

Suddenly, the blonde gives him a fierce hug, and walks away. Edward nods at their table apologetically, before calling to the barman for a dustpan and brush.

'Well. That was dramatic,' whispers Frankie. The argument has caused her to perk up. 'Once the wine starts flowing at these events, it all starts to come out. Do you know them?'

'No. Though I think the man is Edward something?'

'Edward Carter, yeah. Reviewer for the *Daily News*. He's a sweetheart. He's got that whole sensitive air about him. Anyway, the woman was Sarah Parks-Ward, who is a total Scorpio.' Frankie rolls her eyes at Jane as if this should mean something. 'Publicists are all like that. Dramatic. She has the ear of a few powerful people though, so it's always worth getting on her good side.'

Frankie looks back over to where the scene had taken place, furrowing her brow and tracing her finger around the rim of her glass. She, thinks Jane, would be a swan. 'Haven't seen her lose control quite like that before though. I wonder what the story is.

'You know,' Frankie continues, glancing down into her now-empty glass, 'there's something in the air this year. People seem off. You know the moon is in the eighth house right now?' She raises her eyebrows emphatically at Jane, who responds by sipping at the yellow wine. 'It means something big is going to happen. I'd hoped it was going to be a new jo—well, never mind that.'

A notification pings up on Frankie's phone, lying on the table. The editor glances at the screen, then turns it face down.

'Just another new TikTok from Laura Lane. She's a dreadful writer, but I'm still obsessed. Such a star, she can sell anything. She's here, you know? Apparently she's been running around, boasting about her sales figures and chart place and latest advance to anyone who will listen. I wouldn't be surprised if someone strangles her.'

Jane knows all about Laura Lane, though has yet to meet her. A social media star and romance author of medium success, she'd recently turned her pen to crime by adding a murder into what read to Jane like an erotic novel. It had gone viral among young women, shared widely on a social media platform called Tokker, or Face Tik, something like that.

'That American star editor Kimberley Brown is here too. Wouldn't be surprised if she comes to blows with Carrie Marks, the old witch. Don't know *what* it's going to be – I've just got a feeling. Who knows, maybe it will be something good?'

Frankie tips her empty wine glass to her mouth, frowning at it when nothing comes out, then picks up her phone again and jumps to her feet.

'Bugger, I need to run. The panel just ended and I should be there to explain what happened. If I can find it again.'

'But what about—'

'Sorry, Jane, talk later? You are marvellous. A superstar. I'm sure what you've written is the best thing ever.' She is arranging the bags over her shoulders, and gathering the heavy-looking box in her arms. 'See you later, yeah?'

With that, Frankie jogs out of the bar, barging the swinging doors open with her back again. No wonder her skirt is so dirty.

The sky outside has now turned to a deep royal blue, and although the lawn is still bustling, the bar is starting to fill. Day one of the festival has officially come to an end. Panels are finishing up, activities closing, stalls shutting down. Jane knows that the real party is about to start, despite the majority of guests not arriving until tomorrow. She wonders if what Frankie said is true. *Is* there something in the air this year?

Jane has always found socialising difficult, and tonight, especially, she is not in the mood for it. Her conversations with Abi and Frankie have left her feeling flat. Time to drag this old horse back to her Air BnB to be buried in a good novel. Tomorrow is another day.

She heaves her large, polka-dotted frame out of the booth, pulls the festival programme off the table with a sound like tearing a wax strip from skin, and picks up her bag.

When asked the following day, many people would mention that they saw a tall woman in a spotted green dress leaving the bar.

But no one saw her sneaking back in.

Chapter Five

Kimberley Brown is here under duress.

The hotel room she is sitting in, like the rest of the UK, is past its best. Things are old and shabby – much like that cow Carrie Marks. Ha! Sometimes Kimberley wishes that her thoughts were narrated aloud, as if she were on a television show, so people could understand how funny she is.

Most people see her as an über-professional editor, efficient, a bit of a ball-breaker as they would have said back in the day. But underneath, she is a hoot! She is kind! She gave £10 to a homeless person at the train station! Not that this British money is worth anything.

This, however, is a work event, and so she'll stay professional. Which is more than can be said for Brad, who has spent the first day at Killer Lines making a fool of himself.

The publicity department in New York – they don't know how lucky they are still to be back there – pulled a lot of strings to get Brad Levinsky this gig. He is a big name, don't get her wrong, but being awarded the Crime Legend award at the UK's biggest crime fiction festival isn't small fry, even if it is held in *the arse end of nowhere*. She smiles to herself in the mirror, saying the phrase out loud to see if it suits her. She'd learnt that particular British-ism from – never mind. Best not to think of *her*.

When the festival was confirmed, Kimberley had been ecstatic. She's been building Brad's brand at home for years now, for most of her own career, but he could certainly use a few more

sales in the UK. This might be just the ticket. She'd had to persuade him to attend, even resorting to undignified begging. He
had a real bee in his bonnet about the British. Something about
the American Revolution, bad teeth and small doorways.

But *she* wasn't supposed to be here. When the publicist allocated to hold Brad's hand announced she was pregnant, Kimberley
had fought tooth and nail not to be the one put forward.

'You don't have children, correct?' her manager had asked,
one eyebrow raised, eye glasses lowered so they didn't diminish
the icy stare.

'I don't see how – no, I don't have children, but—'

'Well then, it makes sense for you to take this one. Rachel is
going to be off on leave and Steven said it's his four year old's
birthday. You're Brad's editor. You need to go.' It made sense,
but it also wasn't the first time her lack of children had been
used against her at work. 'Cheer up, Kim, take a few days either
side to relax. See some sights.'

'In *Cumbria?*'

'Sheep? Hills? I don't know what they have, just see them.'

Staring at her face in the mirror of her hotel dressing table,
she sighs. The truth is, Kimberley doesn't really have anything
against this country – she'd even spent six wonderful months
in London in her twenties. Unlike Brad, she *likes* the history.
She *adores* the accent. She doesn't even mind the food. She just
hates Carrie Marks.

And now her presence here has turned out to be completely
unnecessary. Brad had moaned non-stop about the trip on the
flight – the British aren't allowed guns, the British eat battered
Mars Bars, the British can't say what they mean – but she's
barely seen him since they arrived. He was swallowed up immediately by a swarm of drunk men and looked to be having the
time of his life.

Every time Kimberley had managed to find him, he'd looked
drunker and drunker, and happier and happier. Before she'd

turned in, she found him standing on a table with his arms around some Scottish author, belting out the English National Anthem until they all shouted at him to stop.

Regretfully, she'd told Brad a little about *why* she hadn't wanted to attend the festival – a slip-up that makes her cringe. She's been his editor for a long time, and sometimes forgets it's supposed to be a purely professional relationship.

The indiscretion wasn't even her fault. Having avoided this entire country for the last few years, she'd been surprised when she entered one of her favourite British shops – the delightful Marks & Spencer's – to see new additions to the drink range. Who knew you could have a *Pornstar Martini* in a can? Sure, they weren't quite the same quality as the ones served at Bemelmans Bar on the Upper East Side, but not too shabby for £2.99 (plus 15p for a carrier bag, which she did find outrageous).

Four hours and four Pornstars into Wednesday's interminable journey between Heathrow and Hoslewit, she'd confessed to Brad exactly what had kept her away from the UK for all this time. Exactly what she had seen eight years ago. Exactly what Carrie Marks had done to her, back when they were close.

Brad had been sweetly furious on her behalf, vowing revenge and retribution and all the rest of it. He was protective of her, she knew that. It was Kimberley who had discovered him after all, her who'd made him a star. But soon afterwards he'd fallen asleep with loud, grunting snores, and it hadn't been mentioned since.

Kimberley, meanwhile, had slept fitfully on the first night in this hotel, unable to shake off the memories. Luckily, she owns a large quantity of very expensive makeup with which to disguise the results of sleepless nights – makeup she slathered on her face this morning and is now preparing to remove. She stares into the hazy hotel mirror. She has survived day one, but is looking old, despite only being 49. She'll have to get a Botox appointment booked in. She'll tell her PA to do it.

Her iPhone says it is only 11.15, but it feels like 2 in the morning. The text icon on her phone shows a single unread message. When had that arrived?

Clicking on it, Kimberley Brown freezes on the rickety wooden stool in front of her hotel dressing table.

Come and meet me. We need to talk.

As she stares at the screen, three dots appear to show the sender is typing something else.

In the book tent.

Chapter Six

Friday, 9.30 a.m.

Jane is furiously sucking on a mouthful of extra-strong mints, a habit inherited from her grandmother that she falls back on in times of stress.

And what could be more stressful than finding yourself in the middle of a murder investigation?

Since finding the body of Carrie Marks a few hours earlier in the book tent, she's sure she's told her story at least 40 times. It has actually only been three, but Jane is also one to exaggerate in times of worry.

It turns out that she *had* called the police almost straight after finding the body – she's pleased about that, because, though she can remember the conversation, she hadn't been sure how long she had waited before dialling 999. She knew that she had stared at the body for what seemed, to her, a very long time. Carrie Marks, *the* Carrie Marks, lying at her feet with a dagger in her chest. The scene had been horrifying and fascinating in equal measure. And, yes, she'll admit it, just to herself, a little bit exciting too.

A dead body! A real one!

She hasn't said that to the police though. She doesn't want to come across as some sort of psychopath, and they already seem to think she is odd.

Sadly, the experience is nothing like that of Sandra Baker in *Death of Last Hope* [title tbc], so she will probably have to rewrite that.

'So please, Miss Hepburn, tell me why you were in the book tent at five o'clock in the morning?' says Detective Inspector Ramos. 'It doesn't open until ten. A bit keen, were you?'

Jane judges that he, the fourth officer to speak to her, is the most senior. He's a little overweight and it has been too many days since he's last shaved, the bristles making his emerging jowls more obvious, but he has an air of weary experience that sets him apart from the previous three.

Jane can see a Mars Bar wrapper sticking out of his pocket, and thinks of the clichés about policemen and doughnuts. It makes her like him, but his general dishevelment doesn't *fill* her with confidence. Behind him, the book tent has been cordoned off with blue-and-white striped police tape, words in bold type repeated along it. POLICE LINE. DO NOT CROSS. Uniformed officers stand outside the tent entrance as though they are guarding a palace, or a tomb.

'I've already gone through this with your colleagues?' Jane says with an attempt at dignified impatience, the rising tone of a question giving away her lingering nerves. 'I don't have to tell it *again*, do I?'

'My apologies, Miss Hepburn. We're grateful. I just don't understand why you were here?'

Jane wonders if they are toying with her now. She is sure the first officer had suppressed a snigger when she'd explained about rearranging the books.

'I was . . . making sure my books were stocked in the book tent? And that they were visible.' She sits up straight on the wooden bench, still damp with last night's rain, to imply this is nothing to be ashamed of. She is a few inches taller than Detective Inspector Ramos, but her height doesn't seem to intimidate him.

'And were they? Visible?'

'Not really.'

He makes a note, then smiles at her. Despite being part of this general humiliation brigade, Detective Inspector Ramos has nice eyes, she'll give him that. They are small and turquoise, like rock pools, and Jane suspects they always appear watery and tired, as if they spend most of their hours staring at a screen. He looks, she thinks, like a camel, or Liam Neeson gone to seed.

'I tried writing a crime novel once,' says the detective. 'Hard, isn't it?'

'Er, yes?' Jane says, taken aback by the sudden conversational tone.

'Mine was a piece of crap, to be honest with you. I had no idea who the killer was. Hoped I'd work it out as I went. Everyone kept turning up dead, but no killer to be found!'

'Hope that doesn't happen here.'

'Well, quite.'

The 999 operator had been serious and almost alarmingly efficient when Jane called the emergency services hours earlier. The police and ambulance had arrived within 20 minutes, and in that time, Jane had mostly continued staring down at Carrie's body. She'd also decided to move a few of her books after all, because that was her original mission and it's not as if she could have done anything to help her recently deceased agent at that point.

Thinking about it now, she wishes she hadn't done that, because the tent probably won't be open for business anytime soon, and the police found it very strange behaviour. She doesn't want to come across as the kind of person who doesn't care their agent's body is lying on the floor with a dagger in the heart. Or worse, as if she was the one to put it there.

Adrenaline and excitement have been buoying her up ever since, but Jane is starting to flag and is in desperate need of a lie down in her Air BnB and proper cup of tea that isn't drunk from styrofoam. She hasn't had much sleep, and uncovering a murder can really take it out of you.

'Detective Inspector Ramos, I've told you and your colleagues everything I know. Would it be okay if I left now? Really, I found the body, and called for help. That's it.' Jane sips at the dregs of the cold coffee that had appeared around the time of the second bout of questioning. She is regretting wearing the purple tea dress she'd put on this morning, one size too small and digging into her ribs. The Air BnB she is staying in is cheap and drab, but now the thought of putting on her pyjamas and climbing onto its lumpy mattress is heavenly.

'Soon, Miss Hepburn, soon. I promise. Two more questions. One, do you recognise the murder weapon?' Detective Inspector Ramos is already turning over a page of his notebook, clearly not expecting an answer that could be useful.

'The dagger? Oh, yes.' The detective looks back up at her with a surprise that morphs into suspicion. Jane tries not to feel resentful – she's heard of people who waste police time in order to be part of the investigation. How is he to know she isn't one of them? 'The murder weapon, Detective Inspector Ramos, is the Killer Lines dagger.'

'Er . . . can you elaborate?'

'It's in the festival logo? See?' She waves her lanyard at him; it shows a thin dagger piercing the words, becoming the I in Lines and dripping blood. Not particularly classy, but effective nonetheless. 'It's presented on the final day of the festival at the awards ceremony, to the winner of the Crime Legend award? You get your name engraved on it and I think you get to keep it for the year. Brad Levinsky is supposed to be receiving it this time. Have you checked above the door of the Dog and Bone? That's where it was yesterday,' she says with a shrug, trying not to become distracted by visions of her own name being scratched into the metal alongside other illustrious winners' – though she supposes they would have to clean off the blood first. Ramos's mouth is hanging open, making him look even more camel-like, and she feels a warm glow of pride.

'Well, okay. Okay then. That's ... that's good to know.' He shouts over his shoulder for another officer, imparts the new information in a hurried undertone, and sends them off to check the door of the pub, before turning back to Jane looking flustered. 'That's very helpful. And before we let you go, can you think of any reason that someone would want to hurt Ms Marks?'

'I'm sure there are lots of reasons.' The sharp crease between his eyes deepens, so Jane rushes on. 'Well, maybe not that many reasons someone would do' – she gestures towards the book tent – '*that*. The whole dagger business. But Carrie Marks is – was – an important woman, Detective. Important people make enemies.' She gives what she considers to be a sage nod.

'And do you know who these enemies were?'

'I don't want to point the finger.'

Ramos waits in silence, his watery blue eyes fixed on hers. Jane knows the tactic from television dramas, but she can feel it working on her anyway. Her skin grows hot and she can feel sweat prickle on her back. She shifts uncomfortably on the bench.

'Her assistant!' she eventually blurts. 'Abi Ellis. She was angry with her? She felt a bit ... unappreciated. I heard a rumour of some professional grudge between Carrie and an American editor too? Kimberley something?'

Detective Inspector Ramos chuckles, looking over his shoulder again to see how his colleagues are getting on. His interest in Jane is over. He pulls a wallet from his inside pocket and slides out a business card.

'Those don't quite sound like murder motives, Miss Hepburn,' he says, closing his notebook and handing her his card as he makes to rise. 'But we'll look into it. And call me if anything else comes to mind.'

'Oh, and the dead horses.'

'Sorry?'

'Carrie Marks had a lot of authors on her list. Some of the less profitable ones, the dead horses, she was sort of ignoring? Dropping them entirely, or palming them off on to her assistant? Or maybe just hoping they would disappear. I . . . I imagine some of them were quite hurt by that.' Detective Inspector Ramos is smiling now, and he gently shakes his head in a patronising manner as he gets to his feet. 'Carrie Marks would have turned down a lot of work from new writers as well,' Jane says, standing too and looking down at Ramos's thinning hair. 'She would have shattered many people's dreams by turning down their stories.'

'With all due respect, Miss Hepburn, I don't think someone would have murdered a woman in cold blood over a *book*.'

Chapter Seven

Friday, 10.45 a.m.

'And I just want to say that murder, real murder, isn't what I signed up for. It's going to take a toll on my mental and physical health but – I'm sorry, I need a second.'

Social media star Laura Lane takes a deep breath, fingers splayed on her breastbone as she looks to the sky, blinking long black eyelashes at speed.

'Okay, I'm okay,' she continues into the screen of her pink iPhone as she exhales. 'I know you guys care about me, and about what is going on here. So, I'm going to try and keep you updated. But I also need to make sure I'm taking time for myself, to make sure *I'm* okay, you know? To make sure I feel centred, and I'm practising self-care. I'll upload again very, very soon, I . . . I promise.'

Her voice had started to crack and her face crumple on the last words, so she clicks the red circle on her iPhone screen to stop recording. Flicking back, she takes a sip of her takeaway cappuccino while watching the video with a furrowed brow, hastily blinking away the glossy sheen of conjured tears.

On the screen, you can see glimpses of the tent behind her, police tape winding between tree trunks, and at one point a crime-scene investigator in a full white suit walks into shot. Perfect. It's a fine line between tragic, pretty crying and full-on ugly though, and at the end she tips too much into the latter.

What was it – the lines on her forehead when she screwed up her face? She practises the action again, this time covering the offending area with her hand, pouting her bottom lip a little more. There we go.

Deep breath, phone up, *action*.

Laura Lane is an opportunist, and she doesn't see a damn' thing wrong with that. Unlike most people here, life hasn't been handed to her on a silver platter. She's made mistakes, sure, but she's worked hard for everything she has, and that isn't anything to apologise for.

The fans she speaks to, many of whom make her shudder, are completely clueless about the business of writing. Whatever she might tell them, she knows being an author isn't about divine inspiration, natural-born talent, or having an artistic soul. It's about hustle. Working hard, self-promotion, knowing what people want and giving it to them.

So many of the authors who get past the first hurdle fall at the second. They think they've made it because they've got a few words down on paper and someone like Carrie Marks thinks it's decent? That's not the half of it. Then they come crying to Laura because their sales are bad and the people around them lose interest. It drives Laura spare – but then again, it also leaves more room at the top for her. Swings and roundabouts.

Laura isn't a fool; she knows the other people here don't like her. They don't consider her a 'real crime author'. She isn't in the gang. As if she cares. She'd gone from romance writer to crime writer because she'd sensed she could attract a wider audience, and it had worked. It's hardly *her* fault if others are jealous of her ability to pull in a six-figure salary. They're welcome to sneer at her as much they like; she'll dry her eyes all the way to the bank.

Sitting neatly on a bench between two large piles of pigeon poo, she rewatches the latest video, makes some adjustments to light and shade, and cuts off the last four seconds that show her dry eyes. Personally, she'd never liked Carrie Marks, and certainly isn't going to lose sleep over her sudden absence from the world. But her alter ego, as she thinks of her public-facing self, is made of sweetness and light. She would be deeply affected. Besides, trauma sells.

'Excuse me?' A small voice pulls Laura's attention away from her phone and to a young woman standing a few feet in front of her, clutching a tote bag. 'Are you Laura Lane?'

'That's me!' Laura grins, then remembers the police tent and tries to dial it back down.

'I'm *such* a fan! Of your Jason Steel books *and* the Sweet Romance series. Ohmigod, I can't believe I'm meeting you!'

'Amazing! That's so lovely to hear; it makes me feel so blessed. Would you like a selfie?'

In her excitement, the girl knocks over Laura's coffee and starts to flap around in horror, her face turning bright pink.

'No problem! Honestly!' Laura says with a smile, gesturing for the girl to sit down next to her for a photo. It *is* a problem, she thinks. That coffee cost £3.99. And Laura hasn't had a lot of sleep.

Putting her arm around the thankful fan and pulling her close, Laura takes a little bit of pleasure in knowing that the girl has sat on the pigeon excrement. Grinning at the camera, Laura expertly tilts her head towards the light and flicks her raven-black hair over her shoulder.

'Can you tell me, please – does Jason get with Rachel in the next book? And does Amanda forgive him?'

The Jason Steel books are mostly erotica, with a dose of gore. Occasionally Laura is baffled by the appetites of the public, but she isn't going to argue with them. If they want raunchy serial killer novels, that's what she'll give them.

'You know I can't tell you that,' Laura says with a wink. 'Who shall I make this out to?' She always travels with a pocket full of Sharpies, and now she scrawls her large, looping signature onto the copy of her latest novel that the girl has produced from her bag. A drop of water falls onto the page and blots the tail of the 'e'. Laura frowns at the sky that has suddenly darkened with threatening clouds. Thank God she got a decent video by the crime- scene tent before the weather turned. A few more selfies later and she sees the fan on her way with a cryptic clue about what might happen next in the series.

The encounter had been typical and uneventful, but the intensity of some of her fans scares Laura. Yes, they made her who she is: sharing videos on TikTok about her books, arguing over which character should end up with which, shedding on-camera tears over and over again, always with handy links to buy at the bottom of the screen. But some of them want too much from her. They want *all* of her.

That isn't something she will ever be able to give.

Even her publishers are aware that most of what Laura shows to the world is a carefully constructed persona. But no one, not her fans, not her editor, and certainly none of the other, hopelessly out-of-touch authors here, will ever know the *real* her.

Because if some of the things about her past got out, she'd be over. Ruined.

In fact, it's quite lucky that the one person who knew anything about all of that bother is now lying dead in the morgue.

Chapter Eight

Jane has not been able to get to sleep. When the police had finally let her go, she'd gone back to her Air BnB and crawled into bed, where she still hides. But lying under the scratchy covers, she hasn't been able to switch off her thoughts. Her whole body feels more alive than it ever has before, and when her eyes are closed, she sees blood and daggers and books rather than fluffy white sheep.

She is angry with the police officers for keeping her for hours this morning and not even taking anything she had said seriously. And what was that Detective Inspector Ramos on about, saying someone wouldn't be killed over a book? Doesn't he understand how *important* books are?

Clearly not.

She tosses and turns, fretting about what exactly will happen now. By the time she had left the scene, a crowd had started to form. The book tent is behind the Dog and Bone, by the back entrance gate to the festival site. Everyone arriving early from that direction saw the police vans, the big white tent, the officers in head-to-toe protective clothing searching for evidence.

At first, it was assumed to be a rather jolly themed event – perhaps a play or some sort of art installation. Someone had pointed out that chubby, poorly shaved Detective Inspector Ramos looked a little like Brad Levinsky's lead character and surmised it was a marketing stunt, before another voice in the crowd shouted that theory down.

'Brad's books are *American*. Detective Stone would not arrive in a *British* police car.'

'He would if he was at a *British crime scene*. Maybe he was on holiday in *Britain* when someone was killed,' the original voice roared back.

'Nah,' shouted someone else. 'He would leave it up to the local coppers!'

'You've clearly not read the books,' came a high-pitched shriek from the midst of the crowd. 'Stone always gets involved!'

The argument had devolved into something about marketing budgets and the suspension of disbelief by the time Jane had managed to leave. But still, on the long walk back to her Air BnB – its low price reflecting the distance from the festival site – she'd imagined the mutterings spreading and had no doubt that, by now, everyone would have heard the news.

If Jane had thought for one second that, on the discovery of Carrie's body, the festival would be cancelled and everyone would flee home in fear and sadness, she was wrong. On the contrary, other than a new, corpse-less book tent being hastily erected it didn't look as though there would even be a pause in the day's schedule and, if anything, the murder had injected a note of febrile excitement into the atmosphere.

The day Jane's mother died, she'd been startled from her bedside by a noise from the street. Out of the window, she'd seen the bin men leaping down from their lorry. They'd dragged over a grey wheelie bin and emptied it, shouting to each other above the din. Why, thought Jane, are you carrying on like nothing has happened? Why are you working, and talking, and laughing when the world has stopped? It took days to understand it had only stopped for her.

And what of Carrie Marks? A woman who had made such an impression on the book world, yet seemingly not enough for her death to make it stop turning. Though there probably would be *someone* grieving somewhere. Despite being her client for so many years, Jane doesn't actually know much about Carrie's life, nor who she really was as a person.

By now, the last few people at the festival will have heard what happened. That Carrie Marks had been murdered, and *Jane Hepburn* had found the body.

Though would anyone know who Jane is? Probably not, she thinks with a wince. They might not care who found the body – though maybe she could get herself on one of the author panels now? Something about *Murder in Novels and in Life: where fiction and fact diverge.* Jane chides herself for the ghoulish thought. But she can't quite get it out of her head.

To make herself feel better, she thinks about Carrie's body. Not in a weird way, of course. But remembering the deathly pallor of her skin and the haunting emptiness of her eyes feels less heartless than imagining her own literary success.

Carrie had still been in the pale green skirt suit and silk shirt from the day before, so the murder must have happened at some point last night, rather than early this morning.

But how could someone have stabbed a literary legend in the book tent while people were drinking just up the path in the hotel bar? And why?

Detective Inspector Ramos didn't think books could possibly be a motive, but he had evidently never been at a pitching event where hopeful authors yelled their ideas at prospective agents with the fervour of the converted. Or in a Stephen King signing queue. Jane had once seen a woman hit over the head with a 600-page hardback for pushing in, and last year there were rumours that an author tried to run down their editor in a car when their contract wasn't renewed.

What chance did the police have of finding Carrie's murderer if they weren't even going to *consider* the very obvious motive right in front of them? Ramos had said he would look into it, but did he mean it? Jane cast her memory back to that careers fair, many, many moons ago. PC Imogen Ross's wild eyes and insistence that the police force was not the career path for her.

As an adult, Jane could see that the poor woman had been overworked and underpaid, burnt out and giving up. Was that how all police officers felt? If so, how could they be trusted to look into Carrie's murder?

Rolling over, she buries her face in the pillow and squeezes her eyes shut. She did not join the police force. She is not her own creation, Detective Sandra Baker, sleuth of the highest order. She is Jane Hepburn, mediocre novelist, perpetual single-ton, socially awkward giant. A dead horse that Carrie Marks will no longer need to flog.

She needs to forget all about the blood pooled under Carrie's stiff body, and the rogue smear of it staining the skin above her mouth. The bright coral of her lipstick smudged across her chin. Her eyeliner, vivid against her pale cheeks, suggest-ing she'd been crying, and her nails, painted to match her lips, chipped on the right hand . . .

No. The murder of Carrie Marks has absolutely *nothing* to do with Jane Hepburn.

Giving up on sleep, Jane pulls her head out from under the duvet. The Air BnB is not the luxury sort with claw-foot tubs and excess house plants, but the sort where you are staying in the spare room of someone's house, avoiding them when you scoot down the corridor to the shower, trying not to leave any evidence of your existence in the kitchen. Her room clearly belonged to a child at some point, and is decorated in pastel pink, with cartoon princesses dancing across the duvet cover.

Jane longs to be away from Hoslewit, tucked up on the sofa of the homely one-bed flat she'd bought after her mother's death. Yes, homely does usually mean small and a little ugly, and it *is* small and a little ugly. But it is also actually homely. It feels warm, like a real home. The sofa, too small for some-one of Jane's height, has blankets strewn over the armrests, and cushions perpetually tumbling to the floor. The walls are crammed with paintings and prints that she's picked up over the years from car boot sales, and while wasting her time on Facebook Marketplace to avoid untangling a plot hole.

The day she'd moved in, Jane had been sick with grief, but she'd also felt a sense of calm and possibility. All a woman needs is a room of one's own, apparently. She had bought six new house plants and spent a whole afternoon arranging her books on her new shelves in alphabetical order. In the no man's land between the living room and kitchen area, she had pushed a small desk against the wall, stacking notebooks on one side, books on the other, her computer proudly in the middle. A dream realised – a real writing station for a real author.

The thought makes her feel sick all over again.

Now Carrie is dead, does she even have an agent? Will Abi kick her to the kerb?

Sighing deeply, she sits up in bed. A cup of tea would go down a treat, but it would involve standing up, and quite a bit of movement of both arms and legs. This is why people have boyfriends or children.

Pulling her phone out of her pocket, she starts to scroll mindlessly through her social media feed to silence her thoughts. An incoming call from an unknown number startles her, and she watches the screen until it rings off and Twitter, or 'X' as she's supposed to call it now, reappears. Unsurprisingly, there is already a lot about Killer Lines on there, and the death of Carrie Marks.

The hashtag #DeadAgent is trending. How utterly ghoulish people are! thinks Jane as she clicks on it, bringing the screen closer to her face to drink it all in.

@LauraLane: Check out my TikTok channel for up-to-date coverage on this tragedy #DeadAgent #KillerLines #Lifeistooshort

Jane clicks on the link, quickly signing up for an account in order to watch the updates. Has she really just left that place to sit in bed and watch videos of it? Yes, she has.

Laura Lane's tear-stricken face fills the screen, the white of the crime-scene tent visible behind her. Odd, thinks Jane. She distinctly remembers seeing her looking rather jolly by the police van earlier. She has milky white skin, glossy black hair and long, thick eyelashes. Her nose is large and slightly bent, but in combination with her full lips and wide eyes, it gives her a striking look. Her voice, breathy and delicate, fills the tiny bedroom.

'. . . *murder, real murder, isn't what I signed up for.*'

'Oh, come *on*,' Jane mutters.

'*. . . and I'm practising self-care. I'll upload again very, very soon, I . . . I promise.*'

Jane flicks to the earlier video. Laura, daintily crying into one hand while the other points the camera at her face. Dramatically, she pulls in a deep breath and looks up, right through the screen and into Jane's eyes.

'*I didn't know how much her murder would affect me. I'd met Carrie, you know? It's really making my anxiety terrible.*'

Jane is about to throw the phone across the room when she stops herself, noticing the numbers on the side of the screen. Surely that can't be right: 3.2 *million* views? She clicks on the comment bubble and sees, in real-time, floods of messages coming in for Laura.

'You've got this! You are SO STRONG grl!'

'We love you Laura Lane. You can beat this!'

Beat what? wonders Jane. *Death?*

Flicking off the app, she notices a red number one on the voicemail icon. Voicemails are never good news. They are never about a lottery win, or someone declaring undying love. In this day and age, the humble voicemail is the weapon of the coward. *Oh, you've not picked up*, the voicemailers say to themselves. *Thank God, I can leave this here, like a hit-and-run.*

Jane hears her late mother's voice in her head for the second time in as many days. *Rip off the plaster. Get it over and done with.* Deep breath, click.

'Janet? Hi. It's Abi Ellis here.' Her voice fills the room, even squeakier through the tinny phone speakers.

'Jane!' she says out loud to the empty room. *Janet?* They'd spent hours together yesterday! Unbelievable.

'I'm sure you heard the *tragic* news about Carrie. Poor thing. I'm just doing a ring round to all of the agency authors to steady the ship.' She gives a practised laugh that she probably thought of as *tinkling*, but comes across as shrill. Even though Jane is sure that Abi will still be at the festival, she can't help picturing her sitting in Carrie's office, feet on desk.

'Now, first of all, don't you worry!' she continues with what is clearly a script she'd written out. 'I'm going to be making sure everything runs smoothly. I've had . . . a *lot* of input into everyone's work, and so I'm best placed to take over Carrie's list of authors immediately.'

Jane breathes a sigh of relief, finally heaving herself out of bed to make some tea in the kitchen while Abi prattles away on speaker phone.

'However, um . . . ' The voice changes slightly, tone slipping from rehearsed professional to awkward teenager. The universal script has ended; what personal message is she about to impart? Jane's hand freezes on the bedroom door handle, her eyes closed in anticipation of the worst.

'It's, er, going to be a lot of work. Without Carrie? So, um, obviously there might be one or two changes. Nothing is set in stone *right now*,' Abi goes on, regaining her confidence. 'But I just wanted to warn you ahead of time that we *may* be looking to trim down the client list, due to the obvious *staffing changes*. But we can talk more at a later date. Anyway, thanks and, um, speak soon.'

Press one to delete. Press two to repeat. Press three to—Jane hangs up.

So, there you have it. Abi has pounced on Carrie's authors hours after her death, implying she has always done all of the work anyway, to stop anyone abandoning ship. Apart from the ones she wants to walk the plank, of course.

Nothing is set in stone right now.

Yeah, right.

Jane flops back onto the bed, looking over at her little suitcase, half unpacked by the door.

She'd had visions of grand things from attending the festival, but no. Instead, she'd ended up being interviewed by Detective Fat Liam Neeson, getting blood on her new shoes and becoming agent-less. All at a cost of £175! Well, she is done with it. Writing crime fiction is a waste of time. Writing *anything* is a waste of time. Jane will give up and throw herself into her admin job at the insurance company. She'll focus on decorating her flat, getting a promotion, finding a boyfriend. There are plenty of other areas of her life that could benefit from the attention.

Unable to move in case tears start to flow, Jane stays where she is sitting on the bed, looking at the now-crumpled business card Detective Inspector Ramos left her with. She thinks back to what Frankie said about Laura Lane. Jane isn't a star. She is a no one, with a few tired detective stories to her name and bad dress sense. What is she doing here? What is the point?

Packing everything back into her suitcase, including the slightly too-tight purple dress she'd worn that morning, Jane slips on a more comfortable one that looks a lot like a sack. At least she can breathe in it. And she will be able to breathe even deeper when she is out of here.

Chapter Nine

Jane yawns, head nodding gently down to her chest. A sudden rain shower is long gone, leaving the afternoon sky a bright blue that whips past outside the train window. British spring weather can give you whiplash.

A loud snore wakes her with a start, and she glares around the carriage for the culprit, before realising it is her.

Shuffling in her seat, she checks the gold watch that used to be her father's – 14.25. The Killer Lines lawn will be filling up with people eating lunch by now, sipping their drinks, making friends and forging useful connections. Will any of the jollity be strained due to the murder, or will all be exactly as it was?

None of it matters now anyway. In a few hours Jane will be back home. Do not stop at the Dog and Bone, do not pass Go for £200. It is high time to put this whole sorry mess behind her. Only seven more stops.

The train is juddering to a halt. The Tannoy announces their arrival at West Barning. Six more stops to go. A skinny man with red hair and pale skin is snoozing in the seat across the aisle, drool leaking from his mouth. Jane hopes to high heaven she hadn't looked quite so unattractive while *she* slept. In the glass of the window, she can just about make out her reflection – tired-looking, sad, the seat next to her loaded with her bags.

'This is your train manager speaking, I'm afraid we are being held here due to some animals on the track.'

The ginger man jerks awake and looks around him in a panic.

'West Barning,' Jane tells him, and he slumps back into his seat. 'But sounds like something is up.'

This is not what Jane needs right now. Murder, being dumped by her agency, and now animals on the track. Do bad things come in threes, or is that just good things? What she wouldn't give for a trio of good things.

'I'm being told,' continues the Tannoy, sparking into life again with a screech, 'that sheep are on the line, and we aren't going anywhere fast. So you are welcome to stretch your legs. Sorry, folks.'

Sheep! It's 2025. If Elon Musk can get into space while having an online meltdown, surely we can manage to keep sheep in their fields?

With a deep sigh, Jane regards the ginger man, who has immediately fallen back into a doze. He's pale and drawn. Is he having a day as bad as hers? Perhaps he's lost his job. Or, no, that's it – the exhaustion coupled with the faint white stain on his lapel marks him as a new parent. Jane tells herself she is lucky, at the very least, to have the prospect of uninterrupted sleep to look forward to. Her eyes wander past him out towards the platform. People are streaming from the train doors, looking frustrated.

A woman with a double pushchair barges past a kissing couple in her way, and Jane is 99 per cent certain she is hitting them on purpose. Some teenagers have almost fallen out of the door, laughing, swigging from Strongbow cans as they skip off towards the platform café. At least they are enjoying themselves. And then, walking past her window . . . was that . . . ?

Before she knows what she is doing or why she is doing it, Jane finds herself out of her seat and at the open train door, staring at the retreating back of . . .

'Daniel?' she calls down the platform.

Daniel the intern, spins around. She gives him a small wave, and he waves back. They meet in the middle of the platform.

'Sheep on the line,' he says with a shrug. 'Not the weirdest thing to happen this weekend. You're Jane, right?'

'Yes, Jane. I didn't get a chance to talk to you properly, with Abi—'

'The great dictator? Yeah.' Daniel sighs, and Jane notices that his brilliant blue eyes look bloodshot and small. Carrie, of course, had been his boss, however briefly. How well had he known her? At last, a sign of sadness at a life wiped from the earth. 'I'm Daniel Thurston,' he says, holding out his hand. 'Nice to meet you properly.'

'Can I buy you a coffee?' Jane asks, accepting his handshake.

'How about *I* buy *you* a coffee?' A shadow of his infectious grin returns to his handsome face. 'But instead of a coffee, it's a gin and tonic in a can.'

Sat on a bench surrounded by Daniel's many bags and boxes, the two of them sip from their cans and crunch away on packets of Quavers while they watch the stationary train. They make small talk for a while, Jane learning that Daniel is 22, single, and a recent English Literature graduate living in an eight-person house share in Crystal Palace; Daniel learning that Jane really, really likes Quavers. Eventually, the conversation crawls around to what they are doing on the platform.

'So, what brings you to West Barning, Daniel?'

'On my way home. It takes an age to get back to London from wherever this is.'

'You didn't fancy sticking around?'

'Not likely. What happened ... it was a shock. This is my first job out of uni, if you can call it a job. I've only been at the agency a month. And the CEO has been murdered! Is this what adult life is?'

'Not always,' says Jane. 'But sometimes,' she concedes.

'And . . . no one seems to care? Everyone just carried on as normal? The Dog and Bone was packed this morning, buzzing with excitement. Abi went straight back to ordering me around after the police told us, immediately grasping at Carrie's authors. It made me feel sick.'

They both take a sip from their cans and watch in silence as a toddler throws his ice cream at his mother.

'What about you?' he says, gesturing at Jane's suitcase. 'Why are you leaving early?'

'Same reasons as you really. I couldn't stay there, drinking and laughing and chatting,' she says, despite not having done any laughing and minimal chatting. 'The police spoke to me, and they wouldn't take anything I said seriously. Anyway, I'm done with being an author. Done with books.'

With another slug, Jane finishes her can and makes to rise. 'Another one, Daniel?' He pulls two more cans from his pocket, hands one to her and cracks the other open. It is that kind of day, she supposes.

'You know,' Daniel begins hesitantly, 'I'm a big fan of your books.'

Jane snorts, sending a spray of gin and tonic into her lap.

'No, you're not. But thank you for saying so.'

'No . . . no, I am! I love Sandra Baker! When she swapped the arsenic with vodka in *The Sweetness of Murder*? Inspired! And when she pretended to be a minor royal to gain access to the mansion in book two, *Murder at Dawn*? And I *loved* the bit in book five, *A Desperate Death*, when she faked a phone call for the killer in order to disarm him. Wow! Just wow.'

Jane has never met a fan before, and she doesn't know quite what to do with the information. From the window of the Dog and Bone, she'd seen Laura Lane pose with fan after fan, throwing an arm around them and grinning at the camera, signing books with a flourish. But that isn't Jane, so she gives a sharp nod, blushes furiously, and gulps at her gin and tonic.

'Hey,' she says, to change the subject from herself. 'Do you know that Laura Lane woman?'

'I know *of* her,' said Daniel. 'She's causing chaos apparently. Telling everyone how much she earns, riling people up. She doesn't even have an agent, so she does the deals herself. Makes the agents look terrible.' He grins at Jane, the idea of drama amongst his superiors clearly entertaining.

'Well, look at this.' Jane pulls out her phone and opens up Tik-Tok to show him Laura's videos. She's posted another one since Jane last checked. Clicking the side buttons on her phone, she turns the volume up full and they bend close together to hear it.

'It's been an emotional day here at Killer Lines. I'm finding this . . . just so difficult. Personally. But I feel so incredibly lucky to have some amazing fans right here by my side. We'll get through this together.'

'Ha,' scoffs Daniel, finishing the rest of his second gin and tonic. He pulls out a third without comment. 'She didn't even *like* Carrie. Apparently Carrie publicly slammed her book, ages ago. And Laura Lane is one to bear a grudge.'

'Look at the comments though! These people adore her, they eat it right up!'

U r in r hearts <3 <3 <3

You changed my life and I love you LL when is your next book coming

Jason Steel and Rachel Woods would catch that killer!

Jane assumes Jason Steel and Rachel Woods are the characters in Laura Lane's latest novels. *Could* they solve it? Were they as smart as her gorgeous, frighteningly clever PI, Sandra Baker?

Of course they weren't. Baker would tie this case up in a matter of days.

'Yeah, right,' slurs Daniel, reading her thoughts. 'Baker could solve it though!' They *cheers* their cans.

Baker would take delight in sidestepping the bumbling local police who were looking in entirely the wrong direction. Where would she start? Probably by looking into the relationships people at the festival had with Carrie. A few grudges were already common knowledge, but was the dislike strong enough to provoke murder?

The views and comments are still racking up on Laura's video, gaining momentum every minute.

Could Baker solve this? And, as her creator, wasn't Baker really just Jane in disguise?

A sharp chime makes them both jump in their seats and a harried voice sounds over the platform.

'Thank you for your patience. The sheep have been removed from the line and the train on platform one is now ready to leave. The delayed 15.11 to York will be arriving on platform two shortly.'

'Jane, are you thinking what I'm thinking?' Daniel definitely looks drunk now and is grinning widely.

'I don't know what you're thinking.' But she suspects she does.

'You should solve this. *Baker* should solve this.'

As she watches the views tick up past 3.3 million, 3.4, 3.5, Jane's mind moves just as fast. All of these people online are *hooked* on Laura, on *this case*.

'Baker's not real, Daniel.'

'But you said it yourself: the police aren't going to understand. They aren't taking books seriously as a motive.'

If Jane can solve this mystery, and she gets the word out there that *she* is the one who did so, these people might just be hooked on *her*. If Jane uncovers the truth, everyone's eyes will be on her books, on Private Investigator Sandra Baker. She'll get a new agent, Frankie will believe in her again, she'll top the bestseller lists, she will finally be a success.

Her eyes flick to platform two, where the delayed 15.11 is pulling in, before heading to York – via Hoslewit, and the Killer Lines Crime Fiction Festival.

But can she do it? Can Jane find out who murdered Carrie Marks? And will someone try to stop her?

There's only one way to find out, and that's to get on the 15.11.

Chapter Ten

Friday, 7 p.m.

Edward Carter is hiding. He has spent rather a lot of this week-end hiding, which, at six foot three, hasn't been easy. Right now, he is wedged behind the door of the Dog and Bone, the handle pressing uncomfortably into his hip.

It would be, he reflects, a humiliating position to be found in. But needs must.

Sarah Parks-Ward is on the warpath, and he is her target. Or perhaps it is closer to a trade mission. Either way, he does not want to be found.

Admittedly, this particular hiding spot was a mistake, he can see that now. When he'd seen her entering the bar, there hadn't been much choice. Now though, he is stuck. He can't see what is happening in the room, so either risks stepping out to discover she's still there – and her guessing he'd been lurking behind doors to avoid her wouldn't help the situation – or being forced to stay here until the end of time, eventually starving to death and slowly rotting into nothingness. It is impossible to choose between these equally dire outcomes.

It has been at least 20 minutes, and he worries he needs to sneeze.

Edward Carter is happy to self-identify as a coward. Bravery isn't all it's cracked up to be anyway. Dead people are always described as brave. No one ever wrote in an obituary 'He was the most cowardly man I knew'. Maybe that's because the cowards, tucked up in the safety of their beds with a book, weren't the ones dying.

No, Edward is firm on the subject. If someone asks for your belongings in a threatening manner, hand them over at once and apologise for not pre-empting their desire. If you hear an unexpected noise, run rather than investigate. And if a woman scorned, famously the greatest asset hell has to offer, is looking for you, you hide.

The choice of whether to move or not is soon taken from him.

'It's bloody cold in here! Close that door will you, Stu?'

The room reappears, and Edward is standing face-to-face with a shocked Scotsman, feeling a little ridiculous. On the plus side, a quick scan around shows him that the shiny white-blonde hair of Sarah Parks-Ward is no longer visible.

'Sorry about that,' he says, tugging at his lapels to make sure he doesn't look dishevelled. 'I'll be on my way.'

Slipping out of the door onto the darkening lawn, Edward slinks towards the bushes and melts into the shadows. The rain from earlier has stopped, but it has left the ground soggy, and there are mud spatters on his trousers in seconds. He'd ironed those as well! With a deep sigh, he lights up a cigarette, the flickering flame illuminating his face like a Hallowe'en pumpkin. Soon, the glowing red dot of his cigarette is the only sign of his presence.

What a day! What a weekend! The atmosphere is remarkably jolly, despite the murder. Edward suspects that some of this crowd don't yet understand the murder was real. So many rumours have been flying around – a marketing stunt, a play, a mistake, a heart attack – that most could make neither head nor tail of it. Edward, however, has spoken to the police and knows the ins and outs of the matter.

Carrie Marks was someone he'd known for a long time, since childhood in fact. Now she is dead and people have barely stood still long to draw breath. This isn't something that surprises Edward. He's already known death in his life, more than his fair share. Both of his parents, ageing when they adopted him, had died when he was in his early twenties. He'd lost a friend to cancer at university. But it was the death of his wife and child that had scarred him irrevocably.

Very few people knew the whole, tragic tale of their passing. Carrie Marks had been one of those few. With her death, Edward feels another part of himself die too.

He blows a slow stream of smoke into the air, taking satisfaction in watching it curl and dissipate. How many times had he stood in this exact spot, smoking Silk Cut and hiding from the world? Not just from Sarah Parks-Ward, though she is a particularly formidable adversary, but authors, editors, publicists – the lot of them. People demanding he review their book, others furious he *had* reviewed it and found it wanting. He is tiring of the whole game. *Has* tired of it, in fact, many years ago. Since his wife Nayla died, he's lost his love of a lot of things.

But reviewing books is his job, and he is aware that, as far as jobs go, it is for the most part a pleasant one.

As any good publicist should be, Sarah is fierce, even about less personal matters than their relationship. He had felt her wrath before when he'd written that an author she was working with was *as tired as an octogenarian, as nutritious as a Big Mac, and as exciting as a tax return.* He had hidden a lot at that year's festival.

Those words had been forgiven over time, but would his most recent transgression?

It was weeks ago now, the night he had mistakenly (after too much reminiscing and even more whisky) invited her into his bed after a book launch. Though they hadn't slept together – he had mortally offended her by promptly bursting into tears as soon as they walked in the door – she had spent the night there, and he's not been shot of her since. And now, after he'd let her down both in the bedroom and in the impossible favour she'd requested of him by way of an apology, she seems to be even *more* intent on tracking him down.

61

Edward pushes his cigarette into the mud, squashing it with his brogue. He isn't ready to sleep, but going back inside feels hugely unappealing. Out here, the air is fresh and cool, the country night beautiful once your eyes adjust to the gloom. Hunching his shoulders, he lights a second Silk Cut and inhales deeply, bringing it to life.

Carrie Marks. Her parents had fostered children, as did his until they adopted him, which was how the two of them met. They'd been through a lot together since. Downs as well as ups. But she'd been there for him when Nayla died, that's for sure. This whole situation makes him feel as though he is floating in a twilight zone. Cigarette in mouth, he rolls his shoulders back and then stretches both long, spidery arms into the air. His body creaks more with every day that passes.

He is never sure if he should be grateful for his creaking bones. After all, his wife will never reach old age. His child, not even teen age. Nayla is a Malaysian name that means *the one who wins*, and Edward had always liked to joke he was her prize. Well, he reflects, stubbing out his second cigarette, she didn't win in the end, did she? Neither did he.

Neither did Carrie.

Chapter Eleven

Friday, 7.15 p.m.

Jane sees the long, lean body of Edward Carter slip outside to the garden, and considers following. Had he been *hiding* behind the door? That would be very odd behaviour. And odd behaviour is exactly what they are supposed to be keeping an eye out for. Next to her, Daniel clinks his glass against hers. On the train platform, Jane had decided that if she was coming back to Killer Lines to solve this murder, she wasn't doing it alone. So the unlikely duo have checked back into their previous accomadation – both of which were non-refundable anyway – and have now seated themselves on perilously high stools in the bar of the Dog and Bone, notebooks open, sausage and mash consumed, ready to catch a killer.

The earlier rain shower has driven people inside and the bar is packed. One table is full of American tourists in anoraks, notepads out and heads together. The psychological thriller writers take up a corner of the room, laughter booming from their midst. The Scottish crime writers have joined forces with some recent arrivals – men Jane recognises as writers of Northern detective novels – and are talking over each other excitedly while steam rises from their wet jumpers.

Looking around, you wouldn't suspect that one of their own had been murdered just metres away. Activities continue as planned, drinks flow, fans ask for autographs and writers pitch their work to agents who are longing to be left alone.

But in the past few hours, the news has spread – Laura Lane's TikTok announcement really stoking the fires. So, if you take the time to listen, you will notice that there is just one subject of conversation: who killed Carrie Marks?

'How about Edward Carter?' Jane says to Daniel in a stage whisper. 'We could start with him?'

'Why him? Does he even have a motive?' Daniel is sipping a Guinness, and it doesn't suit him. Jane wonders if – just as she's in a startling red lipstick she'd purchased in the Boots next to the station – he is trying on a new persona.

'It's not all about motive. We need to establish people's movements. Anyway, I saw him arguing with someone on the day Carrie died. A publicist, I can't remember her name. It might be connected?'

'He's a newspaper reviewer. He's probably always arguing with publicists.' She hadn't thought of that.

'She said something, I can't remember the exact words.' Jane shuts her eyes to summon the memory: Frankie, exhausted and sad, in front of her; Edward at the bar with the beautiful, glossy blonde. 'She was really mad, and she was asking for something?' Jane's eyes snap open. 'Then, she said, *I could bloody kill her.*"'

'I just don't think he's a priority,' Daniel says, putting down his drink and slipping from his stool. 'First of all, let's focus on those we know had bad blood with Carrie. Going to the loo, back in a minute.'

Jane sighs as her new protégé squeezes through the crowd and heads away from her. She had been under the impression that she was to be Inspector Morse in this situation, thank you *very* much, and Daniel was to be the Lewis. The Watson to her Holmes. The . . . well, Poirot doesn't really *have* a sidekick, but she is definitely the Poirot. She is the expert in solving crime, sort of, and in her book, a public argument plus a murderous threat have to be important. But more than this, she feels a pull towards the tall, strange man who had been hiding behind the door.

The door to the lawn cracks open, and in squeezes a man Jane recognises but has never spoken to. In his sixties with neatly combed, thinning grey hair, a strong, set jaw and solid body devoid of fat, Brad Levinsky is dressed casually in a plain white t-shirt, leather jacket and faded blue jeans. Jane thinks he looks like the kind of man who thinks he looks like James Dean, rather than actually looking anything like James Dean.

Despite the care he clearly takes with his appearance, Levinsky's skin is grey and his eyes red, and Jane has a brief flashback to seeing him doing shots at 5 in the afternoon the previous day. At least she hadn't been partaking too freely – finding a body on a hangover must be dreadful.

Brad squeezes past her, the wet leather of his jacket sliding against Jane's arm making her recoil. It is like being touched by a snake. Alarmingly, he stops right in front of her.

'Kim! There you are!'

Jane jumps, and tries to shrink away. Deep in her own thoughts, she hadn't noticed Kimberley Brown perched on the stool next to her.

'Brad! Drink, darling? Should we see if they do those Pornstar Martinis?'

'Don't think it's the sort of place. I'll have a Badger's Foot.'

'A . . . what?'

'It's a beer they've got. They've all got names like that. Crazy Brits.' He barks a laugh that is over before it begins. One sharp note, like a printer has run out of ink after the first *ha*.

Brad squeezes past her to sit on Daniel's vacated stool, and Jane retreats to the very edge of her seat to escape the wet leather. It's as if they haven't seen her at all. People often treat Jane as though she is a piece of furniture. If she were a detective, that would have been a useful quality. Though, of course, she is not.

'What do you think then?' mutters Kimberley. She is speaking quietly to avoid her voice carrying, but loud enough for

Brad, and Jane, to hear over the hubbub. 'Did you hear anything else out there?'

'Not much. Those cops are tight-lipped, but I hung around
the area they've taped off, pretending to make a phone call
back home. They think she was killed around 12.30 last night,
give or take 15 minutes. Then some skirt asked me what I was
doing, and I thought I would actually go and call the old bag
after all.'

'You can't call women that anymore.'

'What? Old bag? She's *my wife*!'

'Skirt. But both, I guess. Anyway, did you get through?'

'There's hardly any cell-service around here – thanks for
this.' He breaks off and Jane hears him slurping noisily at his
pint of ale. 'Yeah, no cell-service, had to walk for ages. And
when I got through, she said she was asleep and to leave her
alone. Ah, that's a good beer. Needed that.'

Jane sips at her glass of wine, staring intently at the bar.
She feels intrusive, despite having been sitting here long before
Brad arrived. At the same time though, her skin is tingling with
excitement.

'Anyway, Kim,' continues Brad, 'how are you doing?'

'What do you mean?'

'Oh, come on. Your mortal enemy croaks it in the night . . .
Feeling good?'

'Brad!' Kimberley Brown hisses, and Jane feels rather than
sees her look around and lean closer to the author. 'Okay, I'll
be honest with you. I've got mixed feelings. We had history, as
you know.'

'Good riddance to bad trash.'

'I wouldn't put it in so many words, but . . . ' Jane hears the
clink of their glasses.

Brad gives the same loud, sharp, one-note laugh, jolting Jane
in her seat.

'Talking of words,' Kimberley continues, 'we sh—'

A cheer erupts across the room, followed by a chant that drowns out most of the conversation happening next to Jane.

'*We like to drink with Simon . . .*'

'. . . story straight . . .'

'*Cause Simon is our mate!*'

'. . . to the cops . . .'

'*We like to drink with Simon . . .*'

'. . . bed at . . .'

'*Cause he gets it down in eight!*'

'. . . but I didn't see . . .'

'*Seven! Six! Five! Four! Three! Two! One!*'

Another loud cheer fills the air, causing Jane to cower where she sits and making further eavesdropping impossible.

'It's too loud in here,' says Kimberley. 'Let's catch up later.'

'Sure thing. Want to come and join the guys over there?'

'You go,' Kimberley says. 'I have a few emails to send.'

Brad Levinsky squeezes out of his space by the bar. When he moves, Jane finds herself looking straight into the long thin face of Kimberley Brown and hastily averts her eyes. The editor sips at what looks like a glass of scotch and starts to tap away on her phone. She is wearing white. A purposeful juxtaposition of the more appropriate black of mourning? Or perhaps just what she'd had in her suitcase. Either way, Jane can admit, it looks good on her. In the dingy British bar with its brown and orange carpets and dark, scratched wood, Kimberley Brown shines. Her long, slender body is draped on the bar stool like a silk scarf, smart black shoes tapping against the footrest of her stool. Jane is self-conscious in her bright lipstick, and the sack dress feels absurd next to the stylish white suit.

Auburn hair pulled back into a tight ponytail and deep plum lipstick on her stern yet plump lips, Kimberley Brown looks, to Jane, perfect, powerful, and entirely unapproachable. Usually, Sandra Baker knocks on a door, catching someone unawares, or else turns up at their workplace flashing her

PI credentials. Somehow, approaching someone in a bar is a lot more intimidating.

Suddenly, the editor glances back up and meets her eye. Jane pretends she is admiring a framed picture of some basset hounds on the wall behind her quarry.

'Can I help you?'

Jane slides off her stool in shock. Kimberley Brown, her phone now face down on the bar top, is scowling at her.

'It's just that you were clearly trying to listen in to my conversation a moment ago, which I don't appreciate, and now you're staring at me. So, what is it you want?'

'Oh, I, ah . . . ' The wine glass feels hot in Jane's suddenly sweaty hand, and she feels her face start to glow pink. 'I'm sorry, I didn't mean to—'

'If you want me to read your work, I only take manuscripts from literary agents. And it's inappropriate to approach me in the evening, in a bar. Honestly, I've had it up to here,' she jabs a manicured finger into the air by her ear, 'with wannabe writers shoving manuscripts at me when I'm trying to relax. Yesterday someone put their manuscript under the door of the *toilet* stall I was in. Now, I need to get back to this.' She taps her phone with one long, manicured nail, her mouth set in a firm line and perfect eyebrows drawn together in a frown.

Feeling pink from head to foot, Jane backs away, stuttering her apology. Leaving the room at a sharp trot, she finds herself in a gloomy corridor. Ignoring the stairs and door to the main foyer, she forges ahead down the hallway, turning corners without thinking, desperate to put some distance between herself and Kimberley Brown. This is absolutely the right option. Running away from problems always works.

Finally, she sees the metal sign reading *Ladies*. Pushing open the door, Jane manages to hold in her tears until it swings shut behind her.

Chapter Twelve

Friday, 7.40 p.m.

Jane Hepburn is staring into a smeared mirror, cracked in one corner. She is surprised, and not a little relieved, to see that her wine has come with her, and she gulps it back in one before slamming the glass down on the countertop. There are tears in her eyes, making them shine brightly in the yellow light. Her skin, though not quite as neon pink as it had felt, is flushed and a light sweat has broken out on her forehead.

She cannot do this. She isn't PI Sandra Baker. She is Jane. Just plain Jane, wearing a sack, looking washed up and worn out.

Jane forces herself to meet her own eyes in the mirror and tries to scrub the red lipstick away.

'You are so stupid,' she tells herself, rubbing at her lips with a scrunched-up paper towel. 'You are stupid, and hideous, and an old fool.' She will go back to her Air BnB, grab her still-packed suitcase and head home. She was right earlier. It is past time to give up on all of this; on solving crimes in life, or even fiction. Time to hang up her pen and find a life more appropriate to who she actually is.

'Um, are you okay?'

One of the cubicle doors has silently swung open, and in the mirror Jane can see an embarrassed-looking woman standing behind her. Light brown skin and scraped back hair, short and a little dumpy, with ears that stick out in a charming yet inelegant way that gives her a raccoon-like appearance; it's Natasha Martez.

'Oh, God, sorry. I thought there was no one else here,' Jane stutters, stating the obvious. People don't frequently shout at their own reflection in front of strangers on purpose.

'For what it's worth,' says Natasha, approaching the sinks, 'I don't think you're hideous. And you don't look old to me either.' She starts to wash her hands, avoiding Jane's eyes. The way Natasha pronounces *don't* as *dawnt* reminds Jane that her press announcement mentioned she was originally from Portugal, though the accent is barely noticeable. 'I can't really comment on you being a fool though. That could well be true.'

She looks up and smiles into the mirror, her perfect white teeth and sticky-out ears making her look even more endearing. Jane smiles weakly back. Remembering this woman's easy, stratospheric success, she reminds herself to hate her. But the kind smile won't allow her to.

'Thank you,' she manages at last. 'I'm pretty sure I *am* a fool though.'

Natasha hesitates for a second, evidently torn between two courses of action. Picking one, she turns around and hoists herself up on the counter, between sinks. Perching there, she swings her short legs. She is still in the casual jeans of the day before, worn with a different plain t-shirt, creased and faded. She looks at Jane with interest.

'Tell me about it.'

It isn't a question. But demand isn't the right word either. An invitation, Jane decides.

She isn't the sort of person to open up easily, and having too many friends was never exactly a problem for Jane. But Natasha looks kind, and the other option is to hide in a bathroom cubicle for the rest of the evening until everyone has gone. Exactly how she spent her school prom after being turned down for a dance by Benjamin Wallace, computer nerd and notorious nose-picker.

When the words still don't come, Natasha continues.

'I don't really know anyone here. To be honest with you, I've been in here for the last 20 minutes, playing Tetris on my phone. So you may as well indulge me.'

'But you're the new big thing!' Jane blurts, immediately feeling guilty about calling a person a thing. 'I mean, you're the big success story everyone is talking about. What have *you* got to hide about?' She tries hard to keep the bitter edge from her voice but it's difficult. Natasha is from the world of six-figure deals and splashy announcements, national book tours and actual marketing budgets. Jane is lucky to get a tweet on publication day, and a *cover reveal* with four likes (including her, her editor and, previously, her mother). Her books never get shiny gold foil on the cover, and the most publicity she's ever had was the time her local newspaper interviewed her for an article on potholes in the area.

'Well, that's kind of you. Doesn't feel that way though.' Jane notices that Natasha is blushing too, swinging her legs and avoiding looking at her. The other woman's discomfort somehow settles her. 'Feels awkward,' Natasha continues in a hushed tone. There is something about bathrooms at night that makes you want to whisper, the church of the female confessional. 'Like, I'm not good at social interactions really, and my publicist keeps pushing me at people. I was on a panel and I totally bombed. Had nothing to say. Came in here to cry straight after.'

Jane finds people complaining about success irritating. *Oh no! You have to talk to people about how great you are and then go and spend some of your lovely money? Boohoo.* But she can also imagine her own horror at being made to sit in front of a crowd and answer questions.

'Anyway.' Natasha looks up and over her shoulder, meeting Jane's watery eyes again in the mirror. 'What have you done that's so foolish?'

Maybe because she is at an utter low – is there much lower than being caught talking to yourself while crying and drinking? – or maybe because Natasha is a particularly attentive listener, Jane wants to tell her everything. All about how she's never been to this festival before, and immediately regretted it when she arrived. About the crushing loneliness she felt after losing her mother. About her editor avoiding her, and her agent preparing to dump her. About finding Carrie's body – even admitting to the reason she'd been in the book tent so early. About leaving, and then coming back with Daniel and a fresh resolve to solve the case. Partially to find the truth for Carrie, but partially, to be honest, for selfish reasons. Because if she solves this, she will be someone, and people will notice her, and she'll be worth something. She looks at Natasha, and Natasha looks back at her. And so, in a stutter, Jane does.

'But I can't do it,' she summarises 20 minutes later. 'Obviously I can't. I tried to talk to Kimberley Brown but she told me to get lost, so I did. I froze.'

'Of course you froze! You're not your character. Baker, wasn't it? You're not Baker.'

'Yes,' Jane mutters, leaning forward on the sink and staring down into the plug hole. 'I get that.'

'You're you! Sorry, that sounds so cheesy. But there is more than one way to do something. More than one way to solve a case.' Natasha jumps down off the sink. 'Wait there.'

Again, it isn't a question. So Jane stays where she is, in front of the mirror in the dingy bathroom. Daniel will be wondering what's happened to her by now, but she can't go out there. Is Natasha coming back? Maybe she's scarpered – no one wants to hang out with the class dunce.

When the door swings open again, Jane jumps, so convinced is she that Natasha has abandoned her. But, no: Natasha has returned and has a bottle of red wine in one hand and two empty glasses in the other.

'Ah, you have one already,' she says, nodding at Jane's glass on the counter. 'Pass it here.' She pours a healthy amount for each of them. They clink glasses, and Jane feels her spirits rise. There really is something about women's toilets. A safe haven away from the real world, a place where bonds are formed and boundaries crossed.

'Cheers. And thanks for hanging out with me.'

Natasha snorts a laugh. 'Thank *you*. You're the first friend I've made at this festival so far.'

Jane flushes with pleasure and looks down to force her burgeoning smile back in its box.

'You know,' Natasha goes on, 'Carrie was my agent too.'

'I'd forgotten that,' admits Jane.

'I almost went with Marabella Rhodes, from the Rhodes Talent Agency? But, yes, I ended up with Carrie in the end, and she was good to me. You want to solve this murder, Jane? Then let's *do* it. First, tell me everything you know.'

Natasha, back up on the countertop, is jiggling her leg with what Jane assumes is anticipation, knocking back her wine with abandon. Jane feels it catch, *possibility* slowly seeping back into her.

'I don't really know anything yet, that's sort of the issue?'

'I bet you *do*. But I can start if you like? Let me tell you everything that *I* know.'

Eyes wide, face flushed, Natasha looks like an excited child. Bouncing up and down, large dark eyes gleaming, Jane decides she is definitely a racoon, and copies her, heaving her own body, with a distinct lack of elegance, up next to the sinks. *Here we go*, she thinks. *Let's do this.*

'What do you know?'

Then the door swings open yet again.

'She said I was as useful as a ham suitcase!' says Daniel. 'A *ham suitcase!*'

Tears of laughter are coursing down Jane's face, and she can't remember the last time she had such fun. Oh, how much can change in one day, she thinks to herself. From finding Carrie's body to the police questioning her, to listening to Abi's ominous message in her apartment, to crying in the toilets, to laughing with new friends.

When you wake up, you never know how that day will end. It's that fact that makes life both terrifying and wonderfully exciting.

In her distress, Jane had run right past Daniel as he made his way back from the bathroom. He'd waited at the bar for her, but when she didn't return had become worried. Seeing Natasha enter and leave again carrying supplies, he'd put two and two together and followed her. Perhaps Daniel will make a good detective yet.

It's now 11 p.m. and Jane has been up since 4.30 that morning. Her whole body aches with tiredness and exhilaration, but the three of them are still in the bathroom, finishing the wine. Natasha and Jane are perched between the sinks, and Daniel has made himself comfortable by sitting cross-legged on the floor like a child at school assembly.

'Like, a suitcase to transport ham, or one made of ham?'

'I mean the latter sounds more useless to me,' shouts Daniel. 'What sort of niche insult is *ham suitcase*? Why not . . . I don't know . . . a paper umbrella?'

Natasha's snorts of laughter echo off the tiles, making Jane giggle even more. She's never thought of herself as a giggler, but you never do know. 'And all because I hadn't realised she wanted the contracts printed out before she asked. Like, I was somehow supposed to know? It was my second day. *I'm not even being paid.*' Daniel slaps the floor in mock fury and Jane wipes the remnants of tears from her eyes.

'Alright, not that this isn't fun – and I do sympathise with your predicament, Daniel, which is probably covered under the Modern Slavery Act – but we're supposed to be solving a murder here?' Jane says, pulling herself together. She is the adult in this group after all.

'We *were*, before you snuck off to the toilets to get drunk with this one,' Daniel says, gesturing at Natasha, who raises her glass in a silent salute. 'What's the plan then, Jane?'

From her perch, she sees the youthful faces of Daniel and Natasha turn to her in expectation. Is she their leader? The Morse? The Sherlock? It's what she wanted, but she has never been a leader before. Unless you count the time she volunteered for the Girl Guides, and quit after getting stuck in the tent and having to be cut out.

'Well,' she begins, slowly, sipping at her wine to stall a moment longer. 'First, we need to understand motive, means and opportunity.' Just like that, the day spins on its axis again. The dingy room, so recently ringing with hysterical laughter, falls completely silent. Her new friends are hooked on her every word. 'That means we need to create a full picture of who had an issue with Carrie Marks – we know a little of this already, but not enough. We also need to establish who would be capable of committing the act, and lastly, who had the *chance* to do it.'

They sit and drink their wine in silence, the gloomy yellow bulb above the sinks emitting a horror-movie flicker.

'Who has a motive?' asks Natasha, her voice dropping to a whisper again, as if the sound of it might scare away the atmosphere.

'Well,' begins Jane, 'she had a known feud with Kimberley Brown. I even saw Kimberley celebrating her death.'

'Abi Ellis,' says Daniel confidently. 'She felt obstructed by Carrie, wanted her clients and a free rein. She's very ambitious . . . I don't think that girl would stop at anything to succeed.'

'Woman,' says Natasha absently, seemingly on reflex. 'Not girl. Pass me Jane's handbag.' Daniel hands it up to her, and she rummages until she finds the red lipstick. On the grimy mirror, Natsha writes *Suspects*, and underneath that *Abi Ellis* and *Kimberley Brown*.

Jane likes the effect, though that lipstick was the one she'd only just bought from Boots and it had cost her £8.99. Probably not the time to mention it.

'How about Laura Lane?' offers Natasha. 'I know they don't like each other, though I'm not sure why. I spoke to Laura last night and she dropped in a few scathing remarks.'

'Yeah, I've heard about that,' says Daniel. 'I know Laura is an advocate for authors representing themselves, and Carrie once wrote an article about authors who are bad writers but good self-promoters, blah blah blah. But there *could* be more to it?'

Natasha adds the name to the mirror. 'You know, this is not what I expected being an author to be like.'

'Maybe they didn't care for each other, but I don't see how those reasons,' Daniel nods at the mirror, 'would result in Carrie's death.'

'There could be more to their dislike than we know. Murder isn't always logical,' Jane says. 'And it's not always planned. They could have argued, and arguments can escalate. I don't think that anyone *planned* to murder Carrie Marks, not right in the middle of a literary festival. That would be madness.'

'Those are our top suspects then,' Daniel whispers.

'There will be others out there,' says Jane. 'Though surely not *that* many harbouring a hatred so strong they would *kill*?'

'You said it yourself – murder is not always logical,' reasons Natasha, 'and often accidental.' Silence fills the bathroom as they stare at the names on the mirror, scrawled in gruesome horror-film red.

Abi Ellis.

Kimberley Brown.

Laura Lane.

Let the hunt begin.

Chapter Thirteen

Saturday, 5 a.m.

Jane is awake. Despite her body feeling heavy from lack of sleep, she tosses and turns and frets, staring at the ceiling of her rented room. She experiments with closing her eyes and opening them in the darkness to see if she can see any more with her eyes open than closed. She counts the drips of the bathroom tap, which she can faintly hear through the paper-thin wall – infuriatingly, it appears to drip every three seconds, but every now and again it will randomly drip twice in quick succession. She is starting to believe it is purely these out-of-sync drips that are keeping her awake.

As well as the dripping and the impenetrable darkness, thoughts of the day just passed are also stopping her from sleeping. On reflection, it's probably more the day than the drips.

The dripping is now interspersed with a new sound – the gentle chatter of birds waking up. Jane thought her eyes were open, but forgot she'd closed them earlier. Maybe she isn't as awake as she'd assumed. Peeling her lids apart, she realises that the thick darkness is paling, but the digital alarm clock on her IKEA bedside cabinet, a relic from the turn of the millennium, tells her it's 5 a.m.

A few more hours, and then she'll get up and try and make it out of the house before she has to speak to her hostess. Mary seems perfectly nice, but also someone, as Jane's mother would have said, who could *talk the hind leg off a donkey*. The kind of person who tells you about their sex life when you've only enquired how their day was. The kind of person to have an opinion on how you make your toast. The kind of person to ask you about your relationship status and, without so much as knowing how you like your tea, have plenty of suggestions for how to 'fix' the terrible affliction that is being single and childless.

Jane can tell, because Jane is observant, that Mary likes to think of herself as a good hostess. Because of this, Jane plans to use the dripping tap to fend her off. If Mary starts to talk to her, she will mention the tap, and Mary will panic and go to look at it. Jane wonders briefly if the fact that she makes escape plans so often to avoid conversation is connected to her rather solitary existence.

Today though, conversation is a must. With Natasha and Daniel by her side, she must find a way to speak to their suspects. It might also be worth buying a new lipstick.

Laura Lane is awake. She is scrolling through the videos she made yesterday, analysing which are the most successful in terms of shares, likes and comments. The videos where she is tearful, but only slightly, are performing best. Her fans like a complex mixture of vulnerability and strength that makes her appear relatable and aspirational at the same time. Lying back on her pillow, she closes her eyes. She should get up soon, go for a run before other people start appearing in the world. Though perhaps she'll give herself a day off, after everything that's gone on.

Breathing in deeply, remembering the lessons she'd been taught on her yoga training course, Laura steadies her heartbeat. Meditation, a daily ritual, had been forgotten the previous day, and she blames that lapse for her being awake now. But as well as that, there is a lightness in her blood that she can't deny. Carrie Marks not looming over her with demands – demands that had recently tipped into threats – makes her feel freer than she's ever felt before in her short, difficult life. She breathes out, loudly, freely, then rolls onto her stomach and smiles into her pillow.

Brad Levinsky is not awake. Having finally crashed into his room at 2.45 in the morning, he is now lying spread-eagled on top of the duvet, hands clenched into fists, arms flung out like a terrifyingly large baby. With his mouth wide open, his snores shake the room. Pity his neighbour.

Back home, Brad lives a fairly clean lifestyle. He writes, works out, eats like a rabbit and sleeps like a log. Just why he's allowed himself to let his hair down so spectacularly on this trip is a mystery. Maybe it's something to do with what Kimberley told him on the way here.

She likes to appear professional and detached, but Brad had seen the torment in her eyes when she'd made her confession, and he knew she immediately regretted it. He loves Kimberley Brown. Not in a sexual way – she's far too metropolitan for his tastes, despite being a gorgeous woman. But she had discovered him, stuck by him, and eventually made him a star. So, he loves her.

Now, however, he isn't worrying about that. Now, after two days of solid drinking during which he's tried valiantly to keep up with the British authors, he is sleeping soundly. In his head, an F-22 fighter jet with the American flag painted proudly on the tail, races through the sky, expertly taking down a Russian Sukhoi Su-57. He is in the cockpit, and in his ear, his commanders cheer his name.

Edward Carter is awake. He'd slept poorly, and is now leaning out of his hotel window – the same hotel that Daniel, Abi, and Carrie Marks had booked into – smoking his first cigarette of the day. He'd managed to quit once. Having started when he was 17 because he'd thought it would help his chances with the ladies, he'd stopped at 30 to help his chances with living to old age. But that didn't seem as important after Nayla died, so he'd picked it back up with a vengeance on the day of her funeral.

There is so much pleasure in smoking. The nicotine hit, yes, but also the excuse to stand outside alone for ten minutes whenever you feel like it. He even finds enjoyment in the sanctimonious shakes of the head people give him.

'Do you know that will kill you?' someone he doesn't even know will tell him.

'Yes,' he'll say cheerily. 'It says so on the packet. That's why I picked them.' They would leave him alone then.

Checking his watch, he sees that it's just past 5. He'd agreed weeks ago to meet a publisher at 8 a.m. that day, someone who thought providing him with some stale croissants and bad coffee would buy his favour in review inches, but there were hours yet. Stubbing out his cigarette, Edward judges that he has just enough time to work on his project before breakfast, so he digs his laptop from his bag and settles into a chair to begin.

Sarah Parks-Ward is awake. Deep under the duvet of her luxurious bed, she holds her phone an inch from her face as she scrolls through her latest bank statement. The number at the bottom is a little alarming. There is a chance that this is a nightmare, but as she can see the offending Fendi boots in the corner of her room, she assumes it is not.

At least she'll look good today while she is shepherding around the talentless Natasha Martez, who somehow bagged that gigantic deal. Sarah's read her book, and it's little more than *fine*. The woman looks a mess too, in her scruffy t-shrts and trainers – if Sarah had that money, she'd look incredible. Even *more* incredible than she already does. She scowls into the darkness, reaches out bravely from the warmth of the duvet, and hurls her phone at the boots.

Whatever. The bank balance doesn't matter too much. She is good at this – putting any little problem to the back of her mind for a while. She's got a plan, and it's a good one this time, one that will keep the lights on for a while yet – and keep her in nice shoes. Absolutely no chance it will fail.

With that thought, she snuggles back down into the bed and closes her eyes, preparing to catch a few more hours' sleep before the world awakes.

Frankie Reid is not awake, though she had been until fairly recently. Late to bed, and now she will surely be late to rise. She is lying, fully clothed, on the grubby sofa in her hotel room with her laptop positioned precariously on her thighs. She'd been up late trying to finish the work she hadn't had time to tackle that day because she'd been distracted by – well, it was obvious what she'd been distracted by.

It had been hard to continue as normal: mingling, support-ing authors, pitching her voice so it had the right amount of sorrow in it whenever Carrie was mentioned. In the end, she'd perfected a line to use whenever the name was brought up in conversation – she would shake her head slowly, and say *a true legend*. It implied respect, and invited no response. It had worked a charm.

Back in her hotel, she'd tried desperately to finish her latest edit while drinking a bottle of warm white wine she was plan-ning to put on expenses. Frankie has not saved the work she did on her laptop, which died an hour ago. The wine glass is now on its side, the liquid it contained soaked into her right trainer.

All over Hoslewit, people sleep and do not sleep – the two main states of humanity. After *alive* and *dead*, anyway. Natasha scribbles notes, while Daniel snores, and Abi dreams of some-thing that causes her to smile under her duvet. Detective Inspec-tor Ramos blearily hits his alarm clock, inwardly begging for ten minutes more, while Kimberley Brown does push ups next to her bed, and Jane continues to stare at the ceiling. Whoever you are, she reflects, you are either asleep or not asleep, for your whole life. That thought feels deep in the darkness, like a lot of nonsense thoughts sometimes do.

Sliding out of the scratchy sheets, Jane picks up the towel that had been left out for her. It's crunchy, which Jane knows is due to its age and Mary's washing procedure. Though perhaps the washing is Mary's husband's job. It's 2025 after all.

In her attempts to move as silently as a mouse, or a Tesla if you're going to be modern about it, Jane misjudges the space and whacks her hip painfully on the corner of the small desk. The lamp, adorned with characters from *Frozen,* falls to the floor with a crash, and she squeals in agony. That will bruise.

Jane Hepburn is now most definitely awake.

Chapter Fourteen

Jane is striding, yes, striding, across Hoslewit towards the festival site. She's holding a cup of coffee that cost £3.50 at the local café, despite being Asda's own brand instant granules. She'd seen the jar. Not only this, but Mary had cornered her on leaving the bathroom, and insisted she have breakfast with her and her husband, which had turned out to be severely undercooked scrambled eggs. They had been poured onto Jane's plate like a slurry of cement filling up a gangster's grave, and she had politely declared them delicious.

Despite this inauspicious start to the day, Jane is buoyant. She is off to meet her *friends*, and together they are going to *solve a murder*. How thrilling! How delightful! And not only that: when they've solved it, she's going to take her career in hand. No more yellow lanyards, no more languishing book sales. She is Jane Hepburn, and she is here to *slay*.

On second thoughts, she thinks, she'll scratch that last bit. It was a word picked up from watching hours of Laura Lane's TikTok videos, but she isn't sure she can pull it off. Given the circumstances, she isn't sure calling herself a slayer is appropriate either.

But she is certainly here to . . . impress. That would do it.

Either way, she's prepared for action, armed with a tote bag that holds a fresh notebook and pen for jotting down any clues, as well as some copies of her novels. She had the excellent thought that Detective Inspector Ramos might enjoy a copy of book one in the series, *Rush of Blood*. After all, PI Sandra Baker may be able to give him some handy tips. Jane's pre-signed it, just in case.

The tote bag is one she uses a lot and got free with the latest Jamie Oliver cookbook, so she feels it to be suitable for a book festival. Jane likes Jamie Oliver, considering him to be a very nice man, a good egg so to speak, and she has an outside hope of him seeing her with the bag and striking up conversation. After all, lots of people like crime fiction, and she's sure he could have wangled a free ticket if he'd asked, so he may well be here. She has a signed copy of *Rush of Blood* in the bag for him too.

Jane walks down the steep hill from Mary's house towards the centre of the village, bag banging against her hip with each step. Down past Tesco Metro and the post office, past the Londis, which has tried to rebrand itself as the Village Shop. She cuts through the graveyard, dotted with ancient tombstones and Heineken bottles, and past the church that watches her judgmentally with tall, stained-glass eyes. In the heart of the village, she goes past the charity shop and the butcher's, outside of which sits a fat, mangy cat who stares at Jane with a hungry expression, and a squat Chinese takeaway, yet to open for business, before climbing the hill on the other side. Eventually, she sees the large banner reading *Killer Lines Crime Fiction Festival*, just glimpsing Detective Inspector Ramos disappearing beneath it alongside a crime-scene investigator.

Stopping to catch her breath, Jane drinks the cold dregs of her coffee with a wince, shading her eyes from the morning sun as she studies the festival site. It's still quiet, but there is some movement. Like 8.50 a.m. at a Wetherspoon's, there are always a dedicated few who arrive for the opening of the doors.

'Heading up?' The voice from behind her makes Jane jump, the empty cup *not* dousing her with coffee being the first bit of good luck she's had that day. Spinning around, she sees the long figure of Edward Carter, who must have come from the Thistle Hotel over the road. Still, she marvels at his quiet approach.

Jane blushes and nods. 'Yes, just catching my breath before I head up the hill.'

'Hopefully, you're up this early to see the panel I'm moderating? *Crime in Heels: the rise of the female gangster.* It starts at nine.' He checks his watch, and Jane registers how nice it is for a man to wear a watch in this day and age. She also registers how, despite her own six foot, she has to look *up* at him. It's a pleasant feeling.

'Oh, yes. Yes, that's it.'

'No, you aren't. But thank you. I'm Edward.'

Shifting her coffee cup, Jane awkwardly shakes his hand, her tote bag sliding down her arm as she does so. 'I'm Jane. Jane Hepburn? I'm an author?'

'Jane Jane Hepburn. Nice to meet you.' He smiles, and Jane feels a rush in her head that is nothing to do with too much caffeine and too little sleep. What looks like croissant crumbs on his shirt suggests that he is single, or at least sleeping alone on this trip. He has grey eyes behind thick glasses, and they lock on to hers. 'Shall we walk?' He gestures to the path and they fall into step, long legs matching each other's pace. 'What do you write?'

Jane fumbles in her bag for a copy of *Rush of Blood*, pulling one out alongside a tampon and a satsuma. She puts the satsuma back in the bag and pretends not to have noticed the tampon that now lies on the grass between them. Jane is aware that getting her books into the hands of someone like Edward Carter could change her fortunes almost as much as solving a murder, though it's always seemed just as difficult.

'I have a detective series? Sandra Baker. She's actually a private investigator rather than a real detective. Here.' She thrusts it at him like an aggressive student looking for charity sign-ups on Oxford Street, regrets it, and pulls it back as he goes to take it. Awkwardly, she offers it again.

85

'Well, thank you. I'll give that a read.' He says it politely, and Jane tells herself not to get her hopes up. He is probably just a very polite man.

'Oh, hang on, could I have that one back? I think it's signed.' Her face burning, she opens the front page to check, confirms that it says *Dear Jamie*, and finds a blank one in the bag. 'Here. Sorry.'

A crash breaks the moment. The Killer Lines banner has come untied and fallen loudly to the ground, pulling down bunting and hitting someone on the head with a *thump*. Organisers scurry over, appearing like ants. They shout suggestions while the victim shouts obscenities.

Jane and Edward walk on in silence, Jane willing her face to return to a normal colour. Not only has she been able to give this man a copy of her book, but she has a unique chance to start her investigation. Daniel may have dismissed the idea of questioning Edward Carter, but she has to start somewhere. And this person isn't actively snarling at her like Kimberley Brown had.

'So . . . Edward. How have you found the festival?'

That's good. She is easing in. Though she's aware she has about five minutes until they reach the site and he disappears.

'Well, it's been okay, apart from a dear friend of mine being murdered, I suppose.'

'Carrie Marks was a friend?' She realises Edward is the first person who has described Carrie thus, and the thought makes her sad. If Jane herself had been the victim, would anyone use that word of her? Her mother had always been Jane's only real friend.

'A very old friend. It's knocked me quite for six.'

'Did you see her that evening then?' Jane's mouth is dry and she tries to keep her voice even. One point of action for the day was to nail down people's movements late on Thursday night. Brad had said Carrie was murdered at around 12.30 a.m. So either the murderer was up late, or they'd snuck back to the festival after most people had gone to bed. Jane hadn't expected this task to start before she was even inside the festival grounds though.

'I saw her, yes. We had a drink together, we usually do.'

'Can I ask what time that was?'

Edward stops walking and turns to look at Jane, a deep crease forming between the grey eyes behind his thick-framed glasses. Jane looks back at him, hoping her pink face appears the picture of innocence. She'd written a character in her fourth book, *The Troubled Knife*, who convinced everyone around them that they weren't a serial killer despite the mounting evidence. Bernadette Shaw had achieved it partly with a sweet smile, which Jane tries to emulate now.

'Why do you ask?' Edward replies eventually.

In the background, Jane is vaguely aware that some festival organisers are now on ladders, others on the ground, as they fight with the unwieldy banner. '*Ted!*' Jane hears one of them shout. '*Get a bleedin' move on, will ya, you daft sod!*'

'I'm just curious,' she says with a small shrug. When Edward doesn't respond, she sighs. 'Carrie was my literary agent. I'm trying to build up a picture of what happened that night.'

'*Ted, you moron!*' the festival organiser bellows. '*Lift. It. Up. And hand it to Brenda!*' Another crash as the banner is dropped by whoever is on the ladder.

'*That's it,*' says maybe-Ted. '*I'm going to Greggs for bacon rolls. But if you think you're getting one, mate, you'll be as disappointed as your mum must be.*'

'And . . . I found her body,' Jane says.

Edward's eyes widen but he makes no comment. After a moment, he continues walking. 'Well, I spoke to her on and off all evening really. We had a good chat at . . . oh, I don't know . . . around 10.30, I think, just before I left. Carrie was upset. I hate to think of her being upset on her last night on this planet, but there you go. My old man didn't choose to fall down dead in Dunelm while looking at new curtains for the living room, but you can't choose these things.'

Jane's heart is beating fast: from excitement, from proximity to a man she finds beguiling, and from the steepness of the hill they are marching up. They have almost reached the festival site now, and the banner is nearly back in place. The woman she supposes is Ted's colleague Brenda is wiping her brow and glaring at the man on the opposite ladder.

'No,' says Jane in a concerned voice, not looking at Edward, 'I don't suppose you can choose. It is a shame though. Why was she upset?'

'Oh, she'd had an argument. More than one. Look, I've known Carrie a long time. She wasn't perfect. Far from it. She made mistakes, and she made enemies. That's who she was.'

Jane has nothing to say to this so she walks on in silence, hoping for more. Eventually, Edward obliges.

'She'd had some bust up with her assistant,' he mutters with a sideways glance at Jane as they enter the site. 'Hello there! Lovely banner! Anyway, you'll know Abi if you're a client of Carrie's? They rowed. Something about her being a drunken disgrace and showing the agency up. To be fair to Carrie, I do think I saw Abi being sick in a plant pot. But Carrie could be . . . harsh. I'll bet she didn't say it too kindly. Then Abi came back at her about all sorts of other things. It escalated.'

'Curious,' says Jane, flashing her lanyard at the hungover-looking woman guarding the entrance. 'That does sound unpleasant. Was it resolved?'

'Not that I know of. She was going on about Laura Lane, after having a bit of a confrontation with her too. But I don't really know what that was about.'

'I've heard they didn't like each other?'

'Oh, they didn't. But whenever I asked Carrie about the specifics, she'd tap her nose,' Edward mimes the action, 'and say she'd tell me one day. Anyway, here we are!' he says, looking around as if to check the coast is clear. 'I'd better go and brush up on my questions. Not that there will be much of a crowd at this time in the morning.'

He stops, turning to look at Jane with what she thinks to be a sad smile. This man has a story, she tells herself.

'Look, I'm not stupid, Jane. You sound like you're trying to find out what happened, and I can't tell you that. If I knew, I'd be at the police station and someone would be locked up by now. Sure, Carrie argued with Laura and Abi that night. She argued a lot.'

'Isn't there any last detail you can tell me? Anyone you suspect? Any grudges Carrie nursed, for example?'

They stare at each other for a few seconds until Edward turns away with a frustrated sigh, plunging his hand into his pocket and pulling out a cigarette packet. 'I don't usually smoke this early in the day. But what with . . . okay, I need to go to this panel. But if you insist on not leaving this to the police, I'd suggest you speak to Kimberley Brown.'

'What happened between them?' Fear strikes Jane at the thought of approaching Kimberley again, and it must have shown on her face because Edward replies in a softer tone.

'It's not my story to tell. Kim's bark is worse than her bite. She'll tell you. We all used to be friends at one time. Though that was years ago now.' He lights his cigarette and turns to leave.

'One last question!'

He sighs again, then inhales deeply and blows smoke into the air. His shoulders relax a fraction, as if he has been tense this entire time. 'Okay. Then I really need to go.'

'When did you last see Carrie Marks alive?'

'Around 10.30, I told you. Speak to Kimberley Brown. And thanks for the book.'

He gives her the sad smile again and lopes off, his long legs crossing the lawn in moments. More people have started to arrive behind Jane now, slowly buzzing past the keeper of lanyards and onto the lawn. Ted is walking back up the path, smugly unwrapping a bacon roll. It makes last night's wine lurch in Jane's stomach.

That *had* been interesting. Carrie had had an argument with Abi *and* with Laura Lane. And there'd been more infuriating talk of this infamous feud with Kimberley Brown.

Jane finds herself drawn to Edward, there is no denying it. But what she had found most interesting about the entire conversation, quite apart from his sweet, sad eyes, was the certain knowledge in her gut that Edward Carter was hiding something.

Chapter Fifteen

The day is bright, and Jane is sitting on the grass with Daniel and Natasha, drinking scalding hot tea from a white foam cup. Daniel has provided bananas. Before they separated the previous evening, he had set up a WhatsApp group irreverently called *Those Meddling Kids*, and Jane experienced a physical thrill when a message had arrived this morning telling everyone to meet under the willow tree at 10 a.m.

'Not bad for an old woman,' Daniel says when she finishes telling them about questioning Edward.

'I'm hardly an old woman, Daniel. I'm 42,' says Jane, her outlook having changed from the previous evening now she has friends at her side and a mystery at her feet. 'Besides, age doesn't impact on your ability to question a witness. If anything, I think you'll find that the more life exper—'

'So,' Natasha says, pulling them back to the point before blowing softly on the surface of her tea. 'He said that Carrie argued with Abi about her drunkenness, and it generally escalated. And she also argued with Laura Lane about something mysterious.'

'Well, those people were already on the list, so it doesn't really help us, does it?' says Daniel through a mouthful of his third banana.

'Actually,' Jane says, unwilling to let him bring her down, 'it *does* help. Our suspicions have been *corroborated*, which is an important part of any investigation. We also now know that Carrie argued with two of our suspects on the night in question. We are building up a picture of her movements.'

'Bravo!' says Natasha with a smile. Balancing Jane's notebook on her lap, she holds her tea in her left hand while she scribbles down the new information.

'Why on earth do you have so many bananas, Daniel?' says Jane. 'Not that I'm not grateful.'

'Pocketed them at the hotel buffet. Prices in the Dog and Bone are criminal.'

'Okay,' says Natasha, 'what did he say about Kimberley again?'

'Nothing much we don't know already, but he was insistent we speak to her. The most interesting thing though, was this. He said when he asked Carrie about Laura, she would tap her nose and tell him he would know *one day*. Now, call me bonkers, but that implies to me that Carrie had some secret information about Laura.'

Jane has been mulling over Edward's exact words all the way through the talk about female gangsters, which made her feel a little guilty for not paying attention. That nose-tapping gesture means secrets; it means *that's for me to know and you never to find out*. And secrets can easily migrate to being motives.

'I reckon that's just Carrie being Carrie,' says Daniel. Jane wonders if he purposely waits until he has a mouthful of food before speaking. 'She liked to pretend she knew things. Always keeping her cards close to her chest.'

'It's a motive,' Jane insists. 'If she had secret information, that could lead to blackmail, and that could lead to murder.'

'That,' says Natasha, 'is a stretch.' But she writes *blackmail?* down next to Laura's name anyway.

It is 10.30 and the bulk of the crowd has now arrived. The lawn is full of people milling around, chatting and laughing, most holding cups of tea but one or two already drinking alcohol. Sun-soaked British people and booze – as doomed and beautiful a pairing as Thelma and Louise.

The doors to the Dog and Bone stand open, the place above the door where the Killer Lines dagger once hung now conspicuously empty. Though most people are taking advantage of the weather instead of holing up in the gloom, Jane can just make out Detective Inspector Ramos talking to the bar staff, notebook in hand. Across the lawn, publishers and bookshops have stalls stacked with promotional material for authors' latest offerings. Someone is organising a game of *pin the knife on the body* to win a copy of a book – it seems they didn't fancy rejigging the game post an actual murder. The woman in charge of it looks exhausted, but sticks a pained smile on her face as she tries to bribe passers-by to participate with mini Mars bars.

The bar tent across the lawn is full of those protecting their hangovers from the blinding light of the sun, and people queuing for coffee or prosecco.

If you didn't know it, you would never guess that a body had been found here the morning before.

'You know what's bothering me?' says Natasha, gazing at the Dog and Bone. 'Someone took down the dagger from above the pub door and carried it all the way to the book tent, without being spotted.' Today, Natasha is wearing a creased pink shirt with red jeans and Converse trainers. It's a strange look, thinks Jane. But there's nothing wrong with strange.

'Edward's about ten foot tall,' says Daniel, now lying back on the grass. 'That wouldn't be a problem for him.'

'Edward didn't kill her,' snaps Jane. 'He was her friend. One of the few who was, by the sound of it. But . . . well, he knows something else. I'm sure of it.'

'If he was desperate for us to speak to Kimberley, maybe it's connected to her?'

Jane sighs. 'Maybe. He did say they all used to be friends. One thing is for sure, a lot of roads lead in her direction.'

In silence, they stare around the lawn, watching people come in and out of the beer tent, the Dog and Bone, the newly contructed book tent and the connected hotel. No one has seen Kimberley yet this morning.

'I can ask Brad where she is?' says Natasha.

'You know Brad Levinsky?' says Daniel, spraying fragments of chewed banana into Jane's lap.

'I wouldn't say I *know* him. But we were on a panel together yesterday. *The New and the Old: from debut to brand author.* Anyway, we chatted a bit afterwards. It wouldn't seem odd for me to say hello.' She shrugs, self-deprecatingly dismissing her status. Jane pushes down jealousy by tearing daisies out of the grass and ripping them to shreds, then nods her approval.

Natasha gets to her feet and marches off in search of Brad Levinsky, last seen vanishing into the depths of the Dog. Daniel and Jane remain in place on the grass, finally able to drink the tea that has cooled below volcanic temperature. Detective Inspector Ramos leaves the pub looking harried, flipping his notebook shut and disappearing in the direction of the crime scene.

'I was in the bar earlier,' says Daniel from his position on the grass.

'*Already?*'

'Not for a drink. For information. Beat the police to it by the looks of things.' He props himself up on one elbow so she can see his face. 'Spoke to the barman – he's a nice guy. A student at my old uni actually. He was working on the night Carrie died.'

'Oh! Good thinking, Daniel!'

'He doesn't remember anything being off. Just a bunch of people getting progressively drunker and more annoying. He did say that the loud group of men were there until about 2 a.m., having an English versus Scottish drinking competition, but he is sure none of them left at any point because when one of them tried to go home at midnight, he was shouted at and made to sit back down. Then there was an American bloke who kept singing and some woman passed out in her chair, but he doesn't know who they were.'

'Great intel. Anything on our top suspects?'

'Sadly not much. Though he said another woman was annoying – kept standing on a chair and speaking into a pink phone all night, so maybe that was Laura Lane?'

Daniel flops back down, pleased with himself. Jane watches Edward Carter blink in the sunlight as he leaves the hotel and is immediately latched on to by a group of people she doesn't recognise, as well as the blonde publicist who threatened him with the wine glass. They are too far away for Jane to understand what the conversation is about, but she gets the impression that he is politely trying to remove himself from it. When she feels Daniel watching her, Jane turns her head to look about generally instead.

It's not that she fancies her chances with Edward Carter, nothing like that. He is too far out of her league. Jane's romantic life, if you could call it that, is about as successful as her literary one. When she was 13, popular David Atkinson had asked her out in front of the whole class. When Jane had said yes, he had, to roars of laughter and applause, responded with a mime of vomiting and the revelation that it had been a dare. She hadn't trusted men since.

In her life, she has had three encounters you could perhaps describe as romantic. The first was at 18, when she went to the cinema with a boy from the school bus, followed by a large bottle of cider, some humiliating fumbling in a park, and then radio silence from him. The second had been a short-lived dalliance with an accountant who used to poke at Jane's stomach and suggest she tried running, and who moved to Warsaw for a job one day without a backward glance. And finally, most recently and most devastatingly, with her former boss at the insurance company.

Stefan Heller and Jane had dated for two years, before he broke Jane's heart, and she'd responded by breaking his. When their dalliance started, she had moved teams from Fridge and

Freezer Insurance to one even *less* interesting so the relationship didn't interfere with her work. The early days had been heady and exciting – hiding in stationery cupboards and staggering leaving times, Jane waiting in a coffee shop nearby. Stefan would ask her to prepare a report in a meeting – cold and managerial – and Jane would feel a thrill zip through her body.

Successful, tall and intelligent, with a nice (if weak-chinned) face, Jane was quite sure that Stefan was *it*. Finally, she had met the one. He made her feel good about herself; even, dare she think it, sexy. Those first six months had been some of the happiest of Jane's life.

It didn't last, of course. But that's okay. The complete and utter joyful abandon of a new relationship never does last. Sooner or later, you start to notice they don't make you tea as often as you make it for them, and they notice that you talk incessantly through television shows. They are rude to the waiter that time, and you are too tired for sex. It happens, and it's okay. But Jane never did stop staring at Stefan when he didn't realise, and thinking to herself how lucky she was.

That was until she heard a rumour in the staff toilets that one of the managers was sleeping with an admin assistant. Jane, out of sight in a cubicle, froze so the gossiping women weren't alerted to her presence. She'd believed they'd kept their relationship private, but this conversation must mean the news had finally got out – which she didn't mind though she worried Stefan would. Unless they were talking about a different manager altogether.

'He's got form,' said a disembodied voice from under the door. 'Apparently, he slept with the last assistant in the Fridge department too.'

'Reeeeallly?' The friend's voice was nasal and lazy, and Jane recognised it from calls to the finance team. It couldn't be Stefan they were talking about then – Jane was sure he would have told her if he'd had a previous work relationship.

'Yeah, they were shagging for ages. She's the big one, you know?' After a beat of silence, the nasal woman laughed shrilly, leaving the cruel mime up to Jane's imagination. They obviously meant her. But then . . . ?

'And now he's screwing Emma what's-her-face. Well, well, good for Stefan. But that's gonna be allll over the office once Doug tells everyone he saw them at it in the stationery cupboard.'

The conversation continued for another ten minutes before the two women decided they should probably drag themselves back to their desks, though it was another half an hour before Jane left the cubicle.

The inevitable showdown revealed that the second affair had been conducted for four months, and that Stefan had simply been *testing the waters*.

'Hedging his bets,' her mother had said at the time. 'The daft sod didn't want to put all his eggs in one basket, but juggling risks breaking the lot.'

Jane had surprised Stefan – and herself – by leaving him, and Stefan had surprised Jane by finding this utterly outrageous. She started working remotely in an attempt never to see him, or anyone else, ever again. By the time she'd been pulled back into the office, he'd been promoted and moved to the top floor, something she felt both grateful for and angry about. He had been the last man to make a fool of her, she'd sworn to herself. From that day forward, Jane had officially given up on romance.

But the sad grey eyes and peppery blond hair of Edward Carter steal back into her mind, and she feels her cheeks flushing.

'Jane?' When she snaps out of her reverie, she sees Daniel sitting up again, his blue eyes narrowed in concern, his forehead furrowed and mouth set. 'You alright there?'

'Oh . . . oh, yes. Just thinking about the case.' She attempts a reassuring grin, and looks around the lawn for something to comment on. Edward, finally shaking off his admirers, glances in their direction and catches her eye. He smiles and gives a nod of recognition. Daniel laughs.

No, romance is officially over for Jane There is no point even considering it. Especially not when she has a murder to solve.

Chapter Sixteen

Saturday, 10.30 a.m.

Abi gives the bin an almighty kick. It hurts, and shoots paper, empty coffee cups and an apple core across the room, but does it help? No, not really.

Her head is aching. It has been hurting for the last few days. She knows this is partly hangover-related, she isn't an idiot. But today she is mostly blaming Carrie Marks.

Yesterday had been spent speaking to police, poring over agency paperwork, reassuring authors, and starting to get to grips with everything that Carrie had kept from her over the years they'd worked together. Now, she finds herself in her hotel room, hopping on one foot to ease the pain in her toe. She flops back down onto the bed, where paper is spread out across the duvet, and the laptop she hasn't plucked up the energy to open yet sits on her pillow.

Abi isn't a natural *people person*, she can admit that. These festivals and author events exhaust her. She's recently ordered a brand-new copper-bottomed roasting tin from Lakeland, and is extremely keen to get back to her Kentish Town studio apartment and try it out. Apparently, they get really hot, with the copper. She will be able to make a cracking Sunday roast, and then eat it alone, in silence.

Despite having been Carrie Marks's right-hand woman for the past four years, Abi Ellis has been kept out of much of the inner workings of the business. Until now. Carrie was protective about her company, and Abi is finally getting some idea of why. It is a mess.

Sitting cross-legged on the duvet, she puts her head in her hands for a moment, an act of pure self-indulgence that no one else is here to see, but the theatrics make her feel better nonetheless. That dopey Detective Inspector Ramos asked her the same questions over and over again yesterday. *What was your relationship like with your boss?* Rocky. *Did Carrie have any enemies?* Are you joking? *We've heard reports of an argument between you both hours before her death, could you tell us what that was about?* My drinking. *What were your movements on the night in question?* I went back to my hotel when I'd done enough networking. *Do you know wh—*No, I don't know what time that was, I could barely see for Pimm's.

It had been humiliating. The detective had to confirm that Abi had been so drunk it had sparked an argument with Carrie, by questioning various people on her movements. All of them agreed that, yes, Abi really *had* been that annoying. Many of them appeared to have witnessed the vomiting in the plant pot episode. Someone reported that she had called them a *fat cow*, and another swore Abi had knocked over a table full of drinks while trying to perform the dance from Beyoncé's 'Single Ladies' – though she was quite sure that last one was not true.

Whatever, it was over now. And despite the humiliation, which that inspector guy clearly got off on, he hadn't worked out any of the *real* reasons for their fight.

Deep breaths, Abi tells herself, remember what the therapist said: 'Wash the anger away with breath.' What a load of bollocks. She pushes the lamp off the bedside table instead; it makes a satisfying *clunk*. Perhaps she will get the copper saucepan, to match the new roasting tin? Quite apart from the practicalities, she'd seen someone on Instagram with a whole copper cooking set and it looked divine. When she's finished up here, she'll find the profile again. It was @PoppyCooks or @PoppysReallyNiceHouse or something like that.

When she finds the strength to open the laptop and move her finger on the trackpad, the screen springs to life. She enters the password Carrie Marks didn't know she'd guessed a long time ago.

People underestimate Abi Ellis. That isn't always a bad thing, even if it does make her blood boil. What she's doing now, for example, would be a lot harder if she registered in people's thoughts as a credible presence. If they thought she had it in her.

Carrie's screen background is a picture of her little white dog, Sheekey. A yappy creature named after a famous London fish restaurant, Sheekey hated most people and was only happy when presented with a freshly cooked sausage. Abi can relate; though she scowled at him when Carrie brought him into the office, in secret she used to pass him snacks under the desk. Abi wonders who will look after the dog now and feels slightly guilty that it never crossed her mind before this. Perhaps she could take him in. She wouldn't mind sharing the roast dinner with Sheekey.

Abi had half expected the police to come back and ask her more questions this morning, but it doesn't look as if they're planning to. They must be as stupid as they look.

Clicking indiscriminately on folders, she starts to pull up contracts, expansion plans, tax records. A lot of the maths looks like Greek to her. Well, not Greek; she can read Greek. Like Klingon.

The battery icon flashes up, and she clenches her fists in annoyance. Is there anything more irritating in life than having to get up and find the cable for a laptop? Yes, she thinks, as she discovers she has to untangle the large knot it has made with the other wires in the box. Carrie always was wildly disorganised. Charismatic, impressive, hard-working, yes. But chaotic to the core.

Plugging in the laptop, Abi returns to the search she started the previous day. She scans through emails, hunts through folders. She could really use a drink, but checking her phone she sees it's not yet 11 a.m. Maybe not. She has a lot to do today. She'll wait until midday. Opening a folder labelled 'Personal', she scans through mortgage paperwork, life insurance documents, JPEGs of Carrie's passport and driving licence.

If she had all of the new copper kitchen equipment, perhaps she would have more followers. At the moment she has 56, which feels respectable to her, but Laura Lane has 2.6 million. Abi hates Laura Lane. At least she has that big nose. Abi would hate to have a big nose.

An Excel document lists all of Carrie's clients, organised in order of importance. She scrolls to the bottom, where those in danger of being dropped are flagged in red; the ones who have already been dropped are relegated to a separate tab. Carrie had been cleaning house, trying to refocus her time and energy on keeping money-making clients happy, as well as pulling in new high earners. It makes a lot of sense to Abi now that she's seen the state of the agency's finances. There are some familiar names there in the netherworld, with some other familiar ones poised at the tipping point. Abi does the bulk of the work for some of these no-hopers that Carrie deemed beneath her, and finds it rather depressing. She needs to start making those goodbye phone calls.

Scrolling back up, she smiles as she looks at the categories near the top. Well-known names alongside exciting new voices, like Natasha Martez. *These* are the people Abi should be representing, and she needs to keep hold of them. Marabella Rhodes from the Rhodes Talent Agency has already been approaching Marks Agency clients, the vulture! Fifteen per cent of an author like Natasha's advance – the agency fee – could get Abi a complete set of Le Creuset cookware.

Pulling up a blank Word document, she stares at the screen for a while, thinking. How did Carrie write? Her style was more flowery than Abi's is. A natural show-off. Abi suspects Carrie of having wanted to be a poet but, having no talent, turning to overly long emails instead. Abi herself isn't much of a writer. She did start a novel, like everyone else, but found it to be an exceedingly dull and time-consuming process, so filed it away for another day. She *could* write one, obviously; she just can't be bothered.

The room is hot, and her hair is already frizzing around her face. When Abi is rich, she'll get a keratin straightening treatment. Get it dyed too, and her lips done. She fancies looking like Monica from *Friends*, though she obviously doesn't have the body for it. Yet. What diet was that woman on?

Rich is a way off, she knows that. But if she plays this right, she will at least not be poor anymore. She'll have enough to buy all the copper kitchen equipment she likes, as well as that new Ninja air fryer she'd been eyeing up, the one with two compartments. *And* people would take her a little more seriously.

Making the finishing touches to the typed-up document, she reads it through multiple times, decides that it will do, and presses print. The ancient machine in the corner of the room rumbles into life with a guttural groan, LEDs flashing.

This is it. Leaping up, Abi steps on the lamp and bangs her shin on the bed frame. Swearing violently and profusely, she figures it's the lamp's revenge. Everything needs revenge once in a while. It'll leave a bruise though, and ruin the outfit she plans to wear later. Nothing makes you look like more of a child than bruised shins.

Paper starts to chug through the printer before it gives a loud growl, grinding to a halt with a noise like a car crash in slow motion, and starts flashing red. Paper jam.

'Just my luck,' mutters Abi. 'Just my rotten luck.'

She fights with the paper, succeeding only in tearing it to shreds and getting black ink all over her hands. Eventually, the light turns green, and she restarts the printing process.

Sitting on the floor by the printer, Abi breathes out in relief, and finally smiles to herself.

It's time for her luck to change.

Chapter Seventeen

Saturday, 11.15 a.m.

'Not too fast for me at all, Daniel,' Jane pants, almost breaking her neck when she steps in a ditch. Despite her long legs, she isn't cut out for the speed with which Daniel moves through the world. 'Though perhaps,' she adds in an undertone, 'Natasha would appreciate us slowing down?'

Natasha, at least half a foot shorter, is a few metres behind them and going red in the face.

'Yes, cool it would you, Daniel? The murderer isn't legging it across Hoslewit right this moment.'

'Well, we don't actually know that,' Daniel says reasonably, but slowing all the same. 'Because we don't know who it is.' He turns and jogs on the spot, in a way that makes both Jane and Natasha want to lamp him.

Natasha catches up, and they move off again at a more reasonable pace.

'I'm not cut out to be a runner,' Natasha grumbles, still breathing heavily.

'It's good for the heart,' Daniel says. 'Cycling too. I did the London to Brighton cycle route recently.'

'Wish you'd kept cycling right into the sea,' Natasha says under her breath, and Jane decides it's time to wade in and keep the peace.

'What's the hotel called again, Natasha?'

'The Old House. It should be around that corner. Not too far. No need to rush.'

It hadn't taken Natasha too long earlier to track down Brad Levinsky, who'd been celebrating the end of a successful panel discussion with a morning pint of Badger's Foot, to which he'd apparently taken quite a liking.

It also seemed not to have been his first pint of the day, because he'd given Natasha a hug she swore burst one of her lungs, and happily informed her that Kimberley had headed back to the hotel after his panel to get some work done. He'd even given up her room number when Natasha had asked, without her having to invent so much as a reason.

Jane couldn't help compare the ease with which Natasha secured this information with her own interaction with Kimberley Brown. Being a celebrated author obviously made people less wary of Natasha than they were of Jane, who could be anybody. Just a yellow lanyard. Or maybe that was her bitterness talking. And Brad's bitter talking.

The Old House is the nicest hotel in Hoslewit, and when it comes into sight as they round the corner, Jane sighs in envy. Square and Georgian, with large sash windows, climbing pink roses and a pretty green rectangle of lawn outside, the Old House looks like the quintessential English country retreat. Their eggs are probably perfectly cooked.

'What's the plan then, Jane?' asks Natasha.

Jane doesn't have a plan; she figured they would make one up as they went. Her mother's voice sounds in her ear – *Failing to plan, Jane, is planning to fail!* – but she ignores it. One thing she does know is that they have a better chance of speaking to Kimberley Brown here, away from prying eyes and ears. Once they are in her room, Jane will make it very difficult for Kimberley to get rid of them.

'Well, I guess we just ask to come in?' she says.

'. . .Genius.'

She ignores Daniel's sarcasm, and is pleased to find that Natasha does too.

'What we want to know is, why she and Carrie hate each other,' Jane continues.

'Obviously,' Daniel says with a cheeky grin.

'And,' she continues as if he hadn't spoken, 'if they had any contact at all that evening.'

'Her movements, too,' pipes up Natasha. 'I can't remember seeing her later on. If she has an alibi putting her somewhere else from 12.30, then she's off the list.'

'Yes! Absolutely,' Jane says with a nod. She should have said that first. 'Motive, means, and opportunity.'

Marching up the path with all the confidence of a straight white man, Jane pushes open the beautiful double doors, leading into a reception room whose glamour has slightly faded with time – just as Jane likes it.

'Can I help you?' A chubby young man who is barely taller than Natasha looks up from the reception desk to their left, giving the gang a sceptical stare. He has a thick German accent, and Jane wonders why he chose the tiny town of Hoslewit to settle in, so far from home. Does he miss it?

She has a sudden urge to hug the poor boy before she is stopped by Daniel muttering, 'I'll handle it.'

A quiet conversation ensues at the desk, after which Daniel returns smiling grimly, nodding them towards the lifts.

'What did you say to him?'

'Oh, just that we were here to see our colleague Kimberley Brown. She can't leave the room due to her terrible diarrhoea, so we are bringing her work to her. I started to tell him about the consistency and frequency of her bowel movements but he didn't seem to want to know and waved us right up.'

'Very good! You *are* clever!'

He tries to suppress a smile, but can't help looking pleased at the praise. Daniel, Jane reflects, has a way with people – when he's not being sarcastic. His charm and age allow him to get answers from the bar and hotel staff, just as Natasha's reputation and smarts allow her to speak to the likes of Brad Levinsky. Other than *leader*, Jane isn't too sure what she herself brings to the table and hopes no one enquires. They squeeze into the lift and soon find themselves in front of room 204, flushed with success. Their investigation is off to a flying start. And now here they are, about to interview their first suspect!

'Leading suspect, I'd say,' says Natasha when Jane voices her excitement.

'You think? My money is on Abi Ellis. She's a nasty piece of work,' says Daniel.

'Well, let's discuss this when we're not outside a suspect's door, shall we?' Jane says. 'Perhaps over a nice cup of tea later. Or a sandwich.' She raises her fist to knock. In the moment before she does, she remembers writing the first Sandra Baker novel. Sandra had recently opened her detective agency and was going to interview the man she suspected knew about the suspicious death of her client's lover. Baker hadn't stalled. She'd knocked boldly, with not an ounce of fear. Zero self-doubt.

Jane knocks.

After a moment of breathless silence, they hear a crash from behind the door followed by a loud burst of swearing. A rattle of the chain announces that someone is coming, and yet Jane is still taken aback when it flies open, revealing an impatient-looking Kimberley Brown.

'Yes? Can I help you?' She is a furious vision in green silk, the long sleeves of her dress snatched in at the wrists, ballooning on the arms. The gown falls fluidly to the floor and catches the sunlight streaming in through her window.

Jane is sure she's never seen someone quite so glamorous in her life. Unless you count celebrities in magazines and on the television, which of course you can't. Have you seen what they wear to those award shows? You can't expect someone normal to match that sort of level. Rhianna went to one of the shows as a sort of sexy pope one year. Jane's grandmother would have passed out at the sight, but luckily she was already dead. God rest her soul.

'Kimberley Brown? We need to speak to you, I'm afraid,' Jane manages, tearing her eyes away from the dress and trying to stop thinking about how you would clean it were you to spill any food on it. Wet sponge and a prayer probably. 'May we come in?'

'No. Who the hell are you?'

This doesn't seem to happen to Baker. Her commanding presence opens doors, metaphorically and literally, wherever she goes.

'Look, Ms Brown,' Natasha says from behind Jane, and she steps to the side to give her some space. Natasha has a kind, calming voice. She couldn't be more different from the towering, glaring, glimmering American editor, but Jane feels her presence immediately defuse the interaction. 'It may not be ideal, but you do need to let us in. We have to talk to you about Carrie Marks. And I'm sure you wouldn't want us to shout our questions through the door, would you? We wouldn't want to disturb the other guests.'

Natasha smiles sweetly, her dimples and sticky-out ears adding to her unassuming charm, despite the fact that she has just laid an overt threat on the table.

Once again, Jane is thankful for her new friends. Who would have thought she would pick up two such capable people as these? What are the chances? It's not like she vetted them. She was much more likely to get stuck with some blundering idiot, a dominant mansplainer, or even a cruel overlord like Abi. That's normally who she manages to attract into her life. But these two? Absolute marvels.

Kimberley Brown is hesitating, eyes darting to each of them in turn with suspicion, and a hint of fear. That's interesting. She doesn't seem the type to give in to fear easily.

'Oh, *fine*,' she says with a theatrical sigh, throwing her hands in the air and turning away with what can only be described as a flounce. 'Fine! Come in! It's not like I've got a ton of work to do before I need to be back at that bloody festival again.' Her voice is heavy with sarcasm.

In reality, Kimberley has been watching Season Six, Episode Nine of *Sex and the City*, 'A Woman's Right to Shoes'. She's watched it at least ten times before, and finds it comforting in times of stress. She'd been branded a Carrie Bradshaw when younger, but now feels like more of a Miranda. Natasha's eyes slide to the image of a pair of Manolo Blaniks on the paused laptop screen, and Kimberley slams it shut.

'We're sorry to bother you, Ms Brown,' Jane begins, standing awkwardly by the wardrobe. She has never felt so out of place as in this elegant room, which smells strongly of peonies, opposite this elegant woman.

'You seem to be bothering me nonetheless,' mutters Kimberley, throwing herself down onto the armchair she'd clearly previously vacated. Resigned, she sits up straight with a sigh and folds one long leg over the other, suddenly the picture of professionalism. 'Go on then. What is it? I know you aren't police, so I've no idea what your game is. And call me Kimberley. *Ms Brown* makes me feel ancient.'

Daniel and Natasha both look at Jane, who is growing hot as though under a spotlight. She feels lumpen and ungainly next to Kimberley Brown, and as though she is swelling in size until she is sure she'll burst from the room. She coughs, breathes, and takes a quick peek in the mirror. Everything looks normal.

Kimberley Brown is bobbing her foot up and down in impatience, or anxiety, Jane isn't sure which.

'Would you like a mint, Ms—er, I mean Kimberley?

'What?'

'A mint. Extra-strong. They're British.'

'Oh. Okay.'

'Natasha? Daniel?'

Jane passes around the packet of mints until everyone is silently sucking away. Bravely, she moves towards the desk, pulls out the hard wooden chair and sits down facing Kimberley.

'Ms Brown. Kimberley. We know you had a grudge against Carrie Marks. We would like to know why.'

Kimberley stares at her non-plussed, then throws back her head in laughter, and chokes on her mint. It isn't until Daniel has thumped her on the back, sending it flying, and Jane has handed out more, that she speaks.

'Yeah, me and Carrie weren't the best of friends. What of it? Doesn't mean I killed her, does it?'

'But *did* you kill her?'

'Oh, please. And what business is it of yours if I did? You're not the police. You're no one.'

'That's unkind,' says Natasha, and Kimberley shrugs.

'Can you please tell us why you weren't speaking?' asks Jane.

Kimberley leans forward in her armchair. 'I know this is a work event, so I'm trying to keep my professional cool, but I'm going to have to tell you, politely, to F off.'

As Kimberley leans towards her, Jane realises the peony smell is her perfume. It's expensive and intoxicating. For one wild moment, Jane wants to kiss her. She sits up straight and coughs.

'We want to know because we've taken it upon ourselves to find out the truth about what happened to Carrie Marks. There are plenty of other people who will tell us the story. Many have already offered,' she lies smoothly. Jane never knew she could lie like this. How thrilling! 'But it felt right to ask you first. Hearsay can be dangerous, don't you agree? It's how rumour starts. But if you don't want to tell us, we'll take someone else up on their offer.'

Jane makes to stand up, the wooden chair creaking ominously under her weight.

'Oh, sit down, enough with the dramatics, Poirot. Yes, I'm sure there are *plenty* of people who would be happy to tell you what happened. So, I suppose you're right, I may as well do so myself. Though I tell you now, it's *not relevant.*'

Kimberley collapses back into her chair, abandoning her rigid posture and staring at the ceiling.

'I'll put the kettle on, shall I?' Daniel says, ever the good intern.

When they all have a mug of tea in front of them, which due to the class of hotel is Yorkshire rather than PG Tips and therefore the perfect colour of a two-penny piece, Kimberley gives another of her deep, victimised sighs, and starts to talk.

Chapter Eighteen

Saturday, 11.30 a.m.

'Carrie Marks and I were very good friends. The best,' Kimberley begins, finally taking a sip from her mug. 'Lovely tea by the way, thank you. You know, it's one of the few things I miss about this country? Proper tea. It's where the British excel.'

'I can agree with you on that,' says Jane with a nod, and Daniel and Natasha oblige with murmurs of assent.

'Well, like I say, we were friends. We met early on in our careers. She was an assistant at some literary agency, I was an editorial assistant in a publishing house. Our bosses worked together, so we worked together. We spoke a lot. It's a hard slog, being on the bottom rung of this industry. Hard work, no money, even less credit for anything you do right. It's a bonding experience.

'When she came to New York with some friends in her mid-twenties, we met and hit it off. From there, we climbed the ladder side by side, meeting whenever she was in the US or I was in the UK. God, we had such a fun time back then. I . . . I can't believe she's dead.'

Kimberley looks up at the ceiling and blinks back what Jane assumes to be tears. Or is she simply pretending? There is something unnaturally polished about this glamorous, beautiful woman. Aren't people this perfect pretending all of the time, one way or another? They must get good at it.

'When I was promoted to Editor, I managed to get in on an exchange posting through work. Went to London for six months, and Carrie became my best friend. They were probably the best months of my life. I loved London, and I . . . loved her. She was gorgeous then. Well, not *gorgeous*, but impressive, you know? Even as an assistant. Just commanded the room. Always got a seat at the table. I was never that sure of myself, but Carrie taught me how to *seem* sure, and then how to *become* sure.'

She speaks without hesitation, as if she's told the story a thousand times, yet the atmosphere in the room suggests otherwise.

Placing her tea on the floor, Kimberley reaches up and loosens her tight ponytail, letting her auburn hair fall around her face, partially hiding it. She swings her legs up and over the armrest, leaning backwards across the seat of the chair, and runs her fingers through her newly freed hair. Jane can't help but compare herself to the woman sitting across from her. Even if Kimberley turns out to be a vicious murderer, Jane would still find herself lacking. She pulls her own ponytail tighter, her fingers feeling the roughness of hair she forgot to brush .

'She would come to New York fairly regularly, the older she got,' Kimberley continues. 'Her clothes became more expensive, the West Country twang in her voice faded, but she was still the same person, deep down. Just as fun, just as adventurous, just as self-assured. She was a bridesmaid at my wedding. Ha! What a joke! But, yeah, she got to know Martin too – that's my ex-husband – and a few of my friends. Whenever she arrived in New York, she'd slide right in.'

Jane pictures the young Carrie and Kimberley, taking London and New York by storm. She can't believe that this woman in front of her was ever unsure of herself. How could someone go from that to this? A thousand questions occur to Jane – where did they go in London? What did they wear? What was the wildest thing they got up to? Who had the nicest shoes? – but she keeps her mouth closed.

'Yeah, she *slid in* alright! Ha!' Kimberley snorts at a joke that no one else understands. Until she spins in her seat, bringing her

114

bare feet down to the floor with a thud, and meets Jane's eyes again. 'Into my bed. Alongside my husband.'

The entire room gasps.

Daniel lets out a whispered, 'No!'

Kimberley is a good storyteller. Maybe that comes from being an editor, or maybe it's a story she repeats to herself over and over again, wondering at the injustice of it all.

'She stayed with me and Martin for a week, not long after she'd set up her own literary agency. This was about eight years ago now. God, I can't believe it's been eight years. We had just started trying for a baby, Martin and I. Can you imagine? Anyway, I came back from the office early, to work on an edit at home. Martin's in finance, he usually works late, and I thought Carrie had meetings downtown that day. We'd planned to meet for cocktails after. But I heard them as soon as I opened the door.

'It's wild . . . even though it was obvious what was happening, I still didn't *know*. I still went to check. Like I needed to see. It was . . . so unexpected. And yet, almost not unexpected? Carrie was like that. She wanted it all.'

Kimberley picks up her tea, which must be cold now, and falls back into her cross-chair position, legs hanging over the armrest. No one else moves a muscle.

'The neighbour called 911 because of the shouting. The cops turned up. But no one knew who should leave and who should stay. Ha!'

It isn't until Kimberley mentions the police that Jane remembers why they are here. She'd been completely hooked on the terrible tale of best friends turning to worst enemies, taken in by this beguiling woman with a sorry past.

'After that, I left Martin, and Carrie and I avoided each other. It's a small industry, but we lived on different continents, it wasn't hard not to speak. Until this weekend, of course.'

'You spoke this weekend?' Daniel asks.

'What? No, I mean we were in the same place. It was the first time for us since back then.' Kimberley sighs and sits up with an air of finality, tucking her bare feet under her body. The wall of terrifying professionalism has crumbled. She looks pale, and her eyes are pink, giving her an air of childlike vulnerability. 'Look, I hated Carrie, I won't lie. Wouldn't you? After that? But I didn't kill her. I . . . loved her once. And even if I hadn't, I'm no killer.'

Natasha, perched on the edge of the bed, clears her throat. 'Would you mind – I'm sorry, but would you mind telling us about Thursday night? It's just helpful, to know who saw what?'

Clever, thinks Jane. Much better than out and out asking where she was when Carrie was murdered. Jane hasn't accused people of murder many times in her life, but she has a suspicion most wouldn't like it.

'Honestly, I went to bed early, so I can't be much help. Brad . . . and don't repeat this . . . was driving me crazy. He was so drunk – singing, dancing on the table. After all of these years, he's a friend as well as one of my authors. We're very close – I even told him about all this business with Carrie on the way over here. But he didn't need me there to hold his hand, and I was exhausted. I'm 50 this year, I don't have the stamina I used to.'

Jane couldn't believe it: 50. And such perfect skin! Perhaps she can bring the conversation around to skin care after they've talked about the murder.

'What time? Do you remember?'

'Ten. I remember it was ten because Brad started singing *Ten Green Bottles* and it was my limit. I didn't really see anything unusual while I was there. Carrie was still around at that point though, I heard her.'

'What do you mean, you *heard* her?'

'Arguing with someone outside when I left. I didn't see who. But, honestly, Carrie argues all the time. I saw her shouting at her assistant earlier in the evening.' Kimberley's eyes widen in a brief flash of panic, and she quickly adds: 'Not Brad though, it wasn't him she was arguing with. He was inside singing his heart out.'

'That was the last time you saw Carrie? Or heard her? At 10 p.m.?'

'Look, I don't know anything else, okay! I don't know why you're asking me these questions! I didn't see anything!'

'And you never *spoke* to Carrie Marks?'

'Why *would* I?'

Flustered, Kimberley rises to her feet again, leaving them in no doubt that the interview has ended. Getting the hint, the others stand too and are promptly ushered towards the door, muttering their *thank you*s and *sorry*s as they go. Opening the door, Kimberley just about refrains from physically pushing them through it, and slams it behind them without so much as a goodbye.

In the softly lit corridor, they raise their eyebrows at each other, wordlessly communicating that they should wait until they are in the fresh air to discuss what they've learnt. Daniel mouths a silent *wow*, and Jane feels a tingle of excitement running down her spine. They'd done well. At the lift, they wait in a tense silence, but before the ding signifies its arrival, they hear a door open down the corridor.

Kimberley Brown reappears, the soft lighting casting shadows across her skin that make her look both beautiful and sinister, hair cascading around her face like a modern-day Medusa.

'I can prove when I came back here, by the way,' she shouts to them. 'Had to ask reception for my keys when I got in. You can check with them on the way out. You shouldn't trust people have alibis just because they *say* they do. Do you even know each *other's* alibis? Someone killed Carrie. It could be anyone. Even one of you.'

Her words hang in the air as they stare back at her. Finally, she turns away and slams the door once again.

Chapter Nineteen

Saturday, 12 p.m.

Jane and Daniel are sitting on the wall of the graveyard, drinking coffees they'd bought after leaving Kimberley's hotel. Natasha regrettably had to run back to the festival to meet her publicist but has vowed to meet them for lunch afterwards.

'Who would cheat on Kimberley Brown?' asks Jane.

'An idiot,' says Daniel.

'A blind man.'

'A gay man?'

'I think that's the total list. And as it doesn't sound as if he's either gay or blind, we must conclude her ex is an idiot.'

'Classic detective work there, Baker.'

They sit in companionable silence as a group of middle-aged Texan tourists streams past them. Judging by their lanyards and programmes they are all on their way to Killer Lines. One of them points enthusiastically at the little church behind Jane and Daniel.

'Oh my Gooood!' the woman shouts to her friends. 'It's *so old* and *so cute!*'

Jane waits until everyone in the group has taken a picture, many of which she suspects she is in, and is out of earshot before she continues talking.

'But what on earth is wrong with Martin Brown is not really the question we should be asking ourselves, is it? What we should be asking is: *did Kimberley murder Carrie Marks?*'

The story had touched Jane and made her feel protective of its teller. She doesn't want Kimberley Brown to be the murderer.

She wants to become her friend, and find out where she buys her clothes. It astounds her that someone like Kimberley could have been hurt, just as Jane had by that toerag Stefan Heller. If even Kimberley Brown can't keep a man, what chance could there be for Jane!? She chides herself for being a bad feminist, and tries to focus on the matter at hand.

Could this woman be a killer? Carrie, her best friend, bridesmaid at her wedding, had had an affair with her husband. It was certainly motive enough. A few drinks, a confrontation, tempers running high, a dagger hanging conveniently above the door frame. It could happen.

'She was agitated at the end there,' muses Daniel. 'You think she knows more than she's saying?'

Jane gives a vague noise of agreement. She'd noticed it too: Kimberley had started to get upset and defensive when probed about the evening Carrie died. Jane is sure that something happened then, something Kimberley is keeping to herself but that isn't necessarily murder. 'Maybe it's the secret to eternal youth.'

'What do you make of her account of the evening?' asks Daniel. 'She must have left just before me. You know, I can't remember seeing her when I went. It's a shame the guy on reception wouldn't confirm for us what time she got back.'

'That's the sort of thing a police badge would come in handy for, isn't it? Someone would probably be able to disprove it if she was lying though. She's hardly inconspicuous, is she? Especially as there weren't many people around on that first night. Why say she left at 10 if she didn't?'

'Unless she just left the *bar*?'

'And hid in the bushes for two and a half hours?' says Jane. 'I doubt it. It was cold that night. Raining on and off. And it would make the murder more premeditated than I believe it was.'

Though is that still true? Jane had previously believed the murder was unplanned because it seemed so strange to kill someone in the middle of a literary festival. But this was the first time Kimberley Brown had come into contact with her ex-best friend since the night of her betrayal, and who knew when the next time would be? Perhaps she left, but her anger was so great that she grabbed the dagger and lay in wait for her chance?

Daniel lies back on the wall with a sigh and closes his eyes. With the April sun on his perfect, sculpted face, he reminds Jane of a Greek statue. It would be called *A Young Man Relaxing*, and it would be displayed by a fountain, one marble hand dipping lazily into the water. They lived the life, the ancient Greeks, always up to something hedonistic. Couldn't trust them.

'That dagger above the door to the Dog,' Daniel muses. 'Not an easy feat to get it down and walk all the way to the book tent without being noticed.'

'I doubt anyone would be outside to see them with it, in the dark and rain. And Kimberley is just tall enough to grab it.'

'The rain will have made it hard for the white-coat guys to find evidence too.'

'The SOCOs? It may have washed evidence away, but it may also mean there were footprints.' Last she'd seen, the scene-of-crime officers were still buzzing around the book tent. 'When they leave, we should check it out.' Jane and her friends may not have fingerprint dust and DNA testing capabilities, but there are other clues they might spot that a professional might miss.

'So,' says Daniel, still with his eyes closed against the sun, 'Kimberley Brown has motive, we're agreed on that. Means . . . To be honest, I'm not too sure of the difference between means and opportunity?'

'Nor am I,' confesses Jane, thinking back to the few Criminology lectures she *did* attend at university. 'I think it's to do with if the person *could* do it?'

'So a person with no arms would find it hard to stab someone, and therefore have no means?'

121

'Well, that's a bit basic.' Jane can't think of anything else to add. 'But in essence, yes?'

'Okay, so she has motive. She has means-slash-arms.' Daniel motions in the air above him to demonstrate a forward slash. 'But she doesn't have opportunity, because she went back to her hotel two and a half hours before Carrie was murdered.'

'Unless she's lying.'

'Unless she's lying,' agrees Daniel. 'Which, if she is a murderer, probably isn't beyond her.'

Is this all there is to detective work? Just see who was angry and around at the time of death? That seems easier than Jane previously thought. Apart from the potential for lying of course. Liars ruin it for everyone else.

PI Baker often just *knows* when people are lying, because she is a brilliant judge of character. But Jane is finding that, in reality, everyone appears uneasy when talking about whether they murdered someone or not, and although she senses there is more to both Kimberley and Edward's stories than they are letting on, she isn't getting the sparkling intuition she ascribed to her fictional detective. *I'd take her story with a pinch of salt,* her mother would warn her. *She could be crooked as a barrel of fish hooks.'*

'She's right about one thing though,' Jane says to Daniel's horizontal form and shaggy dark hair. We need to corroborate stories. Confirm alibis.'

The next question hangs on her tongue unspoken, but the last words of Kimberley Brown reverberate in her mind. *Do you even know each other's alibis?*

A buzzing at Jane's hip tells her that someone is calling her. Could it be Abi again, calling to make sure Jane got her voicemail message? To finally prod her towards the plank?

'Jane? You gonna get that?'

'Um, I wasn't planning on it actually.'

The buzzing stops, and a second later, Rihanna's 'We Found Love' blares from Daniel's pocket, almost sending him over the wall in shock.

He answers. 'Natasha? Oh, okay. Yes, we'll see you there!' Pushing his phone back into his pocket, he jumps to his feet. 'Come on, Jane.'

'What's going on?'

'We're late for a drink with Abi Ellis.'

Chapter Twenty

Saturday, 12.30 p.m.

'Oh, it's you.'

Abi Ellis doesn't look too pleased to see Jane and Daniel.

'Lovely to see you, Abi.'

Natasha, at Abi's side, greets them both with a one-armed hug, holding a glass of Coke aloft with her other hand. They are standing at the makeshift bar of the beer tent that has been erected on the lawn. Jane is pleased not to be sitting back in that drab pub again while the sun is shining.

Someone has tried valiantly to give the drinks list a literary theme – *A Brave New Ale, A Rum of One's Own, The Strange Case of Dr Gin and Mr Tonic* – but they'd run out of steam half-way through. *Wuthering Whites (Wine)* is particularly pathetic, in Jane's opinion.

Daniel is uncharacteristically quiet as he gives Abi a small wave of recognition.

'And didn't *you* leave?'

'Decided to come back,' he mutters, looking at the grass.

'Well, you could have let me know. I've been *swamped.*' Abi swigs at the glass of white wine the barman passes her while fumbling her card out of her purse with her other hand. Before tapping the card reader, she looks over awkwardly at Jane and Daniel and huffs dramatically. 'Just my luck,' she mutters under her breath. 'Would you like a drink?'

The group of four sit on a wooden bench inside the tent to escape the midday sun, Jane sipping at a *Wuthering Whites* spritzer, while Daniel wields a *Master and Frozen Margarita.*

Abi angles her body to exclude Jane and Daniel from the conversation as much as possible.

'So, yeah, I *adored* your novel,' she says to Natasha. 'I actually read it before Carrie even did. And I'll be taking over most of her clients now, so it would be incredible to know if you're sticking with the agency? I know Marabella Rhodes from the Rhodes Talent Agency is already sniffing around, but I assure you that I'm *very* capable.' Abi flashes a huge, false smile.

'I'll have a think,' Natasha says politely. 'It would be nice to share an agent though, right, Jane?'

Abi murmurs something under her breath that Jane can't quite hear, but she is sure it is along the lines of *over my dead body*.

'Absolutely! Let's stick together,' Jane says, the spritzer already making her feel brave, sitting here with her two new friends, sunlight making the white canvas ceiling gleam golden.

Jane trusts Natasha to lead this discussion in the right direction, so she zones out as Abi monologues, desperately pitching herself as an agent, heavily implying that she had been doing most of Carrie's work anyway. Today, she's wearing a long navy dress with white spots, buttoned down the front, but she's made a mistake when putting it on – a missed button means that the whole thing is skew-whiff and the fabric gapes in places, showing her sickly pink bra underneath. One leg protrudes from a long slit in the fabric, revealing a scuffed and bruised shin.

As Abi downs the dregs of her wine, Jane soundlessly returns to the bar and reappears with a bottle of *Pride and Prosecco*. She isn't above using alcohol to extract information. In her second novel, *Murder at Dawn*, Baker got her longed-for confession (on tape no less!) after the eighth shot of tequila. She had been pretending to drink alongside the suspect, but deftly tipping the liquid into her lap. Her dress may have been ruined but her wallet was full once she collected from her client.

Pouring out new drinks to murmured thanks, Jane sits back on the bench and raises her glass, feeling their eyes on her.

'Nice, Jane!' says Abi. 'What are we celebrating? Your first number-one bestseller?'

Jane decides to ignore the sarcasm.

'I thought we should all raise a glass to the woman who has brought us together. Natasha and me as authors; Abi and Daniel,' she nods to each in turn, 'as employees. We all lost Carrie Marks, and in the most horrific circumstances. To Carrie.'

In silence, everyone clinks glasses, muttering *to Carrie* in that way British people do when they have to join in, with all the enthusiasm of singing a hymn at a wedding. Apart from 'All Things Bright and Beautiful', of course. Jane likes that one. But only the chorus.

'She was a remarkable woman,' says Natasha, seizing the line Jane has thrown. 'Abi, you would have known her best. What was she really like?'

Abi shrugs. 'Yeah, I guess you could say she was remarkable, in a way. She knew what she needed to do to get ahead, and she did it. Whatever it took. She wasn't perfect, but who is?'

Abi's button nose is starting to glow with the sun and alcohol, and her hair is becoming frizzier, like one of those speeded-up films of a mushroom growing that Jane's seen on Facebook. As she yawns, Jane notices she has a smudge of coral lipstick on her tiny white teeth. With a jolt, she recognises the colour.

It was Carrie's.

If Jane were a real private detective, she would simply ask the question. If she were in the police, she would *demand* an answer. But she is just Jane. So she'll have to be circumspect. Use her initiative. The beer tent is filling up, the queue at the bar lengthening as people decide that past midday means it is time for alcohol. The buzz makes them all relax.

'I've heard she could be quite . . . argumentative?' Jane probes. She knows from previous interactions that Abi isn't the hardest person to get talking about the negative traits of others. Even, Jane suspects, the dead.

'Oh, yeah, she wasn't afraid to stand up for herself!' Abi says, finishing her glass and groping for the bottle in the ice bucket, topping everyone up. 'If Carrie had a problem with you, you'd know. In business she wouldn't really row much – she was good at getting her own way without that. People said she was charming, which I *guess* was true.' She says *guess* with grudging emphasis and an eye roll, in case they mistake her words for actual praise. 'She could talk people into things. But if you knew her well, you could be less lucky.'

'Sounds like a difficult person to work for,' says Natasha with a sympathetic head tilt. 'I actually think I saw you guys arguing the other night? What was her problem?'

'Eurgh!' Abi flings up one hand dismissively. '*That.* She was being such a hypocrite.' When no one speaks, she continues. 'Said I was *making a scene* because I'd . . . I'd had a few drinks.' She bridles at her own words, becoming defensive and raising her voice in a squawk as if they'd been the ones to tell her off. 'She was *never* without a glass in her hand herself! It's the *job!* It's a *social job!*'

Everyone shakes their heads in sympathy.

'And I told her, I said *you need to back off,*' Abi says, jabbing at the air as if her old boss is sitting at the table with them rather than in a drawer at the morgue.

'Brave,' Jane says, after giving a low whistle.

'Yeah, well. She couldn't push me around forever. And I told her she needed to start treating me with some respect, because I knew she wasn't an angel herself. I knew alllll her secrets. Everyone underestimates me, I'm just tiny little Abi. But I know *everything* that goes on in that agency.' She is panting with exertion and emotion, and her hand trembles as she raises the glass to her lips.

'Wh-what,' Daniel stammers with attempted nonchalance, 'things?'

'I'm not telling *you*,' she sneers, then Abi's eyes flick to Natasha and she visibly tries to pull herself together, sitting up straight and flattening her bushy hair. 'It's nothing anyway. Just some agency stuff. I'd been going through files and found a few bits and pieces. I won't go into it. I should probably stop drinking too. There's a lot of paperwork I need to sort out today. Everything's in my hands now.' She shrugs with a brave smile, as if to indicate that this is a dreadful, unasked-for burden. It's faux-modest, but at the same time the tremor still apparent in her hands hints at how overwhelmed she must feel.

'You're taking over the agency then?' Jane asks in surprise.

What usually happens in cases like these? Does a business simply dissolve when the owner passes away? Either way, Jane is quite sure that the Marks Literary Agency wouldn't automatically go to Carrie's assistant.

'Well, no one knows *yet*. But it was basically just us. Occasionally some interns to do the donkey work. No offence,' she tells Daniel. 'It's up to me to keep things going until . . . until things become clearer.' Abi blushes, the pink spreading from her nose and cheeks to the rest of her face, making it look distinctly tomato-like. She hides behind her glass. 'Which I'm sure they will soon.'

Natasha tops up Abi's glass and, despite her earlier comment about stopping, she nods her thanks. Jane tries Baker's fake drinking trick and can feel the fizzy liquid bubbling on her chin.

'Jane, did you just pour that drink down your top?' Abi is staring at her, eyebrows furrowed.

'Um, missed my mouth. But what happened after you fought with Carrie? Did you leave for the night? It must have been quite upsetting.'

It doesn't seem possible, but the pink of Abi's flushed face becomes brighter. 'No, I hung around. I wasn't about to go running off to bed, tuck myself up for the night, just because she said so. I had *networking* to do.' That line restores a little of her self-confidence – only important people network, after all. The smug smile returns to Abi's face. 'I don't think I got back until about 2 in the morning. I was exhausted the next day, didn't find out about Carrie until the police knocked on my bedroom door.'

'Who were you talking to?' asks Jane, hoping she sounds curious and impressed rather than demanding.

'Oh, I don't know, do I? Everyone. I didn't keep a *log*, Jane.'

Shaking the bottle, she finds there is none left and gets to her feet. Standing, she is about the same height as Jane sitting on the bench. Her frizzy hair is very large now, bursting out in an impressive triangle around her face. A tomato in hay.

'Righto, I need to get back to it. Natasha, I'll call you. Let's discuss where we go next with your career. Daniel, we need copies of the latest *Plempton Hall Mystery* for a panel later; bring them to Room Twelve by three o'clock. Jane.' She nods dismissively at Jane.

In desperation, Jane spins on the bench and calls to Abi's retreating back: 'Who do you think did it, Abi? Who killed Carrie Marks?'

The buzz in the tent has grown loud enough to mask her words, though one or two people nearby throw their table a curious glance. A passing man knocks into Jane's elbow, spilling what smells like a *Tequila Mockingbird* down her back. Abi turns to them, lips painted in Carrie's beautiful coral shade quirking into a smile.

'One of the many people,' she says, with eyebrows raised meaningfully, 'who thought she deserved knocking off her pedestal.'

Chapter Twenty-One

Saturday, 12.45 p.m.

Frankie Reid is late again.

But today, she has decided she does not care. She is sick to death of running everywhere, overflowing with *sorry*s and *thank you*s and *please*s and *that's wonderful!*s. *Sorry your edit is late, sorry I missed this email, sorry I haven't read your book yet.* Well who is saying sorry to Frankie, eh? Who is saying sorry for her wages only increasing by three per cent in the past four years? Who is saying sorry for missing their deadline or writing, frankly, sub-par books? Or for her new shoes being very slightly too small and her head pounding from too much late-night wine? No one, that's who.

But she isn't angry today, far from it. She feels very free. Deciding not to be sorry, to not rush, is marvellous. Her boss calls her, and she turns off her phone. Sitting in the corner of the shady beer tent, she flips open her laptop and takes a sip of her *Great Gats-beer*.

The bushy hair of Abi Ellis comes into view, and Frankie sinks down in her seat. Abi stops and spins back around, her bouffant bouncing like jelly as she moves. Frankie peers through the people milling around and can just about make out who Abi is speaking to – is that Jane Hepburn? Jane is standing, watching Abi storm away. Her top looks like she has spilt her drink all over it – it's only midday, Jane, for Christ's sake! People need to pull themselves together. Jane sits down at a table together with Natasha Martez and some gorgeous young man Frankie doesn't know. The three of them clink glasses.

Abi marches through the crowd, a tiny firecracker, and swishes out of the tent. Frankie exhales, pleased not to have been spotted. She can't stand Abi Ellis. She's the kind of person who will be important one day, despite not having any discernible talent, and who will delight in making assistants cry. Strange how you can tell that about a person no matter where they are on the ladder.

Despite this, she does have some sympathy for the girl. Frankie knows what it was like to work for Carrie Marks – being Carrie's assistant was her first job out of university. She'd languished there, finding it near impossible to get a different employer despite working for a top agency. Finally landing the position at Eagle Wing had seemed like a lifeline at the time – now it feels more like an anchor.

Did Carrie sabotage Abi's career, as she had Frankie's? Had she spread the same rumours of incompetence, untrustworthiness and general unemployability, in order to keep her as a faithful assistant rather than allow her to move on to better things?

Edward Carter's face pokes through the tent entrance, scans the interior, and then retreats. Sarah Parks-Ward scurries past Frankie's table, almost knocking over her drink as she makes a hasty exit.

But back to business. The sight of Jane and Natasha only increases Frankie's determination. Flicking through her folders, she locates the one she's after. Opening *CVs and Cover Letters*, a raft of past applications fills the screen. Cover letter after cover letter, ranging from professionally dull and business-like to creatively witty and, in one misguided example, a little aggressive.

Frankie had been offered none of these jobs, despite being overqualified for many of them. She'd tried to trust in fate, but as the months of applications had turned into a year, her confidence had started to drain away. Working for a small publisher like Eagle Wing meant small budgets, and small budgets meant small books, small sales and small glory.

Peeking over at Jane Hepburn and Natasha Martez again, she huffs. How is she supposed to get a great new job at a major publishing house when she doesn't have amazing authors about whose success she can boast? Her authors are good; some of them great even. It's not necessarily their fault. It's just that she doesn't have the manpower or money to make them bestsellers, or the hours in the day to give them the guidance they need.

Take Jane Hepburn, for example. Jane's a good writer. Creates a wonderful sentence, intricate and exciting plots. But there are issues Frankie doesn't have the time, or the heart, to dive into anymore. She's burnt out.

Each of the documents on her screen represents hours of wasted life. Hours, she reflects, she could have spent helping people like Jane Hepburn go from good to great. A new job would bring her back to life, she knows it. And now – at last – she knows *exactly* why she hadn't got any of them.

After her horoscope told her to take control of her fate and demand answers, Frankie had done just that, cornering someone from a bigger publishing house on that first Thursday morning in Hoslewit. The frightened HR executive had finally told her of the old rumours that stained her name, and careful investigation led Frankie back to Carrie as their source.

At first, Frankie assumes, Carrie didn't want her assistant – and make no mistake, Frankie had been a *brilliant* assistant – to leave her in the lurch. When Frankie had finally managed to secure a new job, Carrie barely spoke to her for her whole notice period, apart from a catty aside about how she hoped Frankie wouldn't 'find the job too ... *much*'. Her head had been slanted to one side, eyebrows raised in concern as fake as her platinum hair. When Carrie had continued with a barely audible, 'Oh, *dear*,' as she turned back to her emails, Frankie had felt belittled – as Carrie had intended – and about two inches tall. Today, the memory makes her swell with rage instead.

Ever the resentful dog in the manger, Carrie had evidently continued to drop the odd nasty comment here and there, mentioned fabricated misdemeanours, feigned relief to be shot of her old assistant, long after Frankie had left the Marks Agency. Publishing being what it is, her lies had been repeated and embellished – until Frankie was unemployable.

She shouldn't be surprised really. No one knows people better than their assistants, and Frankie had always known Carrie to be a spiteful old bag.

Shaking her head to clear it, Frankie forces her eyes back to the collection of old applications. Now she knows exactly why she hasn't been getting these new jobs, she can repair the damage that her first boss did to her career.

With Carrie out of the way, she is finally free to fly.

Chapter Twenty-Two

Saturday, 1.30 p.m.

It's fairly common knowledge that the best sandwich is chicken and bacon, but what if Natasha is a vegetarian? She doesn't *seem* like a vegetarian, but you never know these days. Best get some cheese and pickle as well.

Jane doesn't hold with veganism, which is frankly a step too far. But just in case, she gets Natasha a Twix. Twixes are vegan, right? Probably.

Londis in the village has an impressive array of crisps, but again Jane feels quite qualified on this subject and so confidently picks up four packets of salt and vinegar McCoy's. Ridged.

Being an admin assistant to an office full of insurance people means you become well versed in the hierarchy of meal-deal items.

She strolls back to the festival at a leisurely pace, reflecting on the fact she hasn't moved around this much in years, and she fancies it looks good on her already. Running here and there, up and down hills, chasing killers. Turns out sleuthing is an even more effective weight-loss method than going to yoga every third week.

It's going pretty well so far – two of their top suspects questioned! Not to mention her little chat with Edward Carter (and giving him a copy of her book). At this rate, she'll be running the Metropolitan Police Force by the end of the month.

No, they don't necessarily have many *leads* as such. But some promising clues have come to light. Frustratingly, it transpires it's quite difficult to get the whole truth out of people. They insist on closing their mouths just when it's getting interesting. Absolutely no one has yet said *oh, yes, actually I did the murdering*, or had tell-tale blood spatters on their shoes, which is most annoying.

Though thinking about it, that would ruin the fun.

In her sixth novel, *Killing Time*, PI Sandra Baker spent a long time collecting clues that failed to give her any concrete answers until, at last, one piece of information made everything slot into place. Jane can only assume that something similar is happening here.

She walks past the little church and its crumbling gravestones and thinks again about finding Carrie's body in the book tent. Mint green skirt riding up above the knee, coral lips shining against pale skin. The memory of seeing that same colour on Abi's face today makes Jane shudder. How long did it take Abi to raid her boss's belongings? What else has she helped herself to?

No matter what expensive makeup she plunders or purchases, Abi Ellis will never be Carrie Marks. Kimberley said Carrie had always been impressive, had always commanded a room and been completely sure of herself. Even Abi had said she could charm her way into anything. Abi, with her spite and her messiness and her failure to conceal how she's only interested in people who will further her own aims, will never be described in similar terms.

Jane has planned to meet the others on the lawn, by the willow tree, for a picnic lunch. Daniel has gone to move the books Abi had requested into the correct room, and Natasha has been dispatched to try and find the next suspect on their list – Laura Lane. Jane likes Natasha a lot, so she tries not to let it bother her that, after writing just one book, and even that yet to be published, Natasha already has more contacts in the industry than Jane does.

Deciding she has time to spare, she stops by the same piece of wall she'd sat on with Daniel earlier, and perches to people-watch, averting her eyes from the graves behind her. Would Carrie be buried or cremated? Would her funeral be attended by hordes of glamorous people, or a sparse few? Carrie has been Jane's agent for eight years now – just after starting her own agency around the time Jane started querying – but neverthless she finds it difficult to understand who this woman really is from the pieces of the puzzle she's collected so far. On the one hand, she was the toast of the town; famous, impressive, charismatic. On the other, she was despised by so many. A woman who sleeps with her best friend's husband, an unpleasant boss, an uncaring agent.

Does it really matter who she was? thinks Jane. *Will her death be any more or less tragic, more or less easy to solve?*

A young woman walks past in a t-shirt that reads *Jason can Steel my heart*, the wearer carrying a bulky tote bag stuffed with books. Another Laura Lane fan. When Jane solves the mystery of Carrie's murder, she'll have to make a TikTok video about it, she supposes, and then fans will wear t-shirts with her characters on too. Sandra Baker can . . . put a bun in my oven? No, she'll think about the t-shirts later, best not to get ahead of herself.

Glancing at her watch, she sees that she is supposed to be at their meeting spot in five minutes' time, so heaves herself and her haul of sandwiches off the wall and makes her way up the hill. The walkway is busy now, with crowds wandering in and out of the festival site to find lunch. On the lawn, the huge willow tree stands out proudly like a flag pole, and underneath sits a trio of people. Jane smiles to herself at the sight of her two friends waiting for her, and marvels at how quickly this has come about, and how good something as simple as a friend waiting for you under a tree feels.

As she gets closer, she sees that Natasha has succeeded in her mission and the third person is none other than social media sensation Laura Lane. Daniel is holding a pink iPhone, while Laura, one arm around Natasha, gabbles into the camera, grabbing it back afterwards to watch the clip with a slight nod of satisfaction as her fingers dash across the screen to work their magic.

'Jane!' Daniel shouts up to her, patting the ground. 'Come sit.'

'Aaaand done!' Laura looks up and smiles around the circle. 'Natasha, we need to set you up with a TikTok and Insta. I can tag you, start building up your fan base. Don't listen to the dinosaurs telling you that it's all about the work – it's all about the self-promotion.'

Over the past few days, Jane has watched hours' worth of Laura's videos, and so sitting with her like this is an unsettling feeling – as if she has walked through the frame and perched alongside Mona Lisa. Up close, the milky white skin has red patches blooming beneath foundation, and subtle lines around Laura's eyes hint at her years beginning to show. But the raven-black hair is just as thick and shiny, and the confidence takes on a different quality off-camera.

'I don't think we've met?'

'Oh, yes . . . no, I mean. No, we haven't? I'm Jane?'

'Jane's an author too,' says Natasha kindly, in the sort of voice you might use when talking about a pensioner – *Mary likes biscuits too, don't you, Mary?*

'Yes, I'm an author. Crime novels? Obviously, that's why I'm at a crime fiction festival, haha.' Jane chuckles with a faux-nonchalance that's fooling no one.

'We'll do another video in a bit, and I can tag you too,' Laura says with a smile, and Jane realises that this terrifying media personality is actually extremely kind. It throws her even further off-kilter.

'So,' Laura continues, looking back at Natasha, thick, dark eyebrows aloft. 'You wanted to talk about Carrie Marks.'

Daniel, who'd been rustling in the bag of sandwiches and piling everything up on the grass, freezes.

'That's right,' says Jane slowly. 'We understand that there was some history between you two.'

'And so it may have been me who did her in?'

'Oh, no! That's not . . . that's not at all what we . . . '

'It's fine, honestly. It could well have been. I didn't, but you don't know that, do you? May I?' She points to a chicken and bacon sandwich. Natasha nods, and takes another one. Daniel grabs the third, leaving Jane with the reserve cheese and pickle. That's the last time she tries to cater for unknown vegetarians.

'What do you want to know?' says Laura, taking a large bite of her sandwich and looking around expectantly. 'I suspect,' she says, after swallowing, 'it's why we didn't like each other. And,' she picks up a bag of McCoy's without asking, 'where I was on the night of the murder. And,' she opens the bag and brings a salty crisp to her lips, 'if I saw anything suspicious.' *Crunch.*

'Um, well, yes, that about sums it up. If you would be so kind?'

'When I wrote romance, it was all about crooked smiles and enemies to lovers, blah blah blah. I'm a crime writer now; I know the ropes. My writing life is all murders and motives, questions and answers. Some things I'll tell you, and some I won't – as fellow crime writers, you'll know that's often the way things go.' She nods at Jane and Natasha, munching away loudly on her crisps. As well as a triad of stars poorly tattooed behind Laura's ear, Jane notices a flicker of a scar, a burn mark perhaps, creeping from the edge of her long-sleeved top, and the imperfections surprise her. They hint at a past that this shiny, chirpy media star keeps well away from her online persona.

'Well, I'll begin then, if that's okay?' asks Daniel, looking around expectantly. After hanging back with Abi and Kimberley, it's his turn to take more of a leading role, so Jane nods her encouragement and he sits up straighter. After a moment's pause, he lowers his sandwich self-consciously, wiping mayonnaise on his jeans.

'Laura.' He clears his throat as if he's on stage. 'It's no secret you and Carrie weren't friends. Could you please tell us why?'

She shrugs, returning her attention to her free lunch. 'I don't have many friends, to be honest. Why *would* she be my friend?'

Good answer, thinks Jane. Laura Lane is smart.

'Okay, but it was more than that. You disliked each other. Why?'

Daniel is good at this too though. He has a lovely touch of the dramatic about him, leaning forward as if he is in an interrogation room rather than out in the sun surrounded by crisps.

'Sure. I didn't like her but it's not a huge deal. Carrie was always disparaging of my writing. We once met at an event a bit like this, though it was smaller. She had signed up to have una-gented writers pitch their ideas to her, which I did. She hated my pitch. Nothing unusual in that, but she was foul about it. Really nasty. In public.

'When I became successful, she wrote an article in the trade press about *talentless writers with an iPhone* ruining the industry. I wasn't name-checked, but it was a personal dig.'

Laura chews her sandwich, looking away from the group while she speaks. Her words are matter-of-fact, and lack spite or any obvious sense of grievance. Jane remembers the emotion in Kimberley's face when she recalled her former friend, and sees none of that here. Books are business to Laura Lane, and Carrie simply another player in the game.

'I've had plenty worse in my time, dealt with people a lot bolder and meaner than Carrie Marks. I'm successful. I'm almost rich, at least compared with how I lived before. People like Carrie are – were – the past. I'm the future. She wasn't a threat to me, certainly not someone I'd dirty my hands killing.' Laura shrugs again, perfectly comfortable with her grandiose self-image, and tucks back into her sandwich.

With her pitch-black hair shining in the sun, bold features and slightly hooked nose, Jane decides that she would be a toucan, perched imposingly in a tree.

'May I ask you why you argued on the day Carrie died?' asks Jane.

Laura doesn't give much of a reaction, but you can tell, if you're watching for it, that she isn't expecting them to know this. There is an infinitesimal pause in the motion of her jaw, a quick blink of the eyes. By the time she swallows, she is perfectly composed.

'Sure, sure. It's not a mystery. She wanted to be my agent, I said no.' Laura picks up the second half of her sandwich and continues eating.

Jane's eyes flick to Natasha, bemused.

'Why did she want that? When the two of you don't get on?'

Laura coughs, her bark of laughter obstructed by Londis's finest chicken and bacon on wholemeal.

'Why do you think? I sell. No matter what she has said about me and my writing and my fans, I sell. I make money. And she wanted in.'

'The cheek of it,' whispers Daniel. He's forgotten his interrogation persona and is now lying on his belly, propping himself up on one elbow and staring at Laura in fascination. 'How could she think she even had a chance after the way she treated you? And why would you want to give her 15 per cent of your earnings when you're already smashing it?'

'I know, right?' Laura answers, and Jane fancies she hears the hint of a West Country accent slipping through her polished façade. 'I said no, Carrie pushed, words were exchanged. That was it really. And in answer to the other questions – I spent a chunk of the evening talking to Natasha here. Which she will vouch for, I assume?' Natasha nods. 'I don't know the exact time I left. I can't account for every second of my time, but I know none of it was spent murdering.'

'And the third question. Did you see anything suspicious?'

Laura finishes her sandwich and starts up on the crisps again. She doesn't answer or look at any of them until the bag is empty, as if she has zoned out and into her own private world where all that matters is the demolition of salt and vinegar McCoy's. Carefully, slowly, she folds the crisp packet until it is a square inch and places it back on the grass.

Standing up, she brushes the crumbs off her top and shakes out her glossy black hair.

'Look, I'm happy to help. I am. But I'm also not here to make enemies, no matter what you've heard about me. I'm here to sell myself and sell books, to make contacts and make money. Not to murder or gossip. What I'm gonna say is, if I were you, I would be checking when people left the bar. And when I say check, I don't just mean *ask*. I mean *check*.'

She pulls her phone out of her pocket, fingers swiping and typing at speed. Without lifting her eyes from her screen, she continues, 'Now I've gotta go. I have a panel I'm speaking on. Natasha – our video is doing pretty well. Make sure you set up an account today, yeah? Good luck, you guys.'

Natasha, Daniel and Jane are left staring at each other under the willow tree, sandwiches untouched. Jane is mentally sorting through what she'd heard to see if it's of any use. Laura had been forthcoming, undefensive and unoffended. A cooperative witness. But she'd also managed to tell them basically nothing. Jane is reminded of the time she bought a used car, and the man had looked her in the eye to tell her that the Ford Fiesta had great mileage, four new tyres and perfect bodywork. It was only after she'd paid that she realised he'd specifically avoided mentioning the engine, which might as well have been non-existent.

General wisdom dictates that crime authors are lovely, and it's the romance authors you need to watch out for. Well, Laura

Lane is both. Maybe she *is* lovely, but there is something determined, something spiky, underneath. Something that's telling Jane she isn't quite who she appears to be. And Jane doesn't trust her one bit.

Chapter Twenty-Three

Saturday, 2.30 p.m.

Do you even know each other's alibis?

That's what Kimberley had asked. This, along with Laura's assertion that all information must be checked, has rattled Jane. She knows all about *corroborating evidence* of course. It came up in those university lectures she attended before dropping out. It tends to slow Baker down, so she doesn't always do that much of it. But this isn't a novel, this is real life, and it is sending her into quite a spin.

The Killer Lines lawn has become crowded with picnickers in the sun, so Jane, Natasha and Daniel are heading back into the village to find a quieter spot where they can discuss everything they've learnt so far. Jane is eager to start checking alibis, but is at a loss as to exactly *how*. She is in the lead, long legs covering the distance easily, head full of contradictory thoughts. She wants to demand more information from Kimberley Brown, to find Abi Ellis and shake the truth from her, to outsmart Laura Lane. Natasha is struggling to keep pace, but Jane is oblivious and desperate to keep moving.

'Nothing is adding up yet,' she mutters, almost to herself.

'How so?' pants Natasha.

'I just have a feeling that they're all keeping things from us! Doesn't it strike you as odd that Carrie would try to persuade Laura to sign with her?'

'Not really. Laura's sales figures are inc—'

'But think!' Jane feels agitated, hot-headed, and is aware she is talking loudly. 'Think. How was that allowed to become an

143

argument? How? An agent can't *demand* a writer sign with them, it doesn't make sense!'

'Whoah, Jane, stop. Let's take a moment.' Gasping for breath, Natasha grabs Jane's arm and slows her to a halt. 'Let's talk in here.' She pulls Jane through a small metal gate that creaks for want of oil. They are in the graveyard, the ancient church towering over them. Natasha leads the way and sits down in its shade, back against the cool stone of the wall. Hesitating, Daniel drops down next to her. Jane stays standing, annoyed for a reason she can't quite understand.

'We need to get ourselves together,' continues Natasha. 'We need to gather our facts, make a plan.'

'Laura is right – we need to *check* information,' says Jane. She takes a deep breath. 'We need to know alibis. Even each other's.'

She joins them on the ground and they sit in silence as she picks at the grass, stacking strands of it like a small bird's nest in front of her. She can hear another American tourist exclaiming loudly about the church, demanding her friend take a picture of her by it.

'From my good angle though, yeah? Get that cute grave in.'

'Well, I'm not sure I have an alibi as such,' begins Daniel. 'I was working all day, and knew basically no one. I left around 10, don't know the exact time.'

Jane is distinctly uncomfortable about her new friends having to explain where they were that night, as if either of them could be a killer – though they *have* both shown themselves to be incredibly capable people, so you never know. Every killer must be somebody's friend, somebody's child.

The sound of the tourist's voice niggles at her and she tries to focus. It is loudly suggesting she and her friend swap places so that each of them has a picture by the grave they both find particularly adorable.

'You can ask my hotel?' continues Daniel. 'It's the Thistle, and I spoke to the man on reception about borrowing a toothbrush when I got in, so you could probably check with him. That's a decent enough alibi, I'd say.'

'Excellent, Daniel!' says Natasha. 'For the sake of doing things properly, we *will* double-check, if you don't mind?'

'Not at all. Abi, Carrie and I all checked in there, so you could ask if they noticed Abi getting in that night as well.'

Jane just shrugs. She is frustrated and depressed – it is starting to seem unlikely they will ever find the truth.

'Say English Cheddar Cheese!'

'Make sure I don't have a double chin in this one!'

'Mine is less robust, I'm afraid,' Natasha is saying. 'I was with my publicist for most of the night. She was introducing me to people. And then she left me with Laura at about . . . I don't know, maybe 11.30? Laura was trying to give me tips and pointers. Then she went off to speak to someone else – I don't know who – and I took the opportunity to sneak off back to my hotel. There was no one on the desk though so . . . '

'Upload it to Instagram, Sheryl! But put a filter on first!'

The tourist's voice is grating, the kind that can slice through thoughts and metal alike.

'It's almost impossible to know for certain where everyone is at what time, and as Laura pointed out, you can't absolutely trust what people *say*,' says Daniel.

Jane has the impression that no one – not Kimberley, Abi, Laura or even Edward – has told them the whole truth so far. How can they get anywhere when all they have are words, and words are so frequently *false*?

'I'm tagging you in it, Linda. This one gets the grave and the little church cockerel thing in too!'

'I've got it!' Jane shouts, sitting upright, excitement rushing in like a spring storm. Pulling out her phone, she opens up the latest app on her home screen. 'Look – every time I've seen Laura Lane, she's speaking into her phone. Natasha says she was there quite late. If she was uploading content on the night of Carrie's murder, we'll get a good idea of who was still in the bar. Right?'

The others look impressed and Jane feels taller, but this time, in a good way.

Flicking back through Laura's latest videos, she finds one from the evening of Carrie's death, uploaded at 10.04 p.m. Raising the volume and spinning the screen so that they can all see, Jane presses play.

'*Hey, my babes and baes!*' Laura Lane says to the camera, then spins around to show off the inside of the Dog and Bone. '*The party is kicking OFF at Killer Lines and I wish you could be here with me! Love ya!*'

'Mercifully short,' says Jane. 'Okay, who can we see? Natasha, can you write this down?' She replays the video three more times. They spot Daniel in the background, standing in his coat as if he's about to leave. He smiles in relief, as if they hadn't believed his story. The festival not starting properly until the next morning means the bar was only half full on Thursday night, but there are still nameless faces yet to be identified. Among them, the frizzy hair of Abi Ellis is spotted near the table where the Scots are drinking hard, the shimmering silver skirt of Frankie Reid is at the bar, and the hulking form of Brad Levinsky, who looks so drunk he can barely stand, lurks in the background. Carrie Marks herself is waving to the barman, an irritated look on her face. Natasha is just visible, standing with the woman Jane recognises as the blonde Edward Carter argued with two days earlier.

'That's my publicist, Sarah Parks-Ward,' says Natasha when Jane enquires. 'Like I said, I was with her on and off all evening. Brad is there.' She pauses the video and points at a Brad-sized blur in the corner. 'But no sign of Kimberley Brown. She must have been telling the truth about leaving at 10. I don't remember seeing her later than that. And look, there's Carrie, talking to that tall guy.'

'That's Edward Carter! Remember, he said they spoke that night? They were friends.'

'You aren't here, Jane.'

She tells herself she is only imagining the accusing tone in Natasha's voice. They'd agreed to question each other after all.

'I left earlier, at maybe around 8? I'm not a big party person. My Air BnB host can vouch for me.'

Jane had fended off Mary's chatter and managed to sneak to bed with a book at 9. She'd lain there, staring at the swirls of the Artex ceiling, missing her mother. If she'd been alive, Jane probably wouldn't have been in Hoslewit at all. It was then that she'd heard her mother's voice in her ear, and had decided to take her fate into her own hands by sneaking into the book tent so early the following day. *Fortune favours the brave, Jane. Time to grab the bull by the horns.*

Only instead of horns, Jane's hand had closed around a can that, once opened, was revealed to be absolutely stuffed full of worms.

'Let's see what later videos she has,' says Daniel. 'This is too early.'

Jane flicks back to the home screen. They watch the next one, uploaded at 11.28, which shows Laura with her arm around an uncomfortable-looking woman she introduces as a famous writer of historical crime. The room is emptier in this video, and though there is no sign of Kimberley or Abi, they spot Brad Levinsky heading out the door, and Frankie Reid deep in conversation with the publicist with the beautiful white-blonde hair, Sarah. The table of male writers are all in the same position, looking a little the worse for wear.

Next is a boomerang video of Natasha, *cheers*ing to the camera in a room that is emptier still. It was uploaded at 12.06, and is captioned 'Happy midnight!'

Finally, they click on the last video of the evening, uploaded at 12.45 a.m.

147

'*Well, day one at Killer Lines has been a blast,*' says Laura, looking a little tired despite the filter and makeup. She spins the camera around the Dog and Bone once, and then her face fills the screen again. '*I feel so blessed to be here, and I just wish you all could be here too. It's incredible to meet other authors, book professionals, and of course, some of you amaaaaazzing fans! I love you SO much. Now I'm gonna sleep until a new day rocks my world!*'

She blows a kiss at the camera and the video fades. Natasha starts to scribble down anyone she recognises, including herself and Brad Levinsky, lingering in the doorway again.

Jane is rewatching, scouring the faces for people of interest. Edward Carter has left, as it seems has Natasha's blonde publicist. There is no sign of Frankie. One of their main suspects, Kimberley, is unaccounted for from roughly two and a half hours before the murder. But is that because she had retired to bed as claimed? Or was she, even as Laura filmed, arguing with Carrie Marks in the book tent, her rage rising, her vision blurring to red, her hand reaching for the dagger?

Abi is absent, but Laura, the last of their main suspects, is shown to be in the bar in both the 12.06 and 12.45 videos, straddling the time of the murder – although as she could have just about had time to kill Carrie and return to post, what does this really prove? Nothing. If only Laura had filmed a continuous video, or uploaded more frequently around the time of the murder.

'Carrie isn't in that earlier video, the one from 12.06,' says Daniel. 'She might already be in the book tent with the killer.'

'That, or they're on their way to meet her,' Natasha says. 'Carrie isn't in the 11.28 video either. What was she up to all evening?'

Despondency creeps back over Jane after the brief rush of excitement earlier. They've learnt nothing at all useful from the videos.

Maybe you just can't see the wood for the trees, Jane, her mother's voice whispers. *Chin up, and go over it all with a fine-toothed comb.*

With a deep breath, Jane presses play again, pausing each second to search the picture. Carrie is conspicuously absent, but she can't gather anything else of note.

Finally, on the video uploaded at 11.28, she sees something. Through the window of the Dog and Bone, out on the lawn, is a flash of bright royal blue. She remembers back to that first morning when Abi had pointed out who was who and what was what. The royal blue jumpsuit swathing an impressive figure.

'That,' she says to her friends, pointing at the window, 'is a person. That, is Kimberley Brown.'

'The Kimberley Brown who said she left the festival for bed at 10 p.m.?'

'The very same.'

Chapter Twenty-Four

Saturday, 2.30 p.m.

Kimberley Brown is shaken.

It's been a long time since she was last in the UK, and she'd forgotten how annoying the Brits are. They all say sorry so much, but aren't sorry at all! *Sorry to disturb you,* they'll say, while barging into your room. *Terribly sorry about that,* they'll whimper after they've been pushed down the stairs. *That's fine,* they'll gleefully shout at a suggestion they cut off their own leg with a rusty hacksaw, *no, no, that's perfect, actually.* You can't trust a word they say. And Jane Hepburn has that in spades.

Kimberley had told that weird trio what they wanted to hear, nothing more, nothing less. Certainly nothing more. After all, her husband's affair is an open secret. It's publishing industry lore. They would have got hold of it somehow, and at least this way they get her version of events. Hopefully, it's enough to stop them digging deeper into her past with Carrie Marks.

At the end Kimberley knows she stumbled, almost giving away too much, though hopefully she saved it. If it hadn't been for seeing her name on the mirror in the ladies' restroom earlier she might not have slipped up, even with the tall woman's obsequiousness lulling her into a false sense of security. But spotting it scrawled on the glass in scarlet lipstick had spooked her.

And then, yes, the tall lady hadn't helped, with her striking eyes and wonderful bone structure, like an artwork. If she hadn't been so hunched and humble, she might even have been attractive in an odd, Amazonian way. But it was the way she *looked* at you and the tone of her voice that made you open up almost without realising it.

There had been a moment when Kimberley had considered telling her everything. Not just what happened all those years ago in New York, but also what happened on that fateful night in the book tent. But of course she couldn't do that. If she did, well, she'd probably have to kill her.

Kimberley glances at the clock on the wall: 2.30. She's hidden in her room long enough. As much as she wants to crawl under her duvet for the rest of the day, she knows it's not an option. If there's one thing she's learnt in life, it's that no matter what, you show up. Made a proofreading error that's going to cost the company $15,000 overnight? Put on your smartest outfit and get in early. Find yourself at the heart of an industry scandal where every single person in your circle knows about your husband's affair? Get your hair done, and smile like you own the world. Basically accused of murder by three randoms with an unknown level of information? Sigh. Here goes.

At least the world is sunny today, and it gives her a confidence boost as she walks to the festival to watch Brad's next panel discussion. Kimberley looks good in the sun. It brings out the gold in her hair and eyes, and makes her feel as though she is in a movie. But what sort of movie will it end up being?

That Jane Hepburn would benefit from some highlights in her hair. She would make a marvellous project. It wouldn't take much – some better makeup, a decent outfit, and get her to stand up straight. She has the air of someone sorry for taking up too much space, which is hardly the sexiest aura.

Kimberley pauses to look at her reflection in a shop window. She's still got it – and so she should, considering how much effort she puts in. It's a shock though; with all the talk of Carrie Marks and the past over these last few days, she almost expected to see herself at 27, the way she'd been when she sat across from

Carrie in that cheap cocktail bar on Ninth. Is it still there? It's been many years since she's drunk two-for-$10 drinks in a place with a sticky floor. A long time since she's sat across from her best friend and cried with laughter.

She'll need to speak to Brad and warn him away from those two-bit detectives. She has a feeling he'll be past buzzed and on to loaded by now, and you can't trust a drunk to keep their mouth closed. Then she needs to make sure she's seen acting normally. Not a care in the world, that's her. In two days' time, they'll be out of here, and then they will never mention Carrie Marks again.

If only it was as easy not to *think* of her as it is not to talk about her. That first night of this Godforsaken festival had been the first time they had spoken in nine years. Carrie had looked just as beautiful, still had that easy smile that shone as soon as she relaxed, even if there were new lines around her eyes and her skin had lost its dewiness.

Even when she cried.

Even with the blood . . .

No, Kimberley can't tell Jane Hepburn and her friends about that.

Chapter Twenty-Five

Saturday, 3.30 p.m.

'Get a move on, Daniel! You're slower than my nan on ice skates,' Jane calls over her shoulder. 'And she's dead, so that's saying something.'

Jane's optimism is back, coursing through her blood and pushing her forward. When she solves the crime, she'll talk about this moment in the morning television interviews. The *break in the case*, she'll call it. *When we saw that flash of blue*, she'll say, *we had concrete proof that Ms Kimberley Brown was lying to us. It was the break in the case.* She'll have to lose a stone before any television appearances, but all this running around is probably helping. And her sandwich was vegetarian after all.

Natasha is speaking on a panel at 4 (*Good Friends Help Bury the Body: the role of friendship in crime fiction*) and so has gone to find a quiet corner where she can prepare and learn some off-the-cuff answers. Daniel and Jane don't have tickets to watch their new friend speak – and Jane is privately thankful for the fact it is sold out – so they are embarking on the next part of their mission alone.

They find themselves striding back towards Kimberley Brown and the Old House Hotel, Jane in the lead, long legs covering the distance easily as usual.

'Jane, can you *slow down*? We don't even have a proper plan.'

Jane slows her pace with a sigh.

'I don't think bursting into Kimberley Brown's room with this information is the right idea,' Daniel continues, at her side now. 'What if she's dangerous?'

The Old House Hotel comes into view as they round the corner and they both slow to a halt.

'As we're back here, I could try with the concierge again?' Daniel offers. 'Or the Thistle . . . the hotel Carrie, Abi and I stayed in . . . is down there,' he says, pointing to a small side road. 'We could ask the front desk about everyone's movements? Kimberley might be our top suspect, but I still think Abi is a strong possibility. And it wouldn't hurt to know more about Carrie's movements in general. It would be great to understand what she was doing on Thursday night for all that time she wasn't in the Dog and Bone.'

Jane ponders his words as she stares at the picturesque Old House Hotel, imagining Kimberley where they left her in her room. Maybe questioning her again so soon *wasn't* the right approach. Something everyone can agree on is that there has been a lot of talk. Her throat is dry with it. The last time Jane socialised this much (if you can call questioning people about a murder *socialising*) was when she went speed dating. She'd spoken to 20 men in one evening, including six who still lived with their mothers, one who was crying throughout, two who were married, and one who immediately asked to inspect her feet.

This, she decides, is much more fun.

'You know,' she mutters to herself, 'Abi must have found a way into Carrie's room to take that lipstick.'

'What are you on about?'

'And if Abi can . . . '

Yes, there has been a lot of talk, and so Jane decides the time has come for some action. After all, *action speaks louder than words*, as her mother always said. Which is why, she decides with a flash of brilliance, they are going to break into the hotel room of the great, late Carrie Marks.

Though she's still not *totally* sure if that is the sort of thing her mother had in mind.

'Why not try to get into *Kimberley's* room?' Daniel hisses, as they make their way down the side road towards the Thistle.

'Because she might still be in there. But we *know* Carrie's not in *her* room. And like you said, we need to find out more about her. Trace the links between Carrie and Kimberley, or Carrie and any of the other suspects. Or find a clue to what else she was doing on Thursday night.'

Daniel doesn't take much convincing to become reckless, which, Jane decides, is an excellent quality in a sidekick. Soon, they are happily discussing ways they can gain access to Carrie's room as they walk. Daniel favours a blunt approach – simply going up there and hitting the door with something heavy – whereas Jane would rather use her wits. They discuss everything from dressing up as cleaning staff, to faking a sudden illness and claiming the life-saving medicine is inside, to learning to pick locks.

In the end, it comes off without a hitch, and with minimal lying.

Jane lingers in the lobby of the hotel pretending to peruse the menu on the Lavazza coffee machine – cappuccino or macchiato? Sweet and Low or sugar? – while Daniel works his charm on the pretty young receptionist. From the corner of her eye, Jane watches her giggle and blush when Daniel leans forward over the desk. Five minutes later, they are in the lift heading to the sixth floor.

This hotel is more modern and slick than the Old House but without its charm. Surfaces are shiny and lines are clean. The lift is fully mirrored, so Jane is made to stare at herself for the entire journey, no matter where she turns. A lift for narcissists, or birds.

'They know I was here with Carrie,' explains Daniel. 'And that she was my boss. I said I needed to collect some work things from her room and the police said I could. And I may have flirted a little.'

'Just a little?'

'Okay, I may have promised to take her to Pizza Express next week.'

'You won't even *be* in Hoslewit next week.'

'Oh, dear. Well, I suppose I'll have to cancel that then.'

They grin at each other in the mirror and Jane feels a swell of pride and warmth. Daniel is so very good at charming his way through problems, she feels lucky to have him by her side.

'You know, you're learning much more in this investigation than you would have on the internship anyway. You can file that one away for *times you have used your initiative.*'

'Perfect, I'll crack it out in the next job interview.'

The lift dings and the doors slide open, finally giving Jane a reprieve from her own image. The corridor is long and softly lit. Someone out there has the job of Hotel Corridor Lighting Expert, and they know the exact wattage needed and the perfect placement for each spotlight. A role for everyone in this world.

Rounding the corner, they arrive at the door of Carrie's room. Number 614. Jane is surprised not to see police tape across it, but maybe the hotel didn't want to draw attention to the murder, and the door is locked after all. She is holding her breath in anticipation, and her and Daniel look at each other, steeling themselves. Daniel raises the key card and taps it once against the reader.

The door whirrs as information is processed. The reader flashes red.

'Oh.' Daniel taps it again, and again it denies them entry. The tension drains away.

'These things!' says Jane. 'What is wrong with a good old-fashioned key? Who was calling for *keys* to be made digital?'

Ten minutes later, Daniel is back with a new key card, the LED flashes green, and the door swings open. Jane lets out a long, slow breath. She hasn't been holding it all this time, you understand, but the tension came right back with the arrival of the new key card.

Carrie's room is large, comfortable-looking, and relatively soulless. The walls are off-white, and the bed – made and unslept in – is strewn with soft magnolia throws and cushions.

'Who knew she was such a slob?' says Daniel, eyeing the piles of clothes on the chair, the stacks of paper and notebooks on the desk, the underwear in the corner. A suitcase is open, half unpacked, by the bed, and there's a pile of gleaming jewellery on one bedside table. The cleaning staff had clearly been in to turn down the room on the day of Carrie's death, and done what they could around the heaps of her belongings.

The door shuts gently behind them, making Jane jump. Now they are here, it feels deeply illicit. Probably because it is. She can't imagine Detective Inspector Ramos would be too pleased to hear about this.

'So what are we looking for?' asks Daniel again.

'I'm not sure. Anything suspicious. Particularly anything that links her to our top suspect, I suppose.'

They are both whispering and standing stock still by the door. Taking a step, making a noise, would feel like disturbing the dead.

'Go on then,' whispers Daniel. Jane straightens her shoulders and tries to project Private Investigator Sandra Baker. In book five, *A Desperate Death*, Baker searches the childhood bedroom of a murder victim for clues. Where did she start?

'You check the bedside table and her suitcase. I'm going to go through the desk.'

Daniel nods, and they both get to work.

Jane sits down at the desk, imagining for one moment that she is a literary legend, negotiating contracts and building careers. Who is she kidding? She can't even build her *own* career. An expensive-looking coat, camel-coloured and elegant, hangs on the back of the chair. It is so similar to the one Jane pictured herself wearing all of those years ago, while following suspicious people down dark alleys, that it distracts her.

Okay, to business. How Carrie managed to create order out of this chaos, Jane does not know. She pulls out her packet of extra-strong mints and pops one in her mouth as she inspects an old-fashioned Filofax lying open on a date three months from now. Almost illegible scribbles fill every date.

Simon Kushner contract up for renewal
Lunch with Josh B
Call SPW
Fatima Knox book tour begins

Nothing obvious that would prompt a dagger in the chest. Jane flicks through notebooks, mostly full of *To Do* lists and doodles, with the occasional underlined idea in block capitals amongst them.

SUGGEST 2 LEO THAT HG DIES IN NXT BK

TERM PW TO AUTHORS

MOVE TK HB TO JAN?

She returns to the Filofax, flipping back in time and squinting to make out the words. Those she can read are mainly lunch dates, more contract reminders, and occasionally something so abbreviated it could mean anything at all.

TLD in WTS
KL – KM / LL
YSC / YSD 4 PO

At a loss, she pulls out her own notebook and starts copying out some of the recent lists and diary pages. If Jane thought she would get a better idea of who Carrie Marks really was from looking through her belongings, she is drawing a blank so far. She glances over at Daniel, who has finished with the drawers and is now sitting on the floor by Carrie's open suitcase flicking through a hefty, heavily annotated wad of paper. She softly strokes the fabric of the camel coat, wondering for a moment if she could try it on. Then she remembers something – in *A Desperate Death*, Baker found the hidden will in . . .

'Daniel!'

'What have you found?'

He leaps up and hops over the suitcase to where Jane is sitting, holding an old photograph in a flimsy cardboard mount.

'It was in her coat pocket,' she says, staring at her prize. 'Why was she walking around with this?'

'Looks like an old school photo. How old are the kids . . . like 15?'

'About that, yes. I can't tell when it's from though; they're all in uniform. It doesn't look recent. Bad photo quality, and bad hair.'

They both stare at the photograph in silence. It's faded, with a deep white crease through the centre where it's been folded. Daniel takes it from Jane's hand to look at it more closely.

'Sometimes these things have – yep! Names!' On the back of the frame is a printed list of names, from left to right, identifying each child. They scan eagerly, looking for a mention of Carrie Marks or Kimberley Brown or anyone else they might recognise, but they are disappointed.

'I guess it could be unrelated,' says Jane, crestfallen. *A picture is worth a thousand words*, her mum used to say. But sometimes, it's worth nothing at all. 'How are you getting on over there anyway? Find anything?'

'Not really.' Daniel stands up straight and stretches his arms above his head. 'The drawers are empty. More clothes and makeup in the suitcase.'

'Weren't you reading something?'

'Some manuscript. I don't recognise the title from the agency submissions log, but what do I know? I'm sure Carrie didn't share everything she had in with the intern.'

A noise from the door makes them freeze, wide-eyed. A shuffling of feet, followed by a beep, and the whirr of the door's mechanism. Jane's breath catches in her throat.

The familiar bleep of denial.

'Oh, come *on!*' a voice squeaks through the door.

'Abi,' Daniel mouths at Jane. They hear another beep, another whirr, another negative bleep.

'Quick!' Jane mouths back, looking around in panic. Daniel flops down onto the floor and crawls beneath the bed. Jane pushes herself into the almost empty wardrobe, next to the ironing board and mini bar, hiding herself behind the hangers. Pulling the door shut, she holds her breath and tries to still her wildly beating heart. A slice of the room is still visible where the doors almost meet. Does this ever work? In horror films, terrified young women crouch in wardrobes, waiting to die. And die they do.

Faintly, she hears another beep, a gentle whirring, and finally, a chirp of admittance.

The small, scruffy form of Abi Ellis appears in her line of vision, flashes of hair and polka dots dissected in front of her. Daniel isn't making any noise, but is he visible? Abi disappears from Jane's line of sight, but she hears movement in the room, perhaps something being put down on the bed. The sound of a zip.

Jane has not been breathing, and now she fears making too loud a noise when she has to finally gasp for air. She forces herself to inhale slowly, in and out. Would charmless Abi be capable of persuading an extra key card from reception, as Daniel did? There is a small chance that Carrie *gave* her assistant a spare key to her room, though that does seem odd. There is also a chance, thinks Jane with a start, that Abi slipped the key from Carrie's pocket as she lay cooling on the book-tent floor.

Abi comes back into view at the desk, and she's holding – what is she holding? Jane hears rustling as Abi flicks through some papers, then rifles through Carrie's makeup bag. She moves to the pile of jewellery and picks up pieces one by one.

'Oooh, Cartier!' Abi whispers to herself. 'I'll be back for you.' Jane can see her examining some diamond studs, before she sighs and puts them back down.

Would she move to the wardrobe? It's certainly the next logical place to check for abandoned treasures. Tailored jackets, which cost more than Abi's yearly salary, cushion Jane's body; bags that could pay a month's rent poke against her shins. It was foolish for Jane to take the risk she has. *Actions may speak louder than words, Mother, but isn't safe also better than sorry?*

Abi grabs what must be her backpack from the bed, and leaves Jane's line of sight again. There is the sound of the room door opening, gently thudding shut, then silence.

No one moves for what feels like hours, but in reality is seconds. Jane hears the shuffling movement of Daniel edging out from under the bed, sees him slink into view in the crack between the doors. Still, she cannot bring her own limbs to act.

Finally, the wardrobe door is opened, light fills her eyes and there is Daniel, pale-faced and traumatised.

'That was *close*.'

Jane manages to swallow past the lump in her throat, feels the blood racing through her veins. With a deafening clanking, she pushes past the hangers and back into the room. A hysterical giggle forces its way up her throat, but she stifles it.

'We need to get out of here,' she says. 'This has been a waste of time. And Abi could come back.'

'Well, she shouldn't be in here either.'

'Who cares? Let's go!'

'But what was she up to?' Daniel insists, looking around the room.

'Stealing, by the look of it. But I don't think she actually took anything.'

Jane dusts herself off and glances over at the desk she had been sitting at just minutes earlier. It looks the same, apart from one obvious addition.

'Carrie's laptop! Abi had Carrie's laptop, and she's just put it back.'

'Surprised the police don't have it,' Daniel says in an awed whisper. 'Maybe she took it before they got in here?' He sits down at the desk and opens the computer. 'Password-protected. I have no idea what that might be. What the hell . . . Just what is Abi up to?'

Jane wanders over to the pile of jewellery Abi had gone through. Both of the diamond studs are still there, gleaming in the sunlight bursting through the large window.

'It's not Carrie's dog's name,' says Daniel. 'The password. I don't know what else to try. I don't want to end up locking the computer.'

Jane picks up a necklace, gold with a circular emerald pendant. A pair of pearl drop earrings. A golden bangle, heavy and expensive-looking, engraved on the inside.

'Maybe one of her big authors?' Daniel continues. 'Though my password is Bombastic69, so if it's something like that we've got no chance.'

Jane squints at the inscription. The letters are small, engraved in looping cursive.

'Daniel. You need to look at this.'

She passes him the bangle.

'What does it say?' He takes it from her. 'It's kind of hard to make out.' Holding it at arm's length, he squints, and slowly starts to read aloud.

'"*Carrie – my true love. One day. KB x*".'

Chapter Twenty-Six

Saturday, 4.55 p.m.

In truth, Natasha doesn't think she *would* help a friend bury a body. She doesn't have any friends who have asked, yet, but would she get involved?

She decides it depends on who was asking, who the body belonged to (or used to belong to), and why the friend in question had felt the need to bludgeon them to death. She doesn't have a huge number of close friends, and so mentally flicks through them. Would Angie Ray from university call her if she'd killed someone? Probably not; they haven't actually spoken in eight months. What about Paul Weybrecht? What's he up to these days? He'd probably feel her up while she was moving the body. 'Oh, sorry,' he'd say. 'Wrong leg!'

Natasha can't imagine Jane killing anyone unless they really deserved it though. And in that case, would she step up and help her new friend, or turn her back? Or, worse, shop her to the police?

'Ms Martez?'

Natasha is not a natural at author panels. Questions are asked and theories proffered, but she finds herself dropping in and out of focus, imagining which person in the room looks most like a murderer. That guy in the back – the moustache is suspect. Or, she thinks, looking at the striking auburn-haired woman in the green silk dress, *is it you*? Natasha drags her eyes away from Kimberley Brown.

'Sorry, what was the question?'

'The gentleman in the audience asked whether, in your novel, the friends of the protagonist make them a better or worse person.' The woman chairing the panel is smiling, but her voice is hard. She has had just about enough of Natasha's half-hearted performance.

'Oh, yeah. Um. I guess a bit of both?'

Blank faces and silence tell her that this answer isn't good enough.

'Well,' she continues, hoping inspiration will come as she speaks, 'my novel is about a group of friends who commit a crime together. So in that sense, they make each other worse. They got each other into the position where they have a murder to cover up. But in another sense, they build each other up, make each other funnier and braver, compensate for each other's flaws. In reality, I think that our friends have the ability to bring out the best and the worst in us. That's what people close to you do. They push you to be *more*. Whatever that means. So . . . like . . . that . . . um . . . that is what I tried to do. So, yeah.'

The moderator nods, meaning the answer is acceptable despite the lame ending. Natasha has always found the end the most difficult part of public speaking. Without fail, she will limp off into nothingness, until eventually someone saves her from the never-ending loop of *yeah*s and *um*s and *like*s.

At least she has now answered a question and can zone out a bit more. Brad Levinsky clearly enjoys the spotlight, and has been happy to take up most of the air time. Natasha sees her Chanel-clad publicist, Sarah Parks-Ward, in the audience, scowling. Natasha knows she has disappointed Sarah repeatedly. Her scruffy clothes, lack of social media presence, and general failure to wow a crowd are visibly ageing the beautiful blonde in charge of her. Still, Natasha got the impression Sarah hated her from the moment they met, before she'd even opened her mouth. There had been snide comments about the advance Natasha was paid for her book, and probing, uncomfortable questions about the offer process. Maybe Sarah has a sixth sense for poor public speakers.

'And finally, we have time for one more question,' says the moderator, perking Natasha up. Thank the lord, she is almost free to rejoin her friends. What have they been doing? Have they found out anything important? 'How about you, sir? The man in the blue shirt.'

'Er, yeah, thanks. This is to all three of the authors on-stage. Would *you* help a friend bury a body?'

The author of four moderately successful psychological thrillers goes first. With a booming laugh, she shouts, 'Hell, yeah!' The audience titters – she has been a hit.

'Friendship is very important,' begins Brad. His answers are always over-long and his voice very loud. Natasha saw him downing a pint of ale before coming on-stage, and has concluded he is slightly drunk. '*Loyalty* is important. Yes, we should all strive to follow the laws of our society, but what about the law inside ourselves?' He places a hand over his heart and nods with a show of sincerity. It's the most American thing Natasha has seen all day. 'Some people – let's be honest here, everyone! – some people deserve what they get coming to them. And I for one will never turn my back on a friend who needs me.'

'Very good, Mr Levinsky. Very good. And Ms Martez?'

Natasha thinks of Jane again, imagines her asking for help. Daniel, standing at a graveside, holding out a spade. Who is in the grave though? Kimberley Brown? Carrie Marks? Does it matter? She trusts them to know best.

'I'd grab that shovel.'

'Well, well, well, three authors here to turn to in a crisis! Ladies and gentlemen, please join me in a round of applause for our writers today, who will be available for book signings and further discussion in a few minutes' time.'

Since her debut novel is yet to be published Natasha has no books to sign, so she manages to escape relatively quickly. Starting down the steps at a jog, she pulls out her phone to ring

Jane as she moves, but the stairwell has no signal. She can, however, see a text message and voicemail notification, both from the literary agent Marabella Rhodes. Natasha had nearly signed on with Marabella originally, but in the end she'd flipped a coin and chosen Carrie Marks instead. Now Marabella was on the prowl, trying to scoop up Carrie's clients almost before her body turned cold. If Carrie's rival hadn't currently been in the South of France, she'd have earnt a place on Natasha's suspect list.

Deciding to ignore Marabella for the time being, she tries Jane's number again, but it's not until she's in the bar of the Dog and Bone that it connects. They agree to meet by the willow tree.

As Natasha heads there, she is momentarily overwhelmed by déjà vu. The sun is falling in the sky, and bathing everyone on the lawn in the blinding golden light of a British spring day done good. Seeing the two of them standing there, Daniel's arm outstretched towards her, her eyes flicker towards their feet – no yawning grave. As she gets closer, she sees Daniel is proffering a drink rather than a shovel.

'Got us a bottle of *Wuthering Whites*,' he says with a smile as she draws closer.

'Are *any* of the drinks even based on *crime* novels?'

'Just *A Study in Scarlet Wine*, but I've heard it's undrinkable.'

Natasha takes a sip – even though it's cheap and acidic and a far cry from the lightly sparkling Vinho Verde she used to drink in Lisbon, it's also cold and very welcome. After eight years living in the UK, she's almost used to the wine. Almost.

'So, what have you got?'

'Everything.'

She notices now that Daniel is almost vibrating with excitement, bursting at the seams to tell her what they've discovered. Natasha can feel heat rising through her body, as if it is quite literally contagious and jumping from him to her. Electricity leaping between conductors.

'Maybe not *everything*,' says Jane. 'But certainly *something*. Let's sit. I've got photos.'

'Natasha?' The voice comes from behind her, and she recognises it at once. It's commanding, accentless, and strikes fear into her bones. Sarah. Natasha turns to see her publicist striding across the lawn towards her. 'Aren't you supposed to be in the Q&A, darling?'

The scariest thing about Sarah Parks-Ward is that she pretends to be sweet. It isn't acceptable to swear at an author in your care, shout at them or physically manhandle them. But she doesn't need to. She's found ways around that.

'Oh, I thought that was done? I don't have any books to sign or anything.' Natasha's voice comes out as a whisper, and she senses her friends move closer to her in support.

'I know that, my darling,' Sarah says slowly, with the air of having to explain something to a six year old. 'But it's your chance to reach out to the readers and make sure they are *preordering* your book. Getting you on these panels isn't easy, you know.' Natasha looks down, shame-faced, and wishes she wasn't already holding a glass of wine. 'And it's your chance to get to know the other authors, my love. You have a chance here that some people would kill for . People like Brad can help you be a success.'

'I'm getting to know authors now . . . Look! This is Jane Hepburn!'

'Hmm.'

'Lovely to meet you,' says Jane, stepping in. 'And it's almost certainly too late for Natasha to go back now, so let me pour you a glass of wine. Daniel was just going to get more glasses.' He doesn't move, so she elbows him discreetly.

'Yes! Yes, one moment.'

Daniel runs to the beer tent as Jane pulls the bottle from the ice bucket at her feet. Sarah furrows her brow in frustration, but she looks tempted. Before she can make an excuse, Daniel is back and a fresh glass of wine is in Sarah's hand.

'Well, cheers then,' she says, clinking her glass against Natasha's and scanning the lawn as she sips. Sarah Parks-Ward is undeniably attractive but has a hardness to her face that stops it being beautiful. Despite the evening setting in, her makeup is still flawless and her clothes unmistakably designer.

'Who are you with then?' Sarah asks Jane in a bored voice. 'What publisher?'

'Oh, um, Eagle Wing? Frankie Reid is my editor?'

Sarah titters into her wine. 'Good luck.'

'Sorry?'

'Oh, it's just . . . I've heard things about Frankie Reid.'

Jane's face burns red. Natasha is embarrassed that the woman who has joined the group to find *her* has already insulted her friend. Dismissing Jane's editor, and by extension, Jane, so casually.

'Well, I think she's wonderful,' says Jane. 'I don't know where you heard . . . whatever you heard, but it's not true.'

'Oh, it's just something Carrie said years ago.' As she speaks, Sarah's eyes don't stop moving. She's talking to Jane, but looking over her shoulder in case someone more important appears. 'I'm sure she's improved a lot since the early days. I know she's found it hard to get another job.' As she says this, Sarah's eyes stop roving and her forehead furrows, as if something important has occurred to her. 'Just rumours,' she says then, albeit insincerely. 'Didn't mean to offend.'

The group sips wine in silence under the willow tree, everyone wishing themself elsewhere.

'Hey, Jane,' says Daniel, a hint of laughter in his voice, 'look who it is.' He nods towards the Dog and Bone, where Edward Carter is emerging from the double doors. The red in Jane's cheeks deepens. What is more notable, however, is the publicist's reaction.

'Oh! Excuse me. I-I need to speak to someone,' says Sarah, flustered. She runs a hand through her hair, pushing it back from her face and up at the roots to appear fuller. 'Hold this.' She thrusts her wine glass into Natasha's hand and whips out a Chanel pocket mirror, quickly checking her makeup is still in place, still flawless. Grabbing it back without so much as a thank you, she sashays towards Edward. When he spots her coming, he looks startled, but trapped.

'Well, she's a delight,' mutters Daniel, eyebrows raised. 'At least she's gone. Nat, we need to tell you everything.'

He flops onto the grass and crosses his legs. The others follow suit, Natasha feeling a buzz of pleasure at the abbreviation of her name. You'd only abbreviate a name you plan on saying a lot in the future.

Excitedly, as Jane's face returns to its usual colouring, they tell her about what happened at the Thistle, about Abi nearly catching them, about her having Carrie's laptop, and, finally, about the jewellery they found.

'A bangle. Engraved with a message,' says Daniel, almost out of breath now.

'From Kimberley Brown. Natasha – they were lovers.'

'What? But . . . *what*? But Kimberley was married? To a man?'

'So what? People can like men *and* women, you know,' says Daniel with a roll of his eyes. 'And people have affairs. All the time.'

'She did tell us,' says Jane, thinking back over their conversation in Kimberley's hotel room. 'She told us she loved Carrie. More than once.'

'But this means,' Natasha says, wide-eyed and amazed, 'this means that Kimberley was having an affair with Carrie, and *then* Carrie slept with her *husband*. She was betrayed threefold, by her husband, her lover, and her best friend. And when she saw Carrie here after all these years, on the first night . . . all that emotion . . .'

'Bingo,' says Jane, leaning in so that their heads are inches apart. 'Kimberley Brown left the festival at 10 and returned at 11.30. Why? To take revenge on the best friend who betrayed her, the woman who seduced her husband, the lover who jilted her. To murder Carrie Marks.'

Chapter Twenty-Seven

Saturday, 6 p.m.

Having eaten nothing but a second-choice sandwich and some sickly eggs that day, Jane is starving. After all, there has been a lot going on. Chasing killers, finding evidence, hiding in wardrobes. It's far more than she gets up to most Saturdays, which usually consist of a stroll around the town, reading a good book, and washing her whites. Natasha buys three hot dogs from the Dog and Bone, and they eat them on the lawn, talking excitedly as they do so. Natasha tells them how much her mother in Portugal, apparently an excellent cook, would hate a meal like this, and Daniel manages to get ketchup in his hair and on his shoes.

They know what they need to do now. They need to find Kimberley and confront her about what they have discovered.

'When do we go to the police?' says Daniel, without much conviction. No one is ready for their part in the drama to be over quite yet.

'When we have more,' says Jane. 'Ideally, a recorded confession. We still don't have enough to convince them.'

Everyone looks relieved by this decision, though Jane feels a familiar stab of guilt. Is that statement true? Surely, the police would be interested to know that an enemy of the victim lied about her whereabouts on the night in question, and had such a tumultuous past with her? What will Detective Inspector Ramos say when he discovers how far they've come without informing him?

But this is something Jane can push to the far corners of her mind. She cannot turn her back on the enquiry now.

Though they have all, over the years, shouted at television screens about this exact issue, the gang decide to split up to track down their quarry. Natasha volunteers to check the grounds, beer tent and second bookselling tent (this one without a body in it), while Daniel and Jane search the hotel and inside bar.

It's Jane who spots Kimberley first; a flash of green silk and auburn hair across the same crowded room Natasha had fled an hour earlier. She is watching Brad Levinsky as he continues to shake hands with fans, sign books with a flourish, laugh heartily at poor jokes. Jane's height, the bane of her existence, works in her favour. Craning her neck, she can see over the crowd, and gets a clear view of the show-stopping American editor in all of her glory. As Jane stares, wondering exactly how to reach her and what to do when she gets there, Kimberley turns her head.

Arching her perfectly pencilled brows, she looks Jane right in the eye, reducing her to a child. Then, as suddenly as she was found, she's gone.

Jane panics, standing on tiptoes, for the first time in her entire life wishing she was an inch taller. Brad is still there, signing copies of his latest paperback. But there is no sign of the woman she is here to question. At the back of the room to the right, a door swings open, and she sees a glimpse of green before it slams shut.

Jane is immediately on the move. Polite to the point of absurdity, it would usually take her days to squeeze through a crowd like this. Now, with the scent of truth leading her on, she parts it like the Red Sea, confidently nudging people to left and right. Through the door, she finds a stairwell but no sign of Kimberley. Pausing, she can hear the click of heels echoing from above – Kimberley is heading upstairs.

Racing on, Jane sees the swish of the dress above, too far above. She quickens her steps, but hears the creak of a door opening. Which floor is it on? She picks up the pace again, running as fast as she can remember doing in years, the yellow lanyard banging against her chest with each step. Third floor, fourth floor, fifth floor – which is it? Jane comes to a stop, her breath heaving, a sharp pain in her side. And then – the very soft thud of a door closing. From just above.

Bursting through the door onto the sixth floor, Jane, pink in the face, wheezing, sweating, finally comes face to face with Kimberley Brown.

Who still looks perfect.

Before either of them can say a word, a chirpy young man with grey skin, floppy brown hair and distinctly rat-like features, comes out of a side room. He looks relieved to see them, if a little puzzled by Jane's flustered appearance.

'Oh, brilliant! Some people! Come in, come in!' He shuffles Jane and Kimberley into the room he sprang from, both of them too blindsided to protest. 'It's been a bit quiet up here, to be honest with you. We were a hit on day one, but it's tailed off since. I *told* Melissa it was a mistake to be on the sixth floor. People can't be bothered to come up.' He gives Jane a sympathetic look. 'It *is* a bit of a trek.'

Kimberley seems to gather herself again. 'Sorry but wh—'

'Welcome!' he rallies, puffing out his chest and holding his arms wide. 'To the Polar Bear Publishing Jail Cell Escape Experience! Sponsored by . . . Polar Bear Publishing!'

'No, I do—'

'You are UNDER ARREST!'

'Christ,' mutters Kimberley, lurching backwards.

'And you will be locked in this cell until the state sees fit to release you, as punishment for your heinous crimes. You will be here for years . . . YEARS! Unless that is . . . you can ESCAPE!'

Kimberley and Jane edge towards each other for protection.

'When you say *years* . . . ?' Jane asks.

The jailer looks put out at the interruption and drops his voice to a whisper in an attempt not to ruin the atmosphere. 'After 45 minutes, I have to let you out.'

'Okay.'

'WELL THEN, filthy criminals! Time to say goodbye to your freedom!'

He skips out of the room. The door slams shut with unnecessary force, and they hear the click of a lock.

'Theatre school should be illegal,' Kimberley sighs. She perches on a sparse metal bed, the springs screeching in protest. 'That type of person should simply not be allowed.'

The only time Jane has been in an escape room previously – Baxter's Insurance team-bonding day – she'd had a panic attack and ended up sobbing and trying to force her way through a pretend window. But she won't allow that to happen today. This is her chance. Pushing down the alarm the sound of the key in the lock has sent through her, she turns her attention to her surroundings.

The room is decked out like a jail cell, but it has been done on a budget. On one wall, *Wanted* posters and childish drawings are Blu Tacked alongside, rather incongruously, a poster advertising Sunday's Murder Mystery Lunch. Above it, chalk markings indicate that someone has been in the 'cell' for 34 days. Or years. The single window has had plastic bars jammed between sill and frame, and there is a door marked LOCKED, with CELL BLOCK F stencilled on it in large chalked letters. Against another wall is the narrow metal bed upon which Kimberley sits. Long, narrow face; flowing, glossy hair; elegantly folded limbs: Jane decides she is an Afghan hound.

'This is your fault. Why can't you just leave me alone?'

'Why did you run from me?'

'Because you are an unhinged woman,' Kimberley spits, 'who seems intent on dragging up the past. Which I want to let lie, if it's all the same to you. Now, I'm not spending the next 45 minutes sat here waiting for the theatre-school dropout to open the door, so you better get looking for clues.'

Heart pounding, Jane takes a moment to text an update to the Meddling Kids WhatsApp group Daniel started for the three of them:

With KB in escape room. Meet you in the D&B when I can. Jane. X

Daniel immediately responds.

good work baker! and you don't need to sign off with your name btw

It doesn't seem to have occurred to him that being locked in a small room with a murderer you are about to confront may be dangerous. What if Kimberley becomes violent? Would she try to silence Jane? The man outside would surely do something if so, though he is only young and would be easily overpowered if he wasn't expecting violence. But Jane is here now, and she is going to get on with the job.

She scans the room. She should be good at this. Building complex fictional crime scenes is what she does; how much harder can this be?

A deep sigh comes from the bed.

'We obviously have to get through that door,' Kimberley says. 'So there'll be a key here somewhere.' She flops down flat on the bed, the squeal of the springs making them both wince, and Jane begins to search. Under the bed, she finds a safe and pulls it out.

'Combination lock. We need . . . six numbers.'

Kimberley doesn't respond.

'Look,' Jane says hesitantly. 'It was to tell you . . . that I know.'

'Huh?'

'That's why I was following you. To tell you that I, that *we*, know. Not everything, but enough. We . . . we know that you came back to the festival site that night, around the time Carrie died.'

Kimberley's body stiffens, shifting on the bed almost imperceptibly.

'It's on camera, sorry to say.' Jane continues, after a deep breath, 'And we . . . know that you were together. That you had an affair with Carrie Marks.'

The air in the room is still and thick, Kimberley's body completely frozen. Jane can't see her face from where she is kneeling on the floor, holding the small safe. It is impossible to tell how her words have affected the woman in green silk, perched on a prison mattress.

'Thirty-four.'

'What?'

'I'm guessing that two of the numbers you need are three and four,' she says and leans back against the wall, curling her legs underneath her in way that makes her seem almost vulnerable. Child-like. She nods at the wall opposite. 'Those chalk markings. The other numbers must be around here somewhere.'

Jane puts in the numbers and continues to search the room. Eventually, Kimberley speaks again.

'You think you're so clever, don't you? A regular Miss Marple. You've decided . . . what? I came back to the festival and killed Carrie because of an ancient love affair, long forgotten? Grow up.'

'You lied to us.'

'I told you I left at 10, and I did. I don't owe you every detail of my movements. Oh, and six.'

Kimberley is pointing at something tacked to the wall – a single date page from a desk calendar shows the 6th of May.

'You don't owe us anything, no,' says Jane as she puts the new number into the combination. 'But we're trying to find out the truth, and you're standing in the way of that. What do you expect us to think? Oh, maybe it's five as well? As in the sixth day of the fifth month?'

'Sure.'

With a deafening creak of springs, Kimberley shifts her position and starts to hunt around the bed. Under the pillow is a folded prison jumpsuit in faded orange, which she spreads out on the bed.

'Cute,' she says. 'Put a nice belt with it, and roll up the pants to show the ankles . . . Anyway, it's got a number on it. Eighteen.'

Jane inputs the final set of numbers, but nothing happens. She tries again with them in a different order and the safe clicks open to reveal a key.

'Yes!' Kimberley jumps up, snatches the key from the safe, and inserts it into the locked door. They both hear the click of a lock, and Kimberley twists the handle. Pushing the door open, they emerge into another room, laid out like a prison canteen.

'Oh, for God's sake,' mutters Kimberley. 'I thought that was too good to be true.'

Larger than the previous room, here there is a long table laid with tin plates and mugs, plastic knives and forks at each setting. A huge pot sits in the centre of the table, a ladle protruding from it. Shelves lined with kitchen equipment fill one wall, piles of what appears to be 'prison laundry' sit in one corner, and another door leads off this room. Not looking particularly hopeful, Kimberley tries the door anyway. It's locked.

'I want to get out of here,' she snaps, turning back to Jane. 'I'll search this side of the room, you search that. We need something that leads us to another key.'

'Kimberley,' Jane says softly as the other woman starts to upturn plates and look under chairs with the air of an addict looking for an urgent fix. She kicks at the piles of sheets, then grabs the top ones and throws them across the room. She boots a chair leg, sending it toppling to the floor, and starts to sweep things off the shelf indiscriminately. 'Kimberley!'

Kimberley stops and looks up, exasperated, angry, tearful. 'What?'

'I think . . . I think it's time for you to tell me why you killed Carrie Marks.'

Chapter Twenty-Eight

Saturday, 6.30 p.m.

Kimberley straightens up, panting slightly, pale skin flushing pink in a way that makes her look even more radiant than usual. Jane experiences a thrill of fear. She's confronting a murderer alone, in a locked room. Anything could happen in the next 20 minutes. A confession, a denial, another murder. This is the most dangerous, electrifying moment of her life.

'You lied,' she continues. 'You told us you left the festival at 10 and went to bed. You told us that Carrie Marks slept with your husband and you haven't spoken since. You *lied*. And I'm not the police, but I know guilt when I see it.

'You had an affair with Carrie, we know that is true. Was it still going on? Did she try and break it off that night? Is that why you stabbed her? People have killed for lesser reasons than a broken heart.'

The women stare at each other over the long table, set for a dinner that will never happen, for inmates that don't exist. Jane's whole body is tense, every muscle strained.

Finally, Kimberley laughs, but there is no joy in the sound – it's a laugh of exhaustion, of irony and of bitterness. Jane marvels at what depth of emotion can be expressed in one short, wordless sound. Kimberley pulls out a chair at the table, taking a seat in front of a disordered place setting. She rights the plate, and lines up the plastic cutlery neatly on either side, as if preparing to be served at a dinner party.

'Ha!' she says again, and rests her head in one hand with a sigh. 'Sit down.' She says it quietly, her anger clearly burnt up by the ransacking of the dining room.

Jane does so, wincing at the sound her chair makes on the floor.

'I did not kill Carrie Marks.'

'If you don't mind my saying, Ms Brown, that is exactly what a killer would say.'

'I did not kill Carrie. I *loved* her. I hated her as well, of course. But, famously, it's a thin line between the two, isn't it?' Kimberley fiddles with the fork in front of her, tracing each plastic tine with her finger, one by one. Finally, she looks up and meets Jane's eyes. 'How did you find out? About our relationship?'

'Carrie had a bangle. Gold? Engraved? She had it with her.' Jane doesn't want to mention going into Carrie's hotel room, so hopes this will suffice. Kimberley's eyes widen and she puts down the fork.

'She had it with her *here*?' she whispers to the table. 'After all this time? Oh, Carrie.' She shakes her head, eyes filling with tears. Her distress is evident in the twist of her mouth, the torment in her eyes, the crack in her voice, but *not* in the skin across her forehead. Jane has, at last, discovered Kimberley's secret weapon in the search for eternal youth.

'Yes, Carrie Marks was my lover,' she says. 'Lover. What a wonderful word that is. Romantic. Glamorous. But we were also much more than lovers – we were *in love*. Deeply, wildly in love. It started in our twenties when I was in London briefly. But we were young and living on different continents, confused by the whole thing. We were also best friends, and thought it was best to leave it at that.

'The night before I married Martin, I told Carrie I still loved her, but she told me to walk down that aisle. So I did. She was scared, I think. After that, the affair really began in earnest. She told me she loved me too. She'd come to New York, I'd visit London. Twice we met in Paris. Always at the book fairs too of course – Frankfurt, Bologna. It continued for years. Carrie Marks is – was – the great love of my life.

'In general, Martin was a good man. We had a nice life together. Sure, I know I wasn't the model wife; I was cheating on him throughout the whole thing with Carrie. Somehow that didn't really feel so wrong though. She felt separate from my life with him. But if she had asked me, I would have left him for her in a heartbeat.'

'Why did that never happen?' asks Jane, sitting forward in her chair with her elbows on the table, rapt. The scene feels intimate, despite the plastic forks and 20 place settings around them. They sit opposite each other, as if on a date at a restaurant. Jane can almost believe that glasses of red wine are on their way to the table.

'Carrie. That's why,' says Kimberley. 'Don't get me wrong, we were both nervous about it. I had a husband I'd be saying goodbye to, a messy divorce to initiate, money to untangle. And neither of us would relish being the talk of the industry. Can you imagine? Two high-profile people, known on both sides of the pond, one *married*, caught having an affair? And two women at that? It would have been dreadful. I would have done it though.'

Jane adds this new information to the puzzle. Carrie Marks the enigma. Powerful, intelligent, cruel, charismatic. Capable of inspiring great, everlasting love, but too cowardly to grasp it. How lucky she was, and how foolish.

'Carrie kept putting it off. She was just starting her own agency, and she wanted the focus to be on that, not her love life. I understood. I waited. I would have waited forever. Part of me has.' Kimberley picks up an empty tin mug as if there might be some water in it, puts it back down and interlocks her hands, preventing them from fiddling further with whatever is in front of her.

'But then that day . . . When I came in and found her in bed with Martin? It hurt that he did that to me, sure, even though I know it's hypocritical to say so. But Carrie . . . I just couldn't believe it. At least, I suppose, the fact it was with my husband meant I had a good excuse to publically mourn. People just didn't guess *who* I was mourning the most.'

In the silence that follows, Jane fancies she can hear shouts of people down below on the lawn, drunken revelry picking up now the sun has set. It makes the quiet between them even more fraught. Jane wonders how many times Kimberley has told this story. Maybe never.

'I gave her that bracelet about a year before it all ended,' Kimberley continues, still speaking towards the table rather than meeting Jane's eye. Her voice is steady and soft. Resigned. 'It was sort of symbolic of our promise to each other, almost like an engagement ring, I suppose. The plan was that she would set up the agency, partly with money loaned to her by Martin and me. Then, when the business was established, we would announce we were together and take the negative publicity on the chin. I was going to move to London.

'We didn't really speak after the . . . incident. She tried to get in touch, but I couldn't bear to look at her, or even hear her voice. The first time I've seen her in all of these years was on Thursday. And yes, I did speak to her. Yes, I did lie about when I went to bed.'

The buzz of white noise is building in Jane's head now. This is the moment; she can feel it. The confession. But the rush of joy isn't there. Dreams of her own success, of profile pieces about her – the person who uncovered the truth – in the papers, feel tawdry in the face of this story – the heartbreak and betrayal of it, the sad loneliness that emanates from Kimberley.

'I *didn't* lie about when I left the festival. I did leave at 10, with every intention of calling it a night. Carrie texted me when I was in my room, asking me to meet her, saying we needed to talk. I shouldn't have gone, but I'd never listened to her side of the story all of those years ago, and part of me hoped there was some explanation. Seeing her earlier that day drinking a glass of wine on the lawn, had made me a little crazy, I guess. So I went. She didn't have an explanation – of course she didn't. What could someone say to justify those actions? The conversation was short. I shouted, she cried. That was a shock – she was never much of a crier.

'Then I left. Didn't see anyone, though I did fancy I saw a glint of light in the bushes, like a phone or a cigarette? Maybe a firefly. Didn't think much of it at the time, though now of course I do wonder. The rain had just stopped. I walked back.' She sighs, shaking her head gently. 'I'm sorry to disappoint you, Jane, but I didn't murder Carrie Marks. That woman was the love of my life, and my best friend. Despite everything, I loved her. That is my story.'

Kimberley fans her hands in front of her; nothing left to give. She leans back in her chair and exhales, blinking the tears from her eyes as she stretches her arms up into the air. Jane feels raw, exhausted, and extremely sad. She remembers Carrie's cold, dead body. The eyeliner on her cheeks, the lipstick smudged. As if she'd been kissed.

'If you want to know what I did after that,' says Kimberley in a monotone now, drained. 'I was on the phone to my therapist. She's the only person – bar one other – who knows about me and Carrie. Do you know how ... how lonely that is? How insane it makes you feel? That the most important part of you is a secret from everyone else in the world? Well, I called her. After-hours consultation – it was about 7 in the evening in New York – so she charged me extra. She'll have made a note.'

Kimberley pulls a phone from somewhere in the green dress – the existence of pockets officially making it the best item of clothing Jane has ever seen. After a few swipes, she turns it around so that Jane can see her call log.

'Apart from my therapist, Brad is the only other person who knows. I was out of sorts on the way here and ended up telling him. Stupid really. Here.' She proffers her phone to Jane. 'I called her at 12.37. Just as I was getting to the hotel. This doesn't prove anything, but the police are welcome to talk to her – not that they've tried to speak to me after our first quick conversation, so they clearly know less than you do. She'll confirm the call. That I stopped the conversation a few minutes in when I had to find my key card in my bag and then called her back two minutes later. That one was a video call, so it will be pretty clear that I wasn't standing in the book tent holding a knife. I was in my dressing gown, sitting on my bed, looking like hell.'

Jane nods, staring at the call log. No, it isn't solid *proof*, but she believes what she's just heard. Kimberley Brown is not a killer. But in that case, who is?

Chapter Twenty-Nine

Saturday, 7.15 p.m.

Natasha's phone alerts her to a new message, and she pulls it out of her jeans pocket.

It's from Jane, telling her and Daniel that she'll meet them by the willow tree, and that Kimberley Brown isn't their killer. Natasha is disappointed – they'd been convinced that they'd found their woman. The lying, the bangle, her presence back at the festival near the time of the murder, her husband's affair. There was means, motive and opportunity by the bucketful.

She sits down under the tree – Daniel has gone to get some drinks. The evening is drawing in, but light is spilling out of the doors and windows of the Dog and Bone, people silhouetted against it as they smoke on the threshold. Whooping and laughter float over the lawn to where she sits, alone.

If not Kimberley, then who? Are they back to square one?

Oh, well, Jane will be here in a moment, and will tell them everything she learned from the interview. Natasha can't believe she was trapped alone with a murder suspect. It was foolish and dangerous, and she vows that when they find the real culprit, they will send the *police* after them.

Hopefully Jane has discovered something that'll help them decide on their next step, and they still have two suspects. Abi taking Carrie's laptop is definitely suspicious, and they haven't got anywhere with Laura Lane yet. Of course, it could be any of the people who are attending the event – most of them they don't even have names for. But in all of their conversations, they have yet to hear of another person with a credible grudge against Carrie, let alone one who was also here on that first night, before the festival had really begun. Then again, how much do they really know about the enigma who was Carrie Marks?

Natasha flicks across her phone screen and opens TikTok to see what else Laura has posted. Another video has appeared since she last checked. This woman is non-stop. Do her followers not have jobs? Who is finding the time to watch all of this? Then Natasha realises that she has watched every single video, so supposes that answers her question.

Scrolling back, she presses play on the first video uploaded on the night Carrie was murdered, watching without sound. She sees Daniel pulling on his coat in the background, and smiles. Thank God for friends.

That reminds her of the recent panel on friendship in crime fiction, and she shudders. Brad had been so much better at handling it, making jokes and referencing his past novels. Sure, he's been doing this a lot longer than she has, but she can't imagine him ever having been a shy wallflower, stuttering out an answer about friends being there for each other.

Despite her battery warning it's at three per cent, Natasha flicks forward to the next video on Laura's TikTok. There is Jane's editor, Frankie Reid, talking to someone unknown off-screen. That's possibly a glimpse of her own hair. There's Brad in the doorway. Why's he heading outside? It was cold, raining on and off, and he doesn't smoke – he'd told her so in a long speech about his health.

Some people deserve what they get coming to them, Brad had said on their panel. Does Natasha agree with that? She supposes she does, in exceptional circumstances. Everyone's line is drawn in a different place though, that's the problem. Some people are all forgive and forget after a literal massacre, whereas others think using the last tea bag should get someone sent to the chair. What line did Carrie cross, and for whom?

What else had Brad said? *Friendship is very important. Loyalty is important.* Carrie was disloyal, sleeping with her friend's husband like that. But Jane seems sure Kimberley is innocent.

Two silhouettes appear in the Dog and Bone doorway – one tall and broad, with wide hips and a small waist; one a little shorter, narrow for a man. Jane must have bumped into Daniel in the bar on the way. Natasha can just about make out the lanky form of Edward Carter by the door saying something to Jane, the tip of his cigarette glowing in the fading light. Talking in a low murmur, her friends make their way towards the tree under which Natasha is sitting, both of them carrying glasses.

Friendship is important. Well, yes. It is. She hadn't been too sure when asked, but now she *knows* she would help either of these people bury a body. *I for one will never turn my back on a friend who needs me.* That's what he'd said.

Other snippets of conversation jostle for pole position in Natasha's mind, and her hand holding the phone lowers slowly to the grass.

After all of these years, he's a friend, Kimberley had told them. *We're very close.*

How close? Did Brad know about what Carrie did to Kimberley? Natasha squeezes her eyes closed to bring to mind the conversation they'd had in Kimberley's hotel room. Yes, she is sure Kimberley mentioned that she'd told Brad everything. She looks at the phone screen again, at Brad heading out into the night at 11 p.m. He had been so drunk. Out-of-control drunk? She flicks forward to the last video of that night.

'Well, day one at Killer Lines has been a blast,' says Laura. The camera swings, finally bringing the door frame into view. There, just as before, is Brad. It's unclear if he is coming or going. Leaving at 11, returning at 12.30? What had he been doing in the interim? Or had he come back in earlier, and this is him leaving again? Out into the night just around the time Carrie Marks met her end. How important *is* friendship to this man?

Natasha goes to play the clip again, but her phone battery dies halfway through.

Some people deserve what they get coming to them.

'Natasha!' says Daniel, throwing himself down onto the grass beside her. 'Jane has been *amazing*. Honestly, incredible. She hasn't told me much yet. Waiting until we were all together. Just that she trapped Kimberley Brown in the *escape room*.'

As he gabbles on, Jane sits down carefully next to him, looking both proud and embarrassed. Natasha sees her eyes flick over to the Dog, where Edward still stands, lit cigarette in hand. 'That was hardly intentional,' she says. 'But it did work out neatly.'

Natasha stares at her friends, both smiling, excited, having the time of their lives. She can't manage to say a word.

'Nat? Everything alright?' Daniel leans forward to peer into her eyes in the gloom.

'Jane. Did you say that detective gave you a business card? Hand it over. Quickly.' Daniel stares at her, a little crestfallen at such a serious tone in the face of his buoyant mood, and Jane slowly opens her handbag, brow furrowed in confusion. 'Quickly! I need your phone too.'

Natasha stabs the number into Jane's phone, muttering the digits under her breath. She can hear the blood coursing in her ears, feel her mouth turn dry as a bone.

'Um, can you tell us what is going on?' Daniel says as she brings the phone to her ear, listening to it ring twice before a patently exhausted Detective Inspector Ramos answers.

'It's Brad,' Natasha says, crystallising the fact in her mind: a cold, hard truth. 'The killer is Brad Levinsky.'

The shocked silence that follows her words is short – and broken almost at once by a noise coming from inside the Dog and Bone.

A long, deafening scream.

Chapter Thirty

Saturday, 8.30 p.m.

The whispering crowd stares as two paramedics wheel a stretcher out of the Dog. The sirens have been silenced, but the blue lights on top of the emergency-service vehicles are still spinning, making the faces of the spectators all around appear ill and otherworldly.

The ambulance's engine rumbles, and everyone jumps as the siren wails back to life, drowning out the muttering of rumours spreading. The noise reverberates across the quiet Hoslewit hills long after the vehicle is out of sight.

Natasha's arm snakes around Jane's waist, and she leans into her. Daniel, grey and shaken, appears on Jane's other side and they stand at the front of the group, still staring at the place where the ambulance had parked.

'So,' Natasha says at last, 'maybe my theory *wasn't* correct.'

It was Frankie Reid who had found Brad Levinsky's body in the stairwell, and Jane who had found the sobbing Frankie after hearing her piercing scream. Natasha had taken the shocked editor away while Daniel attempted to keep the crowds at bay and Jane called 999 for the second time in a few days.

'Unless he *did* kill Carrie,' whispers Daniel, his voice raspy, 'and this was someone taking revenge?'

'We don't even know if he was pushed,' says Jane. 'It could have been an accident. He *had* been drinking.'

They continue to stare into the darkness of the lawn. True, they have seen nothing that overtly proves Brad's tumble over the banister and down the stairwell was *not* an accident. But even as she says it, Jane knows she doesn't believe he simply *fell*. Baker never trusts a coincidence.

'What did Frankie say happened?' Jane asks a glum-faced Natasha.

'She was trying to find the bathroom. Then . . . wham! A body falls from the sky.'

Finding the dead body of Carrie had been a nasty shock, but in Jane's opinion, nearly being crushed by one has to be far worse. A real test for the nerves that.

'Brad is connected to this case, I'm sure of it,' continues Natasha. 'And now he has somehow "fallen" over the banister and down the stairwell? Plummeted God knows how many storeys, onto a concrete floor? This isn't a coincidence. This is murder.'

Her words echo Jane's thoughts except in one particular.

'He wasn't dead,' she says, but softly. When she'd bent low to inspect him she'd felt a weak pulse, though his body was entirely still with blood pooling around it. If he wasn't dead already, how much longer did he have? This is, at the very least, *attempted* murder.

'We should have spoken to the police earlier,' says Daniel. His cheekbones are prominent in the light shining from the Dog and Bone, his hair flopping over his eyes as he gazes at the ground. He looks breathtakingly handsome and utterly miserable. 'Why did we think we could solve this case? Someone might have been killed because of us.'

'It's not our fault,' snaps Natasha. 'If someone pushed Brad, it certainly wasn't one of us. And what did we even have to go to the police with in the first place? We thought the killer was Kimberley Brown, remember? We were wrong. There's nothing we could have done.'

'Even so,' says Daniel, kicking at the grass. 'We . . . we shouldn't be doing this alone. We shouldn't be getting mixed up in this.'

Sick dread is rolling in Jane's stomach. A potent mixture of shame and guilt and fear. She scans the crowd again, spotting Abi Ellis's frizzy hair in the window of the bar, and Edward just outside the door again, smoking frantically. He looks up and gives her an uneasy smile.

The thing with murder is that it can be really stressful. Even for a bystander. Poor old Frankie will be in bits after seeing Brad splattered on the floor next to her like that, and everyone else looks quite shaken up too. If Jane was the killer, she wouldn't be able to cope at all. But maybe murderers are made differently? Maybe this particular one can push someone down a stairwell one moment, and happily pour a glass of wine with that same hand the next. You can simply never be sure.

The crowd has mostly moved inside now, everyone keen to discuss what's happened over more drinks. After the shocks of the scream, the blood, and the sirens, people are calming down. An excited buzz is replacing terrified panic.

'*Been drinking all day*,' Jane hears someone say with a rueful shrug. '*Daft sod.*'

'*Deathtrap, those stairs.*'

Jane doesn't share the sentiment of the shrugger. But the truth is, she has no idea who pushed Brad Levinsky to an almost-certain death. Just as she has no idea who stabbed Carrie Marks through the heart with the Killer Lines dagger on Thursday night. There is so much Jane doesn't know. What she *does* know is that this is no game, no easy way to garner interest in her writing career and the PI Sandra Baker series. And that she, and her friends, are out of their depth.

Out of the front door of the hotel walks Detective Inspector Ramos, looking tired. His jowls are more pronounced than the last time Jane saw him up close, and his figure is hunched, making him appear ever-more camel-like. Jane watches him breathe in the fresh evening air, then pull a Twix from his pocket.

Detective Inspector Ramos is different from the police officer who repeatedly crops up in Jane's novel. Detective Inspector Fields is tall, muscular and stand-offish. Often peeved at the success of Baker, a private detective who frequently bests the police force with her superior skills, Fields is perpetually either *bristling* or *smouldering* or *growling*. But in a sexy way, not like a dog.

Ramos pushes almost an entire finger of his Twix into his mouth.

His cheeks are bursting when he catches sight of Jane and points over at her while he chews furiously.

'Ms Hepburn!' he calls through a mouthful of biscuit, marching over and coming to a halt in front of the trio. Everyone is thankful when he decides to swallow before continuing to speak – Daniel could learn a thing or two from him. His brow is furrowed and his mouth, when it finally ceases moving, is set in a straight line. So much for chocolate making you happy. 'I need to talk to you,' he says. 'Now.'

The detective strides away from the group, stopping a few feet away and turning back to look pointedly at Jane. With a shrug at her friends, she follows him.

'Are you a lucky person, Miss Hepburn?' Ramos asks as she approaches.

'Um, I wouldn't say so. Though I did once win £15 on a scratch card, which is more than anyone I know has won. But then I lost the card before I could claim on it, so I don't know if that counts as lu—'

'Because this is the second body you have stumbled upon this weekend.'

Detective Inspector Ramos is frowning in a way that tells Jane he is trying to look stern, but the Twix has left chocolate on his nose, which rather ruins the effect.

'Would you say that is lucky? I suspect most would count it as *un*lucky.'

'And what would *you* count it as?'

Jane knows the usual answer to this question would be unlucky, because few people would *like* to find one body, never mind two. But it *has* resulted in rather a lot of excitement for her, not to mention some new friends, and let no one say that Jane Hepburn is a liar. Besdies, a lie to a police officer is thrice the size of a normal lie.

'Well . . . '

'Oh, never mind. Sorry, I'm tired.' Detective Inspector Ramos takes a deep breath and attempts a smile, which looks more like a grimace. There are bits of Twix in his teeth too. 'Let's walk, shall we?'

They leave the circle of light cast by the Dog and Bone and wander across the dark lawn. The eyes of her friends are on her and the police officer, and it feels uncomfortably as though she is on a stage performing an Agatha Christie play. She was in a play at school once – Tree #3 – and wasn't very good at it. She cried when one of her branches fell off and the facepaint got in her eyes.

'Now, Jane – may I call you Jane?'

She nods.

'Well, Jane. When we spoke a few days ago I was under the impression that you happened upon the body of Ms Marks completely by accident.'

'You were correct.'

'But now, here you are, finding another body?'

'Well actually, Frankie Reid found the body. I believe it almost fell on her head.'

'Quite. Well, she may have been present when it . . . appeared. But reports are that the first person to enter the scene after that was yourself.'

'To answer your earlier question, I would say that, on balance, it's been lucky . . . '

'What is even more strange is that I was already en route . . . '

' . . . though not for the victims, I must say.'

194

'. . . . not only to the Dog and Bone, but on my way to speak to the victim. Because *you* called and told me he was the killer.'

'It was actually Nata—'

'*Tell me exactly what happened, Miss Hepburn.*'

The story of hearing Frankie's scream and finding Brad's body isn't a long one, but it somehow sustains the pair for one full circuit of the lawn, Ramos huffing and sighing at regular intervals.

If part of Jane expected praise when she tells him why they suspected Brad in the first place, she is sorely disappointed. As soon as she gets to the part where they started questioning their top suspects, Detective Inspector Ramos snaps.

'For God's *sake*, Jane. This is *not* a game. You are not . . . Jonathan Creek.'

'I never said I was Jon—'

'Stay *out* of this.' He stops walking and turns to face her in the gloom. 'I mean it. This is a real police investigation. It is not for amateurs.' He speaks sternly, but Detective Inspector Ramos isn't blessed with a particularly intimidating demeanour. When his lips thin in disapproval, his stubbled cheeks swell like a puffer fish, and his watery turquoise eyes are too kind. 'I wasn't good at writing books, so I gave it up. You are, no offence, clearly no good at solving crimes. Leave it to us.'

'But—' begins Jane.

'No! You cannot *question witnesses*! You cannot make up wild theories and report them as fact!' He runs his fingers through his hair, smudging chocolate onto his forehead. 'Has it not occurred to you that we, the police, are actually pretty good at our jobs?'

'To be honest, no.'

'Well, we are. You and your friends may have cooked up some theory about books and writing, perhaps someone is re-enacting a novel, or is upset about . . . pages. Or bookmarks. Or something. But believe me, it is not connected. My officers are testing physical evidence found at the scene, and going through the Marks Agency's finances right this moment. We are on to something that *is* convincing. We'll have this wrapped up before you know it. Just stay out of our way and ... try and enjoy yourselves.'

Physical evidence? Finances?

'No!' says Jane, simultaneously stumbling in a hole in the lawn and feeling thankful she'd left the kitten heels from day one at the bottom of her suitcase. 'No, you have to listen—'

A shrill ringing cuts her off, and Ramos glares at her as he answers his mobile. He turns and mutters into it, and when he hangs up he looks even more exhausted, as if another few hours of his life have been snatched through the receiver.

'Look, I need to get to the hospital. But I'm going to come and find you tomorrow to take down everything you think you've found out. I'll need to know *why* you suddenly decided that Brad Levinsky of all people, probably the best-known and richest person in this entire hellscape – and with the most to lose since you're asking – might have been the killer.

'In the meantime, I am warning you, Miss Hepburn. Stay away from this investigation. Before anyone *else* gets hurt.'

It's late now, around 9.30 p.m. On any other Saturday night, Jane would be found tucked up on her sofa – it's small so requires her to curl into a ball – blanket pulled over her legs, laptop balancing precariously on her knees. She might be watching *Antiques Roadshow*, or a true-crime documentary, or *Married at First Sight Australia*. Saturday nights are for treats, and so there is almost always the remnants of a takeaway on the floor beside her. She alternates – Chinese one week, pizza the next, then Indian. This week it would have been a Chicken Madras from Mr Nicey Spicey.

But this is not a normal Saturday. It's quite a bit more interesting, and so she's pacing the lawn while her friends queue at the bar. Even though it is usually about the time her eyes start closing in a chow mein slump, she feels wide awake. She shivers in the cold night air and wonders where she left her jacket. Probably in a corner of the Dog and Bone somewhere. The dew on the grass has soaked into her trainers and her socks are starting to feel damp. So Ramos is investigating Carrie's company finances – she's *sure* he wasn't supposed to tell her that. Even so, she is convinced he is looking in the wrong direction.

'*Before someone else gets hurt*,' she mutters aloud, echoing his words.

'Huh?' Natasha appears by her side, holding out a coffee to her. Daniel, still grey-faced, is a few feet behind.

'Someone murdered Carrie, and presumably the same person has now killed, or attempted to kill, Brad. Don't you understand? This isn't a one off. It's either a grudge against multiple people or Brad knew something, and the killer will do anything not to be caught. Whoever this is is more dangerous than we ever realised.'

Daniel audibly gulps. 'Jane,' he whispers, not meeting her eye, 'I've been thinking . . . Detective Inspector Ramos is right. You're right. This *is* dangerous. We have no idea what we're doing.'

'No, Daniel! We need to *solve* this. *Before anyone else gets hurt*,' Jane says, taking her marshmallow-dotted cappuccino from a grim-faced Natasha. 'And not so I get to be famous. Nor so I can be interviewed in the newspapers to make people buy my books. But because someone killed Carrie Marks, and someone tried to kill Brad Levinsky, and we do not yet know if they will stop at that.'

Agitated, Jane feels for her extra-strong mints in the pocket of her cardigan. It's at times like this she wishes she smoked. Far classier, and looks much more mysterious. Goes better with coffee too. Maybe she should consider purchasing a pipe? She draws out the almost empty packet, but something else comes with it, a slip of paper, drifting to the grass at her feet. Putting a mint in her mouth, she stoops to pick it up.

It's a note, in black ink, scrawled in an unfamiliar hand and just visible in the half darkness.

Back off.

The words send a jolt of dread through Jane's stomach, and her head feels light and dizzy.

'Whoever it is,' Natasha whispers, 'they know we're on their tail.'

Daniel steps away from the note as though it's on fire, shaking his head in denial.

'They'll kill us. We're next.'

'Don't be melodramatic, Daniel,' says Natasha. 'And keep your voice down. Maybe it's a good thing? We've rattled them. They must be—'

'No. I . . . I'm done.'

The two women look at him in confusion.

'I'm sorry. But I don't want to do this anymore.' Daniel's eyes are glistening, and in the moonlight he looks younger than ever before. The dread in Jane's stomach becomes heavier, spreading through her whole body. Something so much more terrifying than a killer's threatening note seems to be about to happen, and she can't think of a thing to say to stop it. 'I'm sorry,' Daniel says again. He turns and walks towards the light of the pub. After a beat of stunned silence, Natasha runs after him.

And with that, Jane, once again, is alone.

Chapter Thirty-One

Saturday, 8.45 p.m.

To make it out of the gutter, you need the ability to act decisively, a lot of gall, and a little bit of luck.

Laura Lane made her mind up the moment her first TikTok post went viral. The memory of it is still clear as day. She'd been sitting in her local Wetherspoon's, cold cup of tea on the table and a cover of Ed Sheeran's 'Shape of You' on the speakers that was even more nauseating than the original. What's happening? she'd thought to herself as she watched the numbers rising on her video. 'Oh, here we go,' she'd muttered aloud. The comments were multiplying, fake-Ed singing something creepy about bedsheets in the background. 'It's life. Life is happening for me. At last.'

And she'd decided then and there that she would do anything, absolutely *anything*, to keep it happening.

Laura has spent days sitting in cheap indoor locations during cold winters, sipping at single cups of tea for hours, avoiding the increasingly angry stares of increasingly angry waitresses. She has spent nights tossing and turning, trying to forget unpaid bills and court summons. She has worn clothes so far past their best they would have to book an overnight stay rather than circle back and find it. She's taken her chance with writing and influencing, thrown herself all in – and made it. She *will not* go back there.

Now she is sitting in the bar of the Dog and Bone, a cold cup of tea in front of her (old habits die hard), but this time the dreadful cover of a song on the radio is drowned out by some loud book bloggers at the next table. Her dress isn't held together by Sellotape anymore, and her nails are freshly manicured. But she knows luck is still needed, gall essential, and more decisions must be made, all to keep her afloat.

As the weekend has worn on, she'd been increasingly left alone by fans, most die-hards having sought her out on day one to capture a selfie and an autograph. This evening, she is enjoying the relative peace at her table, despite the murder-related hubbub around her. She doesn't resent her fans, don't get her wrong. Yes, they can be a little overbearing, some of them even scary (in particular the one who started posting pictures of Laura's characters crafted with her own hair through the letterbox). But in general, Laura loves them. Her readers make her who she is. The bloggers, dedicated next-level book lovers, spread respect for her work despite the big newspapers and literary journals shunning it. The avid TikTokers make her famous. They *all* make her rich. And so, she loves them like the family she never had. Her biggest, most loving foster family. And, yes, she will do *anything* to keep them.

She finds herself thinking of that tall woman, Jane Hepburn. Out of the window, Laura had seen her and Detective Inspector Ramos walking around the lawn earlier, muttering to each other. They looked like mismatched lovers, or conspiring villains. Laura noticed that Jane kept glancing over to where her friends – Natasha Martez and that boy who talks with his mouth full – were waiting for her, straightening her spine self-consciously, tilting her chin a fraction as though she was performing a part.

Yes, she's a funny one, that Jane Hepburn. Laura had watched her bumbling around on the first day, embarrassed as Paddington Bear. A few places behind in the queue, Laura had witnessed the cow on the entrance gate refuse Jane an author pass – she'd looked so pathetic then, so beaten down. Very sad and all, but come on! Pull yourself together, woman. Worse things have happened, and to better people too. People like Laura, for instance.

Now though, it *does* seem as though Jane's pulled herself together. It even looked like she was *arguing* with the detective at one point, hardly something a wallflower would do. It's amazing what a murder can do for the soul. Or is it two murders now? Laura hadn't hung around to find out the fate of Brad Levinsky, though she has been refreshing the news site on her phone constantly in case of an update.

She looks out of the window again and can just discern Jane Hepburn's imposing figure, standing alone at the edge of the lawn. What has she told the detective? What does she know? And where has her little team gone? The weekend is nearly over, and when it is, Laura should be home-free. She doesn't give a fig about the police, but with the tall lady and friends poking around, she is feeling less relaxed. She'll have to try and get Natasha alone to find out what she knows.

This weekend may have been a little dramatic, but Laura's follower count on TikTok is through the roof, so it's not all bad. Two point six million? Her fans really do love a good murder and some crocodile tears. She allows herself to think of all those views, all those clicks, as coins dropping into her piggy bank.

Will she continue living in South London, or buy an apartment in Chelsea when the new book lands? Maybe she'll get a maid, or at least one of those Roomba hoovers. Does Buddhism allow maids? Probably. As far as religion goes, this one seems to be mostly about making yourself happy, which was why she'd chosen it. Not one of those pesky ones that demands worship and thinking of others all the time.

Maybe, when this is all over, she'll go to some sort of Tibetan retreat in the mountains, full of other business-savvy Buddhists. The last one she'd tried didn't serve wine or red meat and had dreadful wifi, but that was probably just bad luck.

Now, where was she? Oh, yes.

Reapplying her lipstick, she pushes at the roots of her shiny black hair. Is the shimmering eyeshadow a bit much with the red lips? No, it adds a certain drama. A *je ne sais quoi*. Like a Mafia moll at her husband's funeral. The bags under her eyes will have to be edited out. No rest for the wicked.

Laura Lane raises her phone again, angling it at her face in a way that doesn't give her a double chin. Recently she's started to find this constant talking to camera all a bit tedious, even soul-sucking. But she hasn't come this far only to stop now. She imagines again that apartment in Chelsea. She thinks of how she has paid every single bill on time for twelve months straight. She pictures of her bank balance, ticking upwards, upwards, upwards, towards a number that will offer her life-long security. Thinks of the mistakes that have almost hijacked her along the way, and the people who have tried their hardest to bring her down.

'It's another dark, dark day at Killer Lines Crime Fiction Festival.' Attractive flutter of eyelashes, as though to ward off tears. Deep inhale. 'And I'm *so* sorry to be the very first to announce some important news to the public. Brad Levinsky, celebrated author of the Detective Stone series, has had a fatal accident.' True, she isn't totally sure the man is dead yet, but he probably is. And 'fatal' sounds better. 'He fell to his death just moments ago. It's been reported that he went over the banister and down a stairwell. I'm . . . I'm finding this very difficult to process.'

Laura gives herself a little shake and pushes back her shoulders, trying not to be distracted by what she can see through the window, which she *thinks* is Jane Hepburn burrowing into a hedge. 'Even so, I'm not going anywhere. You can *bet* that I'll keep you updated on everything that's happening. Even when . . . when it's upsetting for me to do so. I love you, stay strong, keep safe.'

Got it in one.

Now, to edit and upload this, then back to the small matter of breaking into Carrie Marks's hotel room.

There is something in there she needs, and it's about time she stopped beating around the bush and went and got it. If she's caught, it will spell disaster, but that's a chance she has to take. Laura Lane drains the dregs of the cold, milky tea and gets to her feet. She's made the decision, has the gall, and, fingers crossed, luck will stay on her side.

Chapter Thirty-Two

Saturday, 8.45 p.m.

'Jane,' says the bush. 'Get in here.'

Peering through the leaves, Jane sees glimmering green silk and the ghostly face of Kimberley Brown. She looks pale and drawn, the usually gleaming whites of her tear-filled eyes turned a painful red.

'Come *on*,' says Kimberley. There is a twig in her hair and she looks crazed, more Medusa-like than ever. 'I . . . I need to tell you something.'

Jane steps forward hesitatantly, pushing past branches to find herself crammed next to Kimberley Brown in a small clearing, a few feet of bare ground between the encroaching bushes. Their faces are only inches apart.

If Kimberley looks like this, Jane must look an absolute fright after the day she's had. She's not sure she even *wants* to look in a mirror after chasing a woman up six flights of stairs, finding another body, and forcing her way through a shrubbery.

She remembers how she'd looked that day on the train platform at West Barning; exhausted, sad, laden down with bags. That was before Daniel found her, of course. Has he really left? It feels like she's lost a limb.

Concealed in the bushes with Kimberley, Jane flounders for something not-strange to say. Staring at the other woman, she remembers the list of top suspects they made in the bathroom, the very first time she met Natasha. The thought of her new friend writing out Kimberley's name causes her a second pang of grief. Has she lost Natasha too? Jane also thinks of how, until just hours ago, they'd all been convinced that this woman in front of her was a murderer. And now, here they are together, in the darkness. No witnesses. No back-up team.

'Jane?' says Kimberley, snapping her back to the present. The editor smiles weakly, and her perfect teeth gleam in the moonlight. Jane pictures that name in red, scrawled on the mirror, the engraved bracelet, the note from her pocket. She hears the clink of Kimberley's glass as she toasted Carrie's demise, Frankie's scream on finding Brad's body. Her heart begins to race, a trickle of sweat making its way down her back. She'd swallowed Kimberley's story in that escape room because her emotion had seemed genuine. But emotion is not an alibi. It is not proof.

She opens her mouth to speak, but no sound comes out, and Kimberley reaches out to grab her.

An almighty crash causes both women to whip their heads around as a young man bursts through the bushes and cannons directly into them.

Flat on her back, thorns sticking into places she'd really rather they weren't, Jane looks up to see Natasha peering past some broken branches. Next to her, Daniel is lying on top of Kimberley Brown.

The beer tent is only open in the daytime but, being a tent, it is hardly Fort Knox. The gang sit down at a sticky wooden table. Natasha turns on the torch on her phone and puts it face down on the table, giving the impression they are about to tell a ghost story at a twelve year old's birthday party.

'Look, I'm sorry,' repeats Daniel.

'We bumped into Laura Lane on her way out of the Dog, and she said she saw you going into the bushes, Jane,' says Natasha with a rueful smile. 'We were worried about you being alone after that note, so we went to find you. When we glimpsed Kimberley through the branches, Daniel . . . well, he was concerned.'

'Was that any reason to be quite so enthusiastic?' Kimberley snaps, pulling leaves from her hair.

'You were reaching for her throat!'

'I was grabbing her arm because she looked like she was about to faint!'

'Now, now, Daniel was very brave,' Jane says. 'Though I'm sure he wouldn't mind getting us all something from behind the bar to say sorry.' Having her friends not only back at her side, but willing to take on a potential killer for her, has made Jane feel giddy with happiness. After much clinking and crashing, Daniel hands around four rather large glasses of whisky, placing the bottle in between them. 'We'll pay for it tomorrow,' Jane adds, even though she suspects they might not. How wild she's become: first murder – *investigating* it, that is – now petty theft.

Daniel puts his hand on Jane's. 'I'm sorry about . . . earlier. I panicked. But I don't want to stop being on this team.' He gives her a watery smile and squeezes her hand. 'When we couldn't see you on the lawn, I was so scared something had happened to you. And that it was my fault.'

'You came back, Daniel. That's what matters.' They smile at each other, and Kimberley breaks the moment by knocking back her drink in one and slamming down the glass.

'What is it you wanted to tell Jane?' Natasha asks, her voice gentle, as though she is speaking to a child, or a kitten, or a key that's not quite working in a lock.

Kimberley refills her glass. Noise from the pub can just about be heard through the canvas walls and across the lawn. Jane tries her drink. It burns down her throat and sends heat through her limbs. She could get to like this.

'Kimberley?' Natasha probes. 'Did . . . Did Brad kill Carrie?''

'What? No, of course he didn't,' she snaps, the Hallowe'en-style lighting making her glare terrifying. 'Then what? Jump down the stairwell? Don't be an idiot.'

Though it's hardly necessary to be so rude, everyone looks relieved that Kimberley is back to her old self.

'He did *not* kill Carrie,' she says, taking a deep breath. 'But . . . he did speak to her. That night. And someone did this to him. Someone pushed Brad, like they stabbed Carrie. And *you* need to find out who, because the police have nothing. They think this is an *accident*.'

'Well, of course,' says Jane, to murmured assent from the others. 'That's the general aim.'

'Have you filled them in?' Kimberley nods at Daniel and Natasha, and Jane shakes her head. She hasn't yet had time to tell them everything Kimberley revealed in the escape room. So much has happened in the last few hours that it feels like days ago now.

'Only that I didn't believe you were guilty. Would you like to tell them what you told me?'

'God, no. Once was enough. You do it, I'll drink.' She demonstrates this by knocking back the last drops in her glass and reaching again for the bottle. Jane obediently relays everything she'd learnt earlier, albeit with less panache than Kimberley's delivery. When Daniel looks unconvinced, she blames her own lacklustre performance. She can never get the balance right. Not enough emotion here, but far too *much* emotion when she was Tree #3.

'Daniel, I believe her. She didn't do this.'

'Okay,' says Natasha. 'And I don't believe she would hurt Brad either.'

'Are you quite finished debating whether I attacked my friends?'

Daniel gives a reluctant nod.

'Shall I go on?' Kimberley is starting to slur her words. She scratches the sticky wood with one long, emerald-painted fingernail. 'This place is filthy. Like, what is this?' She holds up a nail to show a thick brown globule of old beer-soaked varnish.

'Look at all the cigarette butts under that table too. I can't wait to get out of here. My plane leaves day after tomorrow. But first . . . I need to know who did this.' She pauses, then sighs. 'Brad's a good guy. I didn't want to get him in any trouble, so I left him out of it. But now . . . now he's . . . he's dead, I may as well tell you.'

Kimberley stares at the table, scratching away with her fingernail, and Jane realises there is a vital piece of information that has not yet reached Kimberley: the fact that Brad was still alive when he was strapped to that stretcher. The Baker in her decides that sharing this information can wait a few moments longer.

'Carrie texted me at about 11.30, as I said,' Kimberley continues, avoiding everyone's eyes and still scratching at the wood. 'Telling me to come meet her in the book tent. Which I did. I told you it was just to talk about the past, but it was also . . . it was also because of a run-in she'd had with Brad.' The intensity of her scratching increases, her nail bending threateningly.

'I'd told him everything on the way here. About how we were a couple, and how she'd screwed me over. How we hadn't spoken since. He was mad. He is – was – protective of me.'

'What happened on Thursday night, Kimberley?' Jane's eyes have grown used to the strange lighting, and she can see her friends sitting stock still, so as not to break the spell.

'Carrie texted me. But when I came to find her, she . . . she was a bit of a mess.' Kimberley holds up her palms, and Jane has a sudden flashback to that morning in the book tent – the mud splatter on the dead woman's skirt, the smudged coral lipstick, the trickle of dried blood on her lip. She'd wondered, even then, how that had got there.

'She was *mad*. I'd always liked Carrie when she was mad. I was the only one who could deal with it. Guess it made me feel special. She was ranting about me needing to keep my author under control. But then I got mad too. Like, after all these years, this is what you've called me here to talk about? My *author*? We had a massive row, and it *all* came out. And then . . . and then we made up.'

'But what has this got to do with Brad?'

'He'd seen her outside in the gardens. God knows what she was doing out there, but he followed her, to confront her about what she'd done to me all those years ago. He'd had a *lot* to drink. But he frightened her when he shouted, and she slipped. She hit her nose, which bled, and there was mud on her skirt. She was okay, but Carrie never liked looking a mess.'

'Why are you telling us now?'

'Because Brad did not kill Carrie, nor did he *fall* down that stairwell. Someone murdered him, and I think the two things are connected. He was outside at least once on Thursday night. I didn't want to get him in trouble, and knew he'd be a suspect if I admitted he'd confronted her. But now he's dead, there's no point keeping quiet. In one weekend, someone has murdered the love of my life *and* my star author and friend. And I want them found.'

There is an awkward pause around the table as she glares at them fiercely in turn.

'Um, Kimberley?' says Natasha in a whisper. 'I don't know what you heard, but . . . Brad isn't actually dead. He certainly isn't well, but he was still alive when he left here.'

After a yawning silence that amplifies the noise from the pub beyond, Kimberley throws back her head and laughs.

'If I wasn't so relieved, I'd throttle the lot of you,' she says, tears springing into her eyes. 'Get out of here. And leave the bottle.'

They get to their feet to give Kimberley some time alone. When they're at the entrance to the tent, she calls out to them.

'One more thing. Brad said when he saw Carrie that night, he heard her arguing with someone else. Something about a book.'

'Yes,' says Jane, turning back. 'That must have been Laura Lane.'

'No. She was outside in the bushes. Arguing with a *man*.'

Though there are rules about no additional guests in the rooms, Jane is the only one staying somewhere without a concierge, so they are in her Air BnB. In Mary's kitchen, Jane is opening the cupboards with the air of someone trying not to set off a rather large bomb. Which, in a way, she is. If she wakes Mary, there's a chance she'll be kicked out of her accommodation. Or worse, Mary might want to join them. She might make them those dreadful eggs.

Finally, Jane locates the mugs and places three of them onto the countertop as softly and quietly as snow on grass. As the kettle approaches boiling, the rumble of the water feels deafening. Tea bags in – Sainsbury's own brand, which she feels more positive about than PG Tips but less so than Yorkshire Tea – she waits while it brews. Daniel strikes her as the type who would like an unappetisingly weak tea, she decides, and so fishes his out almost immediately.

While the other teas reach the right shade of brown – the deep colour of a Hob Nob as opposed to the Rich Tea she'd chosen for Daniel—she leans against the oven and thinks over what Kimberley said.

Had Carrie really been arguing with a *man* that night? There isn't a single man on their suspects list. This is a publishing event after all, and the industry is notoriously female-centric. Unless you look at the CEOs and board members, of course, who are, strangely, mostly male. How about that?

Removing the tea bags, Jane catches the burning drips in her palm as she carries them to the bin, a name in her head that she doesn't want to utter. Edward Carter . . . she was sure he had been keeping something back from her. But the idea of *Edward* being involved in anything sinister is disturbing and, for a reason she can't put her finger on, upsetting. It's also nonsensical. They haven't uncovered a single motive that would cause him to kill his life-long friend.

Jane positions all three mugs in one hand and creeps out of the kitchen, scaling the stairs at a painfully slow pace. When a drop of boiling liquid splashes onto her bare foot, she grits her teeth but doesn't utter a sound.

Kimberley is – *was* – entangled with Carrie in a web of lies and secrets, love and hate. All good reasons to kill. Yet, deep down, Jane still believes she is innocent, of murder at least. She is convinced Carrie wasn't killed because of lies, or secrets, or love, or even hate. She is sure, somehow, the agent was killed because of *books*.

In the bedroom, Natasha is flicking through her phone while Daniel lies still on the bed with his eyes closed. Both look with relief at the mugs being borne towards them. Daniel takes a loud slurp and grins up at her from the princess-covered duvet.

'A perfect cup of tea.'

She knew it!

Jane sits at the dressing table, the chair wobbling dangerously, and puts down her mug. Natasha is explaining that Laura Lane has announced Brad's fall as both fatal and an accident. Jane is trying to listen, but she is tired, and Natasha's voice is washing over her. She spins on the chair, putting her hands into the pockets of the jacket she'd recovered from the corner of the pub.

'Oh!' she says. 'I forgot about this.'

She pulls out the school photograph she took from Carrie's room.

'Why did you take that?' asks Daniel.

'I'm not really sure. I must have just shoved it in my pocket when Abi turned up. Hopefully it won't be missed. I doubt it's important.'

Natasha gets off the bed and comes to stand by Jane, looking down at the now-crumpled photograph of 16 smiling schoolgirls.

'Where did you get that?' she asks.

'Carrie Marks's hotel room. It was in the pocket of her coat. After finding the bracelet, everything else seemed sort of incidental. Sorry I didn't show you earlier.'

'That's very odd.'

'I know! Why would she be carrying this around with her at Killer Lines?'

'And why would she have a school photograph of Laura Lane at all?'

Chapter Thirty-Three

Saturday, 11 p.m.

'What do you mean?'

Jane has frozen in her seat, and Daniel is now sitting bolt upright, wide-eyed.

'Well, look!' says Natasha, leaning down and pointing at one of the girls. 'That's Laura, right?'

'But . . . we checked the names on the back! Laura Lane's isn't there.'

The photo is old and faded so it isn't immediately obvious. But yes, when Jane squints, she can easily identify the large nose and full lips of the social-media-star-cum-author, even as a teenager. Despite the fading print, Jane can tell Laura's hair doesn't have its present-day glossy shine, that there are dark circles around her eyes, and her face is set in a scowl. In contrast to the bubbly, confident woman she has blossomed into, she doesn't look like a happy child. Even so, Jane can't believe she'd missed it before.

Natasha leans down and plucks the photo from her hands. Laying it flat on the desk, she counts the heads along to the Laura Lane look-alike, then spins the print over and counts the names.

'Katie Mack,' she announces. 'But why on earth would Laura be listed as Katie Mack?'

'You're totally sure it's her?' says Daniel from the bed.

'Well,' says Natasha, 'it's an old photo, but it certainly *looks* like her. And Carrie did have it in her pocket, so it's not unreasonable to assume it's related to someone or something at this festival.'

'They argued!' says Jane, her voice too loud in the quiet of the room as excitement takes hold of her. 'Remember?' All of a sudden, she is up and pacing the cramped floor space. 'This is connected, I know it!'

'Hold on,' says Daniel, still sitting on the bed, biting his lip. 'How would Laura reach the dagger? It was above the door frame. It's not like someone wouldn't notice if she got a ladder out.'

'Natasha?'

They both turn to look at her, the voice of reason.

'Well, that's certainly interesting . . . '

'Stop being a politician!' says Daniel.

They discuss the photograph in furious stage whispers. Jane is sure this is the missing piece of the puzzle, but can't exactly say in what way. Natasha finds it *interesting*, but is more keen to discuss the argument Kimberley mentioned Brad overheard.

Their top suspects – Laura Lane and Abi Ellis – are both women. Brad, briefly suspect number one, they now unanimously agree is not only innocent, but a second victim.

'And he saw something. I'm sure about that,' adds Natasha. 'Brad knew enough to get himself pushed down that stairwell. And *I* think what he knew is the identity of the man who argued with Carrie that night. Maybe the same man who killed her.'

Jane doesn't want to admit it to herself, but part of the reason she'd become so fixated on Laura Lane is because she hadn't wanted to entertain the idea that *Edward* was the person arguing with Carrie in the bushes, long after he told them he left the festival. She does not want the grey-eyed man of imposing height to turn out to be a cold-blooded, knife-wielding killer with a penchant for the dramatic. Especially when he's said he will read her book.

'There weren't even many men at the festival on that first night,' Natasha continues. 'Brad we've discounted. A couple of audience members came early, but I didn't see many of them hanging around the Dog after dark. There was that big group of authors though?'

'I'm pretty sure they're in the clear,' says Daniel. 'The barman told me there was an England *vs* Scotland drinking competition. Anytime anyone so much as went to the bathroom they got jeered at. Can't see one of them sneaking off outside for half an hour without notice.'

Natasha nods and finishes the dregs of her cold tea, staring down at the old school photograph.

'I know you don't want to say it, Jane,' says Daniel eventually, 'but we need to talk about Edward.' Her face burns again and she slowly spins on her chair to hide it. 'He was in the Dog that night, he has a long history with Carrie, and you said yourself you were certain he was hiding something when you spoke.'

'And *you* said he was not *a priority*!'

'That was before we *knew* anything.'

Jane rubs her forehead, thinking fondly of her cosy little flat and the comfort of her own bed. 'Anyway,' she says, 'what about Abi Ellis? She's doing quite well out of Carrie's death, in case you haven't noticed. She was on our suspects list, and we've barely scraped the surface with her.'

'Well, I wouldn't put it past her,' Daniel concedes. 'But it doesn't change the fact that it was probably Edward who was heard—'

'Ramos mentioned finding some financial discrepancies – maybe Abi was skimming money from the agency?'

'That's a stretch, Jane. You can't just make stuff up!'

'Now you liste—'

'What we need,' says Natasha, taking charge effortlessly, though Daniel and Jane continue glaring at each other, 'is to get people *together*.'

'A party?' Daniel asks, looking perkier. Jane spins on her pink desk chair.

'You could say so. This trying to track down individuals one by one, listening to the carefully curated information they tell us, and then searching for someone else, is taking forever – and we don't *have* forever. In case you didn't realise, tomorrow is the final night of the festival. Tomorrow is our *last chance*. And let's not forget that note – Jane's been *threatened*. We need to get them all in one place and get them talking. Let the wine flow. You never know what might slip out.'

The last time Jane attended a party, it was a work Christmas bash, which had taken place on a Wednesday in March because venue hire was cheaper then. It was during the period she was secretly dating Stefan. He had danced with multiple women (*all to keep up appearances, Jane, don't be a bore*) but not once with her. She had stood by the sausage roll table, watching, trying to smile at passing colleagues. The night had ended when Cathy from procurement was sick on a board member, and Jane noticed that Stefan had left without saying goodbye. Jane isn't a fan of parties.

But this? This is different. For one thing, it isn't really a *party*, it is a *plot*. And for another, she will have Natasha and Daniel with her. She feels more enthusiastic about anything life has to throw at her with them by her side.

'We'd need an excuse,' Daniel is saying.

'How about memorial drinks for Carrie Marks?'

'That could get too big. It's going to have to be about you, Natasha. "Come meet the great author" and all that. Select guest list.'

Natasha grimaces and shakes her head.

'Abi Ellis will come if you ask her,' Daniel insists. 'She's desperate to hang on to Carrie's clients.'

Some of them, thinks Jane.

'We'll get Edward Carter there with the promise of an exclusive interview,' Daniel continues, waving his mug around dangerously. 'And the promise of food. He looks like he needs fattening up. And Laura Lane would attend the opening of a kitchen bin if she could put it on TikTok.'

'I'm not throwing a party in my own honour,' Natasha sighs, lowering herself to sit cross-legged on the floor. 'That's humiliating. What sort of person does that?'

'Authors. You guys *love* celebrating yourselves from what I've seen.'

'That's so unfair. Anyway, who else do we want there? We should each take a few people as target invitees.'

Jane watches the two of them bickering, throwing names back and forth at the same time, offering ideas for how to tempt them. She sips her cold tea and imagines all of those people around a table together, divulging their secrets. In her mind, Laura Lane is the scruffy, scowling girl from the photo.

'Kimberley Brown,' muses Natasha. 'I know we've spoken to her a lot, but she isn't *entirely* off the table. I'm not wholly convinced there isn't even *more* she could tell us.'

'She knows what we're up to though. She won't be fooled by a party invitation.'

'Well, maybe we can pretend we need her help? She wants the killer caught. Or *says* she does.'

God, that Christmas party had been bloody depressing. Jane had spent money she didn't have on a new dress to impress Stefan. It was forest green, nipping in at the waist and floating out in an A-line. She'd pushed the boundaries of her comfort zone and her bank balance, but had decided it was worth it. Yet the only real communication she'd had with him that night had been the text he'd sent.

O Christmas tree, O Christmas tree . . . ;)

'Jane?'

'Oh, yes. Sorry.' They continue looking at her, and she tries to push the humiliation of the March Christmas party out of her mind. Yes, this is different. This time, she isn't alone.

'Brad was supposed to do a lunchtime talk tomorrow,' she says. 'So there'll be a gap in some people's schedule then.'

'Perfect, Baker!' Daniel raises his mug in salute, dregs of tea sploshing out onto his jeans. 'What do we tell them?'

'Well,' says Jane, slowly spinning on the child's chair, her brain working. 'We could always book a table at the Murder Mystery Lunch?'

'Ideal!' Natasha is beaming at her, and a rush of pride shunts the image of herself by the sausage roll table out of her mind once and for all. She gives another spin on the pink chair, which is followed by a loud crack. Jane thuds to the floor.

'I think it's time to call it a night.'

Chapter Thirty-Four

Sunday, 8.10 a.m.

It's a truth universally acknowledged that a single man in want of a hangover cure must groan very loudly, so Edward Carter groans as loud as he can. He has an appalling headache, and his mouth tastes like a Wetherspoon's ashtray on a Saturday night. Why had he stayed up so late? Why had he taken a shot of tequila with that editor – Frankie something? She'd seemed to be celebrating.

The groaning hasn't changed the taste in his mouth or the pounding in his head, but he tries again as he sits up, and once again as he swings his feet out of the bed and onto the floor, by which point he feels he deserves a rest.

When he lost Nayla, Edward had started drinking. It seemed the obvious solution. Friends talked too much and gave him pitying looks. They did the washing up, unasked, then put plates in the wrong cupboards. Whisky *never* did that. It allowed him to sit and wallow, freely, with his memories and grief and guilt.

These days, he barely touches the stuff. Not since the night he screeched to a halt at a roundabout, inches from a Volvo estate containing a family of four, almost becoming the same sort of person who took Nayla and his unborn child from *him*.

In Nayla's case, though, it wasn't just the fault of the driver – a notorious drunk by the name of Johnno Guinness (presumably not his Christened name). No, the other person responsible for Nayla's death, and that of their unborn baby, is Edward.

Nayla wasn't supposed to be on the road that night. She was supposed to be at home, watching *Celebrities on Ice* and eating

Chicken Schnitzel – one of the rare meals he cooked. But she wasn't because he had been a complete arse.

He'd had a terrible day at work – his editor told him his latest piece on the new Wes Anderson film was *snore-inducing* – and had come home in a foul mood. He had refused to cook, despite it being his turn, and then he had refused to let Nayla watch her show on television because he hated it. His mood had turned into bickering, which turned into a row, which turned into her getting in the car to watch the show at her friend's house and *get some space*. She was angry, and she never can concentrate properly when she is angry. *Could* concentrate. *Was* angry. He still has trouble thinking of her in the past tense.

He doesn't even hate the show. He just pretended to. Who could hate watching idiots fall over on ice skates? He never misses an episode now.

With another groan, he manages to reach a standing position and head to the shower. The Thistle Hotel is charmless but efficient, like a good accountant. Fittingly, the large shower doesn't wow him, but it does wash away a lot of the night-before buzz. The lighting is too bright, but he is willing to admit that's potentially his hangover rather than the hotel's fault.

Thoughts of his late wife and not-quite-child are aggressive today, as they usually are when alcohol or lack of sleep has primed him for melancholy, and he stares at his solitary tooth-brush for a good five minutes before snapping out of it enough to pick it up and clean away the taste of tequila and cigarettes.

Edward had not meant to let the evening get out of hand, but the atmosphere had been slightly hysterical after Brad's fall. Some people had been crying, others panicked; some were unashamedly excited, and yet others shamedly so. It was an atmosphere that lent itself to drinking fast and hard, to ending up in corners with people you didn't know whispering theories and plans.

Edward had spent the majority of it smoking outside, keeping an ear out for updates, but had been pulled into a group of drinkers near the end of the evening and given himself over to it. On the bright side, he was supposed to attend Brad's big speech today, but with the man of the hour now sadly out of action, Edward has an unexpected two hours free in his diary. If anyone tries to invite him to some dreadful book party, he'll scream. At least he's managed to avoid the ghastly Murder Mystery Lunch this year.

Buttoning up yet another blue shirt, he frowns at the bottom of his trousers. Despite his best efforts at brushing off the mud, there's still a trace. It makes him feel untethered. At least his shirt is freshly ironed, having been sent up the night before by the concierge. Cost a fortune, of course, but they never survive train travel in a wearable state. He slips on his jacket, checks for creases, and looks at his watch. He'll have to head over to the festival soon for an interview with some up-and-coming author he'd agreed to months ago. Hopefully that won't take too long. Same old questions, same old answers.

There is still time though, and there really is nothing better to relieve some of the sadness building in his body and mind.

Sitting at the desk in front of the window, he pulls his laptop out of his bag and turns it on. It's an old thing. His colleagues mock him for sticking with such a brick rather than investing in the latest MacBook, but that doesn't matter to him – particularly since it was a present from Nayla. And he knows how to use it.

Clicking slowly through the folders on the desktop, he locates one called *Bills and Forms*. It was the most unenticing folder name he could think of, not that anyone even has access to his laptop anyway. He barely lets people inside his house these days. Inside is a Word document entitled *The Last Summer*.

The manuscript springs up on the screen and he scrolls to the end of it, pausing to reread where he had left off. Oh, yes, the protagonist was staring across the lake, telling the janitor how the ripples reminded him of the futility of life. Bloody good stuff. He inserts a page break, and types *Chapter Twelve*.

Edward's room is on the fourth floor, with a view of the road leading up to the hotel. Movement in the driveway catches his eye, and he peers out the window to see none other than Sarah Parks-Ward strutting up to the hotel. He cowers lower in his seat, though it's unlikely she would see him from down there. She's not here for *him*, is she? She's been trying to get him alone all weekend and he's sick to death of it. He regrets asking her back to his that night after the book launch in March, but he's apologised a hundred times now. Then out of guilt he'd done her that favour, which hadn't ended well. He pulls the curtain across and turns his attention back to his screen.

Edward has been consuming and commenting on the work of others for as long as he can remember. When he was seven, he wrote a blistering review of the latest *Postman Pat* instalment, which saw him labelled as precocious all through primary school. But it is only recently that he has started to write his own novel.

After the drinking stopped, something else had to fill the void and, try as he might, cigarettes could only do so much. So, he'd sat down one day and typed. At first, he'd tried writing a thriller. He'd read enough of them, and they were all basically the same. Paranoid woman, expensive house, slight drinking problem and some medication that means the sinister happenings could conceivably all be in her head. It was slow going, though, and he couldn't summon the enthusiasm to write about expensive Chardonnay and futuristic home security systems.

Then there was a brief, misguided spell of writing a romance novel. An enemies-to- lovers tale where no one seemed to have a very demanding job, all the men had lopsided smiles, and the protagonist had a lovable dog who brought her and her true love together. But with his own personal life so devoid of romance, it made Edward sad.

And so he'd settled on this. Whatever *this* was. He'd completed the first draft in six months, perfected it over the next three, and started on this, the sequel, four weeks ago. He'd told no one that he had written a novel. No one living anyway. He'd told Nayla when he visited her grave, of course. And he'd told Carrie, his oldest friend and the person with the power to get it out there into the world.

The ringing of his room phone makes him jump in his seat. Creaking out of his chair, he flops down onto the bed and answers it.

'Mr Carter? I have a guest here for you. A Miss Parks-Ward.'

Edward groans again. Why did he answer it?

'I'm afraid I'm rather busy at the moment.'

He hears a muttering on the other end of the phone before the concierge resumes in his ear.

'She says she will wait for you in the lobby until you are ready to walk to the literature festival together.'

What? *No!*

'Um, can you tell her not to wait, please? Tell her that . . . tell her that I'll meet her there.'

'She would like to know when and where.'

There really is no getting out of this.

He remembers the shard of broken glass she'd held to his throat on Thursday afternoon. 'Nine-thirty in the tea room.' It seems less dangerous than the Dog and Bone.

'She says that works and she'll see you there. Have a good morning, Mr Carter.'

He puts down the phone and goes to the window, watching from behind the curtain until he sees her heading down the driveway and out of sight. He'll have to have a word with reception about her. Sighing, he sits back at his desk.

When the janitor wakes, he feels to be floating in darkness and sorrow, the memory of the lake lapping at his senses just as it had on its icy shores.

That's good. He really does have a talent for this. But Chapter Twelve is proving tricky, and Edward's brain is fuzzy, so eventually he slams the lid shut and gathers his things for the day ahead – notebook, pen, wallet, phone, two packets of Silk Cut and a lighter.

If all goes to plan, he may be able to come back and have another stab at it over lunch. To Edward, this project is far more than a novel, bigger and deeper than any of the thrillers featured at this festival. It is his wife. He has poured his whole soul into these books – every memory, every emotion, every regret. What more could a reader want than a piece of the author's very soul?

He looks back at his laptop with a grimace.

Apparently a *catchy hook*, that's what.

How *dare* Carrie Marks?

Chapter Thirty-Five

Sunday, 9 a.m.

Today, Jane is thinking of trying a brave new look.

Walking past the Sue Ryder charity shop on her way to the festival after breakfast, she stops dead. Not literally, though that does appear to be an alarming trend around Hoslewit this weekend, but rather in her tracks, at the sight of a red dress. In the window, next to the dress, a poster announces the shop's special Sunday opening hours during the festival, and an old woman is in the process of unlocking the front door.

The charity shop is one of many on the small high street, just along from a Funky Fones and a gift shop selling purposely distressed candlesticks – the kind of places Jane always suspects of money laundering because she cannot understand how they turn a profit. Why would anyone want a distressed-looking candlestick? What do they want to pretend that candlestick has been up to? Crossing the Sahara? Fighting in Ukraine?

With a deep breath, Jane pushes open the door.

Soon, she is standing in front of a mirror, behind a curtain that only half covers the cubby hole optimistically labelled *Fitting Room*. She'd sheepishly requested the dress hanging in the window from the ancient volunteer, who'd made quite a to-do about retrieving it. Six passing pedestrians were roped in to help wrestle it from the mannequin, as well as the butcher who was just opening up next door – blood-stained apron and all.

The clinging red dress is, to a tee, the one PI Sandra Baker wears in Jane's first novel, *Rush of Blood*. That, in turn, was based on the teenage Jane's imaginings of her future self – in a smoky bar somewhere in Europe, beautiful and sophisticated.

This may not be Paris, and the Dog and Bone may only serve cocktails that come in cans, but . . . can she?

No. She cannot.

'You alright in there, my love?'

The old woman's face appears in the mirror, causing Jane to jump and bang her elbow on the wall. With only around three inches of unoccupied space around her, the cubicle isn't designed for sudden movements.

'Oh, very fancy,' the woman says. Her face is so deeply wrinkled it looks like a crumpled paper bag. Jane squints to make out the glint of her eyes under sagging lids, and is surprised to find they're quite mean-looking. 'Though not *quite* Liz Hurley, are you, dear?'

'I'm not sure it's for me.'

'Well, you have to buy it now, with all that fuss you made.'

Fuss! Jane smiles through her indignation. The woman yanks the curtain back across, still leaving most of Jane exposed to the rest of the shop.

With a last, dissatisfied look in the mirror, Jane smooths down the fabric. It's good quality, the sort of thing she could never afford new, and fits perfectly. But she feels attention-grabbing. Silly.

She sighs, and goes to pull the dress off over her head, but it gets stuck, leaving the bottom half of her body on show, with her arms trapped in a tube against her ears. Jane wriggles, smashing her elbow on one wall and head on the other.

'Everything okay?' the crone calls from outside.

'YES!' yells Jane, voice muffled through fabric. Did this happen to Sandra Baker when she bought her dress? Was *she* stuck inside it, large pants visible and top half looking like an embarrassed sausage?

Jane's phone starts to buzz angrily in her bag. Stops, then buzzes again. She takes a deep breath, and manages to wrestle the dress back down to cover her underwear again.

'On second thoughts,' she says with a smile, pulling back the curtain to find the old grouch alarmingly close to her face, 'I'll take it. And I'll wear it now.'

With her old outfit in a plastic bag, Jane leaves the shop to make her way self-consciously up towards the festival. A man leans out the window of a passing white van and wolf whistles at her. She feels a mixture of shame and pride, followed by guilt about the pride. She's a terrible feminist. Sandra Baker would have told him where to go.

She looks at her reflection in the window of a parked car. If she squinted, could she be Sandra Baker? Too tall, too broad, okay. But she pushes back her shoulders and tries to find the confidence that Daniel chided her for lacking. The red fabric is thick, and though it clings to her body it manages to smooth out her lumps and bumps into something resembling curves. She pulls on her cardigan.

Her phone buzzes again in her pocket, and she pulls it out to find two missed calls and a text from Natasha on their Meddling Kids group.

> I've booked us the last lunch table. We all know our targets and we have two spare seats to fill too. Meet in the tea room at 10. x

By the time Jane reaches Killer Lines, she is feeling absurd and planning to go straight to the bathroom to find a way out of this dress. Perhaps if she lies on the tiled floor, she could wriggle out of it like a snake? It's early still, and luckily the lawn is mostly empty, so she slips through the door to the deserted Dog and Bone without incident.

Surprisingly, the stairwell is not cordoned off with police tape. In fact, the only difference between now and this time yesterday is that the area looks a lot cleaner and has a distinct smell of bleach. Jane inspects the spiralling stairs she chased Kimberley up yesterday, twisting around the gaping stairwell someone pushed Brad down. She thinks of his body lying there, the blood pooling around him, the weakness of his pulse. Is he still alive? If so, is he conscious? Jane crouches to inspect a fleck of blood on a skirting board that the enthusiastic cleaner has missed.

'Everything okay there?'

She snaps up straight, almost headbutting Edward Carter, who has evidently appeared from the men's bathroom further down the corridor. Though similarly startling, his presence is less objectionable than the charity shop crone's.

'Oh, I was just, um . . .'

'Poor Brad, hey?'

The two of them stand in a silence that isn't quite awkward, yet not quite companionable. Respectful? Stunned? Jane often wishes you could ask this sort of thing, but has long learnt that you cannot. She can feel the clinging dress against her skin and it floods her with a sense of shame that makes her queasy. Eventually, she finds her voice.

'I'm surprised that the stairwell isn't taped off. And it's been cleaned so quickly. The original book tent is *still* being inspected.'

'But that was murder though, wasn't it?'

Jane dismantles his words, inspecting them for any other possible meaning. It was a statement – confident in its delivery. Flirty? No, talking about murder isn't flirting. *Get a hold of yourself, woman.*

'And this was . . .?' She says it tentatively, feeling for potential support in the theory. As she does so, she meets Edward's eye and flushes. He really is very handsome. In a gangly, bookish way. Couldn't *possibly* be a murderer.

'What are you suggesting, Jane? Brad fell. He was plastered. Blotto. Gazeboed. And he toppled over the railing.'

'Or was pushed.'

'Murder isn't everywhere. It's actually rather rare. Even among writers.'

'You know what else is rare? Fit and healthy people just *dying.*'

'That . . . is less rare than you think.' He says it quietly, sadly, as though he is breaking a great truth to a woman who hasn't yet seen what the world can do. Jane doesn't understand why, but knows she's said something to upset him. The flush in her cheeks intensifies and she fights an urge to give the man a hug. 'Anyway,' he continues, 'Brad isn't dead, by all accounts. He's hanging in there.'

'He's still alive?' Surely if Brad has been able to reveal who pushed him, it is only a matter of minutes until the culprit is in custody. 'Have the police spoken to him?'

'No idea, it's just something I heard. Anyway, nice to see you. I'd better get going. I've got to meet . . . someone.' He gives her a warm smile and turns to leave.

'Oh! Edward?' Despite his lovely grey eyes, he *is* a suspect – and on Jane's designated target list of people to invite to their gathering. 'Are you free over lunch?' He opens his mouth to speak, but Jane cuts in before he can offer an excuse. 'You should be because Brad's talk has, regrettably, been cancelled, and I believe you were planning to attend that.'

'Yes, well, that's true. So I suppose I am free.' He smiles again. Jane's stomach flips and her eyes start to sting – though maybe the latter is due to the strong smell of bleach in the air.

'Great! Some friends and I have secured a last-minute table at the Murder Mystery Lunch.' Is she imagining his face falling? Had he thought she was asking him to have lunch one-on-one? Almost . . . like a date? She is suddenly conscious again of the close-fitting dress, and ploughs on before she loses steam, pulling her notebook out of her bag to write down her number. 'It starts at one o'clock, so I'll meet you outside the Dog and Bone just before.'

'Oh, well . . . as you say, Brad's talk is cancelled. And there is nothing else I can think of that I might be doing.' It looks a little as if he is thinking *hard* in search of something else he might be able to say he's attending, but who *wouldn't* want to attend a Murder Mystery Lunch? 'So, yes, I am free. As you clearly know. There is no polite reason I could have for not saying yes. So . . . it looks like it's the Murder Mystery Lunch for me. How . . . marvellous.'

'Lovely. See you there.' She tears a strip of paper from her notebook and hands it to him, blushing harder. 'That's my number. If you need it.'

Smiling and nodding, Jane starts to walk down the corridor towards the women's bathroom, anxious now to be out from under his eyes. Anxious, too, to get changed into normal clothes.

'Oh, Jane?' Edward calls after her. 'Nice dress.'

Having successfully secured Edward's presence at the lunch at record speed, Jane is in the tea room early, waiting for her friends. In front of her sits a slice of Victoria Sponge cake, because it's a Sunday and the day they are going to apprehend a murderer, so why not? A nervous-looking teenager brings her coffee to the table, spilling more with each step, her face growing bright red with embarrassment and concentration.

Jane flips open her notebook to go over what they have learnt so far. She looks at Carrie's transcribed diary entries and the sketch of the engraved bracelet they found in her hotel room. She adds the threatening note she'd found in her pocket, as she hadn't had the energy the night before, and even tries to copy the school photo found in Carrie's coat pocket. This last one doesn't go so well, so she turns it into a general swirly pattern and writes *school photo* instead, which should be sufficient.

Her watch tells her it is 9:45, meaning she has about 15 minutes until the others arrive. Flicking to the start, she looks at the three names they'd written down two days ago. Abi Ellis, Laura Lane, Kimberley Brown. Is there anyone else to be added? Anyone to be removed? Her pen hovers over the page for a moment before carefully underlining Laura's name, crossing out Kimberley's and slamming it shut.

Leaning back in her chair, she sips her coffee. A 'flat white' the girl had called it, though Jane can't quite see the difference between this and normal coffee. She takes a bite of her cake, then tries to wipe the jam from her nose without getting more of it on her new dress. Putting down the cup, she holds her sticky hands away from her body, eventually spotting a pile of napkins and a water station across the room.

As Jane rinses her hands to save both her dress and her dignity, she spots someone she recognises in the corner. Her editor, Frankie, is deep in conversation with Natasha's unfriendly publicist, Sarah. Drying her hands on a napkin and taking far longer than strictly necessary, Jane watches the two women whispering intently. Sarah reaches into a Killer Lines-branded tote bag and pulls out chunk of paper, pressing it into Frankie's hands. The editor nods, puts the paper into her own bag, and eventually gets to her feet with a smile on her face. It's the happiest Jane has ever seen her look.

The editor is walking her way, though doesn't appear to have noticed Jane lurking by the cutlery.

'Frankie!' Jane says on instinct, making both of them jump.

'Oh, Jane! I was just—'

'I haven't seen you since the first day here. Not since Carrie died. Isn't it awful?'

Frankie suddenly looks solemn and slowly shakes her head. 'A true legend.'

'And I didn't know you were friends with Sarah Parks-Ward?'

'Not *friends* per se. Anyway—'

'And we still need to talk about *Death of Last Hope*?'

'Yes! Totally, yes! It is now my *top priority*. I don't have time *right now* because . . . because I need to call my mother, who is sick. She's having an amputation.'

'As well as your aunt? That's bad luck.'

'Yes, isn't it? Must run in the family. And I'm *excited* to talk about your book later!' Frankie bares her dazzling white teeth in a grin, or an approximation of a grin, and backs away.

'Okay, hope your mum gets better soon.' Jane walks to her table, reflecting on how accident-prone Frankie's family is. It must be difficult for her.

Turning to see a final glimpse of her editor as she makes to slip out of the tea room, Jane also reflects on something else. They need to fill a space at lunch, and it might be a good way to have Frankie in one place long enough to get some answers about the publication of Jane's next book. Not only that, but Frankie was up late on the night that Carrie died; Jane had seen her in Laura's videos. Perhaps she knows something that could be helpful?

'Frankie?'

The editor pauses and turns, clasping her hands together with a look of practised patience.

'I really need to run, Jane.'

'I just thought you might like to join us for lunch?' The lengthening pause is awkward. When Frankie reluctantly opens her mouth to speak, Jane cuts across her. 'Natasha, Daniel and me?'

'Daniel? Is he that handsome boy with the hair?' She mimes a floppy lock in front of her face, to which Jane nods. 'Oh, well. Sure! I'd like that. Email me the details.'

Chapter Thirty-Six

Sunday, 10 a.m.

Back at the table, Jane finds Natasha flicking through her note-book. She looks up with a warm smile, tired eyes, and a guilty expression. Jane notices that the remnants of her cake and coffee have mysteriously disappeared.

'*Bom dia*,' Natasha says with a yawn. Her eyes flick to the empty plate and she grimaces. 'And sorry. I got in late last night.' Jane doesn't really see what that has to do with cake theft, but she's pleased to see her friend nonetheless. 'Was that your editor? Is she still avoiding you?'

'She had to make a phone call about an amputee.'

'Fair enough.'

Jane waves at the embarrassed waitress, orders another flat white, then updates Natasha on successfully inviting Edward and Frankie to their lunch.

'Good work, Jane! I texted Laura too. She says she'll only come if we agree to her live-streaming the whole thing, so I had to say yes.'

'What's *live streaming*?'

'She's going to film it on her phone, and her followers can watch in real-time.' The thought of this makes Jane feel sick, and she's suddenly pleased that Natasha has eaten her cake. 'She told me to make sure you had your own social channels set up by lunchtime, so she can tag you.'

'Um, sure.' Part of Jane's motivation for solving Carrie's murder was so she could mirror some of Laura's success. But now, when it's being offered on a plate, she finds herself

233

pulling away. Is this what she wants? Talking to the camera during parties and live streaming her lunch? Is this what
it takes to be an author? The bestseller charts are half full
of celebrity names and ghostwritten novels, so she supposes
that, yes, it is what it takes. Who you are is more important
than what you produce. If you are enough, you don't even
need to produce it yourself.

'What's this?' Natasha is holding up the notebook she'd been
flicking through, pointing to some scribbles Jane can't quite
make out. She leans forward to peer at them, when someone
lands in the chair next to her.

'Wow-wee, Jane! Nice dress!'

Daniel appraises her look, and she flushes under his inspection.

'You're late,' says Natasha.

'Barely. And I didn't get to bed until gone 2 in the end.'

A rattling announces the red-faced waitress's arrival as she
places Jane's second flat white on the table.

'Thank God!' says Daniel, reaching for the cup. 'Lifesaver.'

Jane sighs and waves the waitress to bring another.

'So what is this then? Something from the hotel room?'
Natasha puts the notebook down on the table, open to a page
of Jane's chaotic handwriting. She recognises it as the notes
copied from Carrie's diary and notebooks, and tells Natasha
so. Frowning at the information, Natasha drags the book back
towards her and pulls out her own ballpoint pen.

'So, Jane,' says Daniel, who has already flicked his legs over
one armrest of his chair like a Roman emperor. 'Tell me about
the look.'

'To be honest with you, I tried it on in a charity shop and
then I couldn't get it off. So I bought it.'

He stares at her in confusion, then bursts out laughing. In
relief, she feels herself grin at the absurdity of it all. It *is* funny
when you are with friends in a bright tea room rather than
sweating in a barely curtained changing cupboard.

'Well, there are worse things to be stuck in. It looks banging. Maybe you can wear it in your next author photo,' he says, still chuckling into his coffee foam.

Jane stops grinning. She doesn't get things like author photos. She barely gets an email response. What she gets is The Tweet. The marketing team will tell you about the coming tweet, do it, and then remind you of it in later weeks to make you feel ungrateful.

'If you remember, Jane, we had that big moment on social media, so we are watching the ripple effects of that for now.' Or the dreaded, *'It's all about the long tail.'*

But occasionally a publishing insider will mention something she hasn't even considered before, so casually, assuming she's automatically on the same footing as them, and she'll be reminded of her real place in the scheme of things. Of course she hasn't had a professional author photo taken, with makeup applied and lighting tweaked. Her Amazon bio has the same one she put on LinkedIn – a blurry selfie taken before her auburn hair had started to salt and pepper.

Hang in there, Jane, she imagines her mother saying. *You never know what's waiting around the corner.* She chuckles along with Daniel.

He is still laughing to himself, but is silenced by Natasha slamming the open notebook back on the table. Jane is perturbed to see she has scribbled all over it. Isn't it bad etiquette to write in another woman's notebook?

'Okay, most of these are obvious. Lunch dates and the like.' Natasha leans forward in her chair and points to the page with her pen. 'I'm pretty sure some are abbreviations for book titles. And a lot of them are clear if you know publishing lingo.

Daniel leans forward. 'Yeah. HB is hardback, WTS is Waterstones, WHS is W. H. Smith, things like that. '

'Oh,' says Jane, feeling out of yet another loop she didn't know existed.

E.C. NEVIN

'I don't understand all of them. But *this* one I find particulary interesting.'

Natasha underlines the note *KL – KM / LL.*

'None of the initials relate to any publishing lingo that I've heard, unless it's something one of you guys recognises?' Daniel shrugs. Jane shakes her head. 'And I've scanned through Carrie's client list; they aren't initials of any author she represents either. So I broke it down. *KL* could mean—'

'Killer Lines!' says Daniel, sitting up straight now, excited and awake.

'Exactly. And where have we seen the initials *KM?*'

'Katie Mack?' Jane offers, seeing it all come together. 'Katie Mack slash Laura Lane. But . . . but this means that Carrie *definitely* knew? She knew Laura's real identity.'

'And,' says Natasha, pointing at *KL,* 'she planned to confront her about it at Killer Lines.'

'We've got our woman,' whispers Daniel.

The group sit in awed silence.

'Um, another flat white?' The embarrassed waitress is back. She now has a large stain down the front of her t-shirt.

'Thanks,' says Natasha. 'I could use that.'

Though Daniel is now certain Laura Lane is the murderer they have been hunting, Jane can't help but be sceptical. After all, they had been convinced that Kimberley was the killer, and then, briefly, Brad. This time, she is holding herself in check until they have all the facts. *Keeping her powder dry,* as her mother would say.

Something she needs no time to ponder is her newfound enjoyment of flat white coffee. Once she had finally been able to drink an entire cup, she went from indifferent to obsessed. She'll have to put one in the next book; that way she can claim tax back on flat whites as research.

It doesn't look *good* for Laura Lane, that much is true. But would a woman on the rise, and with so much to lose, kill someone because they knew her *real name*? Jane still believes the underlying motive is connected to books. Perhaps what Carrie confronted Laura about – and it's imperative they find out exactly what that was – was something that would be ruinous to her writing career?

Jane is enjoying the quiet stroll towards Kimberley Brown's hotel to invite her to their lunch, her old clothing still in a plastic bag banging against her thigh. Daniel – who they agreed had the least enviable target list – has gone in search of Abi Ellis, and Natasha has been called by her publicist to do some blogger interviews.

Being in no particular hurry, Jane stops by the churchyard and perches on the stone wall. Bringing up Google on her phone, she searches for *Katie Mack*. The first page of results is split between articles about a famous cricketer and a famous astrophysicist. The astrophysicist even has a critically acclaimed book (who doesn't these days!). Jane scowls at the screen.

As she is about to put it back into her pocket, it buzzes in her hand. It's Detective Inspector Ramos calling.

'Hello? Jane?'

'Yes, hell—'

'GET BACK!'

Jane nearly topples off the wall in shock, before Ramos continues.

'Sorry, Jane, a bloody seagull is after my pain au chocolat. How are you? I was hoping we could talk. I was perhaps a bit short with you yesterday. I'd had a long day. SCREW YOU!'

'Yes! That would be great. We've actually found out even more since I saw you yesterday.'

'I'LL SNAP YOUR BEAK OFF! That's wonderful, Jane. I'll be over in Hoslewit later this NOT THE CHOCOLATE BIT! morning.'

'Perfect.' Jane hears what sounds like wrestling on the other end, and is about to hang up and let Detective Inspector Ramos return to defending his breakfast, when it occurs to her that he could help them with something.

Being a private eye, Baker had to use her own smarts rather than police resources, though she occasionally sweet-talked officers into lending a hand. It had taken Baker years to build her contacts, but here Jane is, speaking to the investigating officer on the phone.

'Detective Inspector Ramos? Are you still there?'

'Yes I'm VERMIN! BEAST! still here.'

'Well, two things really. One, I'd be most grateful if you could use that clever police database you have access to, to look someone up for us. She's called Katie Mack, and we need to know if she's been embroiled in anything dodgy in the past.'

'I can't go around looking people up at the request of any civilian with AN ACCOMPLICE, DON'T YOU DARE! a grudge.'

'It's not *my* grudge. But this woman is someone intrinsic to the investigation and I'm *sure* she's hiding something. If we find out what happened in her past, it could be the key to the whole case.' Detective Inspector Ramos doesn't answer, but Jane hears his heavy breathing, a frantic rustling, a squawk, and then a deep sigh.

'You do this for me,' she continues, 'and I'll tell you *everything* I know. If you don't think my information is any good, you don't have to pass on what you've learnt about Katie Mack. Deal?'

'Honestly, Ms Hepburn, I know you're trying to help, but we're quite sure the motivation behind the tragic death of Ms Marks was financial.'

'It won't take you long to put the name into the database and press print before you head to Hoslewit.'

Jane's heart is thumping in her chest. She is *never* this assertive, this confident. Perhaps it's the outfit.

'It'll be worth it, Detective Inspector. I promise.'

Eventually, a rumble of assent sounds down the phone.

'Okay. I'll do it. And then you can tell me exactly what is going on. And I'm not promising to share it with you either.'

Yes! She'd done it! She remembers how in *Rush of Blood*, Baker had successfully wheedled information out of DI Fields and feels a burst of pride in herself. She's starting to like this dress.

'You said there were two things. If that was one, dare I ask what number two is?' says Ramos.

'Will you join us for lunch today?'

'Well, the seagull and his friend have successfully mugged me of my pain au chocolat, so I suppose I'm in.'

Chapter Thirty-Seven

Sunday, 11 a.m.

Abigail Ellis is having her mug shot taken, and she hates every second of it. Not for the first time, she considers whether this profession is right for her. The fake enthusiasm and general expectation of niceness drive her to distraction. But needs must, and as she waves goodbye to one of Carrie's – one of *her* – high-profile clients who has somehow *enjoyed* the photo experience, she breathes a sigh of relief. Must keep them all on side.

'Here you go, you no-good scoundrel!' A rat-faced man is waving a photo in front of her face, air-drying the ink. 'I shouldn't let you walk free, but at least we have you accounted for, you dastardly criminal! If you feel like atoning for your sins, you should head right up to the Jail Cell Escape Experience on the sixth floor.'

Abi snatches the photograph from his hand. It is in black and white and shows her against a height marker, just touching the five-foot mark, holding up a blackboard with ELLIS written on it. She scowls and rips the photo in half. The rat-faced man shrinks back, before rallying.

'Ah, that will do no good, you lowlife vagabond! The police will keep another on file until your dying day! They will hu—'

Abi walks away, dropping the pieces of the photo in her wake. She smooths down her hair as she goes, having been quite alarmed by its size in the mug shot. The sooner she can afford that keratin treatment the better.

So much to do, so little time. The police have already been in touch this morning, wanting to talk about some irregularities found in the Marks Agency accounts. She knew it would all come out, but had banked on having more time.

No matter. She just needs to get back on the laptop and make sure everything that should have been deleted *has* been deleted. The doctored documents seem to have been enough to hold off Carrie's lawyer for now, and the authors have yet to get wind of anything untoward. But that, too, has a time limit.

In the corridor, away from the dreadful marketing executive and his mugshots, she pauses to breathe. She has that workshop on how to make perfect dumplings on Monday night, but if she still has various bits of fraud to commit she might have to skip it. Which would be a pain, because it is non-refundable, and she *would* like to up her dumpling game.

She contents herself with the fact that, when she is rich, she'll be able to hire a private chef to teach her.

She also hadn't *quite* expected such an influx of emails since Carrie's death. Abi had assumed she did most, if not *all*, of her boss's work, but it seems there's a tiny bit more to it than she previously thought. Most authors have replied to the news of the murder with horror and grief, but some unashamed money-grabbers have responded with demands for information. *When will my latest contract be ready? When will my advance come through? Has my manuscript been submitted in Germany yet, or was Carrie waiting until the Frankfurt Book Fair? I haven't got my last royalty statement. Has the publisher got back on the South Africa question?*

I don't know! she wants to scream. *It's a mess! And I'm just one woman!* Instead, she's crafted email after email, being apologetic and professional while begging for patience in this trying time. Two authors have defected to the Rhodes Agency already. She doesn't want to say this is all getting out of control, but she does feel like she's heading into oncoming traffic without being able to reach the brakes. What she needs is a dogsbody.

'Hi, Abi!'

Perfect.

'Daniel, where the hell have you been?'

The floppy-haired oaf flushes, but his eternal grin is still infuriatingly in place. Very handsome though, she'll give him that.

'Well, um, sleeping, I guess? And then I got here this morning at about—'

'Look, you've been promoted. You are the new assistant to the Marks Literary Agency. Congratulations.'

'What?! Oh, wow! Does this mean I'm going to get paid now?'

'Yes, sure, whatever. It also means you are officially on the clock and have work to do.'

This is a good idea. Daniel is young, impressionable and clueless. She can get him to sort through the paperwork while she continues schmoozing the authors, and he probably won't even notice anything wrong. That Natasha Martez is being evasive, and Abi really needs to get her nailed down as a client of her own before any other agents get to her.

Daniel has been wittering on while she's been thinking. Something about lunch? After it's all over, she can get rid of him and pretend this conversation never happened. She just needs to get through the next few days and then it'll be dumpling-making and shopping in the John Lewis kitchen department.

'Abi? What do you think?'

'What?'

'The Murder Mystery Lunch? A few of Carrie's authors are coming, and the reviewer Edward Carter? So we wondered if you'd like to join us?'

Abi would rather cut off her own arm than join the Murder Mystery Lunch.

'Will Natasha Martez be there?'

'Absolutely!'

Duty calls.

'Righto. See you at one.'

Chapter Thirty-Eight

Sunday, 11 a.m.

Jane is pacing the lawn, her stomach positively riddled with butterflies. She is almost as nervous as the time she agreed to do a book reading at the local library and only four people turned up. It soon became clear that two were looking for a bathroom and one was a teenager hiding from his mother, leaving a lone old lady to listen to Jane reading an extract from her latest novel and giving a pre-prepared speech. When it came time for the Q&A, it transpired that the remaining guest was deaf.

But today isn't going to be like that. Today she has a captive audience.

It had taken Jane almost an hour to persuade a still red-eyed Kimberley to join them for lunch. When Jane pleaded that it would bring them closer to discovering who'd killed Carrie and attempted to kill Brad, Kimberley had finally, and with great reluctance, agreed. If Daniel has managed to get Abi on board, then all their targets will be in place.

It isn't until Jane is halfway back to the festival site that she thinks to check her phone and finds a voice note from Detective Inspector Ramos.

He has dug up some *very interesting information* on Katie Mack and is planning to get to Hoslewit early to talk to Jane in private before the lunch. He has rushed his words in what she assumes to be excitement, so now she is waiting, anxious in anticipation. It feels as though everything is finally coming together.

She'd texted the news to her friends, but has yet to hear back from Daniel, and Natasha is still busy. For the first time in her life, Jane is happy no one else is demanding her time. She may not have a publishing professional getting her panel appearances and interviews, but that means she alone is able to meet with a real-life detective and progress their case.

She looks at her watch for the fourth time in six minutes. Even if Ramos left straight away, there is still at least half an hour until he arrives. She can't keep wearing a track into this corner of the lawn while she waits. But with her friends otherwise engaged, she feels at a loss.

Think, Jane! What would Baker do?

She wouldn't stand around waiting for others, that's for sure. Questioning suspects, establishing alibis, wheedling information from police contracts. Jane is becoming more like her protagonist by the day. Crouching in that stairwell this morning in the red dress, inspecting the scene, was positively Baker-esque.

The crime scene! For days now, the police have milled around the corner of the festival site behind the Dog, blue-and-white tape marking off the abandoned bookselling tent. But, thinking about it, today is the first day she *hasn't* seen hide nor hair of a police car. True, professional scene-of-crime officers will have gone over everything with a fine-toothed comb looking for fingerprints, strands of hair, errant threads of clothing. But what if there's something they've missed?

She looks at her watch again. There is time.

Thinking over what she knows so far, Jane walks back towards the Dog and Bone. She's going to follow Carrie's footsteps on the final night, so far as she knows them. The lawn is growing busy and the windows of the bar are steaming up. It rained in the night, so the grass is damp and air heavy, even if she's safe from it for now.

Jane stops dead in front of the pub and looks at the empty space above the door. The killer would have taken the dagger from here, but as it was dark and raining on and off, no one is sure when that happened. It could have been taken hours before it was stuck through Carrie's heart.

Jane heads towards the book tent, down a meandering path and around the side of the pub. There are trees on one side of the path, and she shudders, remembering how she made the walk alone that fateful Friday morning, never guessing what she'd discover. She hears the crack of a twig and spins around, but no one is visible She thinks of the anonymous note – *Back off* – and shivers again. Another crack of a twig, and she turns once more. A squirrel emerges from a bush and dashes up a tree.

'At some point,' Jane mutters to herself, steadying her heartbeat, 'Carrie was out here, speaking, or rather arguing, with a mystery man. Brad saw her and shouted out, causing her to slip on the wet ground.' Jane cannot see any signs of where Carrie fell, just debris and cigarette butts. She continues on down the path.

'Carrie goes into the book tent to clean herself up, and texts Kimberley, who comes back to the festival to speak to her.' Jane sees the blue-and-white tape flapping lazily around the large canvas tent. The sign *Killer Lines Book Tent* still shouts from above the entrance, though it's seen no customers since that very first day.

'After Kimberley leaves, someone *else* comes to the book tent. Someone else finds Carrie, and they kill her.'

The tape around the tent is coming unstuck in places, and a tail of it is trodden into the mud. Do the police ever remove this? Can the owners of the tent clear it out, or does this stand forever as a monument to an unsolved murder? That is, of course, if it *remains* unsolved.

Jane looks over her shoulder to check if anyone is watching. For a moment, she thinks she sees a shadow under the trees, but she blinks and realises it's just a bush. This part of the festival grounds is deserted. The wind is picking up, and most people will be watching an author event, taking part in a themed activity, or else cosied up in the tea room, beer tent, or bar of the Dog and Bone, recommending books to each other or begging favours.

She imagines it's not fully kosher to break into a murder scene during an active investigation. But it's not as if she's planning on causing any mischief. On the contrary, she's here to *help*. Jane slowly unzips the entrance, ducks under the police tape, and nips inside.

The last time Jane was in here, she found a body. The place seems oddly empty without it, even though it hadn't been part of the original decor. She is perturbed to see there is no chalk outline on the floor, which is a shame. Glancing around the room, Jane notices her own books on the table directly behind where the body had been. There is a second of joy until she remembers she's the one who put them there. They do look rather handsome though, laid out like that, in series order.

What might the police have missed? Tiptoeing around the ominous space in the middle of the tent, Jane browses the shelves, lined with titles from well-known writers. Brad Levinsky has an entire table reserved for his books, stacked in neat piles. The latest is perched on top, king of the roost.

Another table is dedicated to big-budget novels from television personalities. All ghost-written, all bestsellers, all with twenty times the promotional budget that Jane's laboured-over PI Sandra Baker series will have behind it. A table of psychological thrillers about women, husbands and families being next door, upstairs or generally secret, sits to Jane's left. She breathes in the smell of unread pages. Even if it's uncomfortably mixed with a stringent chemical smell, it still brings her comfort.

The odour jolts a memory of a projector screen at university into Jane's mind. *Chemicals used at a crime scene:*

Luminol, Iodine, Cyanoacrylate, Silver Nitrate, Ninhydrin, Bleach, Peroxide.

Something catches her eye. Jane goes back to the table where she had reached over Carrie's body to place her own novels. She had been a little stressed when she did it, having just found a body and everything, so perhaps she hadn't been as observant as she usually is. And the police officers wouldn't have noticed of course; what do *they* know about books?

But something (other than the PI Sandra Baker series) appears to be out of place.

The central table is dedicated to Golden Age classics, piled with famous titles by Dorothy L. Sayers, Agatha Christie, and Arthur Conan Doyle. Some are bound in expensive cloth with gilt titles, others with sober Victorian drawings adorning the cover, Jane's books sitting among them in a happy line. But one other book stands out. A new title that doesn't belong. The bright yellow of the font, bold and sans serif, is stark against the sinister silhouette of a young woman in an office being watched through the slats of a window blind. It very clearly belongs on the psychological thriller table. So what is it doing next to Christie?

Jane edges closer, prodding it with her finger. There is a mark on the edges of the pages. Is that . . . *blood?*

With a stab of guilt, she realises this cuckoo was partly disguised by her own novels, moved to the table *after* the murder. Would the SOCOs have noticed it if not for her meddling? Gingerly, she picks up the book with the hem of her skirt, careful not to touch it with her bare fingers. *The Assistant* by Sarah Grey. Did Carrie grab this book in her last moments? Was she trying to tell the police something about her killer? And if so, is it time for Jane to speak once again to *Carrie's* assistant, Abigail Ellis?

'Jane?'

She is back on the main lawn, jittery and confused. Detective Inspector Ramos is striding towards her across the grass holding two cups of coffee. She takes a deep breath to try and calm herself. He looks more awake, more alive, than she has seen him before. His turquoise eyes are glittering.

'Let's go somewhere to talk,' he says with a smile when he reaches her.

Jane nods, and tries to hide the smile blossoming on her own face, though she fails. Sure, this is about terrible, bloody murder, but it does feel good to be at the centre of something. No matter what the party, it's always nice to be invited.

They wipe away the water droplets on a bench at the edge of the lawn, far enough from the groups huddled around the beer-tent entrance and the promotional stalls flanked by beautiful marketing assistants. They sit down side by side.

'So. Katie Mack,' Ramos begins, handing her a polystyrene cup. 'Where did you get that name?'

'You found something on her then? A police record?'

'You first.'

'Okay.' Jane sips at her coffee – she recognises by its bitter taste that it's from the café down the hill – and considers how to begin. She'd decided before Ramos arrived that she will have to tell him more than she wants to, though she'll still keep some things back. Hopefully, being useful will mean she won't get in as much trouble later on when the full extent of her meddling comes out.

'I saw the name on the back of a school photograph of the woman now calling herself Laura Lane.'

'That blogger who's ruining my investigation by putting everything online?'

'The very same. She and Carrie weren't friends, and they argued on the night Carrie was stabbed. I have reason to believe Carrie knew Laura's real identity and was threatening to expose it. What I don't know, yet, is if that threat was worth killing her for.'

Detective Inspector Ramos furrows his brow and sits back against the wooden bench, sipping his coffee.

'Dear Lord, what is this muck?'

'It's Asda's own brand granules.'

He tips it onto the grass.

'When you say you *have reason to believe Carrie knew Laura's real identity*, what is that reason?'

Jane shakes her head. 'No. I've shared already. Now it's your turn. What did you find out about Katie Mack?'

Ramos sighs deeply, staring at the fields rolling out in front of them.

'Look, I'll tell you. But this is private, okay? And even if Katie Mack *is* this Laura Lane person, that doesn't mean she's the killer. I'm still sure the reason is financial.'

'Yes, yes, yes – tell me what you know!' Jane is quite literally on the edge of her seat. A quiet *crack* makes her sit back to avoid yet another humiliating tumble to the floor. She doesn't believe Ramos's purported lack of interest. If he really thought this was nothing, he wouldn't have got here so fast, and his rock pool eyes wouldn't be twinkling with excitement. Silently, she pulls out her packet of mints, putting one in her mouth and offering the packet to Ramos.

'Katie Mack has a criminal record, yes,' Ramos begins, his voice low even though no one is near. He takes a mint, and Jane sees it flash white on his tongue. 'Nothing major. She was in and out of foster care as a child, so she pops up at different addresses causing all sorts of trouble. You often see that with the kids who don't have proper homes. Not their fault they get caught up in it all.'

Foster care? For Jane, Laura had come fully formed as a mini-celebrity, selling thousands of books off the back of chirpy social media videos. Recalibrating to meld her with parentless Katie Mack, bounced between homes and in and out of trouble, is a huge adjustment. She remembers the scruffy appearance of the teenager in the faded picture, her angry scowl.

'Mostly,' continues Ramos, 'it's petty theft and vandalism. Stealing food, clothes, CDs, books. Classic stuff for a troubled teenager with no money and no parental guidance. Caught twice for graffiti, in trouble once for keying her foster dad's car. That sort of thing.'

Jane takes another gulp of coffee, winces, and follows Ramos in pouring the rest on the grass. In the centimetre of space between his scuffed brown brogues and his grey suit trousers, she sees he is wearing mismatched socks.

None of what she is hearing fits with Laura's new polished image. Vandalism? Theft? But by the sound of it, she'd had a difficult upbringing. Wouldn't people understand? Plenty of teenagers get a rap on the knuckles for shoplifting or graffiti. Surely this secret isn't worth *killing* for?

'That's it?' asks Jane, experiencing a rush of disappointment.

'Well, until the fire.'

Chapter Thirty-Nine

Sunday, 12 p.m.

'*Fire?* What fire?'

Natasha Martez is staring at Jane open-mouthed, slowly shaking her head.

'Listen, let's . . . let's get a glass of wine.'

Natasha raises her eyebrows at the suggestion. Jane is usually more of a tea and biscuits person than the suggesting-alcohol-at-11.45 kind.

In the beer tent, Jane puts two more glasses of *Wuthering Whites* on her credit card, partly waiting for the troubling sound of it being declined, partly not caring anymore. What's another £14 on top of the rest?

The April wind has picked up, and the canvas walls ripple with it, creating the effect of them being out at sea. The drop in temperature has driven people into the pub, and so not many of the wooden bench tables are populated. Jane shivers and wishes she had a proper coat with her rather than just her cardigan. Maybe there is a nice one back in Sue Ryder?

She's hungry, too. She never did get to finish that slice of Victoria sponge cake. Perhaps she should have accepted Mary's offer of egg slurry again this morning, but she hadn't been able to stomach the idea.

'Laura, or Katie, had been in low-level trouble. Shoplifting and that sort of stuff.' Jane sips the wine, and its acidity hits her empty stomach, making her wince. 'But one day, she started a fire. And it got . . . out of hand.'

'Arson?' says Natasha with a gasp. 'What was it? A car?'

'Do they sell food in here?'

'Focus, Jane.'

Easy for you to say, she thinks. *You who are full of my cake.* She sighs. 'It was her foster parents' house.'

Detective Inspector Ramos had told Jane how Laura had been arrested at age 17, found miles out of town, on the hard shoulder of the M5 trying to hitchhike. When they'd got to the station, she'd broken down and confessed to everything.

'She was a minor,' Jane tells Natasha. 'So she got off with community service.'

'And you think that's worth killing over?'

'The house . . . wasn't empty.'

'No!' Natasha gasps. 'She *killed her foster parents*?'

'Let me finish.'

By all accounts, Katie's foster parents at the time were kind people, but after a life lived among many of the *un*kind, she was a young girl full of rage. Luckily, they'd both been out on the night of the fire, trusting Katie home alone for the first time. She'd set fire to the garden shed, not expecting it to spread to the main building. When it did, she called 999 in a panic. On hearing the family dog barking, Katie had tried to get him out, but he was trapped.

'The fire department stopped the house being destroyed,' Jane finishes, 'but the dog didn't make it. When the police found Katie she had a nasty burn on her arm and was sobbing her heart out.'

'Wow.' Natasha splayed both hands on her chubby cheeks, her sticky-out ears protruding like handles. '*Wow.* The dog died? Never kill the dog. First rule of fiction. No one forgives you if you kill a dog.'

'Exactly,' says Jane. 'Honestly though, do they maybe have crisps or something? Ideally, I'd have eggs and soldiers.'

Natasha rolls her eyes and goes to the bar, returning to drop a bag of peanuts on the table.

'This is massive,' she says as she sits back down, eyes flicking around the sparsely populated tent to check no one is listening in. 'Laura has built everything she has from scratch. From having nothing and no one, to being semi-rich and famous. And Carrie was confronting her about a secret that could bring down *everything* Laura had worked for. It would *ruin* her if this got out. Arson *and* a dead dog? No way would her reputation survive. What happened next?'

Jane chews frantically, choking on the handful of nuts she'd shoved in her mouth. Coughing, she washes them down with wine before continuing.

'Ramos said she did the community service, behaving perfectly, and her name hasn't cropped up again.'

'Maybe it was a wake-up call? She decided to turn her life around. Changed her name and started again? And how did Carrie know about it?'

'No idea.'

The two authors sit picking over Laura's story as they do the salted peanuts. The wind is even stronger now and the tent is almost empty, with just a few people sitting at the far end. Jane gulps at her wine in the hope it might warm her. She is about to tell Natasha they should think about going – after all they have a lunch to get to – when a gust of icy wind freezes her limbs.

'*There* you are!' Daniel has pushed through the canvas door. He flings himself down on the bench next to Natasha. 'Don't either of you look at your phones?'

Jane is about to apologise, but Daniel shoves a handful of nuts in his mouth and then continues speaking, spraying her with fragments of shell. 'I have *so* much to tell you! Do I have time?'

Natasha looks at her watch. 'Just about. We need to catch you up too. Jane has pulled an absolute blinder on Katie Mack. Jane, you tell him what you've found out and I'll get us all a drink.'

When she returns, Daniel is reeling from the news of Laura's past and Jane is as proud as though she's got top marks in an exam, or a four-star review on GoodReads.

'Where have you been then?' asks Natasha. 'Did you get Abi to agree to join us at lunch?'

'I did, she's coming. And as for where I've been, well, Abi hired me as the agency's assistant,' he says, grinning.

'Congratulations!' says Jane, clinking his glass with her own. 'Though, can she do that? It's not her agency after all.'

'Well, that's sort of what I need to tell you about.'

He pulls out his iPhone, opens Photos and puts it flat on the table.

'Abi needs help with the paperwork. It's basic stuff. Going through everyone's contracts and getting things in order. I'm not really supposed to be thinking too deeply about anything and she clearly assumes I'm an idiot.'

'People judge a pretty face,' says Natasha. 'And more fool them.'

'Well, I know I'm not an Oxford graduate or, like, Epstein or anything.'

'Einstein,' mouths Natasha.

'But I did find this.'

With two fingers, he enlarges the image on the screen and Jane pulls it towards her.

'"I, Carrie Marks",' she reads aloud, scanning down the page. '"Blah blah blah . . . in lieu of a will and testament, leave the Carrie Marks Literary Agency to my faithful assistant Abi Ellis, in the unlikely and unfortunate event of my death or incapacitation."' She looks up in shock at Daniel. 'Carrie left it to Abi? *Really?*'

'Well,' he says with a smile, 'this was printed and, apparently, found with Carrie's paperwork. It bears Carrie's signature, but it's not been witnessed, so I doubt it has any legal standing.'

'You think Abi forged it?' Natasha asks, passing the phone to Jane to read.

'It's more likely than Carrie leaving her the agency,' Daniel says with a shrug, sending his hair flopping down in front of his eyes. 'Abi used to sign a lot of letters on Carrie's behalf; she can easily fake her signature.'

'Clever. So by dying, Carrie has assured her assistant of a bright new future with a list of bestselling authors handed to her.'

'That's not all I saw,' says Daniel. 'As an intern, I never got close to most of the paperwork. I just posted out books, answered the phone and made coffee. But Abi's just had me going through royalty statements and everything. It's a total mess, so I can't be completely sure, but I don't think it all adds up. There are records of payments coming in to the agency, but not going back out to authors. I've sent myself what I could.' Taking the phone back, he brings up an email with multiple documents attached and passes it to Natasha.

Jane frowns. 'Detective Inspector Ramos said something about financial discrepancies. So . . . what? We think that Abi knew about those too?'

The clinking of glasses interrupts their conversation as one of the final tables of people left in the tent gets up to leave. Natasha is zooming in on a new document. From where Jane sits, it looks like a sale of German rights. She flicks on to another; an Excel spreadsheet full of numbers.

'If the Marks Agency was in financial trouble, Abi would *not* have wanted to go down with a sinking ship,' says Natasha in a hushed whisper. Jane takes the phone and starts to look through the documents.

'Then why try and pass off a Will leaving herself a failing company at all? You think she didn't know about the finance stuff?' says Daniel with a frown. 'What's this one?' Jane says, looking at a list of names on another spreadsheet. She notices

Natasha's near the top, with the number one next to it. She starts to scroll down, recognising other clients of Carrie's, all grouped into numbered categories. She flicks right down to the bottom.

'Oh, nothing,' Daniel says, yanking the handset back. 'That's nothing important. Just clients in a list, that's all.'

Natasha plucks it from his fingers and scrolls down the screen. Her eyes flick up to Jane and back down again. 'Yeah, doesn't look important,' she says unconvincingly. Jane feels a deep sinking sensation in her heart, and vows to take a closer look as soon as possible.

The final group of drinkers wander past them towards the exit, letting in a blast of cold air as they push through the canvas door. Jane recognises the laughing woman with the big auburn hair, carrying a stack of brand-new paperbacks.

'I almost forgot!' she says. 'The book!'

Natasha looks at her watch again. 'We need to go. It's almost one.'

Jane leans in and whispers, despite no one being near them. 'No, wait. Before I met with Detective Inspector Ramos, I went to the crime scene. Into the book tent.'

'Isn't it still cordoned off?' says Daniel, frowning.

'Technically. But no one was around. And I found something the police would have missed. A book called *The Assistant* was out of place. It was on the table right next to where Carrie's body was found. There was a smudge of blood on the pages. I think she grabbed it before she died. What if, in her final moment, Carrie was trying to tell us that her assistant was her killer?'

'So it's Abi Ellis? Abi is the murderer?' says Daniel.

'What about Laura?' parries Natasha. 'Her motive is just as strong. One woman stands to gain everything she wants, the other to lose everything she's built.'

'Wait,' says Jane, her head in her hands. 'Wait. We've done this before. Jumped to conclusions because we have *some* of the facts. We were wrong about Kimberley, and we were certainly wrong about Brad. We need to make sure we know everything before we point the finger.'

They sit in silence, downing the rest of their drinks. It's time to meet the others for lunch, and Jane's mind is whirling from wine and theories and secrets. Everything is closing in, but the answer is still out of reach. She remembers the note secreted in her pocket: *Back off.*

'Right,' Jane says, with a look at her watch and another deep breath, 'it's nearly 1. And we have a murderer to catch.'

Chapter Forty

They are now dangerously close to being late for their lunch, so Jane is attempting to jog across the lawn. Sadly, her new dress doesn't allow much room for movement so she waddles like a penguin in a rush for feeding time across the wet grass.

As they approach the Dog and Bone, she can see Edward's bean-pole form lingering outside the main door, smoking a cigarette, nodding along to something Abi Ellis is saying a foot and a half below him while Laura Lane stands a few feet away, tapping away on her pink iPhone. Jane's step falters: *the blood-smeared pages of a book titled* The Assistant. *An unknown man heard arguing with Carrie. An identity steeped in scandal.* The reasons why these people have been invited here resound in her head with each step. *Financial discrepancies and a suspicious will. Initials scribbled in a diary.* Will their killer be sitting opposite them in just a few minutes?

'Jane! And you other ones!' They spin around to see Kimberley Brown striding towards them from the direction of the village. She is dressed today in a suit of deep blue velvet, and Jane can't help noticing that something about her is different. For the first time, she is smiling at them.

'It's Daniel and Natasha,' Jane says as Kimberley catches up.

'Sure. Whatever. Let's go get 'em then, shall we?'

For different reasons, Jane finds she can't meet the eye of Edward or Abi as she greets them. Edward looks tired, even more so than earlier – as though he too has gone through a lot since their conversation that morning in the stairwell. Jane looks at Abi's tiny hands protruding from her long-sleeved dress and imagines them wrapped around the hilt of a dagger. Could she do that?

'Who are we waiting for then?' says Edward, dropping his cigarette and stubbing it out with the toe of one brown brogue. He has an old-fashioned way of dressing that pleases Jane. Looking at him, she can pretend she is in a novel where men wear suits and women wear little hats, where no one has sunburn or tramp stamps or drinks Jägerbombs.

'Well, Laura Lane is just over there, and my editor Frankie Reid isn't here yet.'

'Oh, I met Frankie last night,' says Edward with a smile. 'She has great taste in authors.'

Jane blushes a deep red and starts coughing uncontrollably. 'And,' she says, pretending to glance casually around the lawn, 'I asked Detective Inspector Ramos to join us.' Does she imagine the stillness in the air after those words?

'Well, I can only assume he'll be fabulous at helping us solve the murder mystery,' says Kimberley. 'Which is what we want, correct? To solve the case?'

Abi frowns and looks down at the grass. Kimberley rolls her eyes at Jane, and she feels a thrill at having *the* Kimberley Brown on her side. Are they . . . *friends?*

At the start of this festival, Jane counted herself as having precisely zero friends. Now she thinks about it, she did used to *sort* of have some – there was Hilary whom she worked with in her twenties at Retro Jeans, and Priti her old next door neighbour with the annoying cat. But Jane had worried they were only speaking to her out of a sense of obligation, and eventually they drifted away. Or did she push them? For years, it was really only her mother she felt comfortable with. And after she died, there'd been no one but herself and fictional characters.

But now she seems to be picking them up like fleas on a dog. If fleas were less itchy and more welcome. First Daniel, then

Natasha, now Kimberley. And what of Edward and Detective Inspector Ramos?

'Here they are in all of their glory: our crime-solving team!' Laura Lane walks towards them, waving her bright pink phone around. 'Let's gooooo solve a crime!' She taps the screen, puts it in her pocket, and holds out her hand to Edward. 'Laura Lane. Lovely to meet you.'

Detective Inspector Ramos joins them as they walk inside, falling into step with Jane at the back of the group and muttering under his breath, 'That's the one then? That's *Katie Mack*?'

'The very same,' she whispers back.

While she had been speaking to her friends in the beer tent, Ramos had been making enquiries as to Laura's movements on the night of the festival. He tells Jane that he doesn't have anything new yet, but has people working on it.

'I have more for you,' she breathes, Ramos edging closer as they walk. 'Daniel has found some interesting things in the agency paperwork'

'Oh?'

'Perhaps it's what you've already found out. But money that is owed to authors is disappearing. We also suspect Abi forged a—'

'What are you two talking about?' At five foot tall, Abi Ellis has the unnerving ability to pop up anywhere, entirely unnoticed until she opens her mouth. Now, for example, she is bobbing along at Ramos's elbow, and they have very little idea when she arrived.

'Skimming stones?' tries Detective Inspector Ramos.

'I thought I heard something about forging?'

'I was telling Detective Inspector Ramos how . . . I suspect you will be forging a new path for the Marks Agency. Forging on!' Jane says in a jaunty tone. 'Despite the difficulties in your path! Like . . . like Napoleon Bonaparte.'

Abi looks as though she is about to press them further, but they reach the entrance to the dining hall just in time. The same rat-faced man Jane recognises as the one who locked her and Kimberley in the escape room greets them with a sombre expression.

'Not again,' says Kimberley under her breath.

If he hears it, the comment doesn't faze him. The show must go on.

'Welcome, friends. I am sorry to inform you that something dreadful has happened – there has been a *murder*.'

'Bit crass,' Ramos says in Jane's ear. 'When there has been at least one *actual* murder.'

'But DO NOT FEAR!' yells the rat-faced marketer. 'Lunch is still being served. We ask you one thing only: can you help us *solve the case*?'

'Weren't you on mug shots in the tea room earlier?' Abi says.

'As a member of law enforcement, I perform many duties, ma'am.'

'You run the jail, the dining room, and take mugshots?' Kimberley says with another eye roll in Jane's direction. *You know*, thinks Jane, *I'd say we* are *friends*!

'Times are difficult, ma'am. Cost cutting.'

'Yes, we can help,' says Natasha, because it looks as if Abi is about to keep arguing. 'Can we please be shown to our table?'

Edward has already poured everyone at table nine a glass of wine by the time Frankie bursts into the dining hall ten minutes late, scampering over to them full of apologies. 'Sorry,' she says. 'Medical emergency. My mum . . . had to . . . er . . . rush my brother to hospital.'

'Oh, no!' says Jane. 'Wasn't she having an amputation today?'

'Oh, yeah. Yeah, that was all fine.' Frankie holds out her glass towards Edward. 'Can I have the red, please?'

'Already? I thought the operation would take longer than that?'

Frankie doesn't hear her, despite only being two seats away, and instead starts to ask loudly about the menu. Jane picks up the envelope lying in her place setting. On it, in extravagantly swirly penmanship, is written *Jane Hepburn / Madame de Baguette*.

When everyone has been introduced to each other, and they have sat through a brief introductory talk from the rat-faced marketer about the brutal murder of the butler, whose body has been found in the freezer, Jane suggests they all open their envelopes. A rustling ensues, followed by silence while they digest the characters they've been allocated.

Madame de Baguette is a member of the French aristocracy, in the UK to find a new suitor after the untimely death of husband number six. She has her sights set on the noble Sir Kertoffle, and is planning to use her significant charms to ensnare him.

Jane skims down the clues that her character has spotted: the Reverend whispering with Miss Peekaboo the previous evening, a suspicious yellow substance on Lady Flimflam's shoes at breakfast, and a lipstick smudge on the butler's cheek on the night he was murdered.

To her right, Detective Inspector Ramos is frowning at his piece of paper. He folds it, puts it in his pocket, tears off a strip of his napkin and puts it in the front of his collar. The Reverend. To her left, Laura Lane is uploading a photo of her character sheet to her social media and, next to her, Natasha is growing pale in the face, but gives a stoic nod before folding her own paper and taking a gulp of wine.

As she finishes reading, Kimberley gives a loud 'Ha!', making Abi jump. Jane understands the irony of the moment. They are gathered here to solve a murder – but only half of them know it's *not* that of the butler.

While they enquire about alibis and share clues about this fictional death, this is her chance to find real alibis, real clues to the murder of Carrie Marks, and the attempted murder of Brad Levinsky.

She looks at each face in turn. Is one of the people around this table the one who held the dagger? Which of them does she trust? Her friends Natasha and Daniel, of course, and Detective Inspector Ramos. Kimberley catches her eye and winks. Yes, Jane is satisfied now that she too is innocent. Since their evening conversation in the beer tent, Kimberley seems transformed, as though the weight of her final secret has been lifted from her shoulders. And what of Edward? He looks over and smiles at her. She hopes he is innocent, though still suspects he is holding something back. Frankie is just here to make up the numbers, though she may have information. That leaves two people. Laura Lane and Abigail Ellis. *Which one of you is a cold-blooded killer?*

Abi clears her throat. 'So,' she says in an awkward high-pitched voice, 'Reverend, I must say you are looking, um, very handsome today. I, Miss Peekaboo, have always admired a man of the church.' Detective Inspector Ramos chokes on his wine. 'Though I fear,' Abi continues, 'that the secret you told me last night will soon come out.'

Yes, thinks Jane as she looks at Abi. It's definitely time for the secrets to start coming out.

Chapter Forty-One

Sunday, 2 p.m.

The Killer Lines tea room hasn't exactly been *transformed* from its appearance at breakfast, but a token effort has been made. The mug-shot station has been shoved into a corner, and tables have been spaced out to seat groups of up to ten people. Flickering candles sit in the centre of each table to give the illusion of a dinner party in progress – though they are the battery-powered type from B&Q, which somewhat takes away from the glamour.

The previous year, someone's role-playing had become rather vigorous, resulting in three tables catching fire, a fistfight breaking out, and the lunch being called to a premature halt. It had been quite a to-do at the time, but in retrospect, the worst injuries were a blogger with a black eye and a bookseller who lost her ponytail to the flames, so it was a tame year for Killer Lines – compared to this one at least.

The group at table nine have stumbled through their vol au vent starters, and are tucking into their main courses.

'What the hell is this?' says Kimberley, poking at her plate.

'It's Chicken Kiev,' says Edward apologetically. 'It's a British staple.'

'I know I'm but Edith, the humble maid,' she replies in a monotone, 'but isn't this supposed to be a posh dinner party thrown by Lord and Lady Flipflop?

'*Flimflam,*' snaps Abi, who, to Jane's surprise, has taken to the game with gusto. 'Our gracious hosts, Lord and Lady Flim-flam' – she nods to Daniel and Natasha – 'who have provided

264

this most excellent feast even though the household has been shaken by the murder of their beloved butler.'

Frankie attempts to fill her wine glass, only to find the last bottle dry. She shoots Abi a distrustful look, and waves over the waitress to order another bottle of white.

'We're on to course two,' Laura Lane says into her phone. 'And it's a totally gooooorgeous Chicken Kiev!'

'Can't someone shut her up?' mutters Kimberley, poking at her chicken and recoiling as something green oozes from it.

'Let's get to it, boys and girls,' Laura continues. 'Let's solve this murder!' She winks at the camera and then spins it around to face the table. 'Madame Peekaboo!' she calls dramatically to Frankie, while expertly slicing into her Kiev one-handed. 'It's time I asked you about something I saw last night. You, locked in an embrace with . . . Lord Flimflam.'

'Never!' shouts Abi, loud enough to make the neighbouring table stare. 'My mother would never cavort with a married man. Don't you know she is famously virtuous? She believes in the sanctity of marriage, just as I do, Reverend.' She flutters her eyelashes at a confused-looking Detective Inspector Ramos.

'Um, yeah,' says Frankie. 'Maybe I was comforting him about his dead butler. Did you think of that, um . . .' she squints at Laura's name badge ' . . . Madame Cauldron?'

'You'd think,' says Kimberley, leaning over to address Edward, 'that with all of these writers around, they would be able to come up with something better than this tosh.'

'Wine.' The waitress slams a bottle down on the table.

Laura props her phone against a water glass so she can eat.

'I love my wife!' says Daniel, pointing at Natasha, who gulps at her water, looking awkward. 'Though, yes, I admit, I . . . enjoy the company of Madame Cauldron.'

'Oooooh,' says Laura, to the phone. 'Things are *really* hotting up now!'

'Christ,' Kimberley says under her breath, pouring herself a glass of wine from the bottle and waving to the waitress that they will need more than one.

The presence of Laura's live streaming is not only annoying most people at the table, it is also making Jane's real job – that of solving the murder of Carrie Marks – rather difficult. You can hardly question someone in front of thousands of fans. They are already on to the main course, and she has yet to ask a single question about Carrie, Laura's past, or Abi's role in the agency. In fact, all questions so far have been either wine- or butler-related.

Jane gives Natasha a wide-eyed look of panic. This isn't going to plan.

'Laura,' says Natasha softly, 'I've got an idea. Why not pass the phone around so everyone can record a bit of the lunch from their point of view? Your fans will catch snippets of everyone's conversations that way.'

'You genius! I knew you were cut out for this. Here, you start.' Laura offers the phone to Natasha, who points it half-heartedly in Abi's direction.

With a sigh of relief, Jane turns to Laura.

'Lady Cauldron. An interesting name.'

'As is Madame de Baguette,' Laura says with a smile through a mouthful of Kiev.

'True. Not one I would have chosen myself.'

'Oh, I don't know, it's better than Cauldron. It has a certain . . . delicious quality.' Laura swallows and gives Jane such a genuine smile that she almost retreats. Almost.

'What would you choose, Laura?'

'Sorry?'

'If you could choose your own name. A new identity even. Would you choose Laura Lane?' Laura's smile drops, and a pink tinge comes into her milky white cheeks. 'Or how about . . . Katie? What do you think of that as a name?'

'I – I don't know what you're talking about, Madame de Baguette. But I would like to know more about the suspicious substance you saw on the Butler's shoe on the ni—'

'Laura,' Jane whispers urgently. 'I know your real name is Katie Mack. And I know Carrie knew too. That she confronted you the night she was killed.'

'I – you must be mista—'

'I have proof, Laura. So talk.' Jane flicks her eyes towards Laura's phone, Daniel now using it to film the congealing garlic butter on his plate. 'Before *I* do.'

Across the table, Kimberley is purposely riling Abi by continually forgetting her own character's name. Frankie turns decisively to Edward and starts questioning him awkwardly about his relationship with the fictional butler, though her eyes dart towards Daniel once or twice.

'Okay,' mutters Laura, with a nervous look around the group. 'Okay.'

Laura puts her head in her hands, and Jane gently touches her arm. 'I'm sorry, but you *do* need to tell me about you and Carrie Marks. This is your one chance.'

Eventually, Laura looks up, her face set.

'I've worked for everything I have, Jane. Everything. I grew up in care, moving between foster homes for years. I won't give a sob story, that's not me, but you can probably guess it wasn't the nicest childhood. I caused some trouble as a teenager. Stealing, vandalism, that sort of thing. Small stuff.'

Jane nods but doesn't interrupt as Laura confirms what she already knows. She saw this same moment in Kimberley: the final resignation before the truth comes out.

'You get paid to take a foster kid. Did you know that? A lot of people do it for the money. They take you in, collect their cheque, and ignore you. My therapist told me that's partly why I was acting out. To be seen. But whatever, the reasons don't matter.'

Much as with Kimberley in that escape room, Jane starts to feel unease creep up on her. She has been so desperate to find this killer, so determined. But now, when the moment feels inches away, there is fear. In her novels, the killers are villains. They are men with pure evil in their blackened hearts, ice-veined women who run on cruelty. They aren't people like this. People with hard pasts, sad stories, heartbreaking twists to their tales. People she doesn't want to see in jail, not really. Her hand twitches towards Laura again. *Stop,* she wants to say. *Please stop, before you tell me too much,*

'When I was 15,' Laura continues, 'I was sent to stay with a new family. The Markses.' She sips her wine while Jane slots this new information into place. *Marks* family? 'Mr and Mrs Marks were kind people. Really kind. But by that stage . . . Well, I didn't know how to react to kindness. They were older, and it was easy for me to sneak out at night, drink, get into trouble. They tried their best, but I was a lot to handle.

'As you've probably guessed, Carrie was their daughter. She was an adult and didn't live with them, so I only met her once or twice. I wasn't really interested, then, in being involved in the family. So, yes. That's how I knew Carrie.'

'And the fire?' Jane asks. 'Why did you start the fire?'

Laura's eyes widen as they meet Jane's, the colour disappearing from her cheeks. 'The fire got out of hand. It was supposed to just be the garden shed. I'd thought it would be dramatic, but not that bad, you know? But it spread. Ended up causing quite a bit of damage to their house. And – and their dog didn't make it out.' Her voice cracks, and she is staring at the table, and Jane sees her hands resting there, notices again the flicker of an old burn on the skin. 'God, they were so nice about it. So kind. Their daughter, though . . . Carrie was furious. And I understand why. She reported it to the police, but Mr and Mrs Marks said they didn't want to press charges.

'I'd killed their dog and almost burnt down their house, and they responded with understanding. Everything could have gone from bad to dreadful, with me ending up behind bars. But instead, it ended with a cup of tea and my freedom. For Carrie, that made it all worse. Her parents rallied around me, showed me love. It made Carrie jealous, I think.

'It wasn't long after that that I turned 16 and was able to live alone. The shock of what I'd done, and their reaction, changed everything for me. I turned my life around. I chose a new name, got a job in a café, wrote my books and built up my TikTok channel in the evenings. I wanted to leave my past behind me.'

'But Carrie wouldn't let you?'

'Occasionally I visit Mr and Mrs Marks still. I try to make it up to them by showing them how much I've changed over the years, you know? Show them what they did for me? But Carrie . . . I forgot all about her. That is until I walked into a pitching event around eight years ago. You know the sort. Hopeful authors have five minutes to pitch their novels to literary agents and publishers in front of a roomful of people. We recognised each other at once, and she *tore me apart*.' Laura gives Jane a rueful smile. 'She didn't mention who I was, but she was cruel about my work in front of everyone. After that, I self-published and did very well, eventually finding myself a publisher even without an agent to back me. Carrie has never missed an opportunity to bring me down though.' Laura shrugs. 'Can you blame her, after what I did?'

'She confronted you this weekend, though? Privately?'

Laura frowned. 'Yes. It was strange. A few weeks ago, I had an email from her out of the blue. It didn't acknowledge our past, or that I visit her parents now and again. But she offered to represent me as a literary agent, all cold and professional. You can imagine how confused I was. She *hated* me, *hated* my work. I'm not her biggest fan either, though I understand why she was so mad about the fire. But many years have passed, I'm a new person. I emailed back thanking her, but saying no.'

'And then she approached you here at Killer Lines?'

'She did. She'd emailed me multiple times after that first one, and I stopped replying. I didn't understand what she was playing at. Then she came up to me on Thursday night. Said she was going to tell the world what I'd done if I didn't sign with her agency.

'I said I'd deny that Katie Mack was me, and she said she had some sort of proof. Even so, I didn't understand *why* she wanted to represent me when she clearly hated me.'

Jane does. With her *financial discrepancies*, Carrie needed money, and quickly. The sort of money that signing Laura Lane – and arranging a huge multi-book deal on her behalf – would provide.

'The truth getting out would ruin me. Killed a man? People could forgive that. But killed a *dog*? Never. My fans wouldn't like me lying about my name either. Everything I've built would come crashing down.'

'So what did you do?'

Across the table, Abi is loudly questioning Edward. Jane can sense Natasha on the other side of Laura being unnaturally still, straining to listen in on their conversation. Is she about to hear a confession to Carrie's murder? They sit in silence while the waitress removes their plates.

'Nothing,' Laura finally says. 'Sorry to disappoint you, Jane, but I'm not a killer. New name, new leaf, remember? And I wouldn't hurt Mr and Mrs Marks like that, after all they did for me. I turned Carrie down and went back to the bar. I was panicking, yes. Freaking out. But I'm well practised at putting on a brave face.' She pauses. 'Can I ask you a question now? How did you work out who I really am?'

'A school photo. Your name – your old name – is on it.'

'Ah, I see. I thought Carrie's "evidence" was something like that. I've been trying to get it back. Even tried to get into her hotel room last night, but couldn't manage it. Can I trust you to keep the photo safe? To keep my past a secret?' Laura has tears in her eyes, and her full lower lip wobbles. She looks more like the girl in the photo than ever before.

'If I can trust you were not involved in Carrie's death, you can trust me to keep your secrets.'

'Lady Cauldron!' Abi aims the phone at Laura, her round face once again tomato red. 'You are . . .' She glances at her notes. 'Notoriously rich, and yet you keep your money locked firmly away. I've heard from Edith the maid that the single pair of shoes you brought to the Flimflams' were extremely muddy on the morning after the butler's death.'

Laura blinks back her tears and pastes a grin on her face, lighting up like a true superstar. 'Well, isn't Edith the nosy maid! It's true, I was in the grounds that night.'

'Then I accuse you of murder!' slurs Abi, leaning forward and resting her arm in garlic butter.

Could it be true that Laura just walked away when Carrie was threatening to ruin her? Jane catches Natasha's eye and gives the smallest of shrugs. Either way, she feels significantly closer to understanding what happened that night. A drunken assistant telling Carrie she knew about her dodgy dealings, per- haps making demands in return for her silence. A desperate Carrie begging an old enemy to sign with her and help the agency out of a financial black hole. An angry and confused Laura saying no.

However, it's the final day of the Killer Lines festival, and although they have made strides, this is not enough. It's the final day Jane will be able to speak to those she suspects of being involved in Carrie's death. The final day to catch a killer.

271

She's managed to bring them all together, but they are now two courses down, with the dessert – what looks like a towering Red Velvet cake – already making its way towards their table. And although Jane has a lot to think about, she still doesn't know who put the dagger through Carrie's heart.

Chapter Forty-Two

Sunday, 2.45 p.m.

'You've got cake on you.'

Daniel tries to wipe icing from around his mouth.

'On your forehead,' Jane says.

The cake has been half demolished, and Abi has ordered brandies for everyone, waving a Marks Literary Agency company card over her head. Jane isn't sure about the morality of putting everyone's drinks on the card of a dead woman, but she's relieved it isn't going on hers so stays quiet.

Kimberley, trying to avoid Abi's sloshing glass, suggests everyone move seats for the final part of the lunch, an idea that Jane pounces upon. She has all she needs from Laura Lane, for now.

Happily, she finds herself sandwiched between Edward and Kimberley, though she had been hoping to question Abi on the business while she is substantially under the influence. She raises her eyebrows at Daniel, who has the pleasure of sitting next to the woman who is now his boss. They'll have to rely on him to extract the information they need. Is he up to it? Daniel visibly steels himself, and gives her a determined nod. Of course he's up to it.

'So, Ramos,' says Kimberley loudly. Though her voice is crystal clear, the wine seems to have increased her natural swagger.

Abi frowns. 'That's the Rever—'

'How are you getting on,' Kimberley cuts across her, 'with the murder of my friend Carrie Marks?'

The table falls silent, save for a quiet hiccup from Abi. Next to her, Daniel freezes with a forkful of red velvet cake already halfway to his mouth.

'Well,' says Detective Inspector Ramos, 'I'm not supposed to discuss open investigations.' Kimberley sips her brandy. The tense silence stretches. 'Unless it's the investigation into the fictional murder of a butler.'

'Ha!' Kimberley downs her brandy and waves the glass at the waitress. Jane is aware that the Killer Line awards ceremony is taking place later in the evening, and is a little concerned at the state of half the people around table nine.

'How are you finding things, Madame de Baguette?' Edward is speaking in a low voice, so as not to involve the rest of the table, for which Jane finds she is grateful.

'Well, it's been quite . . . intense, hasn't it?'

'I've heard from multiple people that you plan to seduce me.'

Jane feels heat flood her face. 'What? I – I mean—'

'Edith the maid said she heard you saying as much to . . . Lord Flopsy or something.'

In a rush, she remembers the instructions on her character sheet. 'Oh! Yes. Yes, that's true. I quite forgot about that.' Jane laughs nervously, sipping at her brandy to fill the pause.

'You know, Jane, I try to get out of this lunch every year. And every year, somehow, I fail.'

Relieved to be talking as herself for a change, she smiles at him. 'You have me to blame for that this time, I'm afraid. I did wonder if you were trying to get out of it.'

'To be honest with you, when you asked if I was free, I thought you were asking me to lunch with you. As in, on a date.'

'Oh, I, um, did you?' All of a sudden, Jane's tongue is too big for her mouth. She doesn't know what to do with the hand not holding her glass, so she puts it on her lap out of sight.

'Which is why I said I was free.'

The last man (apart from a drunk on a bus who unbuttoned his flies while drooling in her direction) who made advances to Jane was her ex-boss. Edward doesn't seem at all like Stefan. Nor does he appear to be drooling or unbuttoning his flies. He seems kind, intelligent, and gentle. He loves books. Stefan never read books; he was more of a podcast man, and dreamt of having his own show one day.

Jane casts her mind around wildly for something to say, but, despite being someone who lives in words so frequently, can't find a single one.

'Enough brandy for me,' says Edward. 'I'm getting a coffee. You want one?'

'Flat white, please.'

As Edward is waving down the waitress to order their coffees, Jane catches her breath. She mustn't get distracted when she has work to do. But maybe when all of this is over, she can think about going on a date with Edward. Maybe she'll even ask *him*. *It's a brave new world*, she fancies her mother saying. *Maybe you can teach an old dog new tricks.*

Shaking herself, Jane surveys the scene. Abi is leaning on Daniel's shoulder, her eyes half closed. Detective Inspector Ramos is laughing at something Kimberley has said. Laura, a little paler than usual but with that professional smile fixed in place, is talking into her phone camera. Frankie and Natasha, on the other side of Edward, are discussing Natasha's novel. Red cake crumbs dot the white tablecloth, which is also splotched with flowers of red wine. It would look sinister, if not for the smears of garlic butter.

The door to the dining room opens, and Natasha's publicist Sarah slips into the room. She casts her eyes around, and they land on table nine.

'Coffees coming up,' says Edward. 'You and Laura Lane looked deep in conversation over there. What had you so interested?'

Only half listening, Jane is watching Sarah walk towards their table. She remembers the argument between the publicist and Edward that she witnessed on the very first day of the festival and wonders if Sarah is here to confront him once more.

'Jane?' asks Edward. 'Was it about your own future as a social media star?'

'The past actually,' she says, distracted. Edward is facing away from the entrance, and hasn't yet seen Sarah's approach. Arriving at their table, she leans down and whispers something in Frankie's ear that makes her smile into her brandy. Before leaving the room, Sarah glances up at Edward, and then shoots a quick look at Jane, the viciousness of which makes her flinch. How curious. Edward, she notices, has slung his arm over the back of her chair. 'Sorry. Anyway, tell me, how did you meet Carrie? You said you were friends a long time?'

'We were, yes. Met her when I was a teenager. Her parents used to foster children, and they met mine in the foster parents' community.' He raises his glass and taps it against his chest to signal himself. 'Mine adopted me along the way. Carrie was older than me, but our parents were friends, and over the years we became friends too. Of a sort. More like siblings in many ways.'

Promises had been made to keep secrets wherever possible, but the clock is ticking on this case. Time to take some risks.

'So, you knew Laura too back then?' Jane holds her breath. It is a leap, but not a wild one.

He appraises her, the permanent line between his eyebrows deepening. 'No, I didn't know Laura. This is the first time I've met her. I told you – Carrie never told me much about their connection, but you seem to know more?' He pulls a packet of cigarettes from his pocket and taps it absently on the table.

The screeching of chair legs against floorboards announces Abi getting to her feet. At full height, she is as tall as Jane and

Edward sitting down, but the fact that she is standing is made obvious by her dangerous swaying. Daniel holds her shoulder.

'Everyone! We have all . . . detected. Done our detecting,' she begins, stopping to quietly belch and then hiccup. 'And now we must reveal the killer!'

'I bet the authors have got this,' says Ramos with a genial smile, straightening his napkin dog collar. 'I don't usually detect after so much alcohol.'

'Yes!' screeches Abi, pointing at him and making half the tea room spin round in their seats to stare. 'Okay, authors, you go round and guess the killer!' She lands back in her chair with an audible *flump*.

'Um, I'm not sure,' says Natasha. 'Maybe Edith the maid, because the butler knew she was stealing from the Flimflams?'

'Okkaaaay, everyone at home!' Laura trills into her phone. 'Who do *you* think killed the butler? Put it in the Comments! I'm going to say . . . the Reverend! You heard me! Oh, I can see some of you disagree, but remember, you've heard more of the secrets than I have! Or maybe you are just too clever.' She winks at the camera, then spins it around to show the table again.

'Next author!' screeches Abi, pointing at Jane.

Jane, who has barely been paying attention to the game throughout their lunch, has no idea. But she can feel the things she *does* know, about the *real* murder investigation, colliding in her mind. She has also realised that getting everyone together here was a dreadful idea, and it's time to end this.

Abi's eyes are still on her. 'Yes, I think Edith the maid as well. Same reasons as Natasha.'

'Next author!' yells Abi.

'Abi!' says Jane, getting to her feet, her impressive height silencing the table at last. 'There are no more authors. Let's just . . . let's just end this now.'

'What about Edward?' Abi says, swaying. 'Edward's an author.'

'He's a *critic*.'

'He wrote a book,' Abi insists. 'About his wife. Heard Carrie
– *hic!* – talking to him 'bout it.'

Everyone's eyes turn to Edward, who is shredding his napkin
into tiny pieces.

'His *wife*?' Daniel says, now holding Abi up straight on her
chair, eyes darting to Jane. Her heart skips a beat, and she feels
Chicken Kiev and red velvet cake fighting in her stomach.

'It's called, like, *Early Spring* or something – *hic!* – like that.'

'*The First Spring*?' Daniel asks. 'It was in Carrie's room,' he
says to Jane. 'The manuscript. In her suitcase.' Jane remembers
him sitting on the floor in the hotel, turning through a chunky
manuscript he didn't recognise.

'Was it you?' says Kimberley Brown, whose face has turned
as hard and white as marble. 'Brad heard Carrie that night,
arguing with someone in the darkness about a book. A man.
Was it you?'

Everyone is staring at Edward now, his spindly fingers reducing
the last fragments of napkin to snowflakes. Why hadn't he
told them he had *argued* with Carrie? Or that he'd written a
book he was presumably hoping she'd represent? Jane thinks of
the dagger above the door of the Dog and Bone. Abi or Laura
would never have been able to reach it without a stepladder.
But Edward . . .

Next to her, Edward Carter opens his packet of Silk Cut,
drawing one from the box and getting to his feet.

'My *deceased* wife. I wrote a novel inspired by my deceased
wife, yes. And now, if you'll excuse me, I'm going for a cigarette.'

'What brand are those?' Detective Inspector Ramos mirrors
Edward, pushing his chair back and rising to his feet. He leans
forward and takes the cigarette box from the table. 'A cigarette
stub was found in the book tent that morning. Silk Cut.'

That must be the physical evidence that Ramos mentioned,
thinks Jane. *If only he'd told her what it was, she would have*

known exactly where to point him. The roiling in her stomach increases.

Kimberley Brown stands too, the deep blue velvet of her suit catching the light. How has Edward not turned to stone under her Medusa glare? Jane has been scared by Kimberley Brown every time they've met, but she has never seen her more powerful, more terrifying, more full of fury than she is now, as she stares across at the man who murdered her lover.

'I believe I was the second to last to see Carrie that night,' she says. 'I left her in the book tent. I – I shouted at her. I made her cry. And then I left her there, waiting for her killer.'

Kimberley's voice is hard and cold. There is no trace of the vulnerability she had shown in the escape room or the beer tent. 'When I left, I saw something outside the tent. I didn't think much of it at the time, thought it was a firefly, or a phone torch. But it was a cigarette tip, glowing in the dark. You were there.'

Edward's skin has turned grey, and he shakes his head slowly, mute. The whole *room* is mute. Every chair at every table angled their way

'You argued with Carrie about your book,' Kimberley continues. 'and you left her, but you couldn't let it go. So you went back to find her. You were waiting outside that tent, you went in after me. And you killed her.'

'Is it because,' Abi rasps in an attempted stage whisper, 'she said your book was – *hic!* – rubbish?'

'Edward Carter,' Detective Inspector Ramos says, walking around the table, 'you are under arrest for the murder of Carrie Marks.'

Chapter Forty-Three

Sunday, 4 p.m.

Frankie Reid is watching *Homes Under the Hammer*. After everything imploded at lunch and Edward Carter was arrested, she didn't know quite what to do next. There are lots of things she *should* be doing. She should be finally logging in to her emails and answering her boss's voice notes. She should be finishing the edit that was due last Wednesday. She should be figuring out what's going to happen with her career now. She should be finding a plumber to fix the boiler. And she should be telling the police everything she knows.

That's too much to do all at once though, so instead, she has snuck back to her hotel room, got under the covers, and turned on *Homes Under the Hammer*. A nauseatingly smug couple are slowly being broken down by their money pit of an investment home which, ironically, is also being broken down. It's nice to think about other people's problems. She'll deal with her own after this finishes. Maybe.

The duvet cover is scratchy and an ugly shade of beige. Her first visit to Hoslewit had been as Carrie's assistant, and they'd stayed at the Thistle. Eagle Wing Books can't afford the Thistle, with its fancy coffee, and mini bars in the rooms with miniature bottles of champagne. All her room in the Traveller offers is a plastic kettle, a teabag and sachets of long-life milk. Not even a free shortbread biscuit.

At least there is a television. '*With property,*' the presenter is saying, '*every day is a school day! The best way to start is by doing your homework!*'

Frankie sinks further under the covers until just the top half of her face is showing above the blanket. There is a chance her flatmate has sorted out the broken boiler, but it's a small one. How will they pay for it? she wonders. Perhaps if she gives the plumber a sob story, he'll reduce the bill.

'*Oh, some serious cracking in the plaster here, Bill. That's something to ponder on.*'

Is she foolish to believe this scheme she's embarked on with Sarah Parks-Ward could be her ticket out of here? Out of being overworked and underpaid, out of being embarrassed about her job. Out of the Traveller. Everything feels balanced on a knife edge, and she has no idea which way it will fall.

'*But we could be quids in! Let's find out, when we go under the hammer!*'

It's not long before the jaunty theme tune of *Homes Under the Hammer* draws the show to a close, and the screen flicks to an advert for herbal constipation medication. Up next is *Bargain Hunt*. Frankie can settle in here for the rest of the afternoon, miss the final Killer Lines dinner, and pretend the outside world doesn't exist. That would be ideal. Who says she even needs to go back to work ever again? She is done.

Poor old Jane Hepburn. She's lost her agent, her editor is planning on going off-grid, and her face when Edward Carter was arrested implied she'd lost something in him too. Frankie feels guilty about Jane. She could have been so much more successful, if Frankie had had the time and the energy and the passion. Perhaps Jane will be better off without her.

She remembers reading her work when she was the assistant at the Marks Literary Agency. She was one of the authors Carrie had signed right at the start, when the agency was new and needed clients, stat. Carrie had been dismissive of what she called *old-fashioned detective stuff*, but Frankie had seen something in the way Jane created tension and crafted sentences.

281

When she'd got her job at Eagle Wing, she'd signed her as an author.

Where had that passion gone? The drive that had led her to see potential buried under lack of experience? Sucked dry by meetings and electricity bills, by too-small budgets at home and at work.

Frankie finds her iPhone deep within the bed, takes a breath and opens her email. Quickly flicking past the ones she's been ignoring for days, she finds one from Jane, sent a few months previously. Opening the attachment, she starts to read Sandra Baker Book Seven, tentatively titled *Death of Last Hope*.

Chapter Forty-Four

Sunday, 4 p.m.

Jane sure can pick 'em. To think, she'd been planning on going on a *date* with this man once the murder investigation was wrapped up. Looks like the date will have to wait 20 years or so, 15 if he stays polite to the guards.

After Edward's arrest, the tea room had burst into rapturous applause. It sparked quite a trend, and as table nine filed out, each of the other tables started dramatically 'arresting' *their* top suspects, clearly believing this exit was all part of the game.

Now most of table nine is muttering amongst themselves excitedly on the lawn, but Jane is standing slightly apart, staring out over the hills. After the drink and the buzz of the tea room, the bright daylight feels wrong. It feels as though it should be the middle of the night.

Natasha and Daniel are talking to each other, heads close, words rushing like rapids. Jane can't make out what they're saying, and feels oddly outside of the group, of herself, of the world. Abi is leaning back against the wall, bleary-eyed, while Laura tries to make her drink coffee. Frankie slipped away straight after the lunch, and Jane, discreetly, decides to follow suit.

One person sees her go though. On her way down the hill, marching towards the churchyard, Jane hears Kimberley Brown call her name.

'I'm heading back to my room,' Jane calls over her shoulder. 'Our work here is done! Thank you for coming to lunch. You were instrumental in catching our man.' She is speaking in a chirpy, upbeat tone, but doesn't stop walking. With a start, she recognises her voice from the days after her mother's death. *All good! Let's get cracking on those team expenses, shall we!*

The halt of the click-clacking heels tells her that Kimberley has stopped following, but she calls down the hill after her.

'I just wanted to say, I'm sorry. I know what it's like when people you care about . . . aren't who you thought they were.'

Jane feels a lump in her throat, and raises a hand in farewell.

She wants to be back in her room, tucked into her single bed with Disney princesses dancing across the duvet cover – or better yet, at home, curled up on her too-small sofa. She wants to forget the pride she'd felt when Edward had mentioned a date, and the warm flush when he'd told her he liked her dress. Now she is once again desperate to change out of it, even if she has to cut it off with shears. She wants to forget the cold, pale body of Carrie Marks on the floor of the book tent, the Killer Lines dagger plunged into her heart. Jane's unenthusiastic agent. Laura's blackmailer. Kimberley's lover. Abi's tormentor. Edward's oldest friend.A woman Jane knew, but not really. About whom she has heard so many conflicting opinions and stories that it makes her head whirl.

Why is Jane involved in this in the first place? Who is Jane Hepburn, after all? Just a failed author and an average admin assistant. Why would she, over anyone else, be able to catch a killer?

Vaguely, she remembers Daniel on the West Barning train platform. *You should solve this.* Baker *should solve this.* Jane had thought that if she solved the case, the publicity might push her and her books into the limelight. A stupid idea, and far beyond her capabilities. Edward Carter was never even on her list, and now he is unmasked, she feels nothing but sadness and confusion. Daniel was wrong, and Jane is too tall and broad, too clumsy and shy, to be the glamorous PI Sandra Baker. Natasha was wrong too. Jane truly is stupid, and hideous, and a fool.

She passes the charity shop, the mannequin in the window now dressed in a yellow poncho and white pedal pushers to replace the dress Jane robbed it of this morning. Such a long time ago that seems now.

How could she have missed the clues that Edward was a killer? He had told her he'd left the pub around 10 and this was reflected in Laura's TikTok videos. But they had never got around to confirming the time of his return to his hotel. She remembers the cigarette butts under the tree near the book tent – had he argued about his book with Carrie there, cigarette in hand, just before Brad caused her to slip?

With a start, she remembers more butts under the table in the beer tent, the one they had managed to sneak into so easily when it was supposedly closed. Had he sat in there after the argument, avoiding the party inside and the rain without? Had he smoked cigarette after cigarette, stewing on his oldest friend's rejection of his manuscript? Had he stepped outside when the rain stopped, and seen Kimberley leave the book tent, Carrie standing in the doorway alone? She said as much to Detective Inspector Ramos right back when she found the body, but now she can hardly believe it to be true. Has murder really been sparked by a *book*?

Writing is a game of rejection. Rejection from agents, and editors, and reviewers and readers. Over and over again. You get past one hurdle, and you are rejected at the next. You think you've got through the gauntlet, and then you'll see your reviews on Amazon. *What a load of tosh!* one will say; *How did this rubbish ever get published? One star.* Or even: *I hate crime fiction. One star.* Once she got: *Haven't read this yet. One star.*

Jane is inundated with rejection and knows the burning shame and sorrow of it. Had Edward felt this same anger and embarrassment and disappointment rise up in him that night?

With a heavy feeling in her stomach, Jane remembers Abi's words: *She ignores the dead horses. We may be looking to trim*

285

E.C. NEVIN

down the client list. She might not be ahead, but she knows when it's time to quit. *Death of Last Hope* will be Jane's final novel. She has quite lost her appetite for this world of words.

Walking past the little church, her footsteps grow heavier and slower. The thought of the final stretch to Mary's Air BnB is exhausting. With a sigh, she pushes open the metal gate and enters the graveyard. The stained-glass window of the church looks down on her, and she can't tell if it's offering protection or judgment.

The door is a dark, heavy wood, with ancient metal studs, the handle a ring of twisted iron on a simple latch. To Jane's surprise, it's unlocked. It is, she realises, Sunday.

A service must have finished earlier, because hymn books lie scattered on the pews where people had been facing the altar, praying for salvation. Does Edward pray? Did Carrie?

Jane has never been a religious person, but the chill of the ancient stone and the incense-heavy silence still imbues her with a sense of reverence, so she drops down into a pew.

Her mother's funeral had been held in the local church, though it had been built in the seventies and so felt more like a location for an HR procedure than a passage to the beyond. Jane had been in the front row. Behind her sat their neighbours Edina and Giles, Mr Collins from the newsagent's, and her mother's bridge club – Patricia, Elizabeth and Jeremiah. After the service, Jane had served everyone sandwiches and tea in the living room. The gathering had been quiet, and small, and very, very sad. She had never felt so alone as when the last person left that day.

What would her mother say if she was here now? *I may be sleeping with the fishes, my dear, but you are alive and kicking. You said you were going to solve a murder, so why are you sitting here with a face like a wet weekend?*

'It's been solved!' Jane says into the empty chapel. 'It was ... it was Edward. He killed Carrie Marks when she

286

wouldn't represent his novel. Perhaps she said some horrible things about it and he lost control, I don't know.' Jane thinks of her latest manuscript. Her mother died not long before she started on it. It had been her companion through grief, and loneliness and fear. She'd put a lot of herself into this book, more than she ever had before. 'Part of me understands,' she tells the empty aisle. 'His book was about the death of his wife. If Carrie was cruel about it, and I've learnt enough about her to know she could be cruel, then he may have seen red. Grief can do funny things to a person.'

Just look at her, after all. Grief had turned her from a social recluse to an actual hermit, then to a two-bit detective running around a Cumbrian village solving murders.

Well, she hears her mother say in her head, *that last bit doesn't sound too bad.*

'No. It hasn't been too bad.' She thinks of Daniel's contagious grin, Natasha's kindly logic.

With a sickening swoop in her stomach, she remembers how they had huddled under the willow tree, suddenly so certain they'd found their killer, on the night Brad fell. First Carrie, then Brad, who was pushed over the banister and down the stairwell. Edward must have been worried Brad saw him the night he killed Carrie, and decided to silence him for good. With a shiver, Jane remembers seeing Brad's body on the concrete floor, blood pooling around him.

It had been just after she'd questioned Kimberley in the escape room, and she'd bumped into Daniel on the way to meet them under the tree.

With a start, she looks up at the altar. Her hands grip the wood of her seat as she visualises that night. She and Daniel had walked from the Dog, chattering excitedly, when Edward had called out to her. She'd said a quick hello, but when she'd reached Natasha, under that tree, she'd looked back over at the pub. Jane closes her eyes tight, trying to see everything as clearly as possible. Natasha had been distracted, then demanded a phone. Jane scrunches her eyes even tighter shut – and then, yes! The glow of a cigarette across the lawn, the tall outline of Edward Carter behind it. Just before a scream tore apart the night.

If Edward was outside when Brad was pushed, he is innocent of at least one crime. And if innocent of that . . .

When Jane reaches the festival, clutching a stitch in her side, she is taken aback by the change. She has been gone longer than she realises and the lawn is filling up for the evening ahead; everyone appears to be dressed in their best outfits. Of course, it's almost time for the festival highlight – the Killer Lines awards ceremony and the presentation of the coveted Killer Lines Dagger. Hopefully, they've cleaned Carrie's blood from it by now.

Under the willow tree, she can see her friends waiting for her. Good, they got her message. As she gets closer, Daniel steps towards her and envelops her in a hug that makes tears spring to her eyes.

'Are you okay?' Natasha asks, suddenly at her elbow. 'You vanished. Thank God you're back. We didn't know what to do without you.'

'I—' Jane begins, falters, taking a deep breath. 'I just needed some time.'

'Well, we did it, Baker,' Daniel says, flashing his trademark grin. 'Culprit unmasked.'

'Actually,' Natasha adds, 'it was more that his mask fell off, wasn't it? Though we *did* bring everyone together. So that helped.'

'Whatever,' Daniel says with a roll of his eyes. 'The gig is up. Now we just need to see you win an award tonight, Nat. Aren't you up for Best Newcomer?'

If Edward *isn't* the killer, what then? Surely the police will discover it in due course, and he'll be released. They'll find the real culprit eventually. In Jane's sixth book, *Killing Time*, the police catch the wrong man and the killer walks free into the night. Until Baker discovers the truth, of course.

'We don't know I'm going to win. I'm only nominated.'

'Jane,' says Daniel, clicking his fingers in front of her face. 'Stop staring into the distance like some sort of oracle. There's an awards ceremony to look good at. You're a crime writer, and you need to be there. Luckily you already have your Baker dress on.'

'It's not Edward,' she says in little more than a whisper.

'What?' says Daniel.

'Edward was outside when Brad fell. I saw him. This means someone *else* pushed Brad down the stairs. And why would someone do that unless they wanted to stop him talking? Edward kept things from us, but . . . I don't think he is Carrie's killer. I need to speak to Detective Inspector Ramos.'

Natasha opens her mouth, but no words come out. Daniel frowns, slowly shaking his head.

'Jane!' The shout comes from across the lawn, though she's not sure from where. Then, through the crowd, comes her editor Frankie Reid. 'Jane,' she calls again, panting slightly. She is wearing a silver dress that skims her ankles and chunky pink heels with scuffed toes. Striking as ever, she looks dishevelled, as though she has rushed out of the door half-ready. '*Death of Last Hope*. It's *marvellous*.'

Frankie talks in a rush, brushing her fingers through the tightly coiled hair that stands in a halo around her face as she speaks. 'I'm only a third in, but I already know it's your best yet. *Honestly* this time. And I have thoughts on how to make it even better.'

It's been a long time since Jane heard anyone speak about her work with enthusiasm or vision, but after everything that's happened over the last few days, it feels like too little, too late. She has already made her decision.

'Frankie,' she says, cutting off the editor mid-flow. 'I've decided to change the ending of that book. I'm going – I'm going to kill off Sandra Baker. *Death of Last Hope* is her final outing.' Behind her, Daniel gasps and Natasha emits a small squeak.

'I couldn't agree more,' says Frankie with a grin.

'Hey now,' Daniel, Baker's biggest fan, says, stepping forward.

'Jane, Sandra Baker is wonderful,' says Frankie, holding up her hand to fend off an approaching Natasha. 'But the series has run its course. It was only ever going to work to a certain level because people don't connect with your protagonist. I always knew you could be bigger. And it came to me, in my hotel room just now, what's missing – Baker's flaws. She isn't real enough, Jane.' Frankie pulls a pair of square-cut pink earrings from her bag and puts them on while she talks. 'She isn't real. She's *perfect*. She's smarter than anyone else in the room. She's beautiful. She's super slim, yet eats like a horse and drinks like a fish and is *never* on a diet. Her hair is glossy and never frizzes.' Frankie pulls a lipstick out of her bag and, somehow, applies it while still speaking. 'She runs in heels and her feet never hurt. She never spills her drink. She never has her heart broken.

'Kill off Baker. This book is great, so you'll end the series with a bang. And then you start again. It's not just you, Jane. This industry is deeply flawed and unfair. Some people sink and some people swim, and it's not always the ones who deserve it. But you have to keep trying. With your *incredible* way with words, create a new character for a new series, someone brilliant and clever and beautiful and deeply flawed. And then call me. People like Baker don't exist, Jane. *That's* why people don't connect with her. People like *us* exist. People like *you*.'

'But no one will want to read about someone like me!'

'Why!?' shouts Natasha. 'You're *amazing*.'

Jane looks around at the small group under the willow tree. Her heart feels full and her eyes are brimming with tears. Did her editor really just say she had an *incredible way with words*? Did Natasha call her *amazing*?

'I hate to interrupt,' says Daniel, 'but Jane thinks Edward Carter didn't put Brad in hospital *or* kill Carrie Marks, which is good enough for me. And we're running out of time to discover who did.'

Chapter Forty-Five

Sunday, 6.40 p.m.

The awards ceremony is due to start in the tea room in 20 minutes, so the group has a lot of work to do, fast. At a corner table in the bar of the Dog and Bone, Jane sits with Daniel on one side of her, Natasha on the other. Also around the table are Kimberley, Frankie and Laura.

It is remarkable, thinks Jane, how her social circle is growing and growing. She remembers the feeling of travelling back to Killer Lines with Daniel at her side and how much more powerful he had made her feel. Now, with these five people in her corner, she is invincible.

When Jane finishes telling the group her reasons for believing Edward is innocent, she puts two extra-strong mints in her mouth to suck anxiously. Kimberley, Laura and Frankie are stony-faced.

'You're sure?' says Kimberley. She appears outwardly calm, but is gouging chunks of wood from the table with one fingernail.

'I'm sure,' says Jane. And she is. The more she's thought about it, the more certain she is that Edward is not the killer. He was not in the stairwell with Brad when he fell, and there is still too much that doesn't add up, like the book that Carrie pulled from the table in her dying moments.

'That could have been a coincidence,' says Laura, reasonably, and Jane agrees.

'Abi's movements are unaccounted for that night, and the book most likely points to her,' says Natasha. 'Daniel, do you want to tell everyone what you found?'

He nods, taking the reins. 'Going through Marks Agency paperwork, I found financial discrepancies,' he says with the confidence of a world-weary DI. 'The agency was in trouble, and Carrie had been stealing money from clients to plug the gaps. Skimming money off royalties, in some cases not even reporting foreign deals that had come in but just keeping the money herself.'

Kimberley tilts her head to the side in thought. 'I wonder if Martin – that's my ex-husband – called in the loan. It was always the plan she should repay it after ten years. The date's coming up soon.'

'*That's* why she was so desperate to sign me,' says Laura.

'I think this is what they really argued about on Thursday night,' says Jane. 'Apparently Carrie told Abi off for being drunk, but it escalated. What if Abi responded by telling Carrie that she'd found out about the missing money?'

'While we were waiting for you guys, I've been back through the paperwork I emailed to myself.' Daniel pulls a laptop from his rucksack and opens it, clicking while he speaks. 'The document stating that Carrie left the company in the hands of Abi Ellis in the event of her death was in there.'

Kimberley snorts. 'No way would Carrie leave her precious company to that little idiot.'

Daniel spins the laptop around and everyone skim-reads the document on screen.

'Well,' he says, clicking through to the document's properties, 'it looks like you're right. Abi isn't brilliant with computers. She obviously didn't realise that if you check here' – he clicks on a dropdown menu, and through to Properties – 'it will show you when the document was created. In this case, two days *after* Carrie's death.'

'So, what are you saying?' asks Laura, frowning. 'That Abi murdered Carrie to take over the company? And a failing company at that? This' – she waves at the screen – 'doesn't seem like much forethought.'

Jane leans forward. 'No, I don't think she *would* expect an unwitnessed Word document to go unchallenged in a court of law. I think Abi created this document after Carrie's death as a way to gain some immediate legitimacy while she convinced Carrie's authors to trust her. She didn't want Carrie's *company* but she did want her big-name clients.'

'Strip the troubled agency of clients and stand aside before she's tarnished by association,' Frankie says slowly. 'All of the advantages, none of the legal fall out. Clever.'

'She was desperate to build a relationship with me,' says Natasha with a self-deprecating shrug. 'I think you're right, Jane; she's planning to start her own agency, then leave the sinking, debt-ridden ship of the Carrie Marks Literary Agency behind her.'

'That's all well and good,' says Kimberley. 'But did she kill Carrie?'

The group falls silent.

'I've been rewatching the videos from that night on Laura's TikTok channel,' offers Natasha. 'It's not much, but Abi was here in the bar until quite late.'

'Oh!' says Laura. 'Would it be helpful to see more from the night? I only upload a fraction of the footage I capture.'

Jane's heart leaps. Why didn't she think of this sooner? Every time she sees Laura, she has her phone in her hand, and yet there is only about six minutes of footage uploaded to her channel each day.

Everyone shuffles around the wooden corner bench until they are uncomfortably close together. Laura scrolls back through her gallery.

'Let's start here, shall we? This is around 10 p.m.' They watch blurry footage of the Dog and Bone. Jane finds the experience of sitting in the booth, the light failing outside, watching the same room on the tiny screen, quite uncanny, as though she is time travelling. There is Edward, leaning on the bar, there is Brad talking at him, and Abi sitting at a table. Laura's face bursts into view to kiss at the screen, and then it goes black. 'Okay, next.'

Laura scrolls through videos until she finds one taken at midnight. Similar scenes of late-night revelry come to life in front of them, though the numbers in the room have shrunk.

'Wait,' Natasha says. 'Rewind it.' Laura does, and Natasha reaches out to pause the footage at the right moment. 'Look who it is.'

Jane follows Natasha's finger, and her heart sinks. In the very corner of the screen, she can see a stubby leg sticking out of a familiar floral dress. Laura slows down the speed, and plays the video from the start. There is no doubt about it. Abi Ellis is passed out in the corner of the pub. Jane puts her head in her hands, and Laura slams her phone on the table.

'We should have known,' says Natasha. 'We keep forgetting the dagger. Abi would never have been able to reach it.'

'I'm going to get us all a drink before we have to go through to the awards,' Laura announces. 'Jane, will you double-check a few more of the videos? Try and find that same spot, we need to know how long she was asleep in that corner for.'

Daniel and Frankie offer to help with the drinks, and a dejected Kimberley goes to refresh her makeup in the bathroom, taking Natasha with her ('What if you win? You can't collect an award with no lipstick on'). Alone, Jane scans through the videos, catching glimpses of Abi numerous times. Unless she sprang up unobserved, went and murdered her boss, then came and passed out in exactly the same spot and position, it appears impossible that Abi is the killer. Jane watches one of the earlier videos again, eyes drawn to Edward standing at the bar with Brad. Natasha's scary publicist, Sarah, is watching them intently while sipping her glass of wine. Abi is still upright at this stage.

Jane rubs her temples. What is she missing?

295

With a sigh, she puts down the phone, pulls Daniel's open laptop towards her, and starts to click through the documents he had emailed to himself from Carrie's computer. One titled CLIENT LIST catches her eye, and she remembers the moment in the beer tent when Daniel whipped his phone from her hands. A nervous glance at the bar tells her the group are stuck in a queue of excited punters getting their last drinks in before the ceremony begins. With a deep breath, Jane opens the document.

An Excel document shows a list of names, many of whom Jane recognises. But Carrie's client list is not, as expected, in alphabetical order. Natasha Martez is in fifth place, under a well-known romance author called Sabrina Roberts. Sabrina, Natasha, and the others near the top of the list all have a number one next to their names. Scrolling down, Jane sees slightly less well-known names with a number two beside them. Lower still, there are fewer known names, with a number three.

'Ah,' Jane says to herself. 'It's in *priority* order.' Deciding to bite the bullet, she types her own name into the search bar, and the page whizzes down, down, down. There she is: *Jane Hepburn* and a number eight. Unlike the earlier groups of authors, category eight names are in red, and there's an extra column. Some names are flagged as *To Go*, and others, like Jane's, have a question mark instead. It hurts to see her name in red, but there is slight solace to take from that question mark. Her fate still, *just*, undecided.

Jane is about to click out of the document when she notices, at the bottom of the page, two more tabs titled PROSPECTIVE and PARTED. Over at the bar, Daniel is waving at the exhausted, bird-faced barman, leaning so far forward that his feet come off the ground. Jane opens the Prospective tab.

Another list of names appears, each with notes detailing the date the submission was received, what the book is about and Carrie's thoughts. These must be new authors Carrie was considering signing as clients. Jane recognises only one name.

Edward Carter is listed with an asterisk beside his name. His note is far shorter than the others, simply reading: *'Needs editing, has no real hook. But it's Ed's so will make it work!'*

She remembers Edward's words at dinner: *more like siblings in many ways.* Carrie may have offended Edward by suggesting his book needed work, but she'd been willing to take him on. Even though she'd needed to focus on saving her business, she was prepared to help her old friend.

Jane moves to the third tab: PARTED. These names, like the category eights, are in red, and a separate column proclaims each of them TERMINATED. A little dramatic, Carrie, she thinks. You're hardly James Bond.

There aren't many names on the list and even fewer Jane recognises. Maybe Carrie never managed to get them a book deal at all, or perhaps they haven't produced work in a very, very long time. Vaguely, she has a memory that *Arthur Kellaway* wrote a book about a talking typewriter.

One name, though, definitely *does* ring a bell. In fact, it rings a lot of bells. A Notre-Dame's worth of bells is pealing, crashing, ringing in Jane's mind.

Slowly, as though it's all happening in outer space, she slides Laura's phone towards her, still open on her videos. She replays the one she'd last watched, focussing on the exchange at the bar between Edward and Brad. And Sarah Parks-Ward watching it keenly.

Jane moves to the previous video, locates Edward – and, yes! There Sarah is again, watching him intently from a few feet away. And on the one before that. Frowning, Jane rewatches the videos from around the time of Carrie's death. Snatches of Abi are occasionally visible in the corner, Edward is absent, Sarah too. Had she gone to bed, or was she watching Edward while he argued with Carrie outside?

Six wine glasses appear in front of her, and Frankie slides into the booth, followed by Laura and Daniel.

'Any joy?' Laura asks, gesturing towards her phone. 'Did Abi move from her chair at all?'

Jane shakes her head. 'No, she was in the bar the entire time.'

Daniel gives her arm an affectionate squeeze. 'We've done good, though, Baker. It's not our fault time's run out.'

'Here we go,' Frankie says, pouring out the wine. 'We better hurry, we have to go through in a second.'

Natasha – looking even more racoon-like but surprisingly glamorous with mascara coating her lashes, and her lips painted a glossy maroon – takes a glass as she sits, a breath-taking Kimberley following. Jane continues flicking back through the videos, every time she spots Edward, finding Sarah nearby. Picking up her own phone, she opens the photo gallery. There it was, the last picture she'd taken.

'Um, everyone?' she says, trying to break through the conversation.

'Honestly, Nat,' Laura is now saying loudly, 'you can't go through life without lipstick. Murderer on the loose or not.'

The photo on Jane's screen shows a book stained with a drop of Carrie's blood. She realises that Abi gave her the answer days ago, out on that lawn with a sticky glass of Pimm's in hand. '*They're all at it*,' she'd said.

'Top me up again,' Kimberley says, holding out her glass, her resigned expression a mixture of disappointment, sadness and anger.

'Everyone!' says Jane.

The Assistant by Sarah Grey. *Sarah.*

'More than that,' Kimberley is saying, 'it's really not been a good weekend.'

'Everyone! I – I think I've found it.' Finally, the table falls silent and five pairs of eyes fix on Jane, her phone clutched in her suddenly-sweaty hand. 'I've found who killed Carrie Marks.'

'Ladies and gentlemen!' The rat-like man, looking a little tired after his shift at the Murder Mystery Lunch, is standing in the doorway of the bar. 'Please make your way through to the tea room. It is time for the presentation of the Killer Lines awards!'

Chapter Forty-Six

Sunday, 7 p.m.

Jane grabs Natasha's hand as the crowd surges towards the tea room for the awards ceremony.

Though there are still crumbs of red velvet cake dotting the floor, the tables have been removed and rows of chairs have been set out in lines for maximum capacity. On-stage, a trestle table displays awards ready to be handed out, as well as a display of Brad Levinsky's new novel, *Stab the Night*, despite neither Brad nor the Killer Lines dagger being present for the Crime Legend award.

As they sit, Laura pulls a second bottle of wine from her handbag and puts it on the floor.

'These things tend to drag,' she says with a shrug, and clinks her glass with Daniel, who laughs and pulls another bottle out of his own tote. 'Now quick, Jane. Before it starts. *Tell us.*'

With the crowd around them chatting and laughing as they find seats, Jane doesn't bother lowering her voice. She passes her phone around as she lays out the pieces of the puzzle.

'Edward was on Carrie's client list as a *prospective* author. But he wasn't the only one secretly writing a book,' she says to the group, each of them leaning forward in their chairs in anticipation. 'Sarah Parks-Ward was too. She was on Carrie Marks's client list, but had just been dropped by the agency. She's a *dead horse.*'

'*That's* why she hates me!' says Natasha. 'She kept asking questions about Carrie, and my advance, and how I'd done it. I thought it was weird, but I'd never had a publicist before, so I wasn't sure.'

300

Jane has never had a publicist before either, so can't comment. She gives Natasha a small smile before carrying on.

'I noticed Sarah has been following Edward around all weekend, and I overheard them arguing the day of the murder. I wonder if she asked him to put in a good word with Carrie, seeing he was her friend, and persuade her to change her mind? But when it didn't work, Sarah reacted badly?'

'Potentially,' says Kimberley Brown. Jane could just about tell she was frowning, despite her line-free forehead. 'It's quite a convincing theory. I've had authors react in extreme ways when I tell them I can't continue publishing them. But murder?'

'Then,' Jane continues, 'think about the book I found, the one near Carrie's body? We all focused on how the title, *The Assistant*, could point towards Abi Ellis, but perhaps Carrie used her dying moment to grab it because of the *author's name*.' Jane pulls up the photo of the book, the killer's name in neon yellow on the cover. '*Sarah* Grey.'

While Jane's phone is passed from hand to hand, she notices Frankie's pinched face, her eyes widening as she fixes them on the screen. When everyone else starts to fire questions at each other in excitement, Jane keeps her eyes fixed on her editor. In the tea room that morning, she'd seen Frankie talking to Sarah, whispering over what looked like a printed out manuscript. Then Sarah spoke to Frankie at the Murder Mystery Lunch. Is Frankie shocked that a friend of hers could have commited such an act? Or does she know something more? Jane leans across and gently places a hand on her thigh. Frankie jumps, splashing her wine over Jane's cardigan.

'What is it, Frankie? What do you know?' Natasha sits in between them, but the others are still talking, yet to notice.

'Well, I – I didn't *know*,' Frankie stutters. 'I promise I didn't know!'

'Ladies and gentlemen! Please take your seats!'

'Frankie!' says Natasha. 'Spit it out.'

301

Daniel sees the commotion and leans in to listen.

'I – well . . .' She looks frantic now, panicked. 'Okay. Sarah gave me her manuscript,' she hisses as the volume in the room starts to fall. 'That's all! Carrie had been bad-mouthing me all over town making it *impossible* for me to find a new job. Sarah came to me promising me an interview at Polar Bear Publishing *and* saying she would put in a good word. In exchange, her book would be the first thing I brought to Acquisitions when I got the job. But that's it, I swear! She didn't mention Carrie – I didn't think this had anything to *do* with Carrie! Sarah didn't even tell me she'd been her client!'

'Did this arrangement happen *after* the murder?' Jane asks, Frankie squirming in her seat. 'Perhaps after a potential plan to have Carrie talked around failed?'

'It did. I . . . shouldn't have. But I needed a new job, I needed – I didn't know—'

'Okay, Frankie,' Jane says, patting her hand. 'It's okay, we understand. You didn't know you were doing a deal with the devil.'

Frankie sits back in her seat looking deeply ashamed of herself. She has, after all, been caught trying to cheat her way into a better job, and by her own author at that.

'Sarah sounds guilty,' says Daniel with a hesitant nod at Jane. 'Though is being dropped by her agent strong *enough* motive for murder?'

'The dagger!' hisses Natasha. 'We're forgetting about the murder weapon again! Sarah could never have *reached* it.'

Jane sits back in her seat, mind full of secret manuscripts and unreachable daggers. She has a strong sense that every puzzle piece is on the board and, if the noise would just stop, she could slot them together.

The rat-like man from the escape room makes his way up onto the rickety stage and taps at the microphone, causing booming static to fill the room. He is wearing his finest clothes for the event, too-tight trousers and some sort of woollen poncho. Whatever happened to a good tuxedo? Near the front, Jane spots the frizzy bouffant of Abi Ellis, and a few seats along, the white-blonde ponytail of Sarah Parks-Ward.

Despite not being able to explain how she obtained the dagger, Jane is *sure* she has found their killer. She remembers the argument she overheard on that first day, the morning before the murder. *I could bloody kill her.*

'Welcome, welcome.' The marketing executive smiles around the room like a gameshow host, but his voice cracks on the second welcome, and Jane can see his Adam's apple bobbing with each nervous swallow. 'Um, welcome. Yes, I've said that. Okay. Welcome, um, to the Killer Lines awards ceremony!'

A smattering of unenthusiastic applause fills the room, only slightly louder than the clink of glassware as people top themselves up. Jane silently takes her mobile phone out of a shame-faced Frankie's hand.

'We have many awards up for grabs this evening, from Twistiest Twist to Most Unreliable Narrator, and each of our winners will receive one of these SHOW-STOPPING awards!' He raises one to show the audience – a wooden plinth supporting a brass plaque, topped with a transparent glass dagger. There is one appreciative *ooohh* from somewhere in the audience, which the compere looks happy enough with.

'And of course,' he continues, 'at the end of the evening we will be presenting the coveted Bloody Dagger for the Crime Legend award!' A frantic whisper from the corner of the stage gives him pause, and he leans over to listen before returning to the microphone. 'Though, um, we won't have the actual dagger to present today, because it's . . . engaged elsewhere. But we can still cheer!'

Jane scrolls to Detective Inspector Ramos's name on her phone. She taps out a text update, asking him to come back to the festival site as soon as possible.

The evidence, and this time there *is* evidence, seems clear.

Daniel is right to question it though. *Is* being dropped by your agent a strong enough motive for murder? Jane thinks back to that first day with Abi. Carrie *ignores the dead horses*, she'd said, and Jane had felt as though she had been slapped. That was her, a *dead horse*. All the dreams, and planning, and effort she'd put into becoming an author, and that was what she was. Yes, she thinks, it is a strong enough motive.

Natasha's words niggle at her though. She is right about the murder weapon being too high for Sarah to reach, unlike towering Edward Carter. If Brad *did* fall by accident, as unlikely as it may seem, then does that bring them right back to Edward as their number one suspect? Jane pushes this thought from her mind.

On-stage, Rat Man is announcing the Sneakiest Thief award. In the row in front of Jane, the bushy auburn hair of the psychological thriller writer with the loud laugh is bobbing around as she sniggers into her glass. The woman next to her whispers something in her ear, and they both dissolve into snorting giggles.

Jane's phone screen flashes up a message.

Ramos has replied.

EC's singing like a bird, but still denying murder. He's insistent Carrie was *helping* him with his book. Has been going on and on about her edits missing the point . . .

It's not him, she texts, her phone hopefully concealed from the people around her. There may be life and death at stake, but that's no excuse to be rude.

The room is applauding, and a short, middle-aged man staggering towards the stage. He takes the microphone and thanks the room in a thick Scottish accent, toasting the group of men cheering at one side. He starts to say something that may be insulting about the host, but is luckily indecipherable.

'Okay, okay. I need that back now.' The compere wrenches the microphone from the Scot's hands, and there is another cheer as he falls off the stage. 'And now,' Rat Face shouts above the din, 'for the Most Paranoid Fictional Wife award! The nominees are . . . '

He falters as the doors to the tea room are pushed open. Heads swivel, and someone lets out a small gasp. Whispers slither through the crowd like a snake. A clunk tells of a glass being kicked over – it's followed by someone swearing loudly, and someone else giving a quiet, mournful *wahey*!

Along with everyone else, Jane's eyes turn to the door, but unlike the others she immediately turns back to the front of the room, seeking out her quarry. Sarah Parks-Ward has spun around in her seat. Her face is ashen, her plump lips parted in an expression that looks a lot like fear. Her eyes, wide and panicked, are fixed on the person who has just walked in.

The screech of Kimberley's chair sends a shudder through the surrounding guests, as though the whispering snake has bitten. She's standing, and swiftly side-steps past the others in the row, soft blue velvet brushing against Jane's knees. Once in the aisle, she strides up to the newcomer at the door, and enfolds him in a firm hug.

'Brad,' she says. 'Welcome back.'

Chapter Forty-Seven

Sunday, 7.15 p.m.

Kimberley downs a scotch, hitches herself up onto a bar stool, then orders two more. The barman looks put out; presumably he'd been looking forward to a bit of a break during the awards presentation.

Brad, on the other hand, looks delighted as he takes his pint of Badger's Foot from the bar. He also looks, thinks Kimberley, like hell warmed up. And even then, only in a microwave on the lowest setting. His skin is the pale grey of old concrete, and just as dry and cracked. His clothes, the same he was wearing on the night he fell, are crumpled and bloodstained. If it weren't for the fact that it is April, you could be forgiven for thinking he'd come straight from a Hallowe'en party.

When he turns, Kimberley flinches at the sight of a patch of shaved head and some gory stitches. Brad paid a fortune for that hair transplant. He must be livid.

He's leaning heavily on the bar, so Kimberley hops off her stool and guides him to the same booth she and the others had sat in earlier, while untangling clues to the killer's identity. Brad eases his way in with the tentative grace of an old bear hooking a salmon from the stream.

'What are you doing here?' She goes to down her next scotch but thinks better of it. Someone needs to keep a clear head, and as Brad's is battered and bruised, it should be her. 'Not that I'm unhappy to see you. But I thought you were unconscious in a hospital somewhere?'

Theirs has never been the hugs and kisses type of relationship. If they did exchange birthday cards, hers would read: *To Brad, Happy Birthday, From Kimberley*. When Kimberley's mother died, Brad simply texted her to say *That's crap*. The hug in the tea room had been one of spontaneous, joyous relief, but that was *quite* enough of that.

'I was,' he says, taking a gulp of his drink and closing his eyes in pleasure. 'My God, that's good. We need to look into getting a case of this sent back home.'

'Brad, focus! Should you even be drinking alcohol?'

'Yeah, yeah, alright.' He sits back in the booth, slowly exhaling in a way that makes Kimberley worry. 'It was bleak in there, Brown. I was fine, so I left.'

'You left? You mean, they discharged you?' The pause says it all. 'For God's sake.'

'I'm not a pansy. They wanted me to lie there feeling sorry for myself, eating a Goddamn' potato covered in some sort of beans in ketchup. I said, "I want that toad in the hole, please. And a pint of Badger's Foot." But no, nothing doing. I was bored as hell, so I got dressed and hailed a cab.'

He grins at her, winces, then tries to hide the wince with a long draw from his glass.

'Anyway,' he continues, smile fading, 'I knew you'd still be here and, well, I suppose I needed to tell you some things. Because someone here is a murderer. And I didn't go falling over a banister by accident, whatever that nurse thinks. Chastising me for drinking so much that I fell! Like *I* can't hold my alcohol. Hey, are they doing food here? Hey!' he shouts over at the barman, making Kimberley flinch at the volume. 'You doing food? Can I get one of those pies with steak?' He turns back to her. 'You want one?'

'No, I need you to tell—'

'Make it two pies! And another scotch, and another of these.' He holds up his almost empty pint glass.

'Brad! I need you to tell me what happened, then I need you to go back to the hospital. We are not eating steak pies and getting drunk.'

'We damn' well are. And I'll be right as a peach after I've eaten. It was only a bang on the head.'

'Weren't you in a coma?'

He waves his hand dismissively, finishes his pint and thanks the barman as he delivers their new drinks. The phrase *if you can't beat 'em, join 'em* comes into Kimberley's mind, as it so often has with Brad over the years. There is no telling this man what to do. She knocks back the drink in front of her, and pulls over the fresh glass.

'Besides,' says Brad, 'I don't trust this healthcare you don't even pay for.'

Despite the purple bruising on his temple, and the diminished power of his usually booming voice, Kimberley lets herself feel the relief washing over her. This strange, rough- around-the-edges man is, she realises, one of her closest friends. She couldn't have coped with losing him this weekend. Not after Carrie.

'Someone tried to *kill you*, Brad.'

'They did! The nerve of it. I was starting to like the old tea drinkers, then one of them goes and pushes me down the stair-well. Wake up in a bed that's too small, lights too bright, nurses mad as hell. Might be time to go back home soon, after I've got my award.'

'Who did it?' Kimberley's mouth is dry, heart thumping, but her mind is strangely calm. She thinks back to seeing Carrie that night, how they had shouted at each other, then cried. How they had kissed, for the first time in eight years, and sworn to speak in the morning. She had gone to bed full of dreams of reconciliation, forgiveness, and love. Someone took that from her, and she needs to know if Jane's theory is right.

'Don't know if I'll be getting that fancy dagger though!' Brad is still speaking, and she pulls herself back to the present, forcing the image of Carrie's face from her mind. 'It was nice. Real heavy and solid. Everyone's names engraved on its blade. Would look good on my study wall. Next to the framed reviews, you know?'

Something clicks in her brain, and she looks up from the wood, fixing her eyes on the author. 'What do you mean, it was *heavy*?'

The double doors leading to the tea room swing open, and they both look up to see Jane Hepburn, tall and resplendent in her marvellous red dress, followed by her rag-tag bunch of followers. The voice of the irritating compere trills through the open door, listing nominees in the Bloodiest Murder category. Kimberley feels sweat prickle under her arms and her mouth goes from dry to a certifiable desert. The group is making their way over to the booth, and Kimberley snaps back to Brad, speaking in an urgent whisper.

'Tell me. How do you know the dagger was heavy? When did you hold it?'

Brad looks blankly at her, and the others reach them, sliding into the seats around the table. Kimberley's lost one person; can she lose another? Even if he's responsible for the loss of the first? The hard-won calm in her mind has been replaced by a storm, and the chatter of her new friends is as indeterminate as the noise of crashing waves. She becomes vaguely aware of someone saying her name, and sees Jane staring at her, mouth moving.

It's time for the truth to come out. Whether she wants it to or not.

'Two pies.' A repulsive-looking plate of pastry, meat and very liquid gravy lands in front of her. 'Careful, love,' says the barman with a resigned sigh. 'It's hot.'

Chapter Forty-Eight

Sunday, 7.25 p.m.

Jane is on the edge of her seat. Literally. She starts to slip off, but saves herself just in time. She is squished into the booth, Daniel one side of her, Natasha the other. Laura, Kimberley, Frankie and now Brad, are all crowded around the same table, her circle of friends expanding by the second.

Her phone is in the pocket of her cardigan and she can feel it vibrating against her thigh, but can barely move her arms and so has no chance of retrieving it. Is it Edward, calling to plead his innocence? Is it Detective Inspector Ramos with important news? Is it the Amazon delivery driver trying to drop off her new stationery set? It doesn't matter. Nothing can be as important as what's happening right here, right now.

Kimberley pushes her unwanted pie into the middle of the table. Daniel gingerly reaches out and pulls it towards himself. Brad is shovelling forkfuls into his mouth, pausing occasionally to wash it down with beer. He doesn't seem hugely surprised by the crowd of people, most of whom he doesn't know, joining him for the meal.

Jane catches Kimberley's eye and gives her a reassuring nod. She is pale, and looks shaken by Brad's arrival. It must feel as though she's seen her friend come back from the dead.

'Um, Mr Levinsky?' Jane begins. 'I'm Jane? Jane Hepburn? An . . . an author?' Brad looks up at her, chewing. She takes a breath, and tries to find the confidence that has flitted in and out of her life over the last few days. She feels Natasha press her thigh harder in support, silently conveying what she said outside. *You're amazing!* 'I'm Jane. An author.' Better.

'Nice to meet you, Jane. You been making friends, Kim?'

'Well,' says Kimberley with a doubtful look at the motley crew around her, 'I suppose I have.'

I knew it! thinks Jane. *We* are *friends!*

'We, my friends and I,' she continues, 'have been trying to find out who killed Carrie Marks.'

Laura taps record and slowly raises her phone. Kimberley slaps it down onto the wood.

'To be honest,' says Natasha, 'I briefly thought it was you, Brad, but—'

'But we think we finally know who it *really* was!' Jane interrupts. Through the now-closed double doors, she can just about hear the compere arguing with a prizewinner whose speech has overrun.

'*You need to get off-stage now!*' he is saying. '*We have twelve more of these things to get through!*'

'*Bugger off!*' yells the winner, and the crowd cheers.

'But,' Natasha is saying with a meaningful look at Jane, 'that person couldn't have reached the dagger above the door. So, it *can't* be her. What we are saying, Brad, is that we need to know what happened to you. *Were you pushed?*'

'And if so,' says Daniel through a mouthful of steak pie, 'who did it?'

'And *why?*' finishes Jane, wiping gravy splatter from her eyebrow.

Everyone's eyes fix on Brad as he slowly chews some pastry. He dips a chip in the gravy, swirls it around and squashes it to soak up as much as possible. Jane is wondering if the bang on the head has affected his mental capacity when, at last, he speaks.

'Couldn't reach the dagger, huh? Well. About that.' He swallows the chip in one and begins the process again. It's almost hypnotic. 'I *was* pushed, and I do know who did it. But let's start at the beginning. If it's the issue of who took the dagger that's troubling you, then let's solve that bit first. *I* took the Killer Lines dagger from above the pub door.'

Everyone around the table gasps on cue. Daniel chokes on his mouthful of pie, which cuts through the tension a little bit.

'Why?' says Kimberley. Her face is hard, a slight crease forming between her eyebrows – which is saying something as it's been immovable thus far – and her lips pursed. She reminds Jane, quite suddenly, of a video she'd seen on Facebook where a honey badger fights a wolverine. She's not sure if Kimberley Brown is the honey badger or the wolverine, or a terrifying combination of both.

Brad shrugs, pushing another chip into his mouth. 'Thought it would be funny.' Kimberley puts her head on the table.

'Did you . . .' Natasha falters, so Jane picks it up.

'Did you kill Carrie Marks?'

'What? No! Look, I've told Kim most of this. But I maybe forgot about the dagger. I'd had a few drinks that night. These ales are lethal! Speaking of which – *Hey! Bar guy! Another over here!* – yeah, so I'd had a few.'

'How unusual,' mutters Kimberley. In her left ear, Jane hears Daniel recommence chewing.

'And I went outside to get some air. And I vaguely remember seeing that dagger, and thinking it would be funny to take it, you know? So I did.'

'Riiight,' says Laura Lane. Jane notices that she has subtly propped her phone against her glass to film the conversation. 'And then what happened?'

'Well, I was having a go on the sword outside.' He mimes swinging a dagger around, thrusting at imaginary enemies, jabbing Frankie hard in the chest with his elbow as he does so. The barman leaps back, saving the full pint glass he is delivering to their table by an inch. 'Then I heard that woman Carrie.

She was going on about some book needing better pacing or whatever, and a guy snapped at her that he wasn't changing a thing. You know how annoying authors can be.' He turns to Kimberley with a rueful smile as he says it. 'It sounded like the guy stormed off, so then I . . . ' He glances at his editor as if to check for permission.

'They know about what happened between Carrie and me.'

'Oooh, what did happen?' says Laura. Kimberley reaches over and pushes her phone off the table.

'Okay then,' says Brad. 'I wanted a word with her. So I went after her. But on the way, I realised I still had this dagger. And I was annoyed, but I didn't want to terrify the old witch. So I dropped it. Meant to find it later, but I was blotto, and I guess I . . . forgotto.' He laughs – that same short one-note laugh – into his glass as he gulps down a third of his beer.

'So *anyone* could have picked up the dagger,' groans Natasha, putting her head in her hands. 'But what about last night? In the stairwell?'

'I'm getting there,' says Brad. He looks as though he is enjoy-ing himself, and takes his time swirling another chip in gravy. In the other room, the compere is trying to announce the award for the Best Dressed Villain but, by the din, it sounds as though he has lost the crowd's interest. 'I shouted out to her, and turns out I *did* terrify the old witch even without the dagger, and she fell. She had some choice words for me. Got a real mouth on her. So I left her to it and came back in here. Fell in with some Scottish blokes who can *drink*.

'At one point, I went out for some air and barfed in the bushes.' He chuckles as Kimberley makes a tut of disgust. 'Yeah, yeah, I know. Fifty-eight and still chucking up on the rhododen-drons. Sorry, Miss Perfect. While I was out there though, I saw something. Some*one*.'

Jane is squeezing her wine glass so hard she's worried it may break, so she tries to relax. This is it, though: the moment they've been waiting for. All of their investigation has led to this. Her phone is vibrating against her thigh again. She hopes against hope that Ramos is on his way.

'Some tall guy,' Brad continues, 'comes marching across the lawn from over by the book tent and leaves the festival site. Not long after – don't ask me exact times – some blonde comes from the same direction. She didn't notice me, but she was all frantic-looking. She ran past me and down into the village. She had red stuff on her, like here.' He motions to his chest. 'Thought it was wine. In retrospect, could have been blood.

'I didn't think much of it, truth be told. I was three sheets to the wind that night. The next day was a blur. I felt like the walking dead, and Carrie Marks was, well, *actually* dead. Bit of a hair of the dog fixed me, though can't say the same for her. I wasn't too fussed about the murder, if I'm honest with you. That woman didn't treat my friend here very well.' He nods at Kimberley, who gives him a weak smile. 'And when you treat one person badly, you often treat others badly. I'm sure plenty of people wanted Carrie Marks's head on a platter.

'Well, on Saturday, my memories are coming into a bit more focus. And Kim here seemed actually quite upset about the whole murder business by that point, so I have a think, and realise I need to talk to this woman I saw. Not a big fan of the cops, me. I didn't want to bring trouble down on her head if there was an innocent explanation. So I find her, and say "We need to talk about that night." Nothing heavy, you know.'

Innocent explanation? thinks Jane. *For running from a crime scene covered in blood?*

'She says she's busy and to meet her later on the seventh floor. Bit odd, but sure, whatever tickles your fancy. She's only as big as a tom cat, so I'm hardly scared of her.' He swigs at his beer and burps *almost* politely into his fist. 'But I found her waiting for me on the stairs. I asked about what I saw that night, and she came barrelling at me like a tiny bullet. Quite a

314

woman that one. Over the banister I go, down seven storeys and *wham*. Wake up looking like Frankenstein and feeling like Wile E. Coyote.'

'I think you mean Frank—'

'Oh, I *know* I mean Frankenstein's monster,' Brad cuts off Frankie. 'Editors are all such bloody pendants.'

The table sits in silence as he finishes his chips.

'I was right, then,' whispers Jane. 'She didn't need to reach the dagger, she found it in the grass and used it on Carrie.' She glances at a wide-eyed Daniel, a nervous-looking Natasha. 'The killer is Sarah Parks-Ward?'

'That's the one!' Brad agrees, cheerfully. 'Sarah whats it. Posh. Mean-looking.' He downs the dregs of his drink and turns to Kimberley, speaking directly to his editor and friend.

'She killed her, Kim. That Sarah woman killed your friend. Or enemy, or girlfriend, whatever she was. And she tried to kill me. Where is she now?'

'In there,' says Jane, nodding towards the door to the tea room, from which the sound of booing is emanating, punctuated with appeals to CALM DOWN from the compere. 'At least we've got her cornered.'

'You know,' says Frankie, 'that's not the only entrance, right?'

Chapter Forty-Nine

Sunday, 7.40 p.m.

When Jane Hepburn pushes open the doors to the tea room, she doesn't expect the pimply-faced waitress to have been moving about the room in her absence. She doesn't expect her to have been collecting glasses on a trolley. And she doesn't expect that trolley to have been parked in front of the main entrance she has just burst through. So, instead of arriving in the room with minimal noise and fuss, she instead crashes in with all the elegance of a dumper truck.

Thirty-six glasses crash to the floor, along with Jane herself, who now glitters like a snowball and is damp with the dregs of thirty-six drinks. The move does, however, succeed in finally making the audience fall silent.

'Right,' says the compere as Frankie and Daniel dust Jane off and pull her up into a seated position. 'Welcome, um, late arrivals. If you are, um, quite alright, I am about to announce the award for the Best Newcomer. And the nominees are . . . '

'Jane,' Daniel hisses, 'are you okay?'

'Are you hurt?' Natasha asks, brushing splinters of glass from Jane's arms.

'I'm fine,' she says, feeling as un Baker-like as it is possible to be. 'I can't see Sarah. Has she gone?' At the front of the room, heads are slowly turning away from Jane and back to the stage where the compere is opening an envelope with all the energy of a teacher on the last day of the worst school year of their life. Jane's eyes flick back and forth along the row of chairs, zeroing in on the spot where Sarah had been sitting. The white-blonde head is no longer present. Sarah *has* gone.

'And the winner is,' the compere calls, trying to force some of his old enthusiasm back into his voice for the final few awards, 'Natasha Martez!'

Natasha is still kneeling in broken glass, pulling limes out of Jane's hair.

Daniel prods her in the ribs. 'Um, Natasha? I think you have to go up there.'

'Well done,' Jane whispers to her friend, and this time, she is pleased to find she feels only happiness for Natasha. No jealousy, no bitterness, just pride that this spectacular young woman is being recognised for the talent she is. They may still have a murderer to catch, but Natasha also deserves her moment. 'Go on. Daniel and I will go after Sarah.' Jane nudges her shell-shocked friend towards the aisle, and Natasha eventually starts to walk up to the stage.

There is a sharp pull on Jane's shoulder. Kimberley is heaving her up. Jane's whole body hurts and she pictures her too-small sofa in her cosy living room with a pang of desire. She lumbers to her feet, sliding on a lime and nearly going down again. She would have, if it weren't for Kimberley's grip.

'She must have gone through that exit,' says Kimberley in a furious whisper, gesturing towards the far end of the room. 'You two go that way. We'll search outside in case she's already out the building.' She pushes Jane and Daniel towards the rear door, then disappears back into the bar with the others.

Jane feels the room's eyes on her and Daniel as they walk down the aisle after Natasha, whispering apologies to people as they squeeze past a row of seated book bloggers and through the aforementioned door into a dark corridor. Daniel looks at Jane, eyes wide and fearful, waiting for instruction. She sets off in silence with him following, but when they reach some stairs Jane nods for him to go up while she goes on.

Yet more doors lead off the dark corridor, and Jane opens them one by one, revealing empty function rooms and cupboards stuffed with boxes. This part of the building is like a maze, and Jane imagines Sarah's panic as she desperately tries to find another way out while the clock ticks down to her capture. Has she heard them come through from the tea room? Is she still running, or frozen in a hiding spot behind one of the many doors? Or has she already made it out?

One room is still set up from the last author panel; chairs in a line, piles of books on the table, a large free-standing advert for a novel called *The Unhappy Thief* lying on the floor. Jane is pulling the door closed to continue onwards when she hears something, and stops dead. Could it be Daniel on the floor above? She peers into the darkness of the room once more.

On the far wall, another door stands ajar, visible in the dim light coming through the single window. Jane takes a tentative step into the room, then freezes again, straining to hear any noise. The faint click of heeled boots on wood.

Jane strides towards the door, pulling it open to reveal an empty anteroom and yet another open door. She definitely hears movement now and dashes towards it, knocking her hip painfully against a desk. The crash dispels any pretence of subtlety, and she hears the sound of running footsteps ahead.

'Sarah!' Jane calls. 'Sarah, stop. It's over! We know!'

She finds herself in an almost identical function room, entering it just as another door leading back into the corridor slams shut. Pushing past a life-size cardboard cut out of the actor playing Brad Levinsky's Detective Stone in an upcoming TV series (*very handsome*, she has time to think), Jane reaches the door, wrenches it open and flies out into the corridor, where she sees the white-blonde hair of Sarah Parks-Ward disappearing the way she'd just come from.

'Sarah!' Jane shouts. 'Daniel! Down here!'

She takes off after Sarah; her long legs would usually make up for Sarah's headstart but she's limping now. She'd hit her hip in exactly the same place she'd whacked it against her bedside table. The bruise will be a picture tomorrow. Jane can hear the clatter of Daniel racing down to meet them. Sarah pauses at the stairwell, sees him barrelling towards her, and instead ploughs on, back towards the tea room.

She pulls open the door as Jane is mere feet away from her, and runs out into the midst of the ceremony. Jane and Daniel follow suit, once again feeling all eyes turn their way. On-stage, Natasha is holding a glass dagger, the compere looking over at Jane with undisguised fury.

'Now look,' he begins, but he doesn't get a chance to tell them what they should be looking at because the doors to the bar burst open again, revealing Kimberley, Frankie, Laura and Brad. Finally, the audience appears rather entertained.

Sarah looks between Jane and Daniel blocking one door, and Kimberley's group blocking the other. With a scowl at Jane, she marches towards the stage and up the steps. An *oooooooh* sounds from somewhere in the audience.

'Hey, you!' shouts Brad from the back of the room. 'You owe me an explanation! And either a new jacket or a premium dry clean.'

But she isn't going down without a fight. Wrenching the glass dagger from Natasha's hand, Sarah steps neatly behind her. She slides one arm over Natasha's shoulder and holds the dagger against her throat. Sarah's eyes are wild, and she's panting from the chase.

'I thought I'd already told you to *back off*!' She presses the dagger hard into Natasha's windpipe, staring back at the approaching enemy in defiance.

'Sarah?' says Jane. 'You know that's not a real knife, right?'

Rolling her eyes, Sarah smartly whacks the dagger against the podium. The end shatters, leaving a jagged point, glistening in the spotlight. The sight pulls Jane right back to that first day, watching Sarah thrust a broken wine glass at Edward Carter, and she wonders how on earth they didn't seriously suspect her before.

Sarah yanks Natasha's head back by her hair and presses the now razor-sharp edge to her throat. Glass may not be as elegantly efficient as steel, but it can still do damage when wielded by a psychopath. The rat-faced compere is flapping around on the edge of the stage. Natasha's eyes are bulging in their sockets, her red-painted lips parted in panic. A rabbit caught in a trap.

'I told you,' Daniel whispers in Jane's ear. 'Publicists are always so dramatic.'

Chapter Fifty

Sunday, 7. 55 p.m.

'Why did you do it, Sarah?' Jane calls up to the stage. Her friend's eyes are imploring her to help. All Jane can think to do is get Sarah talking until she calms down, realises she has no way out and may as well come quietly.

That, or she'll cut Natasha's throat.

'You know why,' says Sarah. 'That woman deserved all she had coming to her.'

'We *don't* know why, Sarah. Though I suspect it's something to do with Edward Carter, and with you not being Carrie's client anym—'

'I *am* a client! I *am* still a client!' She stamps one white-heeled ankle boot as she speaks, jolting the dagger. Natasha squeaks in fear or pain or both. 'And it's nothing to do with *Edward Carter*.' She spits his name, disgust morphing her face and the spotlight bouncing off the interlocked Cs of her Chanel earrings. 'Talentless womaniser.'

'We saw Carrie's list, Sarah. The agency was in trouble; it needed money. She was dropping authors who weren't bringing in cash, and we *know* she'd already told you it was happening.'

'She had *no right*!' snapped Sarah. 'Carrie told me editors *all loved it but weren't in love with it*, but then she CCed me in on an email by accident. It said my writing was . . . shoddy, and my plot was, my plot was . . . '

'Pointless and confusing?' squeaks Abi's voice, from somewhere in the audience.

'Shut up! It's not fair how these know nothings like Carrie Marks can decide what does and doesn't see the light of day. Gatekeepers . . . letting through the same old rubbish over and over again while dismissing works of true genius. It's not *fair*.'

A trickle of blood is making its way down Natasha's throat. Winding Sarah up even more is dangerous, so Jane clears her throat and takes half a step forward.

'Tell us what happened that night, Sarah. Tell us what happened the night you killed Carrie Marks.'

Sarah's eyes flicker between the two sets of doors, eventually fixing back on Jane. Tilting the hand holding the dagger, she gives a deep, exhausted sigh.

'Carrie called me, a few weeks ago. She said she was trimming down her client list and . . . and I hadn't made the cut. I reacted to the news with dignity and grace.'

Abi snorts from the crowd.

'But then I spent the night with Edward Carter, and I saw an email on his computer, from *her*. She was giving him feedback on his novel, putting loads of work into it. She said she would represent him if he made some changes, and she'd help him, and all this drivel.

'How *dare* she? I thought she didn't have time for *existing* clients, and there she was, expending so much energy and effort on someone shiny and new? How dare she! And it's not just that. I'd seen the announcement for *her* too.' She jabs the glass further into Natasha's neck on the word *her*. Natasha's blood drips faster. 'Six-figure deal? I *need* that. I just needed Carrie's help. Her support. I have . . . I have debts.'

While Sarah speaks, Jane is desperately trying to think of a way to get Natasha away from the blade before Sarah slips up and cuts her throat, or even decides to kill her on purpose. Could she rush the stage? She'll never make it in time if Sarah decides to act. Is there any way to take her out from afar, with no gun? The nearest ammunition to hand is old lime slices.

'Why kill her if you wanted her help? And why here, at Killer Lines?'

'Because she *wouldn't* help! I didn't plan to kill her. I . . . persuaded Edward to put a word in for me. To ask her to reconsider. Seeing as they were *so very close*, and he *owed* me. When I found him on Thursday afternoon, he told me he'd tried and she'd said . . . she'd said *no*.

'I didn't believe he'd tried very hard, so that night I tracked him down to where he was hiding in the beer tent, smoking and avoiding conversation. I've seen Edward at enough of these events over the years to know where to look for him. Carrie was in the book tent – I'd spotted her going in there looking a right mess. So I sent him in there to try again. But this time . . . I listened.

'She was crying about something at first, some woman. And when Edward *eventually* mentioned me, she . . . she said such horrible things. About my writing. About me.'

Sarah flushes a bright pink, and Jane sees the truth of it for the first time. A woman scorned.

'Carrie was just one person,' Jane says, as softly as she can. 'You could have got another agent, written a new book?' Sarah's flush deepens.

'I know,' she snaps. 'But when Edward left that tent, barely looking at me, it was the final straw. How dare they just . . . discount me? I went in there to confront her myself. Carrie needed to focus on her finances, she said. To sign authors with *real money-making potential*. My book was *never* going to be published, she said. She was . . . so *rude*. And I *needed that money*. The money Carrie got for *her*' – she jabs at Natasha's neck once more – 'she could have got for *me*.'

The entire audience is silent now, frozen as they watch the hostage situation play out before them. No doubt some think it a performance. When will they realise, wonders Jane, that all of this is real? When Natasha's blood soaks the stage? When she falls down, unmoving? At the back of the room, she can see Laura Lane, shameless as ever, recording the scene on her mobile. Kimberley's face is paper-white, her mouth open in horror or disgust or shock. How must it feel to hear that the love of your life has been murdered because they refused to represent someone's novel?

'Did you already have the dagger?' Jane asks.

'I'd seen it,' says Sarah with a nonchalant shrug. 'It was lying in the grass, just outside the tent. I went and got it, walked back into the tent, and stabbed her right in her cold heart.'

A gasp ripples through the audience, and the glass dagger glides lightly across Natasha's throat, a thin red line appearing on her skin. Jane can sense Daniel moving next to her. He leans a fraction closer and whispers something in her ear that she doesn't quite hear. She is vaguely aware of her mobile phone buzzing against her hip and hopes against hope it's Detective Inspector Ramos trying to tell her he's nearly here. Or is the buzzing in her ears? The sight of blood on her friend's throat has made her feel dizzy. She can't see how she can do anything to stop what's happening.

'Why was *I* let go but *you* weren't?' Sarah says from the stage.

'I don't know,' says Jane carefully. 'Maybe I would have been, eventually. But I would have continued, I would have found another way.' Was that true? Just hours before she'd been intent on hanging up her pen for good. But now she sees that would never really have happened. She would always press on, always write, no matter who was listening or not listening. Again, she hears Daniel whisper something urgently, but can't make out the words. All she can focus on is that dagger against Natasha's skin. Her *friend's* skin.

Pull yourself together. That's what her mother would say. Though maybe she would also say, *Looks like you bit off more than you could chew.*

Sliding one foot to the left, Daniel edges closer to her.

'Jane,' he hisses. 'Book five.'

'What?' she mutters back.

On-stage, the drops of blood are increasing in frequency and volume as they trickle down Natasha's neck and stain her clothes. Her eyes are wide and round in fear.

'Book five,' Daniel whispers. '*A Desperate Death*.'

What *is* he talking about? Her phone is buzzing again against her thigh, distracting her. On-stage, Sarah is telling the rapt audience the plot of her novel. From the back, Jane hears someone shout, 'Hey! No spoilers!'

'Think,' Daniel whispers. 'The phone call?'

What happens in *A Desperate Death*? She wrote her fifth book around the time Stefan told her he was taking her to Paris on a minibreak. But on the weekend in question, he said he had to watch the football instead, and she'd unpacked the little suitcase she'd packed with such excitement the week before. Instead of seeing the Eiffel Tower and eating croissants on the Champs-Élysées, she'd settled down with a Terry's Chocolate Orange and finished *A Desperate Death* in one whirlwind night of tears and typing. Her phone briefly stops vibrating, then starts up again with a vengeance.

She's got it!

Now she realises what her mother would really have said. She sees her, clear as day, sitting at their old kitchen table. *It ain't over, Jane, until the big lady sings.*

Turning her head a fraction to the left, she gives Daniel a small nod to show she's understood. She senses him deflating with relief next to her – message imparted, job done. On-stage, Sarah's voice is rising in pitch, and Natasha is shaking, tears filling her eyes. It's now or never.

Jane slides her hand into the pocket of her cardigan and pulls out her phone.

'Sarah?' she says, interrupting the flow of praise for her own literary genius. 'It's Marabella Rhodes on the phone.'

Jane waves it, showing the flashing screen. With her thumb, she flicks the switch to turn on the volume, and the theme tune of *Jonathan Creek* fills the room as it rings. 'From the Rhodes Talent Agency? I think . . . it's for you.'

Chapter Fifty-One

Saturday, 8.05 p.m.

Laura Lane expertly zooms in on Sarah's face, suddenly open and hopeful. Almost innocent-looking. Panning out, she brings Jane back into frame. The lighting, lowered for the awards ceremony, adds to the overall drama of the scene. The warm glow lights Jane from the front and, in her structured red dress with her impressive height, holding the phone out in challenge to a murderer clutching a glass dagger, Laura knows she has a killer shot. After this is over, she's going to make Jane Hepburn a star.

Comments are racking up on the edge of the screen, mostly variations on *OMG* and *Is this real?*, along with emojis of shocked faces and hearts. She's not sure what the hearts are representing – love for the killer or for her downfall – but it's all engagement at the end of the day.

She can sense Kimberley at her elbow, but for once the interfering old crone is letting her film undisturbed. She clearly has some kind of personal stake in this case, and seems happy for Sarah's undoing to be broadcast to the world. Behind her, Frankie is biting her nails nervously, and Brad is leaning heavily on the back of a chair belonging to someone who looks too starstruck by his presence to say anything about it. The low creak of a door causes Laura to turn – someone new slides silently into the room. In the gloom, she can only make out that it's a man.

Zooming back onto Sarah's face, Laura watches hope turn to suspicion in the narrowing of her eyes.

'Why would she be calling *you*?' she shouts down to Jane.

'I told her about your novel,' she replies, and Laura zooms out again to catch the exchange. 'Marabella has been scooping up some of Carrie's clients already, haven't you heard? She got in touch with me yesterday and I mentioned a few other people she should talk to. My editor, Frankie Reid? I know you gave her your book, and she was telling me how *brilliant* it was, so I gave Marabella your name. She said she'd call to discuss. You can talk to her yourself if you like. This might be your last chance, if you're going to be arrested.' The phone had briefly stopped ringing, but in the silence it starts again, causing the audience to flinch as one.

Sarah bites her lip, and the hand holding the glass to poor Natasha's throat begins to tremble. Her lips move, but no sound escapes.

'What was that, Sarah?' says Jane softly.

She'd make a great hostage negotiator, thinks Laura. Or anything really. Jane Hepburn clearly underestimates her own power.

Sarah raises her chin. 'Okay,' she says, her voice cracking. 'Let me speak to her.'

Jane nods, and steps tentatively forward. Laura tracks her movements, slowly zooming in as the frame shrinks. Jane is walking up the wooden steps to the stage, and everyone in the audience is holding their breath. You can feel it, the stillness in the air.

'Lower the knife, okay, Sarah? Just a little?'

As Jane steps forward, Sarah drops the glass blade from Natasha's throat a fraction. The only sounds in the room are the tap of Jane's feet on wooden boards and the incessant shrill of the *Jonathan Creek* theme tune coming from her phone. Slowly, she continues her advance.

Laura is a successful content creator. As well as her bestselling novels, which are just content after all, she's filmed countless personal videos that have racked up many millions of views. She's staged emotional scenes and 'spontaneous' japes, entertainingly furious rants and funny skits. But – and she doesn't know it yet but still suspects – she will never capture a better piece of footage than what she films next.

Which is that Jane Hepburn abruptly stands still, throws the still-ringing phone to Sarah with one hand, and grabs a hardback copy of Brad's new novel *Stab the Night* with the other, bringing it down fast and hard against the back of the publicist's head.

Chapter Fifty-Two

Sunday, 8.15 a.m.

Jane has slogged through writing climactic scenes in all seven of her books. She's never enjoyed that part. Having not experienced too many climactic moments in her own life, she finds the process a little tricky to ape.

She's relieved to discover she has got it somewhat right though. It really does go past in a blur of movement and sound and adrenaline, with rational thought reduced to base animal instinct. You really do come to with the world changed and people looking at you in awe. In real life, however, there are rather more fruit slices in her hair than she'd included in any of her books.

When the copy of Brad Levinsky's latest novel connects with Sarah's pretty blonde head with all the force of Jane's mother entering the M&S January sale, she jerks forward and drops the broken dagger, which shatters at her feet. Natasha hooks her ankle around Sarah's and sends the publicist flying to land flat on her back. Jane promptly sits on her legs, and Natasha, blood smeared across her neck, pins down her arms.

'This jacket is *Gucci*,' snarls Sarah from the floor.

Daniel whoops in delight, jumping up onto the stage to help restrain their prey, and the crowd, having first gasped in shock, are now cooing with admiration. From the back of the room, a voice Jane recognises shouts out as a figure comes striding forward.

'Sarah Parks-Ward,' says Detective Inspector Ramos, pushing his way through the people now standing in the aisle. 'You are under arrest for the murder of Carrie Marks, and the attempted murder of Brad Levinsky. You do not have to—'

'What about Natasha?' shouts Daniel from on top of Sarah's left arm. 'She held her at knifepoint!'

'Okay, okay. And for the assault on Natasha—'

'Martez,' Natasha provides from on top of Sarah's right arm.

'—Martez. You do not have to say anything, but it may harm your defence . . . '

Detective Inspector Ramos continues cautioning Sarah as he mounts the stage, and removes Daniel, Natasha and Jane from her various limbs so she can stand and be cuffed.

'I'll need to speak to you three at some point,' he mutters.

'Don't you mean *well done*?' asks Daniel, pushing his floppy hair out of his eyes and dusting glass fragments from his knees. 'For figuring out the identity of the murderer, catching them, *and* potentially saving Natasha's life?'

'Okay, that too. But the interviews still stand.'

As Sarah is led away, the room breaks out into a cacophony of whispers. Jane Hepburn, still glittering with particles of glass from the drinks trolley and, now, Natasha's ruined award, is sitting on the stage. Her yellow lanyard is stained with beer and blood, but it still reads GUEST.

'You okay, Nat?' Jane whispers, stretching to reach her phone. The screen is shattered, but she puts it in the pocket of her cardigan nonetheless. Natasha, kneeling next to her, answers with a nod and a weak smile, and accepts Daniel's offered hand. When she is on her feet too, Jane feels exposed and taller than ever. Though she can accept it is usually all in her head, this time there really *are* hundreds of eyes on her. In the crowd, she finds some she knows, and feels Natasha's hand squeeze hers, so she straightens her spine, and they make their way down the wooden steps.

'Wait!' The rat-faced man comes forward from the shadows. Jane had forgotten he was there at all. *Thanks for the help.*

'Congratulations,' he says, bending over and retrieving a stump of sharp glass attached to a plinth engraved with Best Newcomer. Blowing on it to remove some of the shards, he hands it to Natasha. 'Maybe you can . . . glue it?'

At the back of the room, the group of standing spectators part to let the detective and his prisoner through, closing behind them like water. Jane, Daniel and Natasha follow them down the aisle, but instead of passing through they are met with ferocious hugs from Kimberley and Frankie. It presses a shard of glass rather painfully into Jane's back, but she doesn't complain.

On-stage, the compere is desperately trying to carry on, despite not a single person in the audience paying attention. Over the din, he shouts that this year's Crime Legend is Brad Levinsky and he will receive his trophy in the post when the police are done with it, then scuttles off-stage.

Jane expects that, by the time he retells this story, he'll play a rather more pivotal role in the action.

Chapter Fifty-Three

Under the willow tree, Jane, Natasha and Daniel pass a bottle of warm white wine between them. It's late, but the air still holds a little warmth, and it's fresh with the smell of the surrounding countryside. The moon is not quite full, but along with the handful of stars and the glow from the pub window, it lights the lawn. It is a perfect spring evening to spend with friends. Even if Natasha does have dried blood and a large plaster on her neck, and Jane is sparkling with powdered glass.

Natasha has wiped off her lipstick and is leaning back against the tree trunk, swigging Pinot Grigio straight from the bottle. Daniel lies on the grass, the dampness staining his jeans. And Jane Hepburn, a little faded, a little tired, a little old, a little covered in old beer and sticky lemon juice, feels a deep sense of contentedness. She takes the bottle from Natasha. Her mother would have hated her drinking from the bottle. But can a leopard change its spots, if a change is as good as a rest?

After promising to come and collect their statements in the morning, Detective Inspector Ramos had loaded a cuffed and crying Sarah Parks-Ward into his car. Before leaving, he'd told Jane that if she ever considered joining the police force, she should give him a call. She'd said she might consider it in the future, but right now, she has a new detective series to write.

'What's going to happen then?' says Natasha, closing her eyes and resting her head on the tree trunk. 'Have they let Edward go?'

'Yes,' says Jane. 'And it sounds as if he was lucky. Apparently Sarah has been trying to get him alone ever since that first night. Perhaps she was worried he suspected her involvement and wanted to silence him, like she tried to Brad.'

'Close shave,' says Natasha with a low whistle.

'I still don't really understand his part in this,' says Daniel, holding out his hand for the bottle.

'Well,' says Jane, who'd been mulling it over herself, 'he told us that he spoke to Carrie at 10.30 and then left the site, didn't he? I think that was partly true, but instead of leaving the festival entirely, he went into the beer tent to sulk after Carrie told him how much work he needed to do to his novel, just like Sarah said. That's where she found him and persuaded him to ask Carrie about her own work one last time.'

'What I don't understand,' says Natasha, 'is why didn't he *tell* us that? Why lie?'

'Maybe he didn't want to admit to being the last person to see Carrie alive,' says Jane. 'Maybe he was scared.'

She takes the bottle back from Daniel, and they watch people mill about on the lawn. Abi Ellis walks across it, looking exhausted and cross, in the direction of the exit.

'Well, I guess I'm out of a job,' says Daniel. 'Once we give our statements tomorrow, Abi will probably be told to stop running an agency she has no right to, and if it really is in a lot of debt, I imagine it will close. My paid employment at the Marks Literary Agency was pretty short-lived.'

'Poor Abi,' says Natasha. When she senses her friends looking at her, she opens her eyes wide. 'Well, she's not *all* bad. She's just . . . lost. Trying to make a place for herself in the dog-eat-dog book world.'

'I'm sure she'll get another job somewhere. She might even manage to bring some of Carrie's clients with her in the end,' says Jane. 'I wonder what will happen to us, Natasha? Agent-less authors, lost in the abyss.'

'We'll be fine, Jane. Don't you worry about it.'

For some reason, Jane believes her.

'Yeah, Jane,' Daniel says, scrolling through his phone. 'I don't know if you're aware, but you're actually pretty famous right now.' He holds up his screen to show Jane a picture of herself mid-action, clobbering Sarah over the head with a book. '*And* you're a great writer.'

Noise from the pub washes over the group. The chatter is almost hysterical as people go over what happened during the ceremony again and again.

'That was such quick thinking in there, Jane,' Natasha says. 'Lucky your phone kept ringing too.'

'Not luck exactly,' she says with a smile. 'We have our friend Daniel here to thank for a lot of it.' His grin widens, his teeth glowing in the darkness. Even Brad would approve of his pearly whites. 'Tell her, Daniel.'

'Well, it *was* lucky Jane's phone was ringing. That's what sparked the idea.'

'It was Detective Inspector Ramos,' says Jane. 'He'd been calling for a while, trying to tell me he was on his way. He was worried we might *do something stupid*. The cheek of him!'

'But it reminded me of something that happens in one of Jane's books, when Baker fakes a phone call to distract the killer,' says Daniel, rolling over onto his front and propping himself up on his elbows. 'The Baker books are so good, Nat, you have to read them. So I suggested it to Jane.'

'But wasn't Ramos there by the end? Why was he still calling?'

'Oh, that was me.' Daniel's grin broadens even further, pushing his chiselled cheekbones higher still. 'When Ramos rang off, I called Jane's phone from mine, behind my back.'

'Genius!' Natasha says with a laugh. 'Absolutely genius, the pair of you.'

'Couldn't have done it without you being so brave and stoic up there, Nat,' says Jane, 'and taking her down the moment you had the chance.'

She sighs and swigs again from the bottle, mentally toasting both her mother and her deceased literary agent. Everyone has had their part to play, and Sarah is in custody. *All's well that ends well* rings in her head.

It's almost midnight by the time Jane says goodbye to her friends and starts the long walk back to Mary's house for the final time. Until next year at least. Her legs and throat are tired – used to spending her free hours curled up alone with a book, her body is protesting the sudden switch to chasing suspects, tackling murderers, and protracted hostage negotiation.

She passes the churchyard, remembering sitting there with Daniel and Natasha, scanning through Laura Lane's videos. She passes the butcher's and the charity shop, the mannequin, still in its yellow poncho, in the window. It all seems like it happened years ago, not mere hours.

What seems *impossibly* long ago, however, is her train ride to Hoslewit on Thursday afternoon, nervous about what she would find. What if no one spoke to her? What if people told her they hated her books? Turns out those worries were unfounded. In retrospect, there were other things – like becoming embroiled with murder for example – she should have worried more about instead.

Climbing the steep hill in the darkness, Jane finally sees Mary's house in the distance. She is looking forward to crawling into her single bed, guarded by Disney princesses. She needs to try and fix the tiny desk chair, but that can wait until morning. What will happen when she returns home tomorrow? She'll continue writing, that's for sure. Now that she knows she has people in her corner. Hopefully, she'll be able to say goodbye to Kimberley and Brad before they fly home, though she somehow doubts it will be the last time she sees either of them.

She doesn't know what will happen with her books, who will be the star of her new series, or even if anyone will publish it. But she does at least know she has some friends by her side now, and that makes a world of difference. Jane doesn't know what will happen in her life next, but she knows it won't be small, or quiet, or lonely. The time for small, and quiet, and lonely is over.

As she approaches Mary's door, dragging her weary feet, she pulls off the yellow lanyard identifying her as a Guest. It has a fleck of blood on it. She'll keep it for the memories.

Acknowledgements

[text to come]